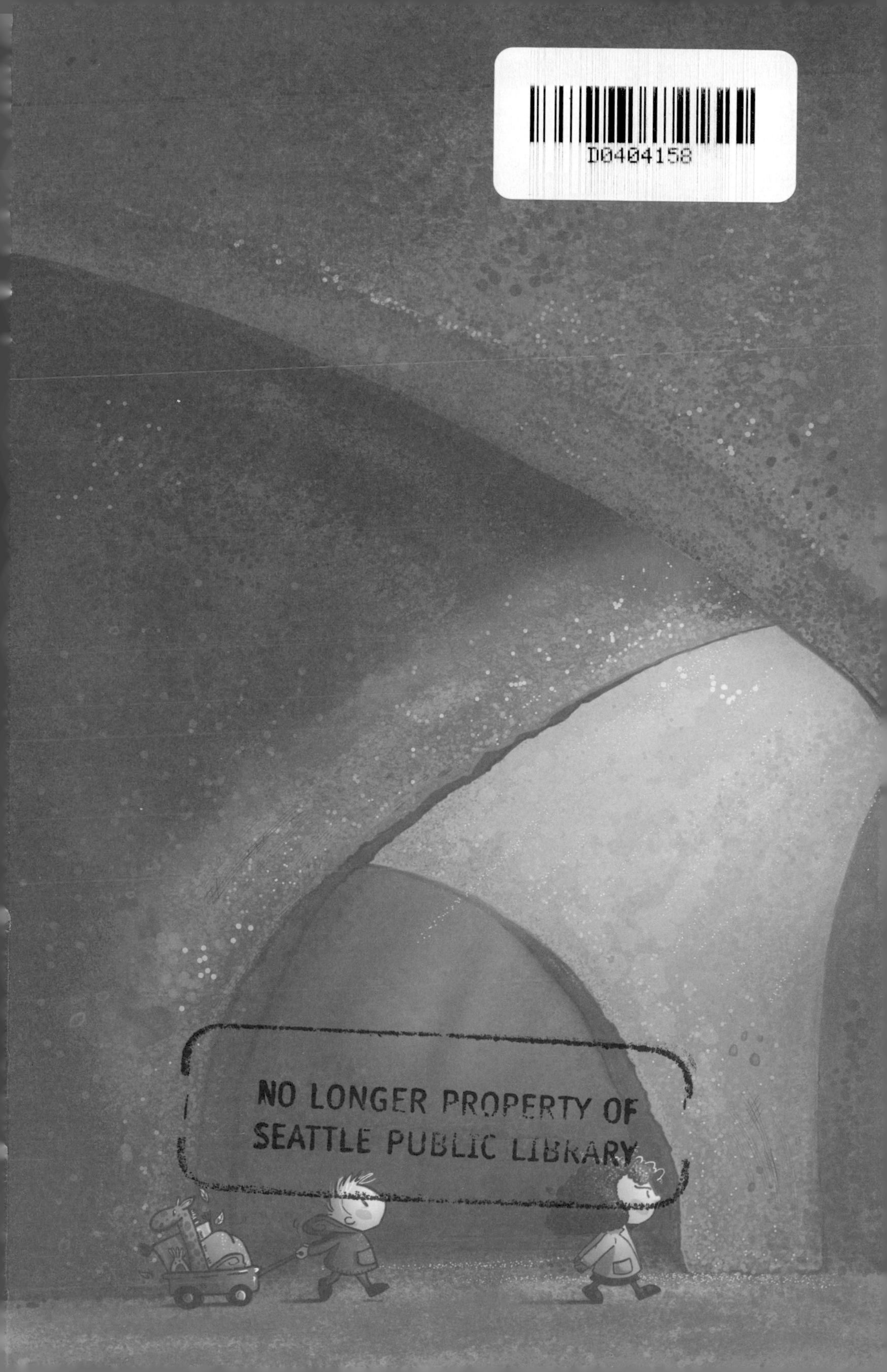

Editor-in-Chief: Chris Staros.

Published by Top Shelf Productions, an imprint of IDW Publishing, a division of Idea and Design Works, LLC. Offices: Top Shelf Productions, c/o Idea & Design Works, LLC, 2355 Northside Drive, Suite 140, San Diego, CA 92108. Top Shelf Productions®, the Top Shelf logo, Idea and Design Works®, and the IDW logo are registered trademarks of Idea and Design Works, LLC. All Rights Reserved. With the exception of small excerpts of artwork used for review purposes, none of the contents of this publication may be reprinted without the permission of IDW Publishing. IDW Publishing does not read or accept unsolicited submissions of ideas, stories, or artwork.

Visit our online catalog at www.topshelfcomix.com.

ISBN 978-1-60309-522-8

Printed in Korea.

26 25 24 23   1 2 3 4

SHELLEY FRANKENSTEIN!

by Colleen Madden!

"CowPiggy"

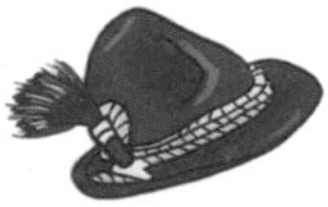

For P and my boys.
For the crazy-chatty-bunny thundersnow journey
we all went on~together!

Here's to the next one. "" xoxomom

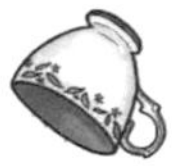

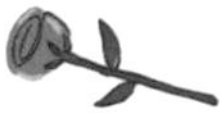

"There is a love for the marvelous."
M.W. Shelley

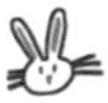

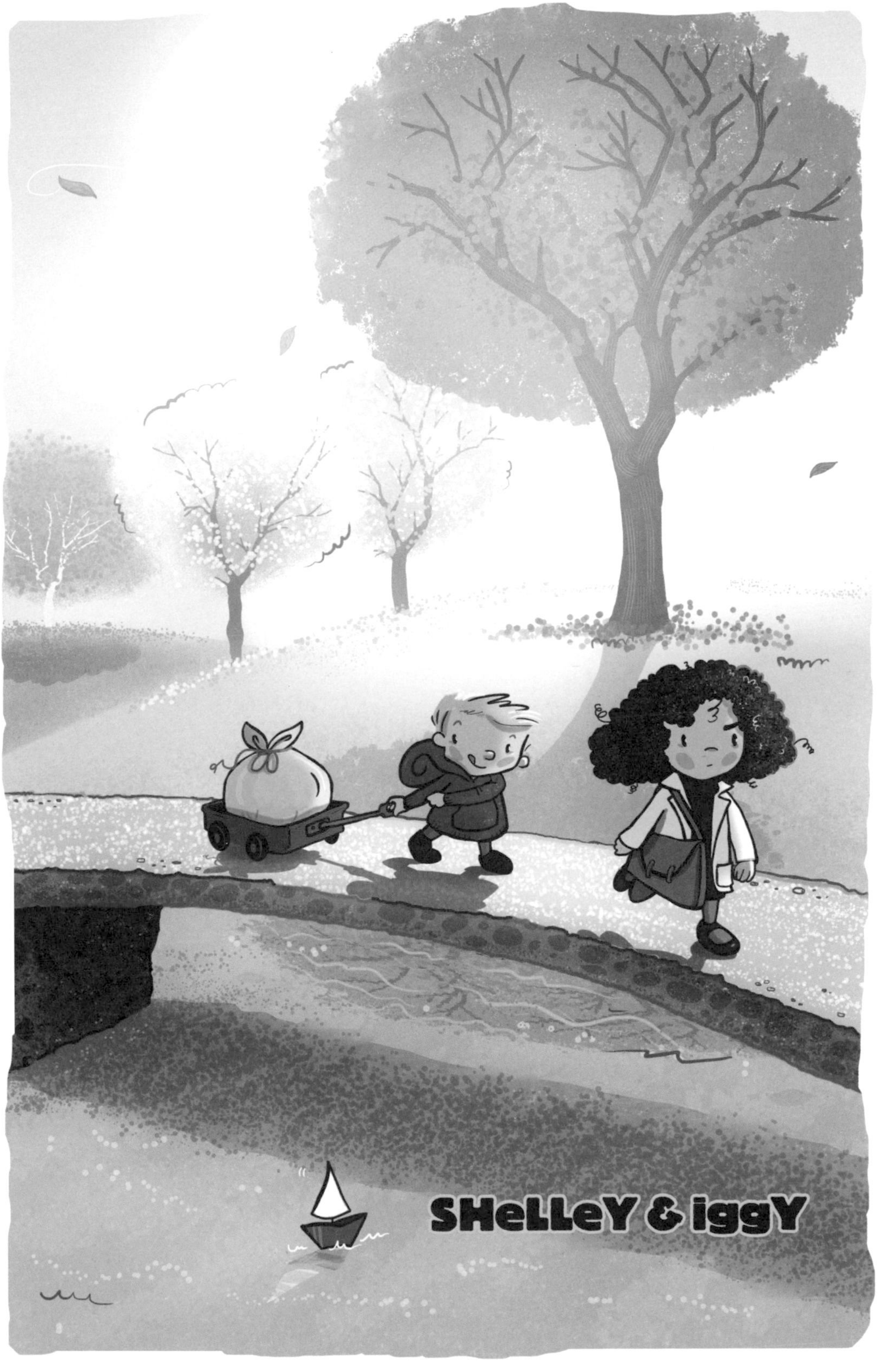
SHeLLeY & iggY

Once

there was a girl named Shelley...

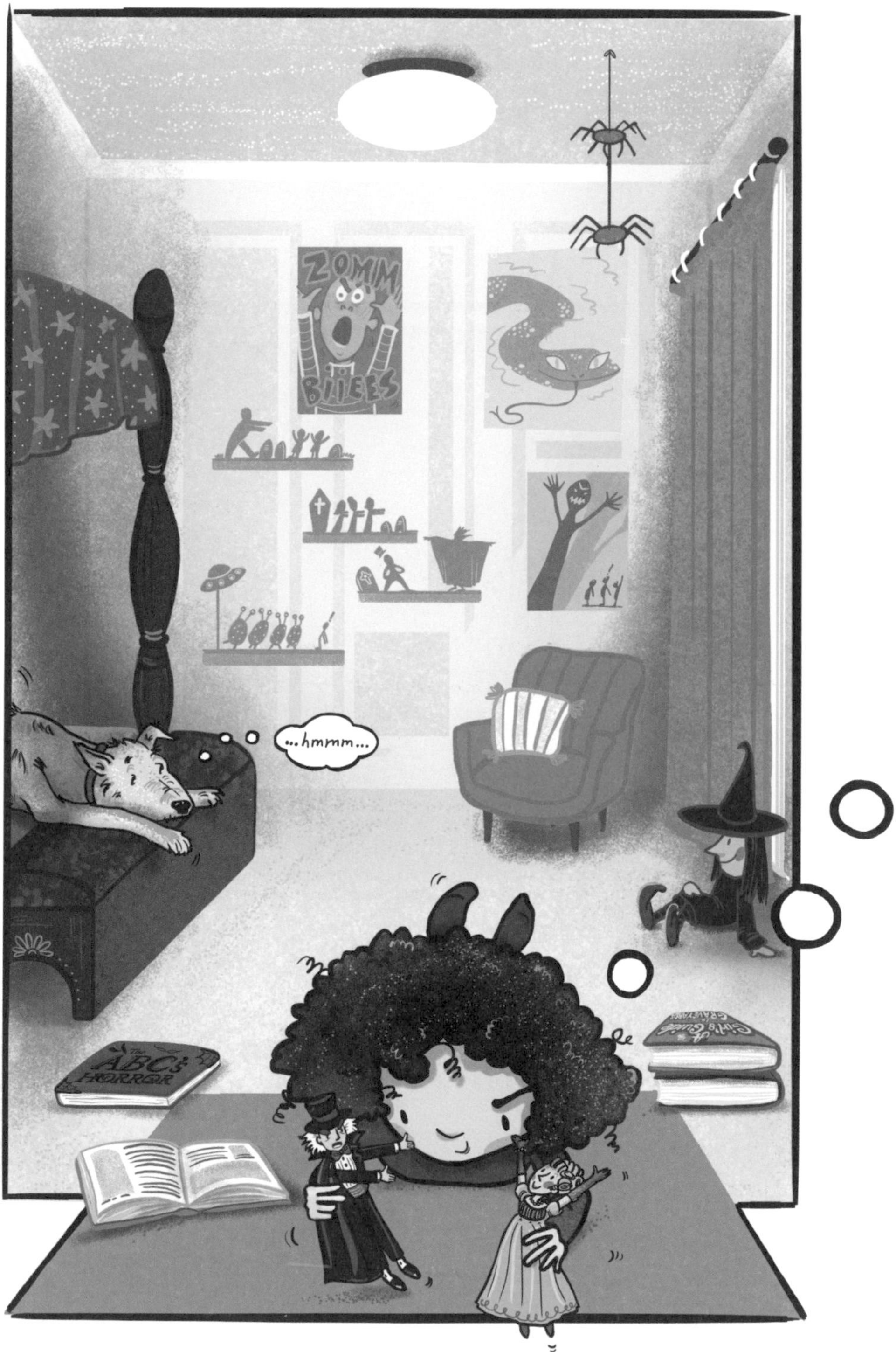
ZOMM
BIIEES
...hmmm...
ABC's HORROR

...who liked scary things.

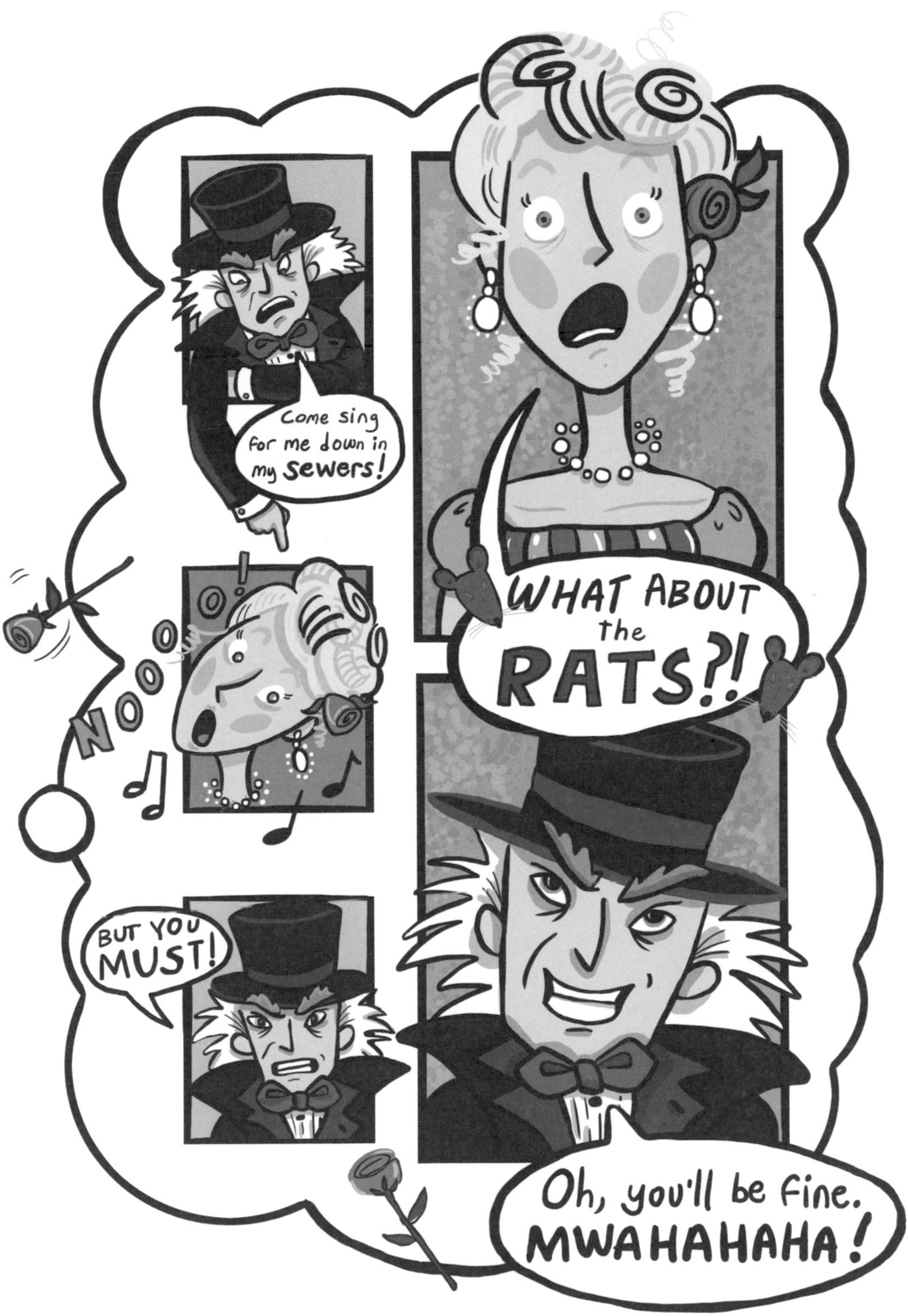
Come sing for me down in my sewers!
NOOOOO!
BUT YOU MUST!
WHAT ABOUT the RATS?!
Oh, you'll be fine. MWAHAHAHA!

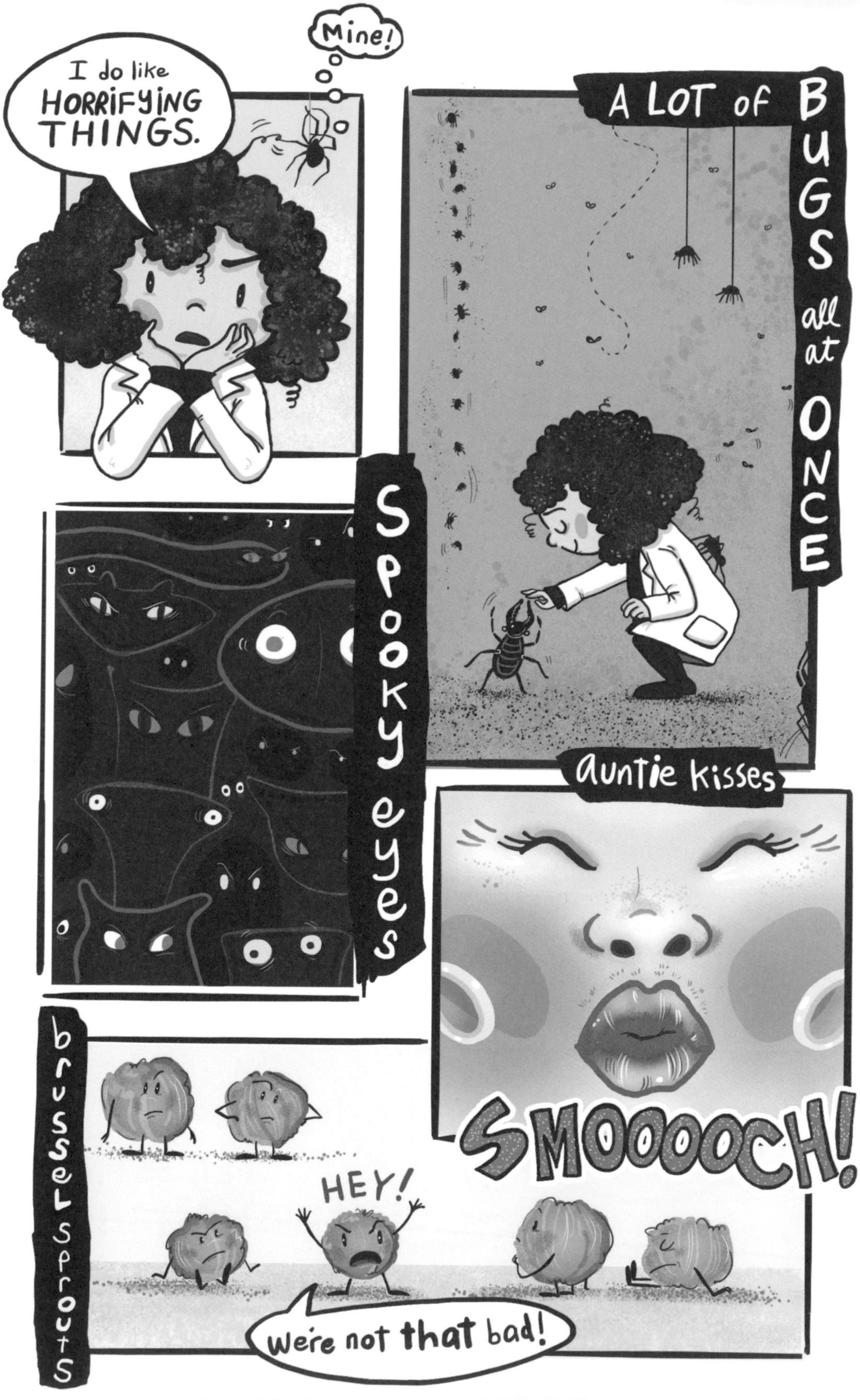
Mine!
I do like HORRIFYING THINGS.
A LOT of BUGS all at ONCE
Spooky eyes
auntie kisses
SMOOOOCH!
brussel sprouts
HEY!
We're not that bad!

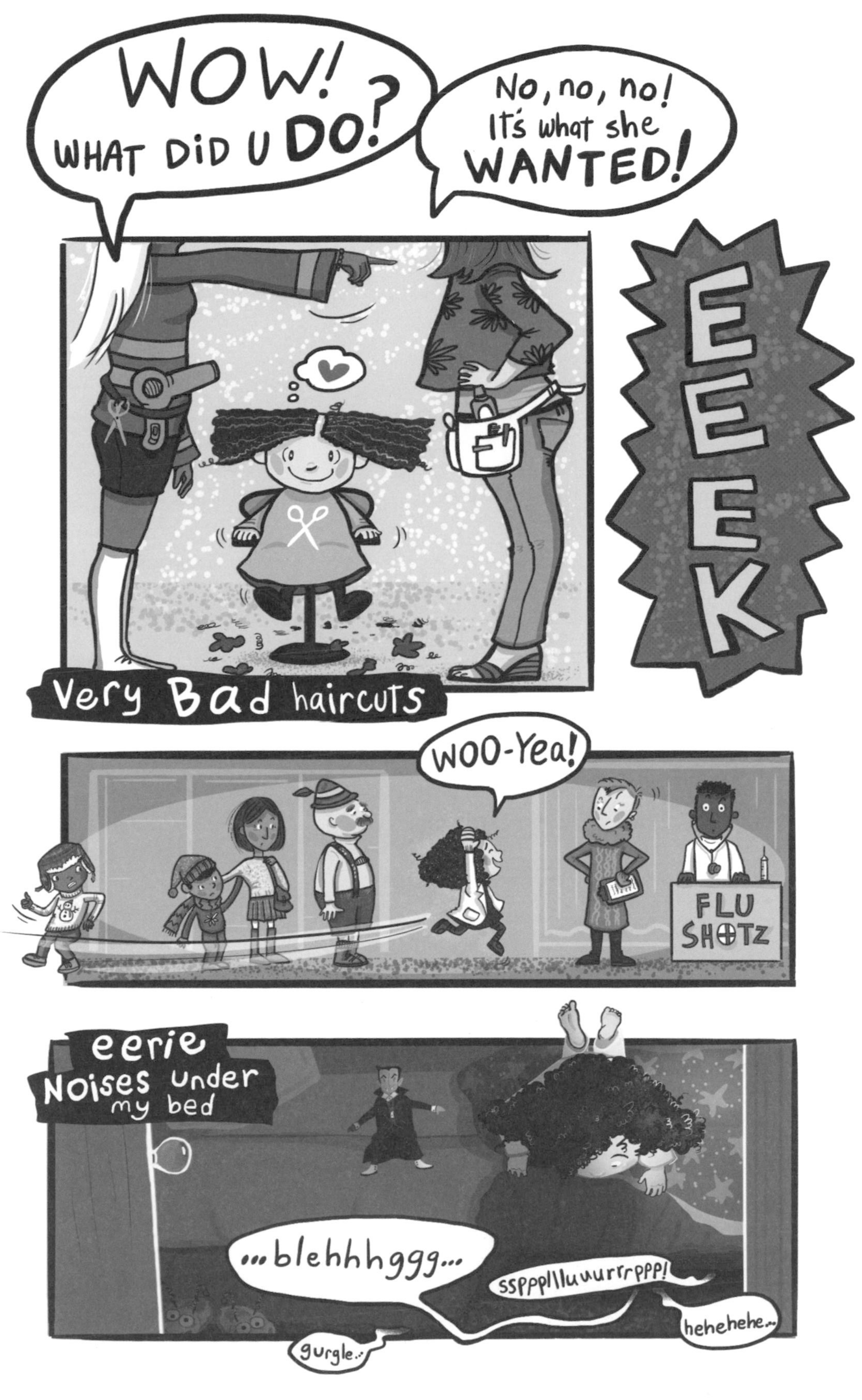
WOW! WHAT DID U DO?
No, no, no! It's what she WANTED!
EEEK
Very Bad haircuts
WOO-Yea!
FLU SHOTZ
eerie Noises under my bed
...blehhhggg...
sspppllluuurrrppp!
hehehehe...
gurgle...

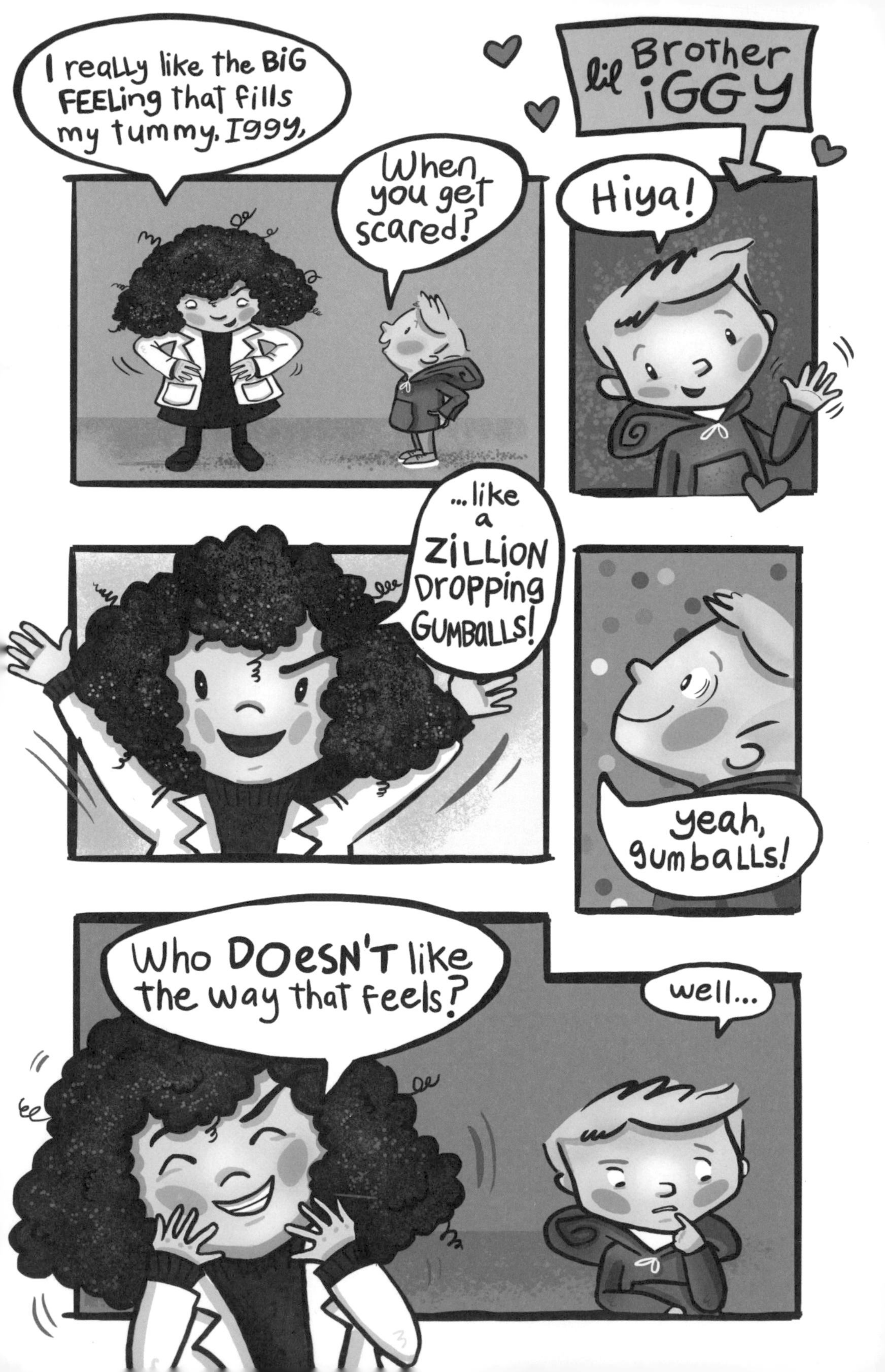
I really like the BIG FEELing that fills my tummy, Iggy,
When you get scared?
lil Brother iGGY
Hiya!
...like a ZiLLiON Dropping GUMBaLLS!
yeah, gumbaLLs!
Who DOeSN'T like the way that Feels?
well...

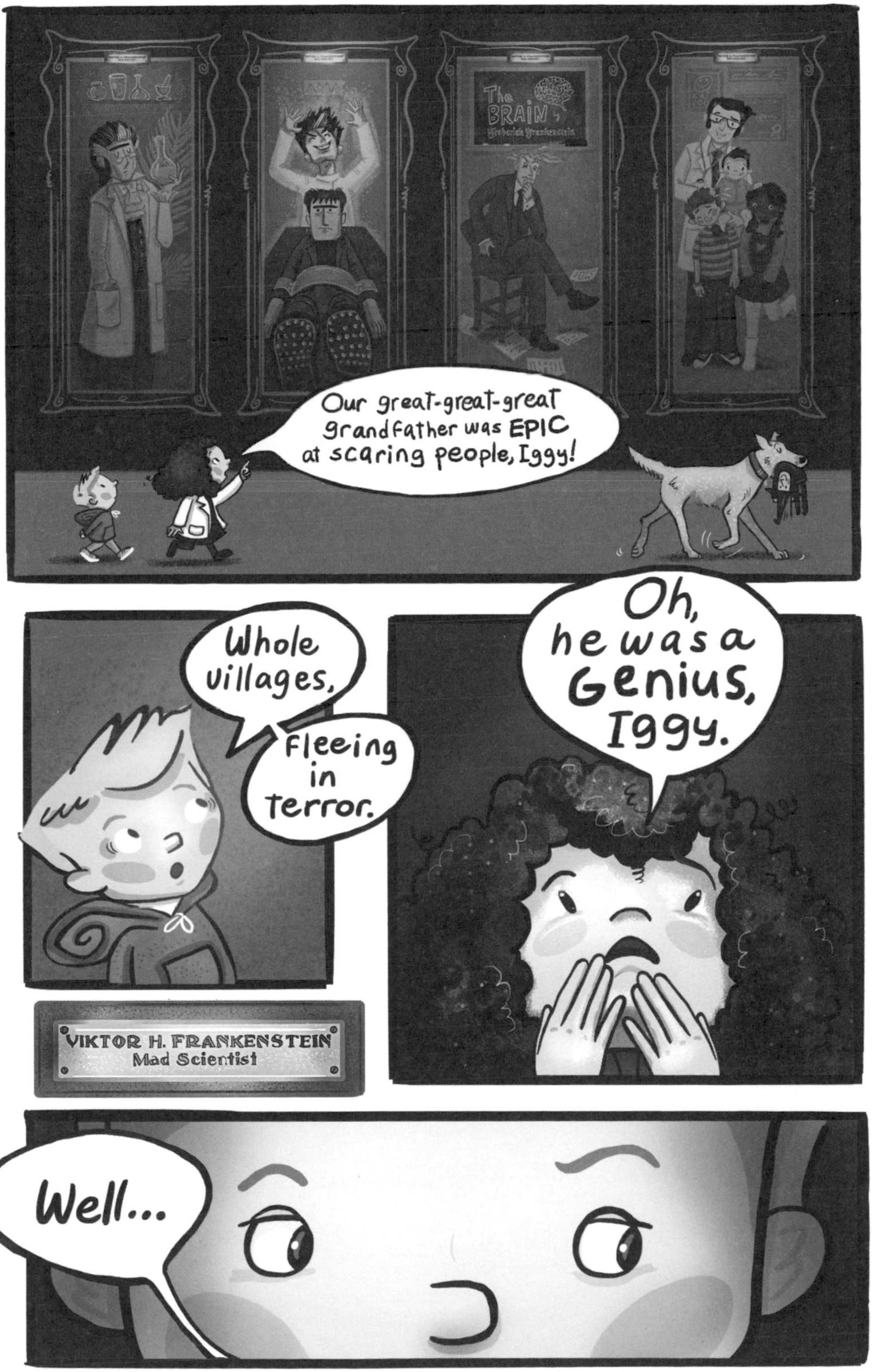
The BRAIN
Frederick Frankenstein
Our great-great-great grandfather was EPIC at scaring people, Iggy!
Whole villages,
Fleeing in terror.
Oh, he was a Genius, Iggy.
VIKTOR H. FRANKENSTEIN
Mad Scientist
Well...

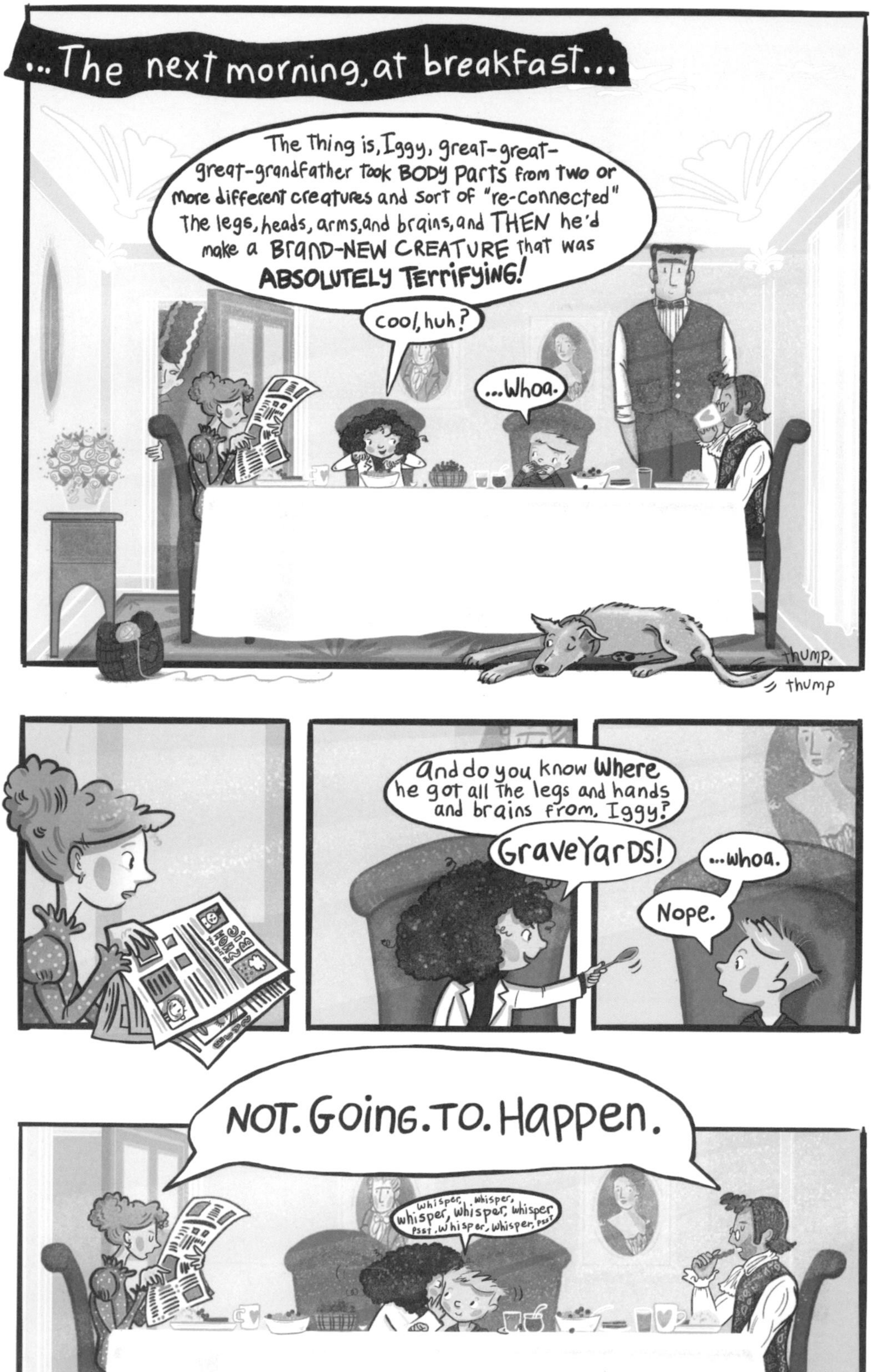
...The next morning, at breakfast...
The thing is, Iggy, great-great-great-grandfather took BODY PARTS from two or more different creatures and sort of "re-connected" the legs, heads, arms, and brains, and THEN he'd make a BRAND-NEW CREATURE that was ABSOLUTELY TERRIFYING!
Cool, huh?
...Whoa.
thump.
thump
And do you know where he got all the legs and hands and brains from, Iggy?
GraveYarDS!
...whoa.
Nope.
NOT. GOING. TO. Happen.
whisper, whisper, whisper, whisper, whisper
psst, whisper, whisper, psst

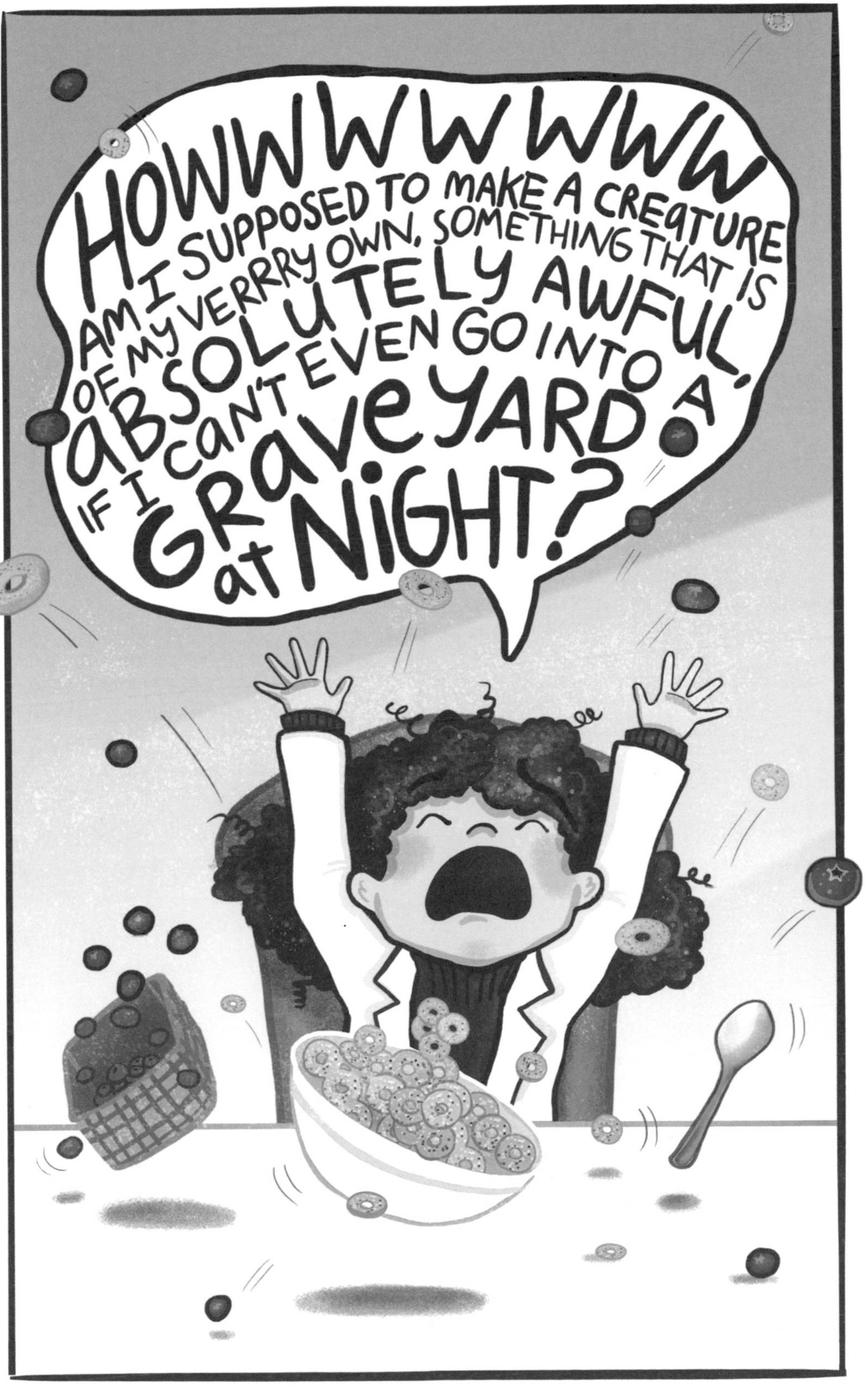
HOWWWWWWWW
AM I SUPPOSED TO MAKE A CREATURE
OF MY VERRRY OWN, SOMETHING THAT IS
ABSOLUTELY AWFUL,
IF I CAN'T EVEN GO INTO A
GRAVEYARD
at NIGHT?

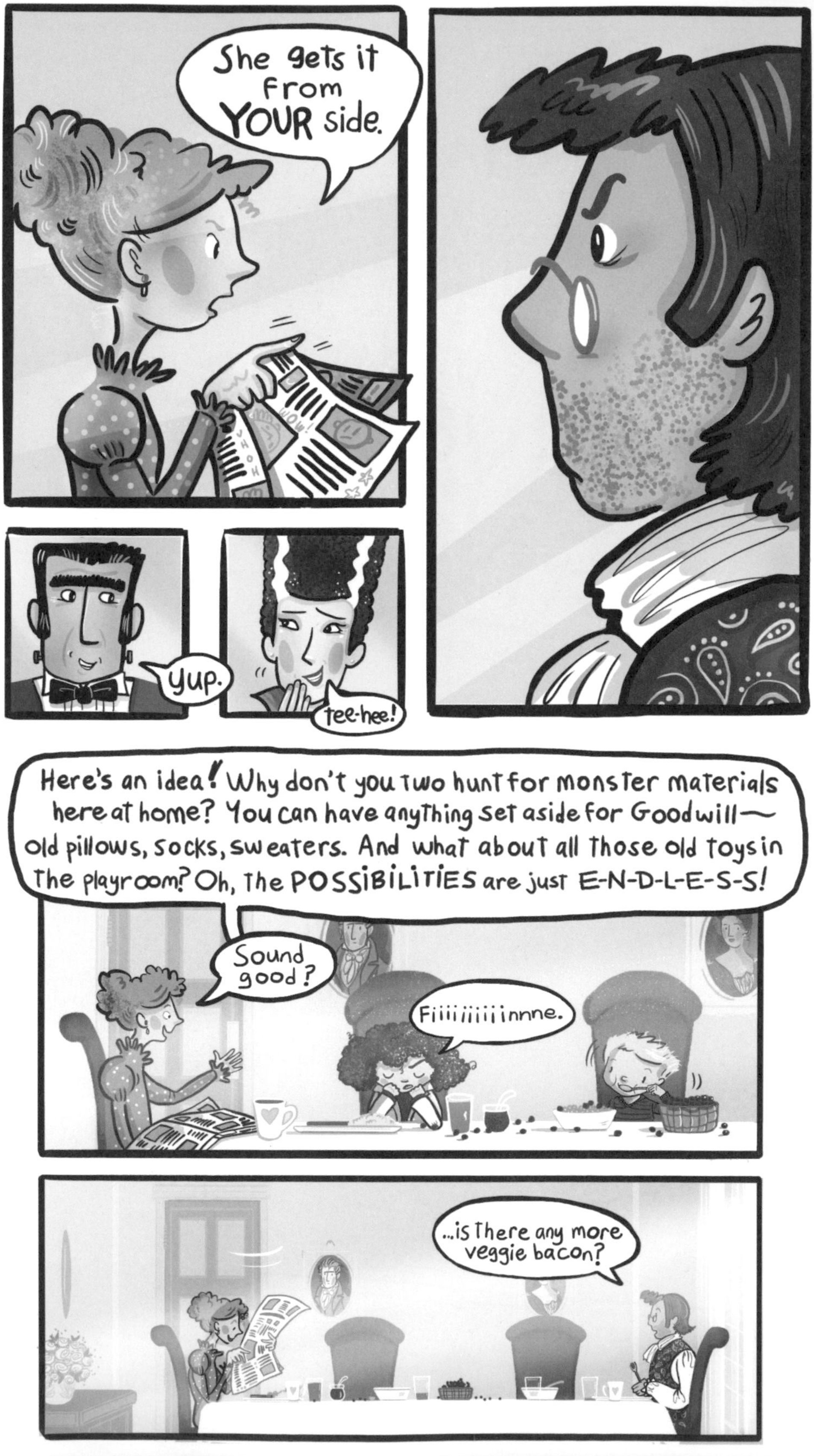
She gets it from YOUR side.
yup.
tee-hee!
Here's an idea! Why don't you two hunt for monster materials here at home? You can have anything set aside for Goodwill— old pillows, socks, sweaters. And what about all those old toys in the playroom? Oh, the POSSIBILITIES are just E-N-D-L-E-S-S!
Sound good?
Fiiiiiiiiinnne.
...is there any more veggie bacon?

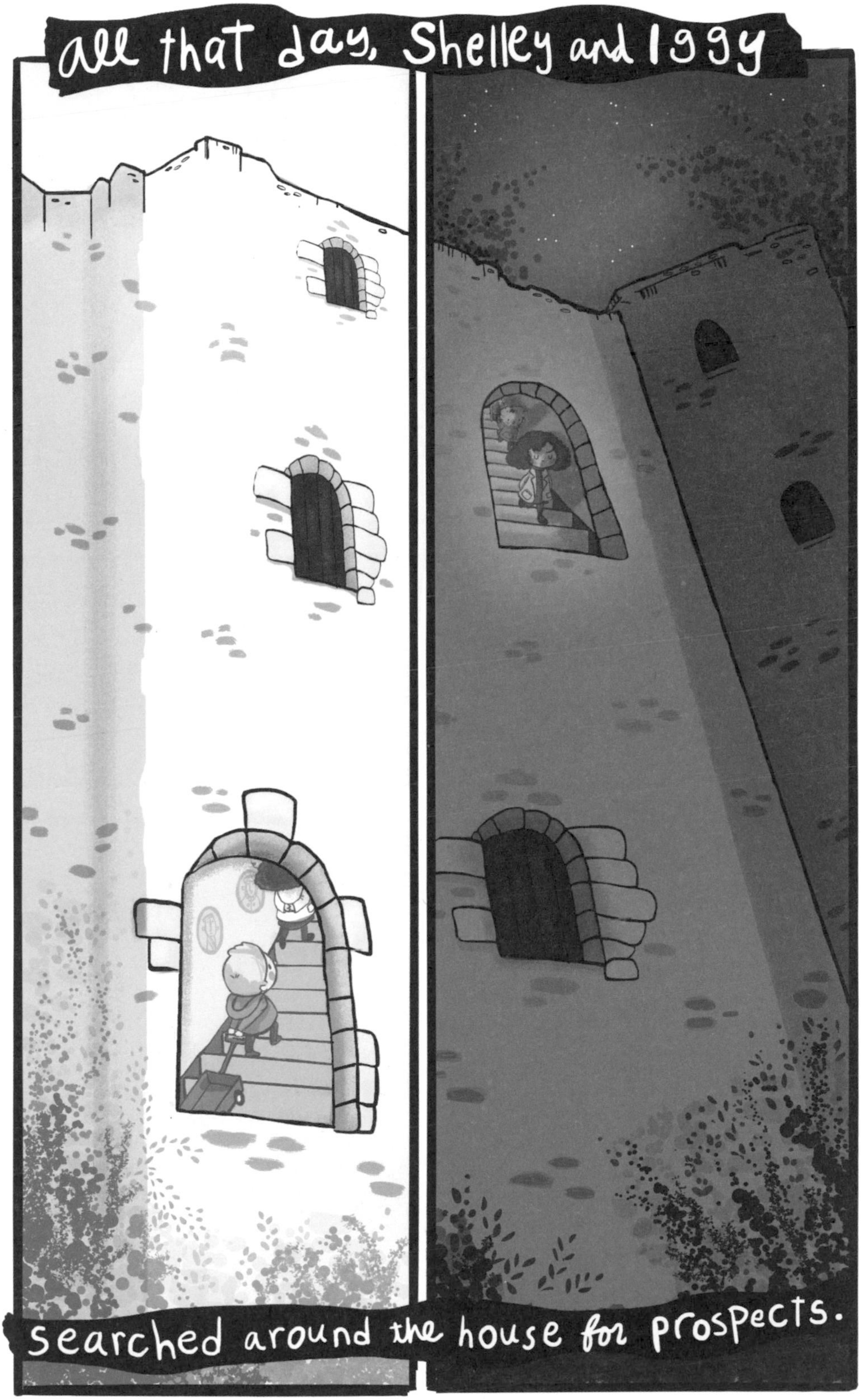
All that day, Shelley and Iggy
searched around the house for prospects.

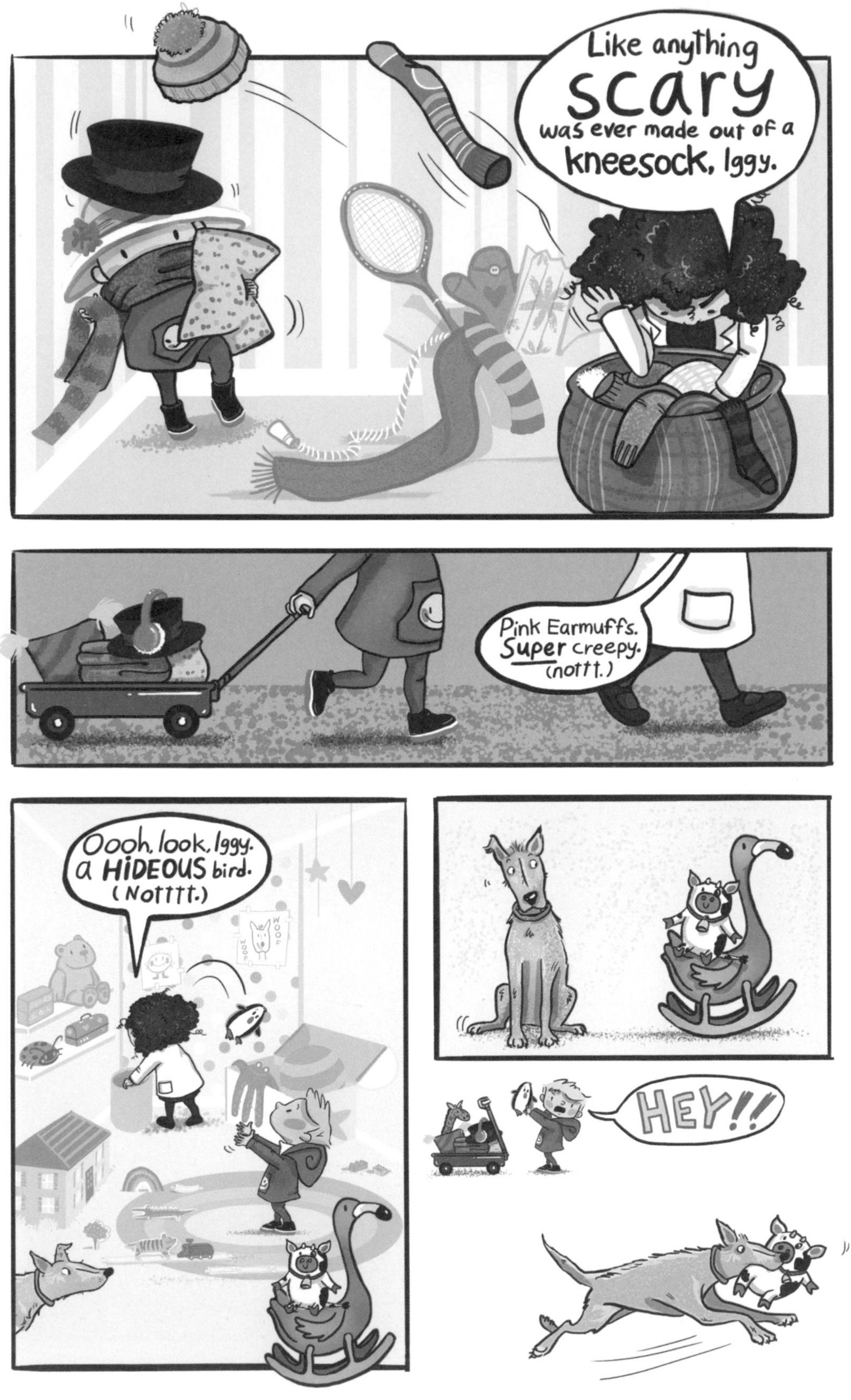

Like anything scary was ever made out of a kneesock, Iggy.
Pink Earmuffs. Super creepy. (nottt.)
Oooh, look, Iggy. a HIDEOUS bird. (Nottttt.)
WOOF
WOOF
HEY!!

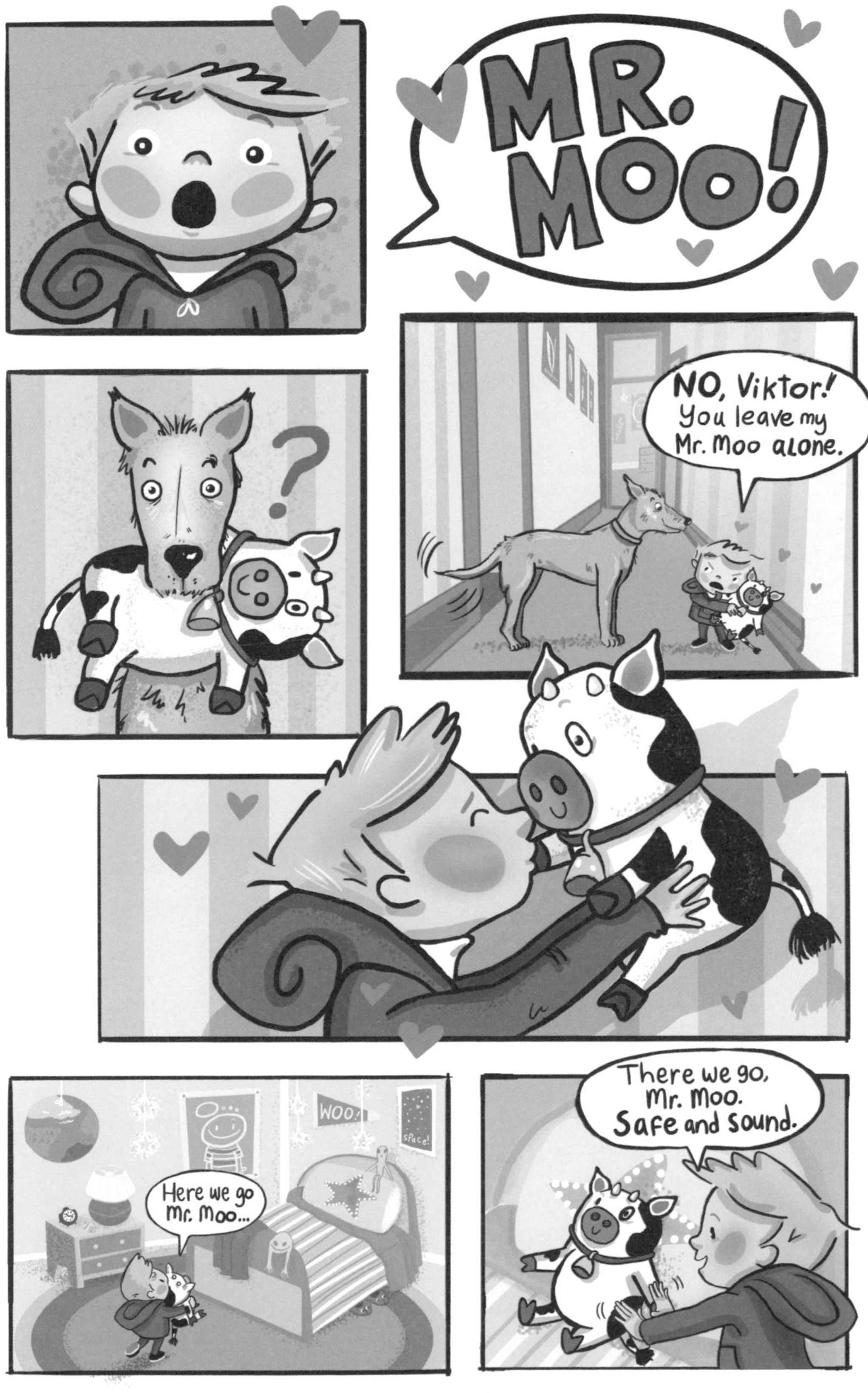
MR. MOO!
NO, Viktor! You leave my Mr. Moo alone.
Here we go mr. Moo...
WOO!
space!
There we go, Mr. Moo. Safe and sound.

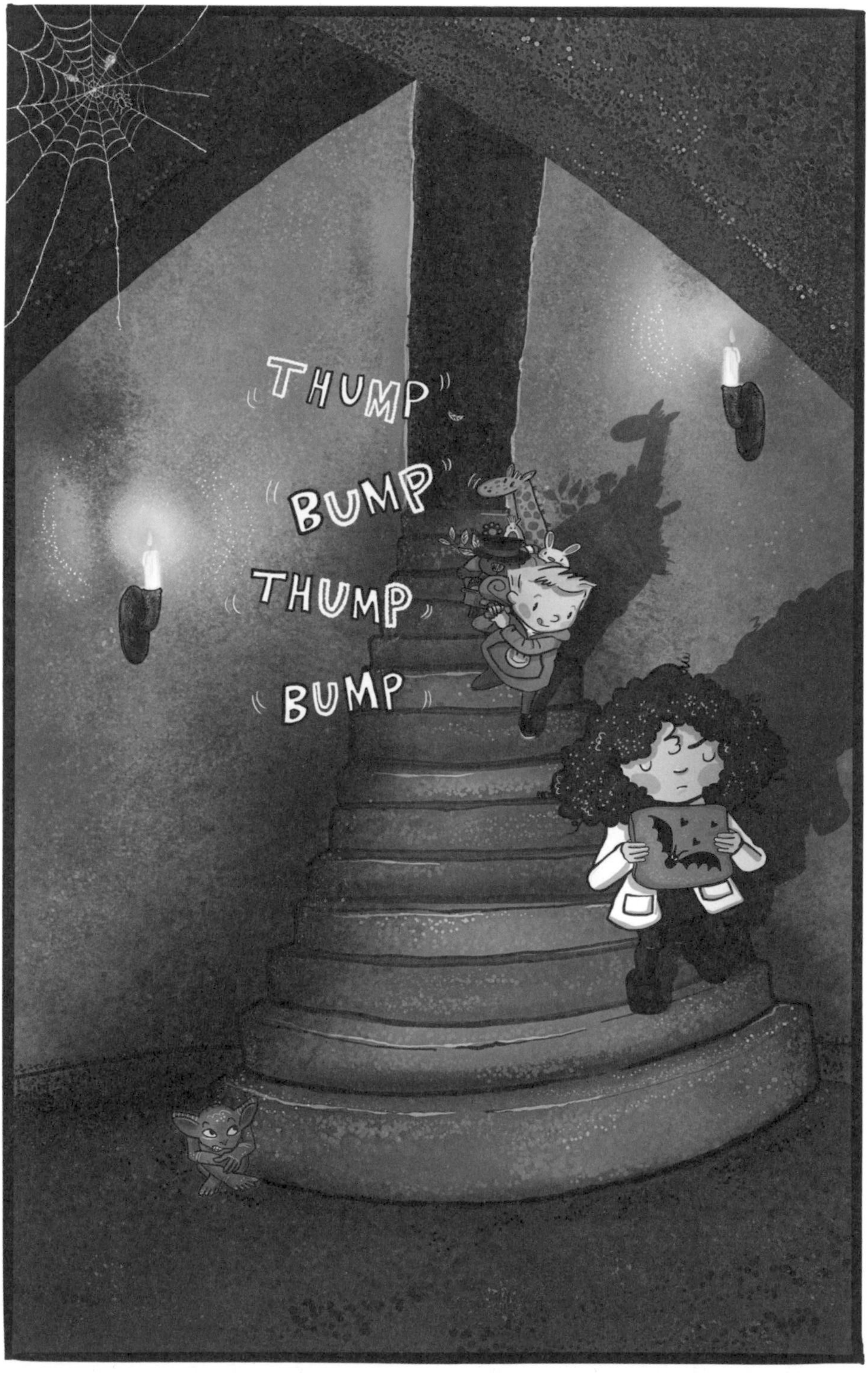
THUMP
BUMP
THUMP
BUMP

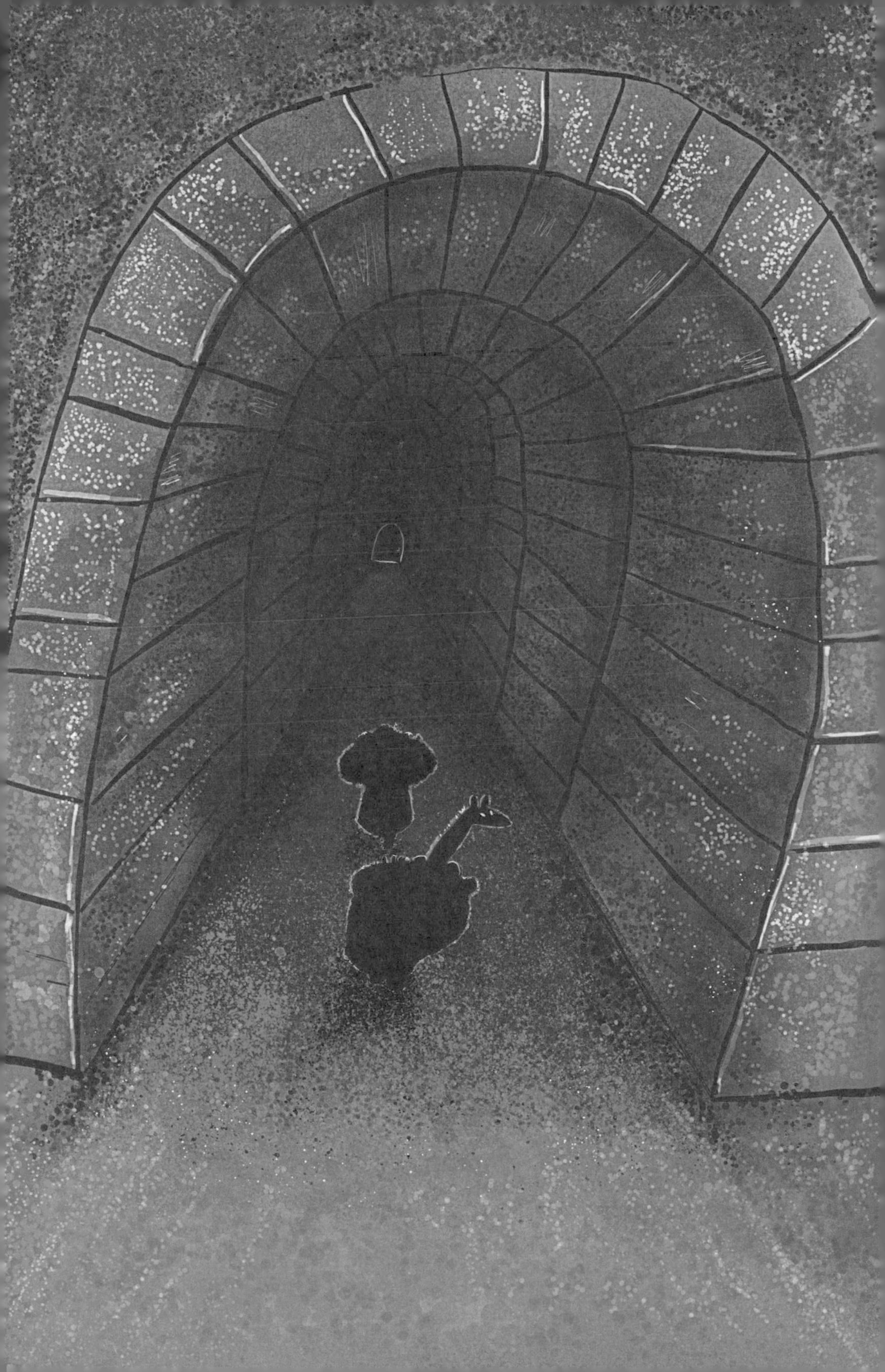

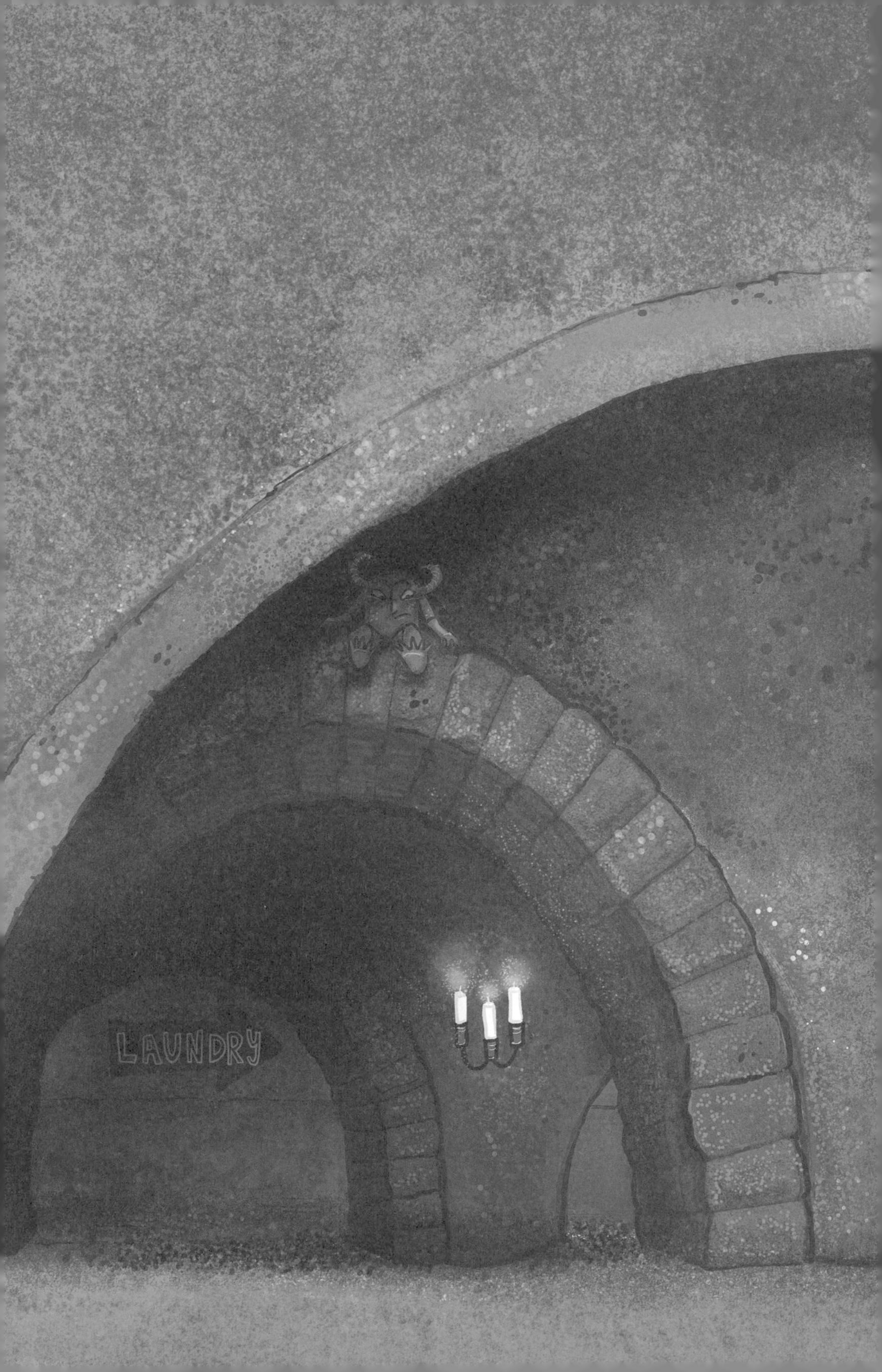
LAUNDRY

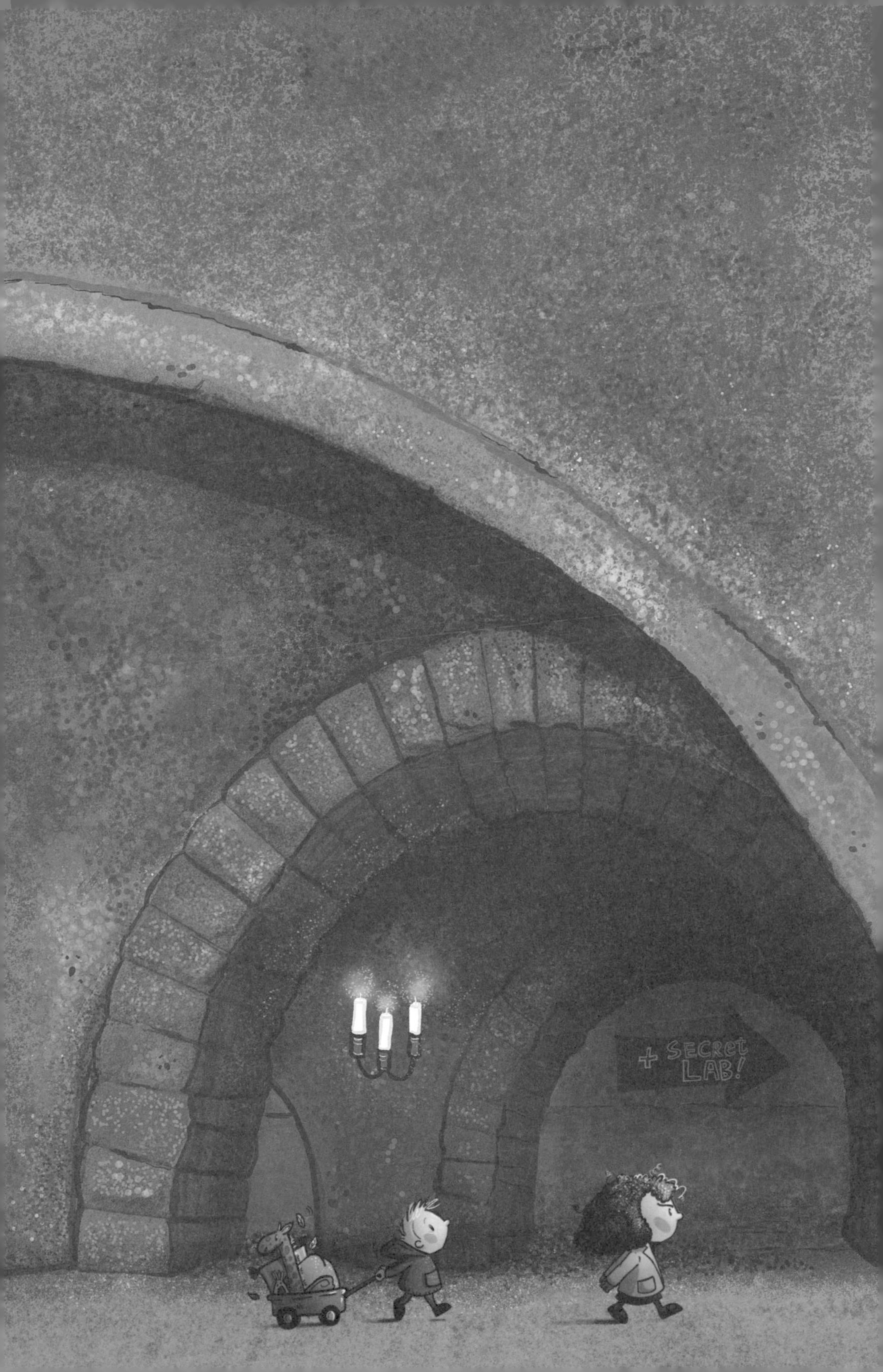
SECRET LAB!

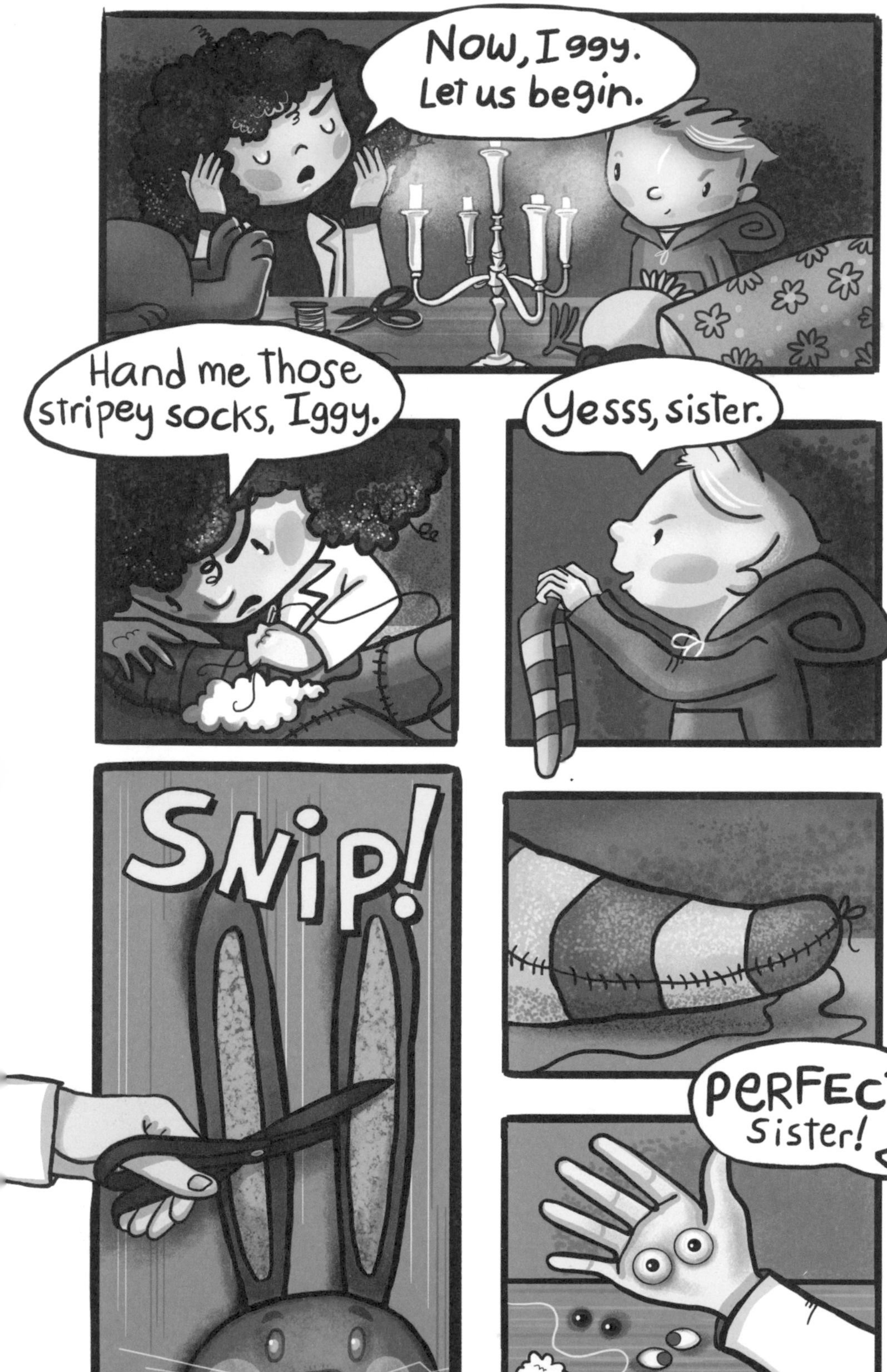
Now, Iggy.
Let us begin.
Hand me those stripey socks, Iggy.
Yesss, sister.
SNIP!
PERFECT, Sister!

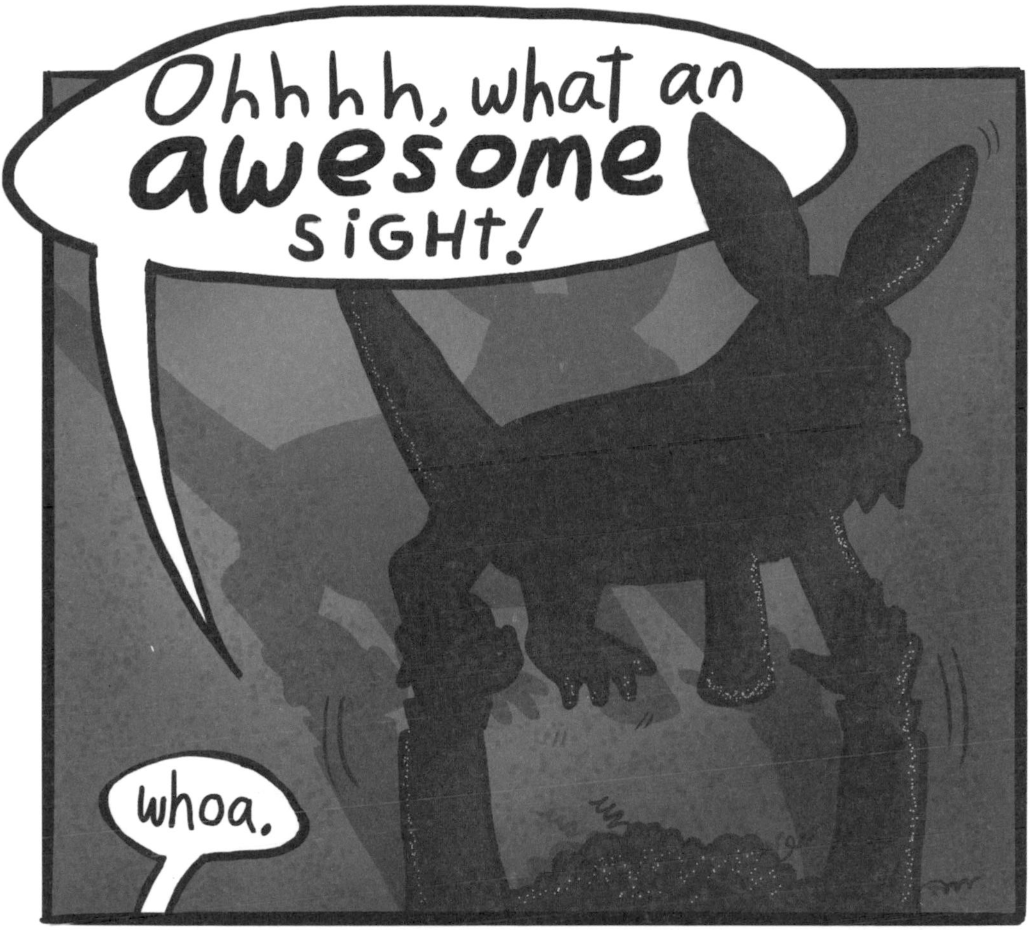
Ohhhh, what an awesome SIGHT!
whoa.

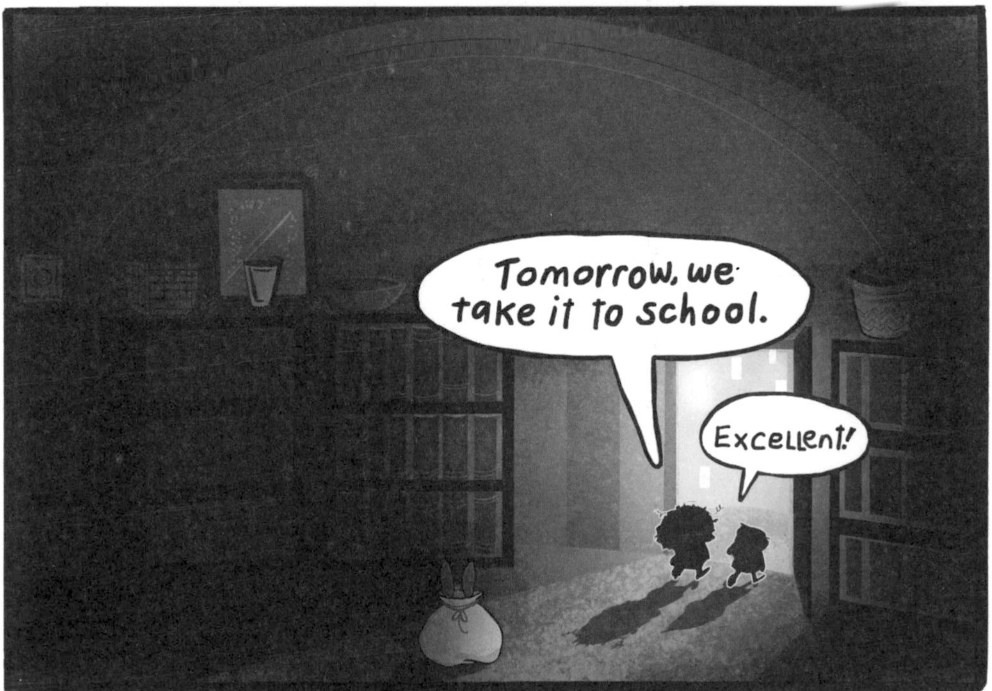
Tomorrow, we take it to school.
Excellent!

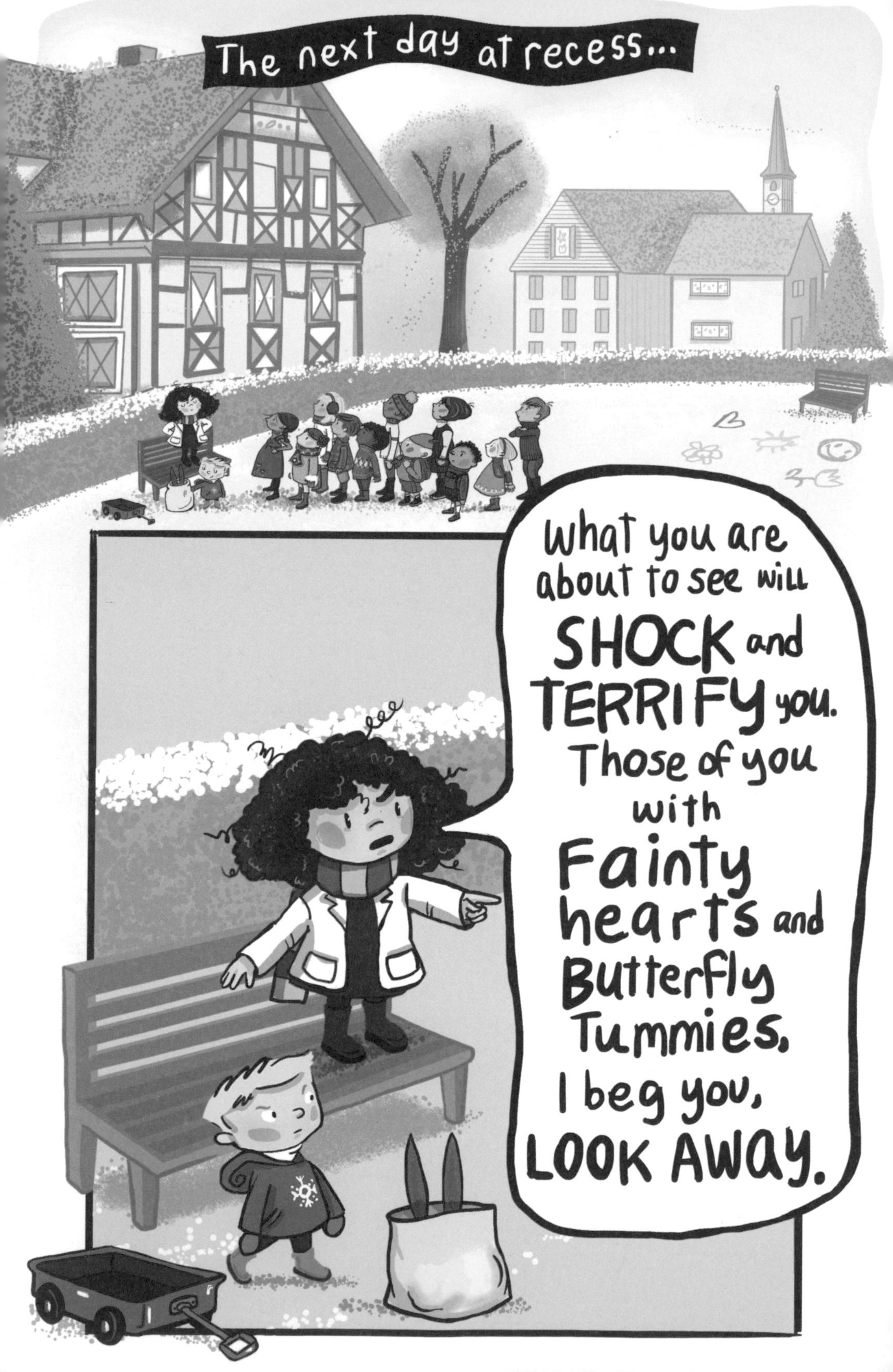

The next day at recess...
What you are about to see will SHOCK and TERRIFY you. Those of you with Fainty hearts and Butterfly Tummies, I beg you, LOOK AWAY.

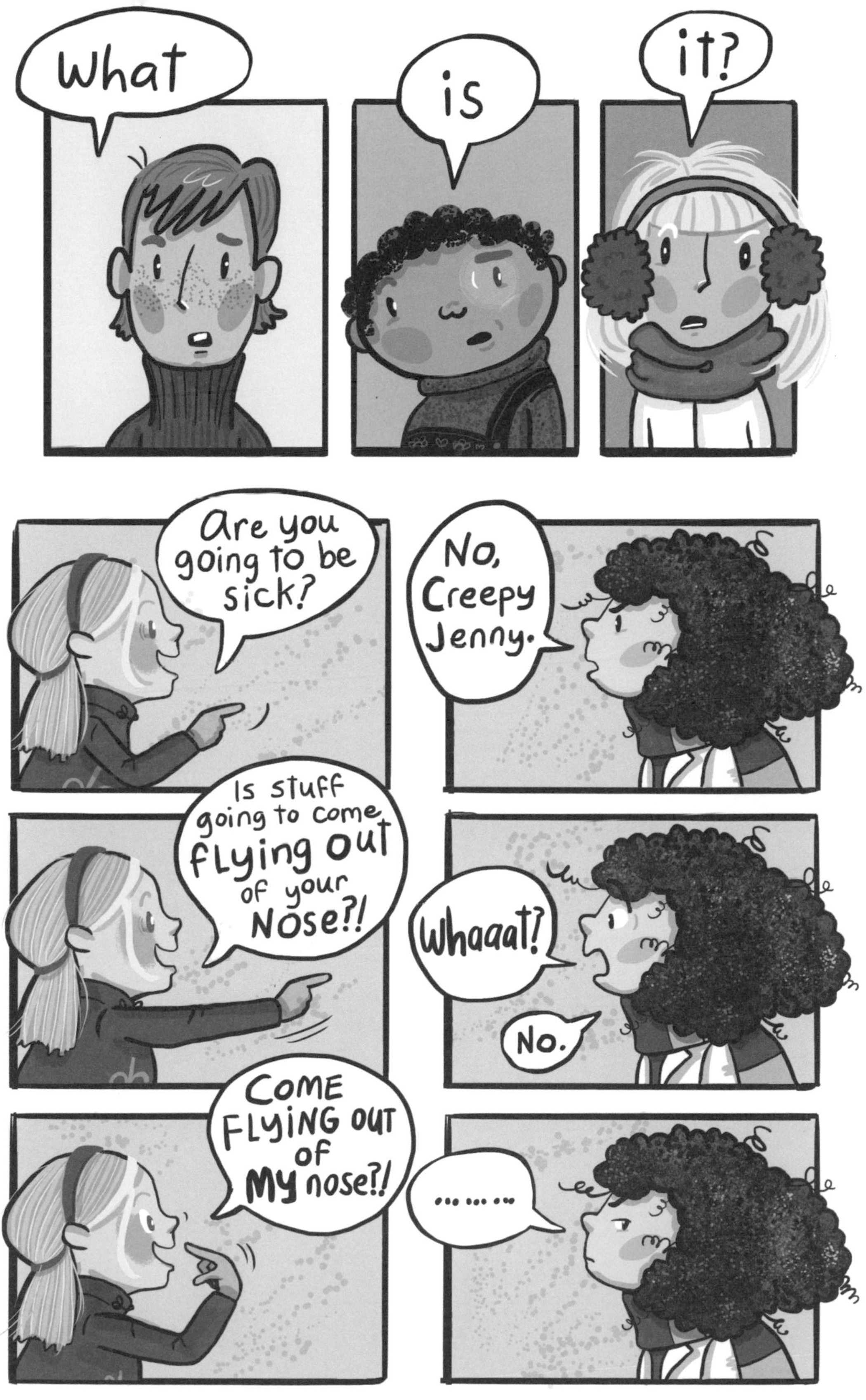
What
is
it?
Are you going to be sick?
No, Creepy Jenny.
Is stuff going to come flying out of your nose?!
Whaaat?
No.
COME FLYING OUT of MY nose?!
....

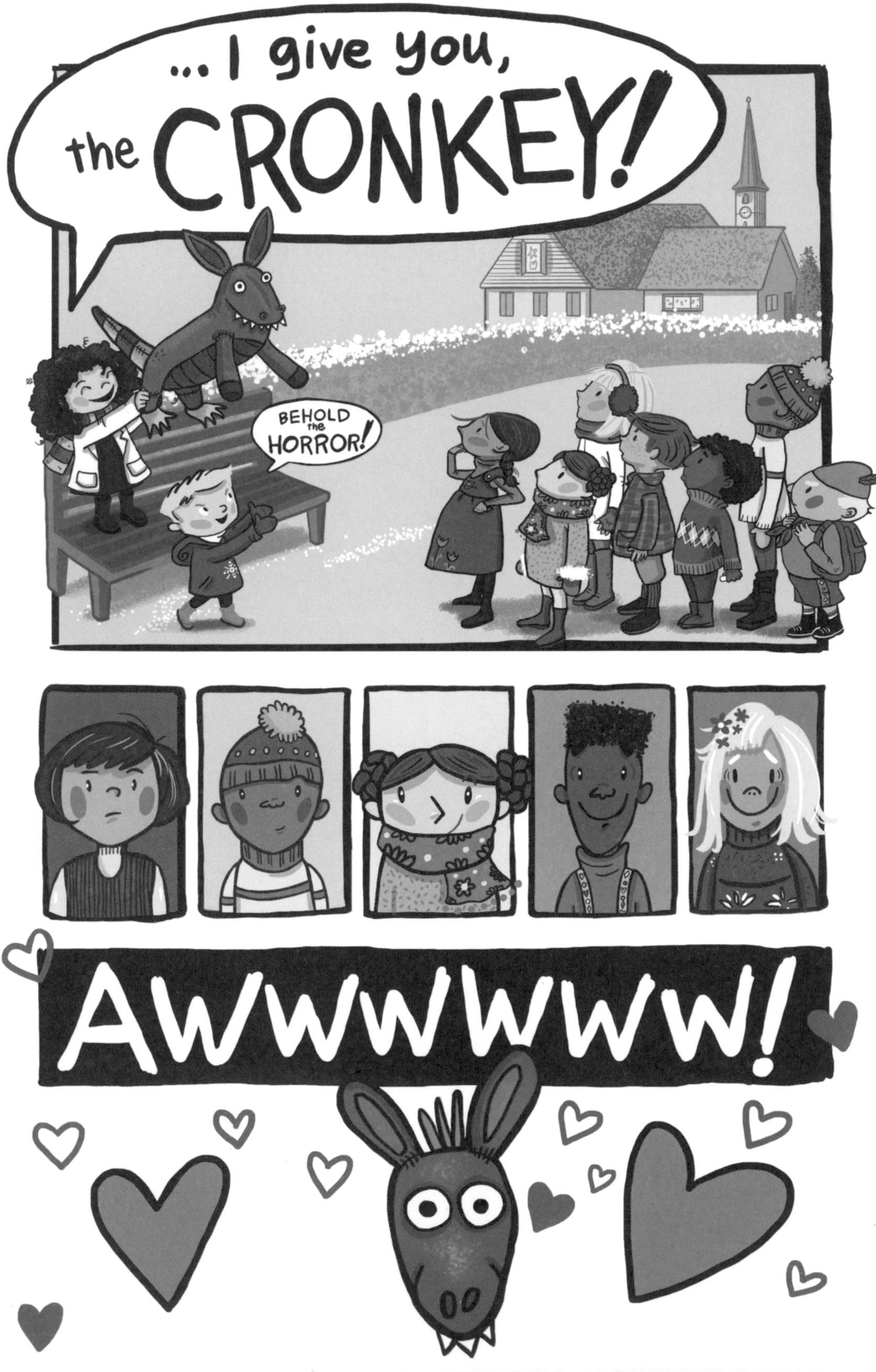
... I give you, the CRONKEY!
BEHOLD the HORROR!
AWWWWWW!

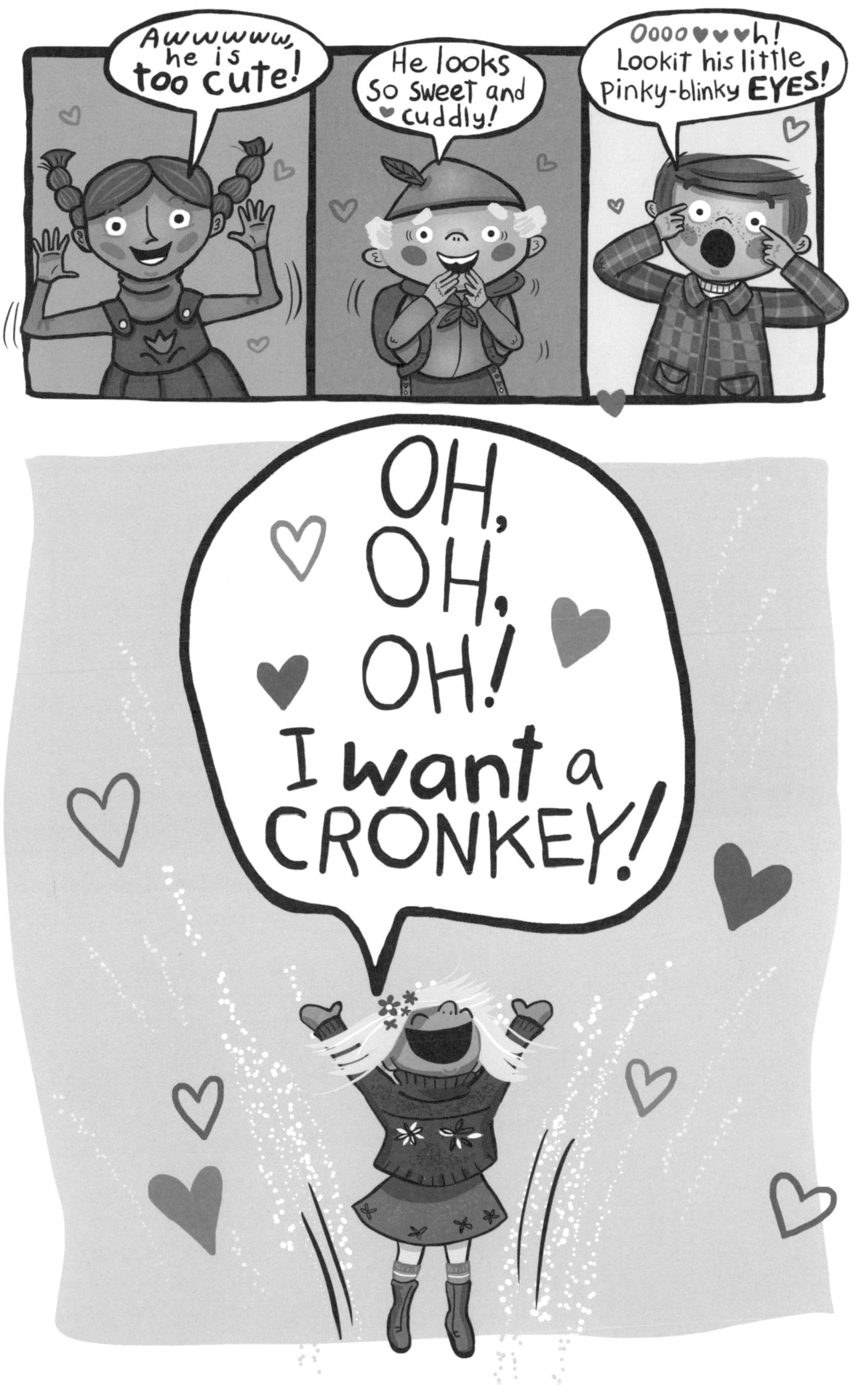
Awwwww, he is too cute!
He looks so sweet and cuddly!
Oooo♥♥♥h! Lookit his little pinky-blinky EYES!
OH, OH, OH! I want a CRONKEY!

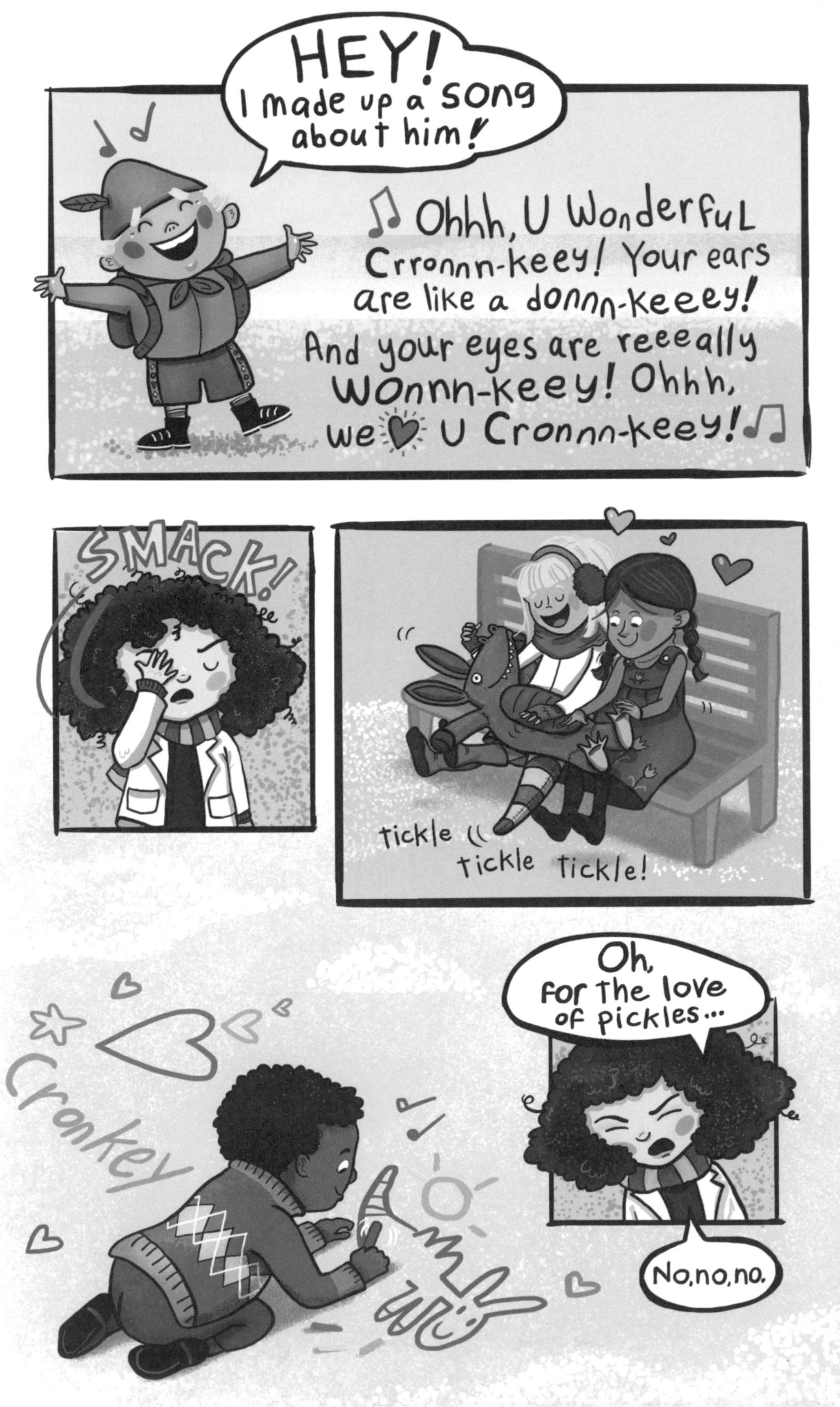
HEY! I made up a song about him!
Ohhh, U Wonderful Crronnn-keey! Your ears are like a donnn-keeey! And your eyes are reeeally wonnn-keey! Ohhh, we ♥ U Cronnn-keey!
SMACK!
tickle
tickle tickle!
Cronkey
Oh, for the love of pickles...
No,no,no.

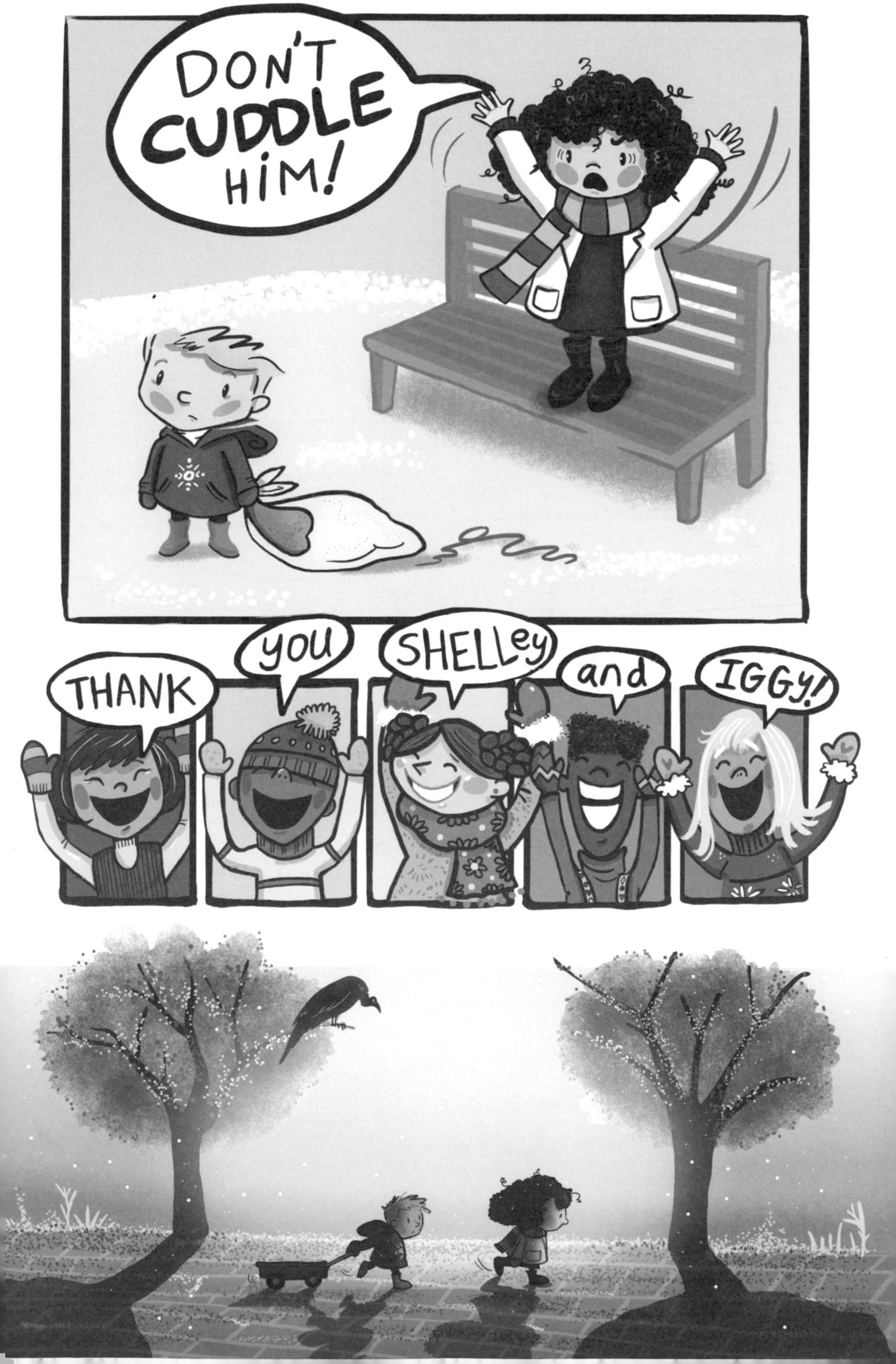
DON'T CUDDLE HIM!
THANK
you
SHELLey
and
IGGy!

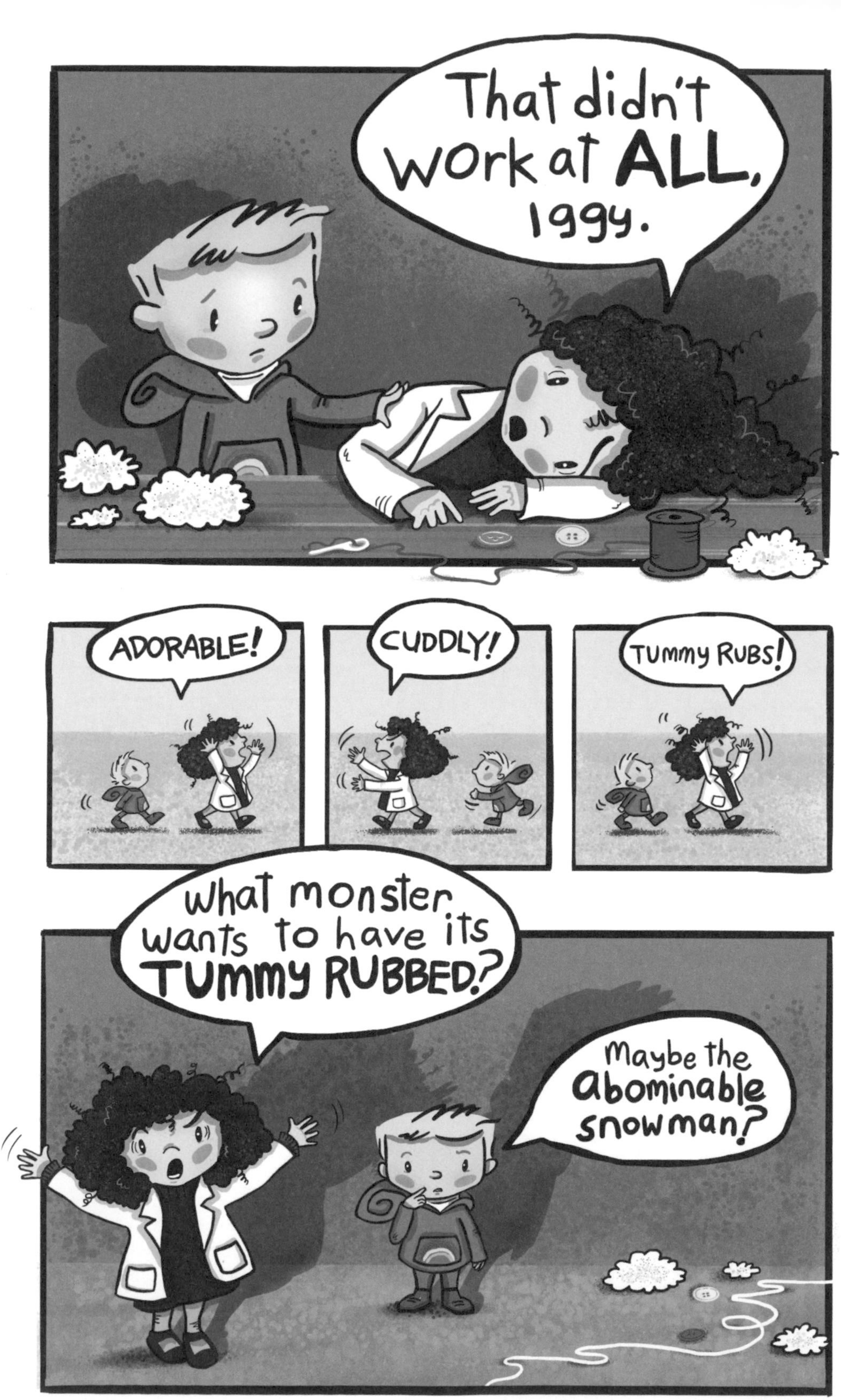
That didn't work at ALL, Iggy.
ADORABLE!
CUDDLY!
TUMMY RUBS!
What monster wants to have its TUMMY RUBBED?
Maybe the abominable snowman?

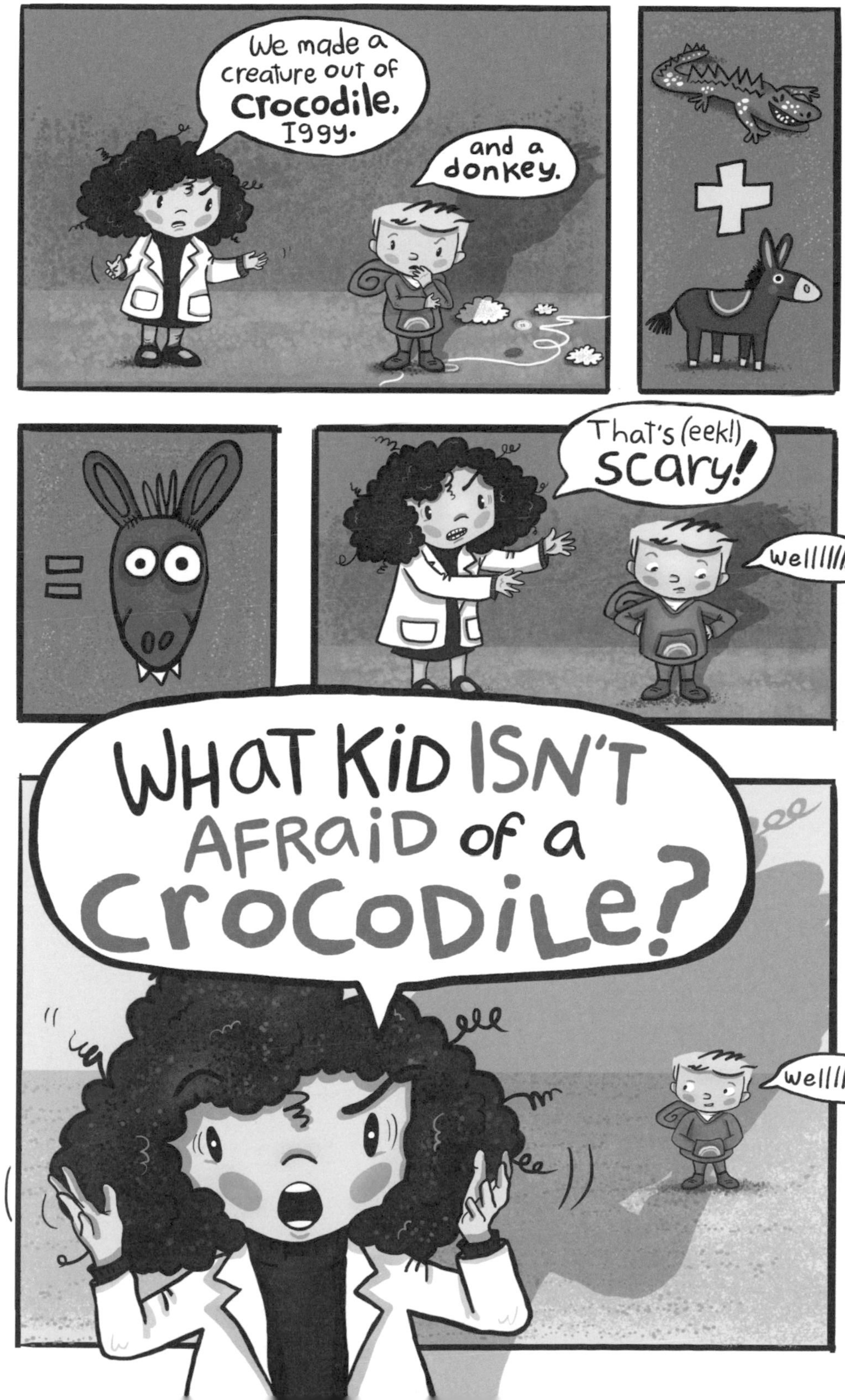
We made a creature out of crocodile, Iggy.
and a donkey.
That's (eek!) scary!
welllll...
WHAT KID ISN'T AFRAID of a CROCODILE?
welllll...

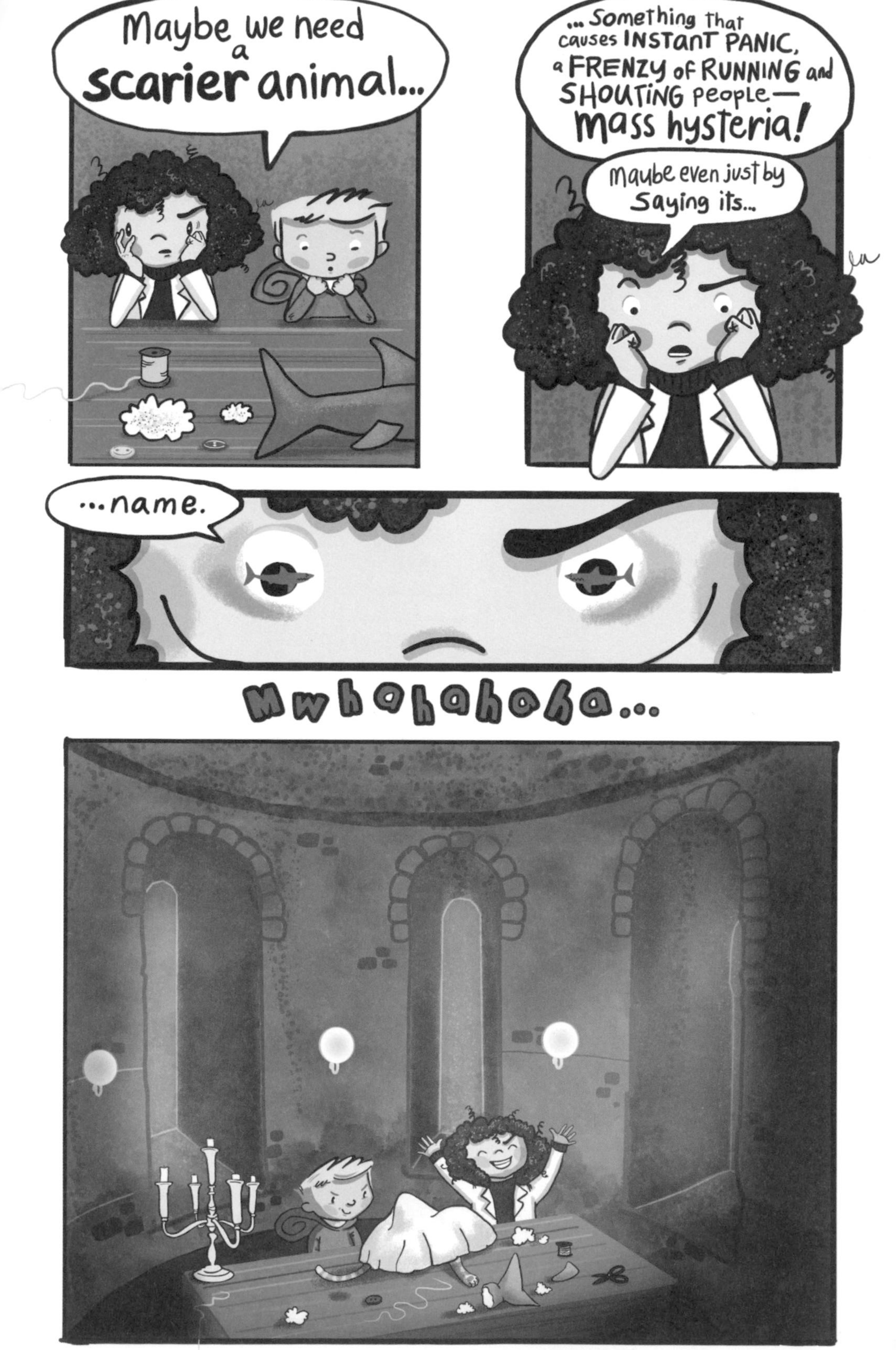
Maybe we need a scarier animal...
... Something that causes INSTANT PANIC, a FRENZY of RUNNING and SHOUTING people— mass hysteria!
Maybe even just by saying its...
...name.
Mwhahahaha...

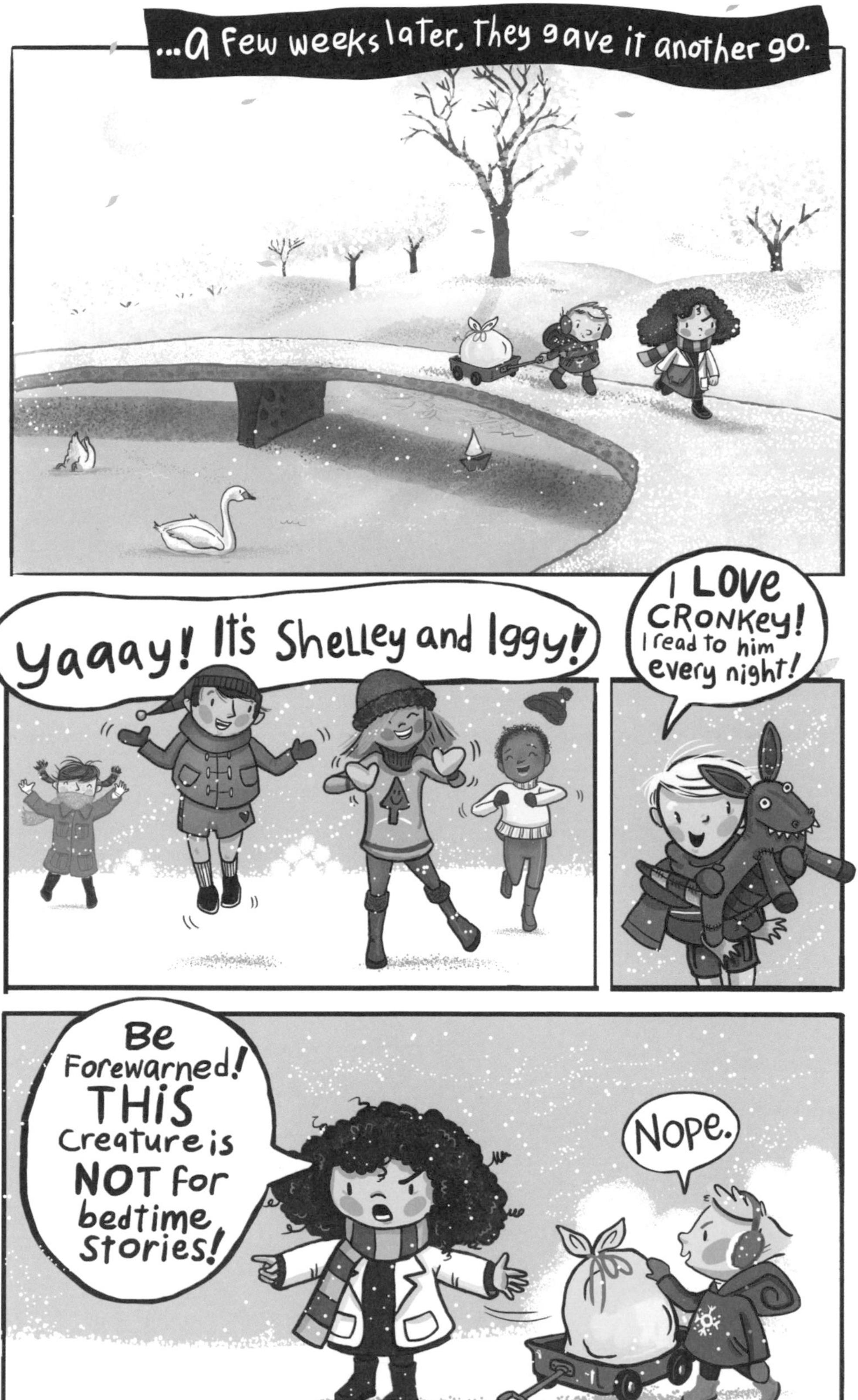
...a few weeks later, they gave it another go.
Yaaay! It's Shelley and Iggy!
I LOVE CRONKEY! I read to him every night!
Be Forewarned! THIS Creature is NOT for bedtime stories!
Nope.

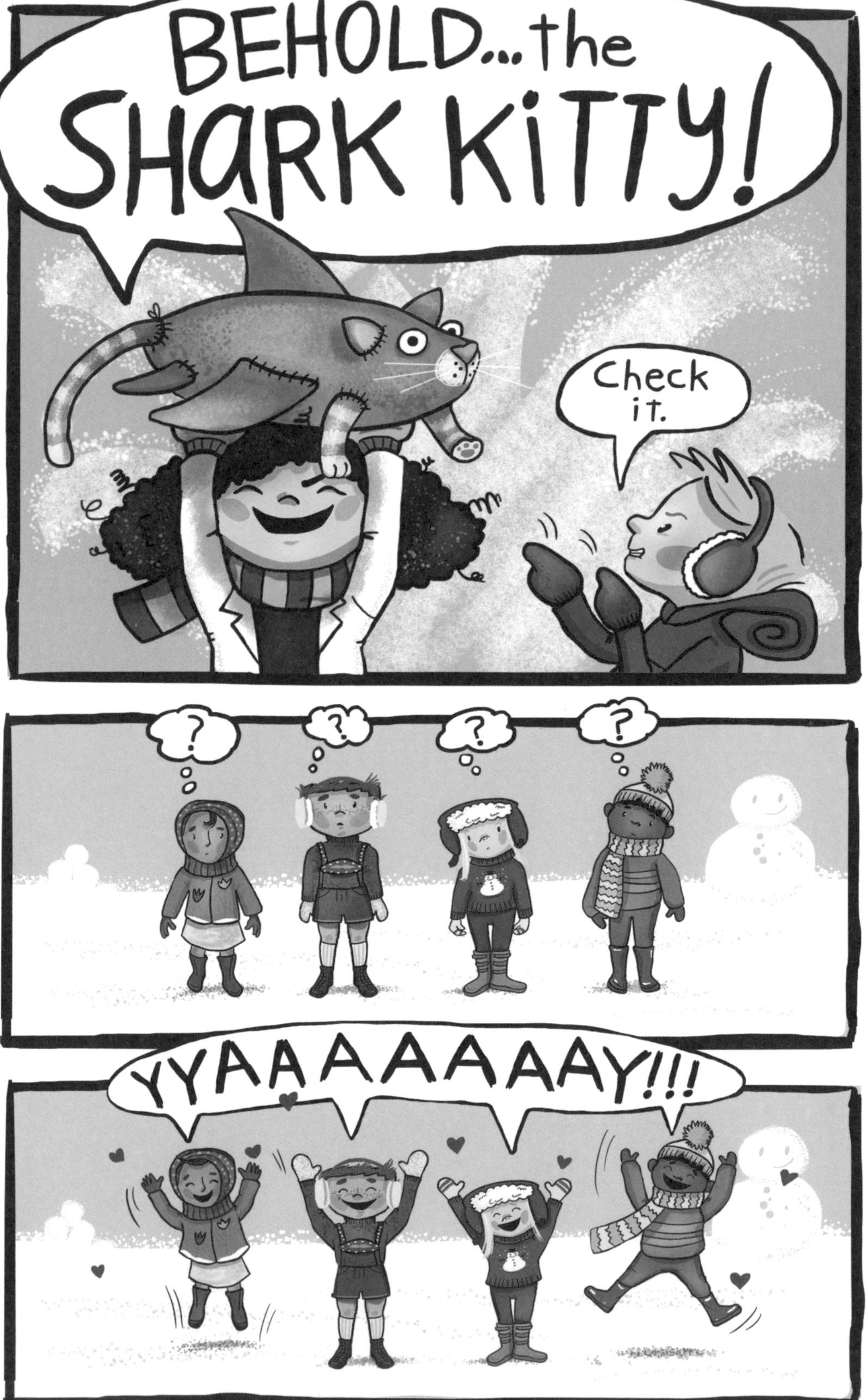
BEHOLD... the SHARK KiTTY!
Check it.
?
?
?
?
YYAAAAAAAAY!!!

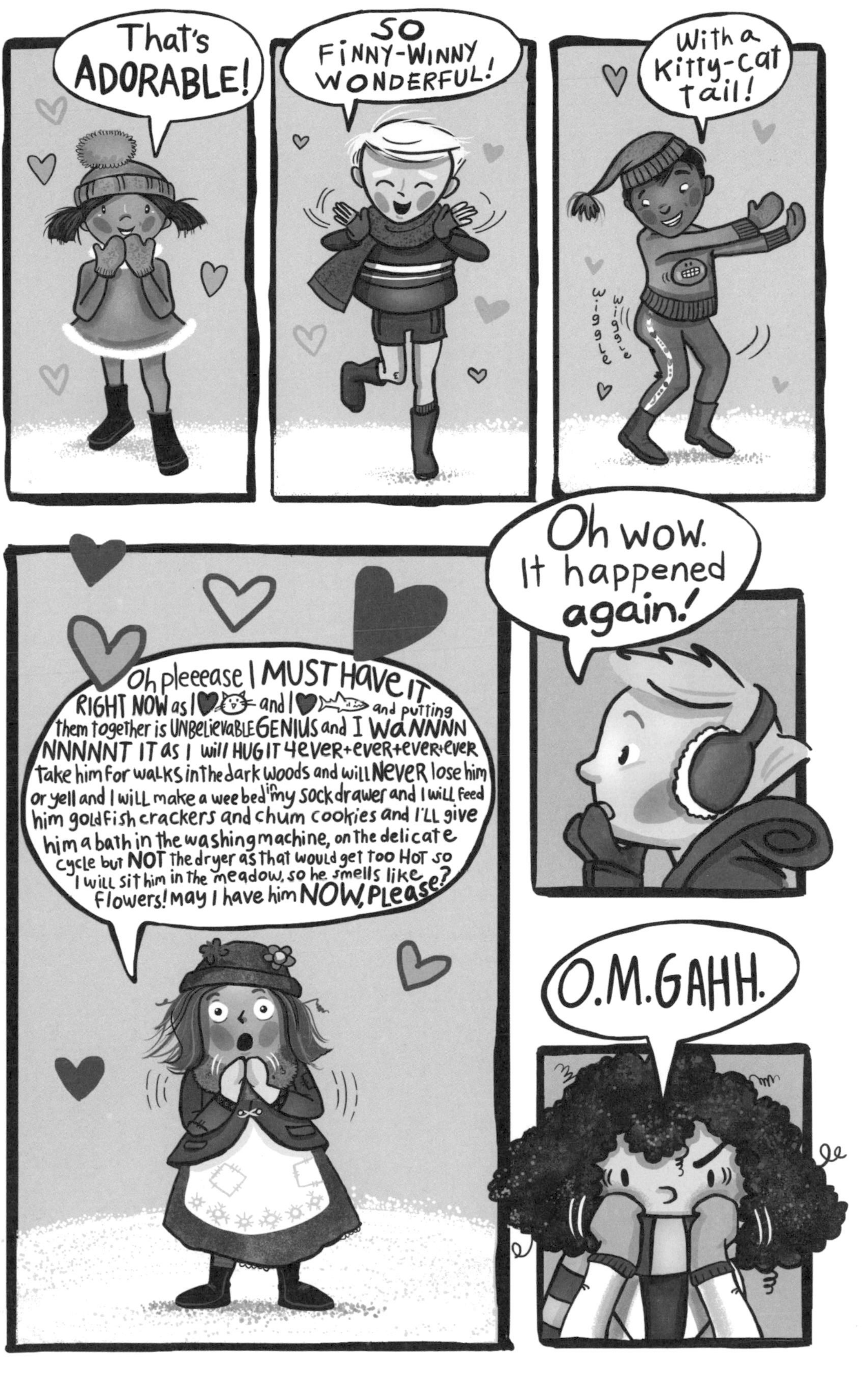
That's ADORABLE!
SO FINNY-WINNY WONDERFUL!
With a Kitty-cat tail!
wiggle
wiggle
Oh pleeease I MUST Have IT RIGHT NOW as I ♥ and I ♥ and putting them together is UNBELIEVABLE GENIUS and I WaNNNNNNNNNT IT as I will HUG IT 4ever+ever+ever+ever take him for walks in the dark woods and will NEVER lose him or yell and I will make a wee bed in my sock drawer and I will feed him goldfish crackers and chum cookies and I'LL give him a bath in the washing machine, on the delicate cycle but NOT the dryer as that would get too HOT so I will sit him in the meadow, so he smells like Flowers! May I have him NOW, Please?
Oh wow. It happened again!
O.M.GAHH.

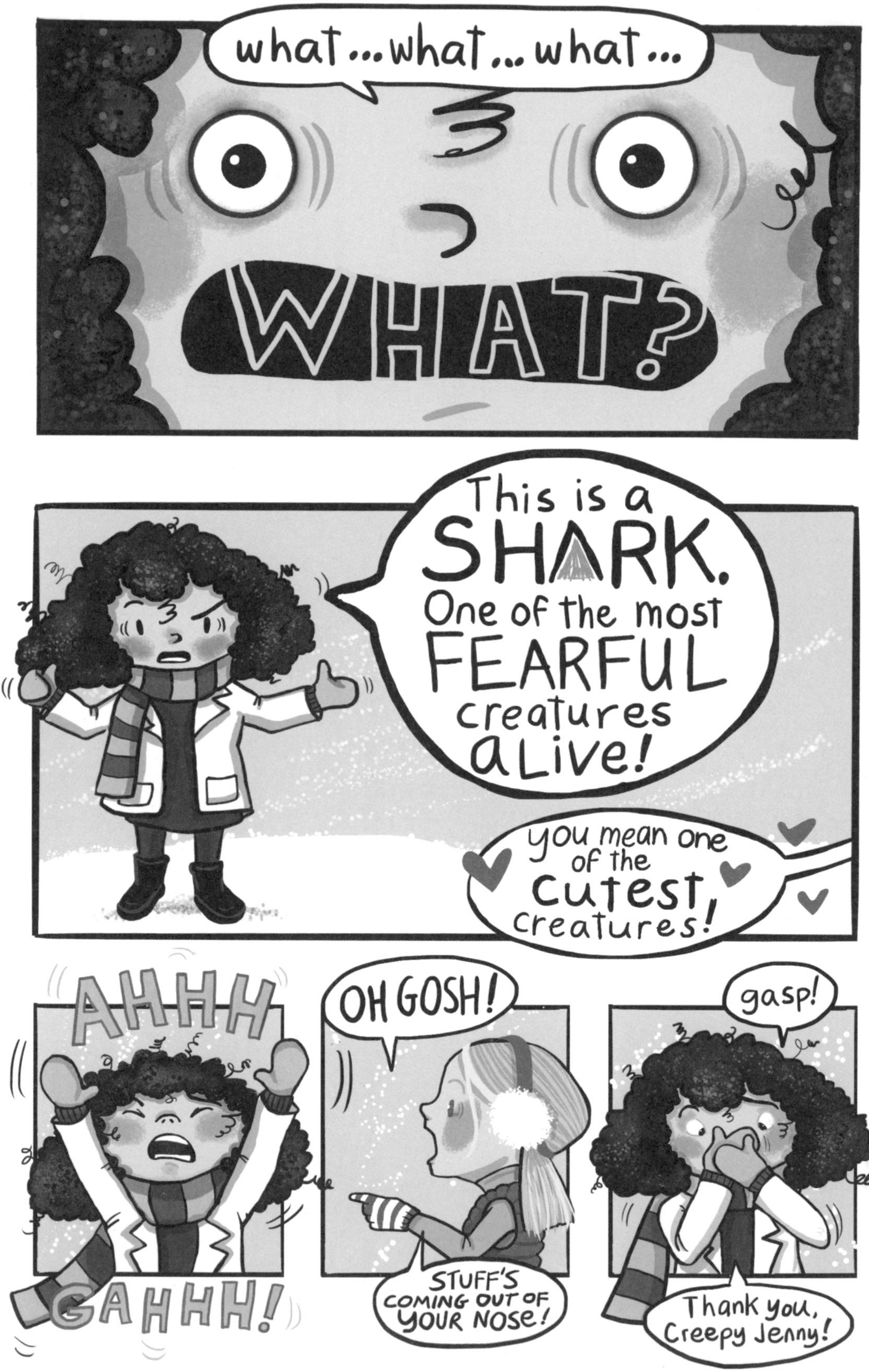
what...what...what...
WHAT?
This is a SHARK. One of the most FEARFUL creatures alive!
you mean one of the cutest creatures!
AHHH GAHHH!
OH GOSH!
STUFF'S COMING OUT OF YOUR NOSE!
gasp!
Thank you, Creepy Jenny!

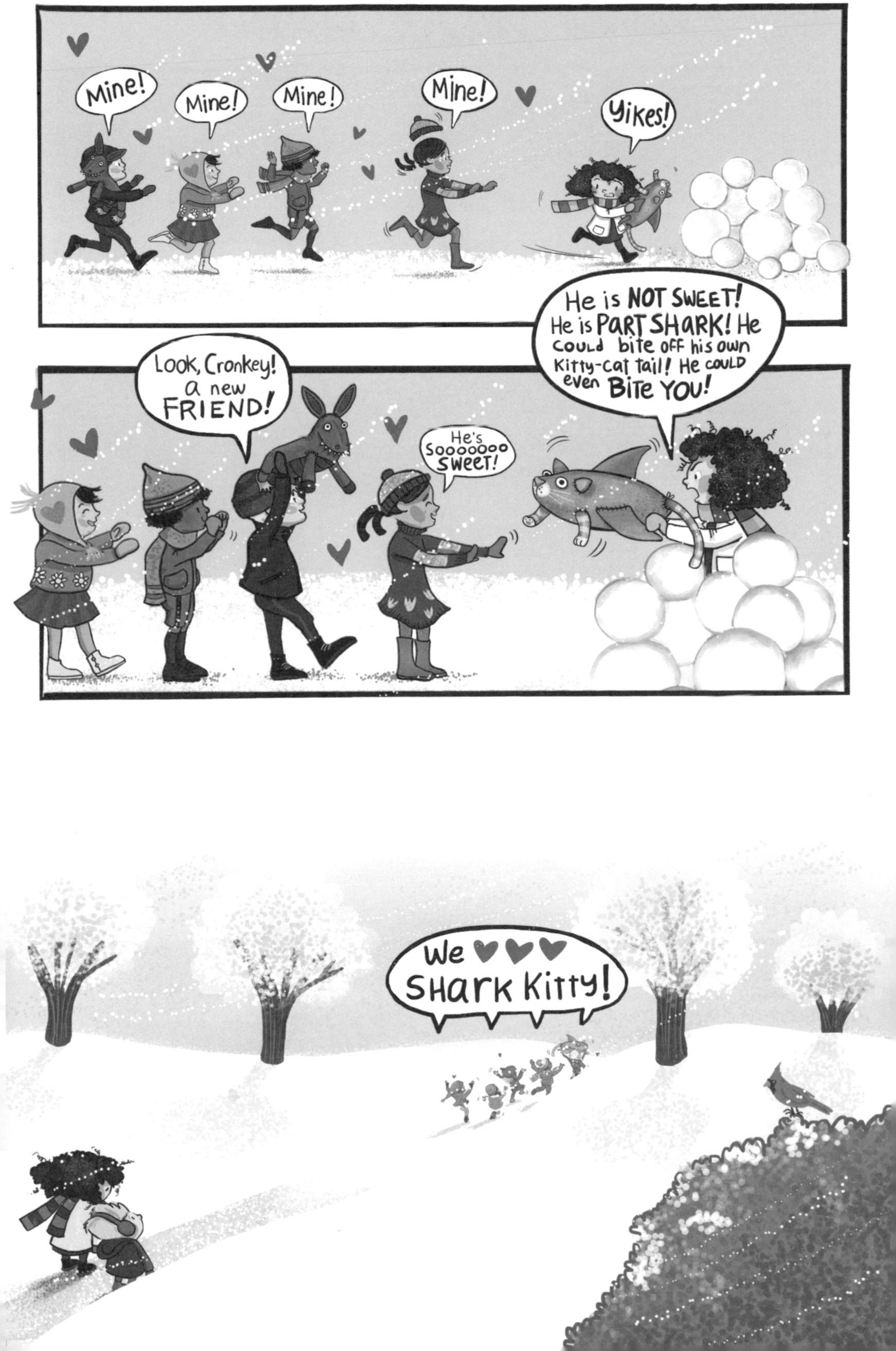
Mine!
Mine!
Mine!
Mine!
Yikes!
Look, Cronkey! a new FRIEND!
He's Sooooooo SWEET!
He is NOT SWEET! He is PART SHARK! He could bite off his own Kitty-cat tail! He could even BITE YOU!
We ♥♥♥ SHARK Kitty!

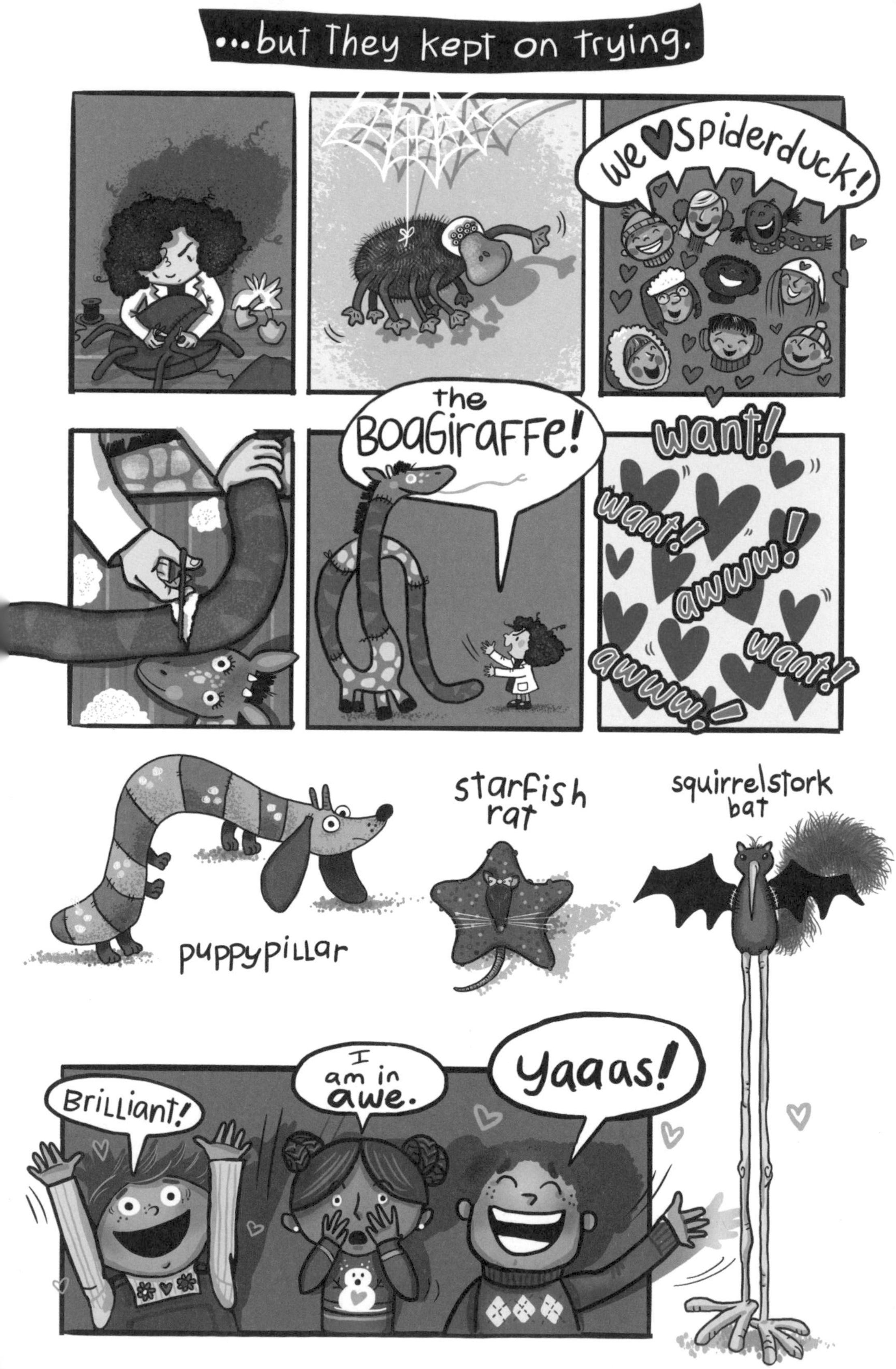
...but They kept on trying.
we ♥ Spiderduck!
the BOAGIRAFFE!
want!
want!
awww!
want!
awww!
puppypillar
starfish rat
squirrelstork bat
Brilliant!
I am in awe.
Yaaas!

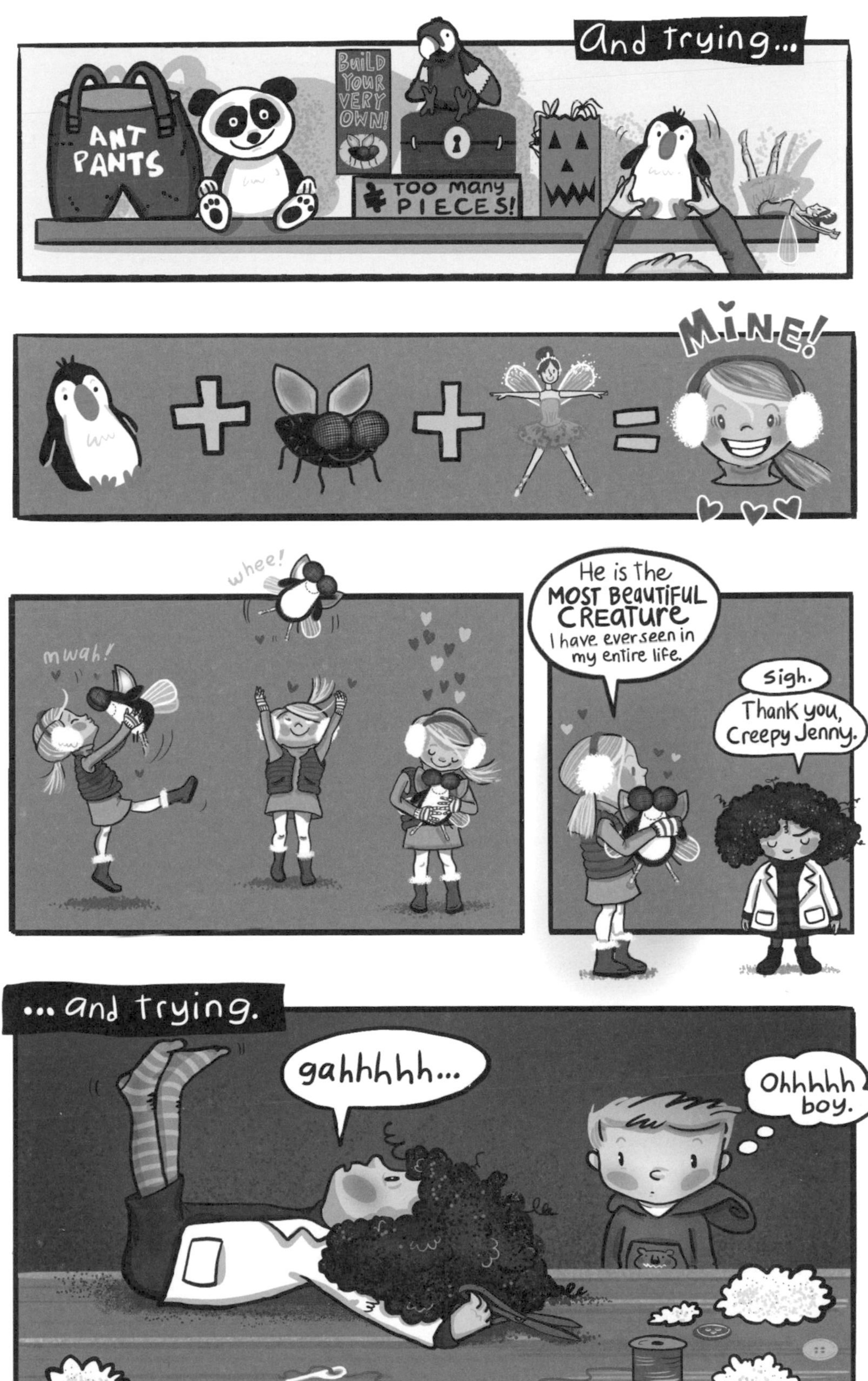
and trying...
ANT PANTS
BUILD YOUR VERY OWN!
TOO MANY PIECES!
MINE!
whee!
mwah!
He is the MOST BEAUTIFUL CREATURE I have ever seen in my entire life.
Sigh.
Thank you, Creepy Jenny.
...and trying.
gahhhhh...
Ohhhhh boy.

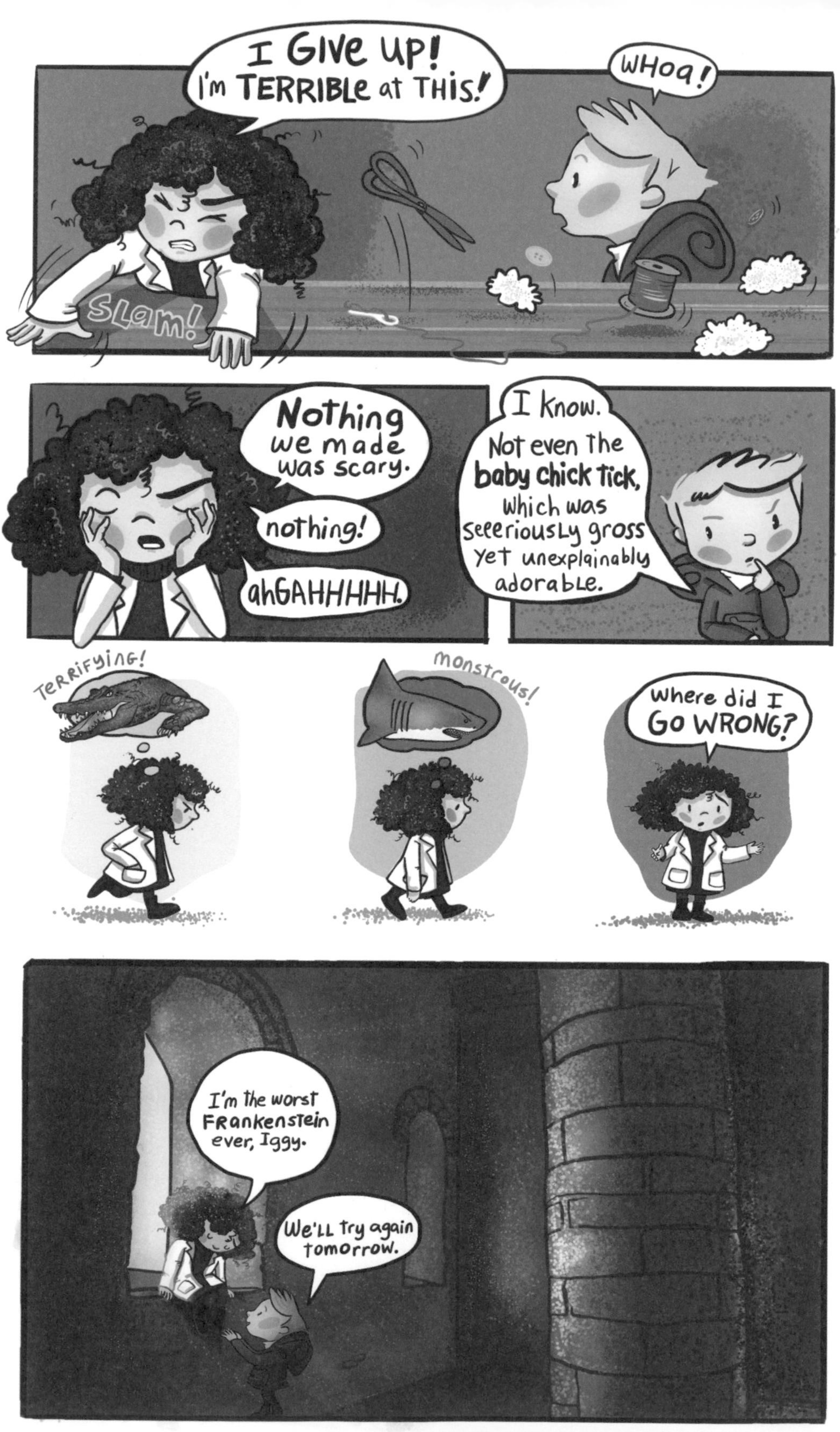
I GIVE UP! I'm TERRIBLE at THIS!
WHOa!
SLAM!
Nothing we made was scary.
nothing!
ahGAHHHHH.
I know.
Not even the baby chick tick, which was seeeriously gross yet unexplainably adorable.
TERRIFYING!
monstrous!
Where did I GO WRONG?
I'm the worst Frankenstein ever, Iggy.
We'll try again tomorrow.

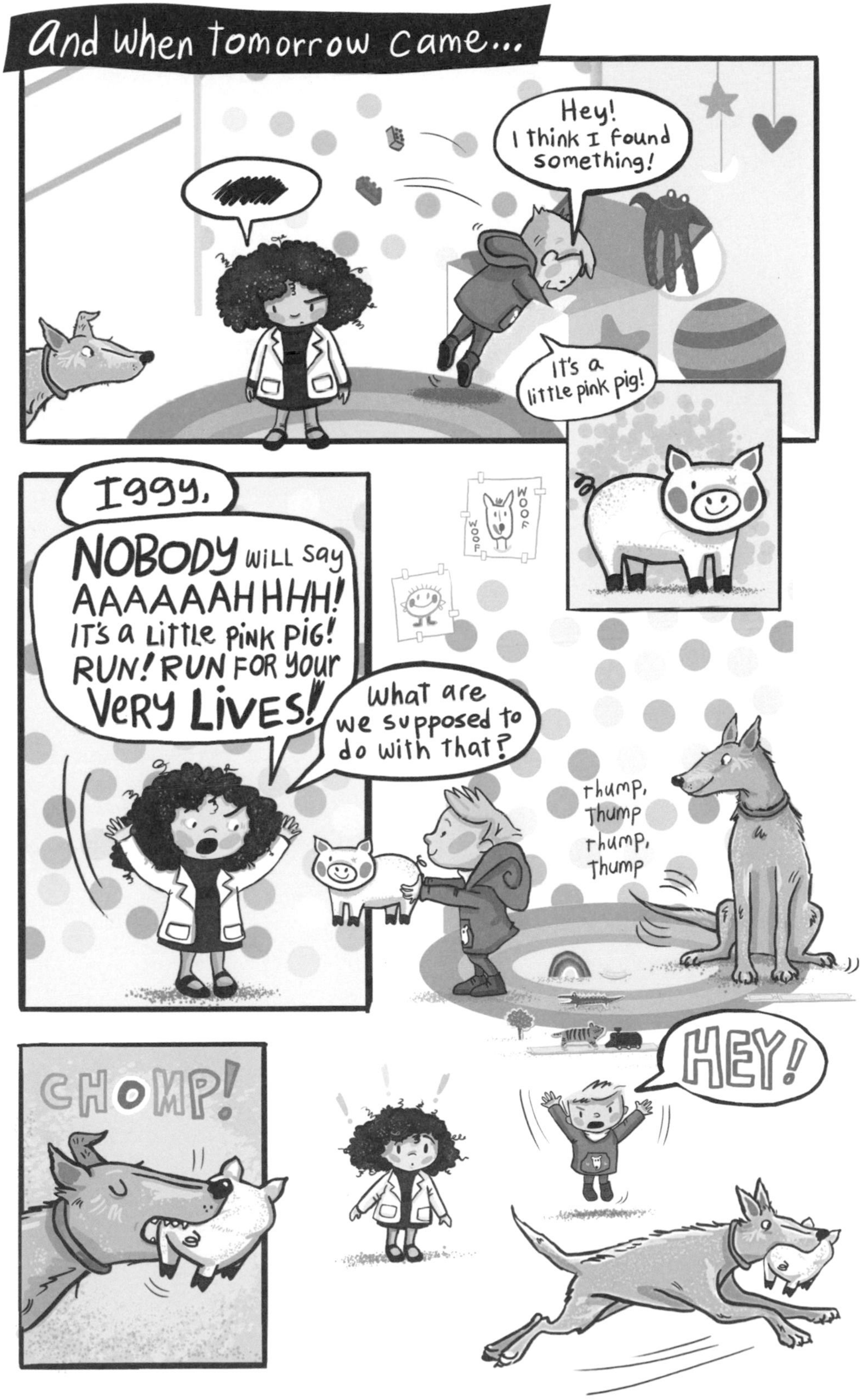
And when tomorrow came...
Hey! I think I found something!
It's a little pink pig!
Iggy,
NOBODY will say AAAAAAHHHH! IT'S a little pink PIG! RUN! RUN FOR your Very LIVES!
What are we supposed to do with that?
thump, thump thump, thump
WOOF WOOF
CHOMP!
HEY!

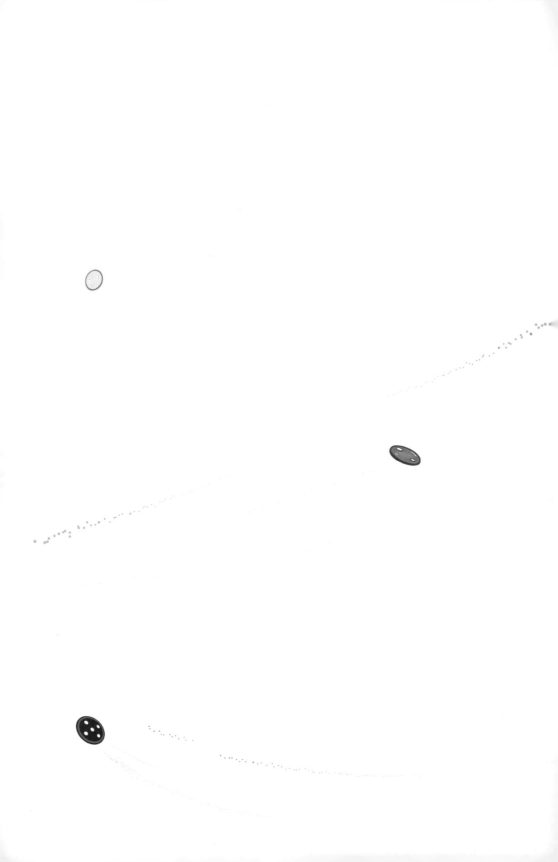

COwPiggY

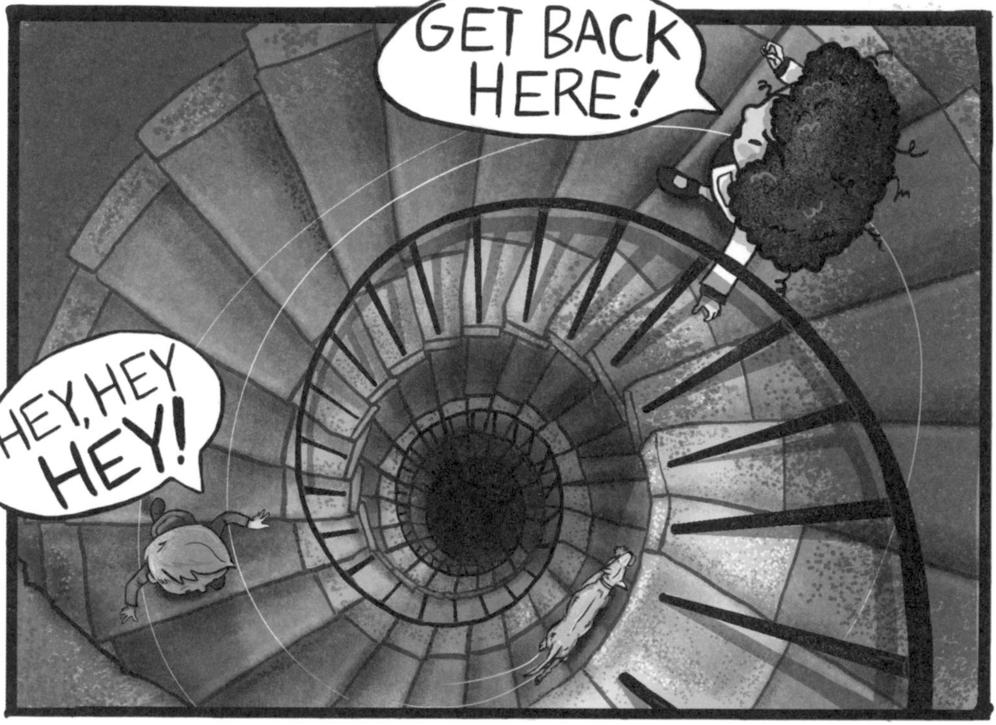
GET BACK HERE!
HEY, HEY HEY!

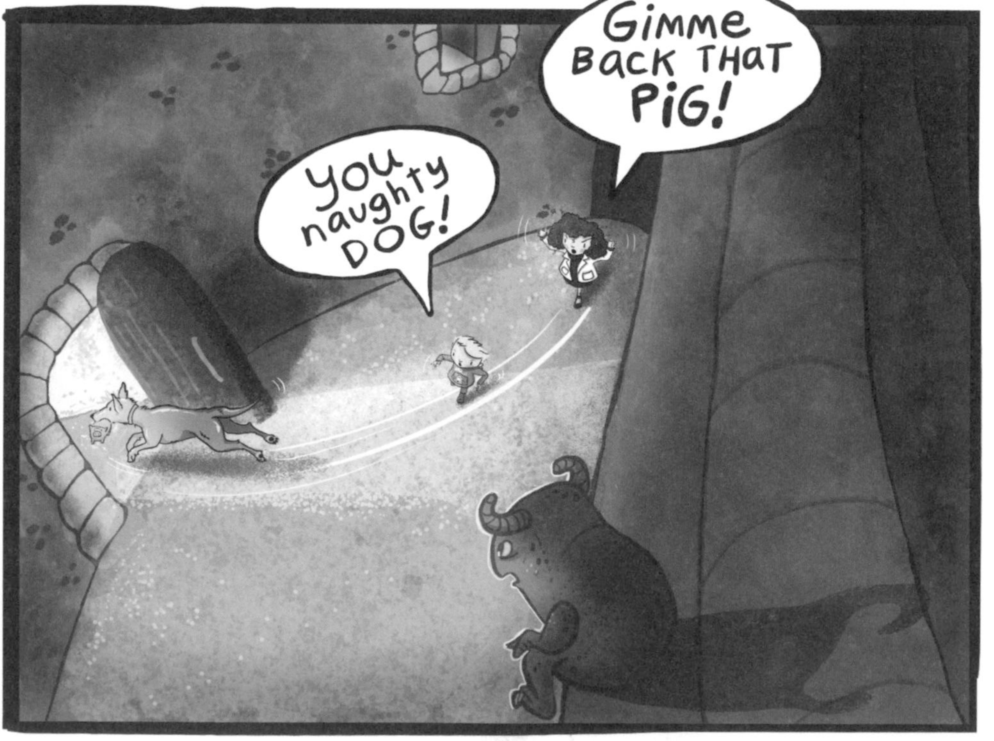
Gimme Back THAT PiG!
YOU naughty DOG!

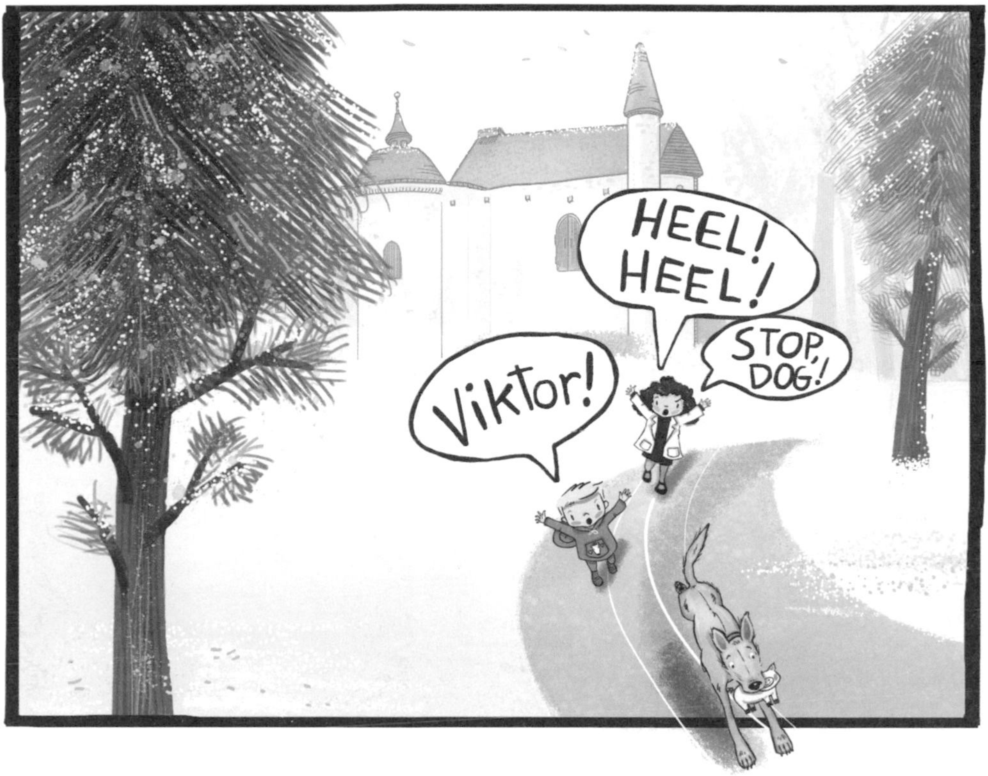
HEEL! HEEL!
STOP, DOG!
Viktor!

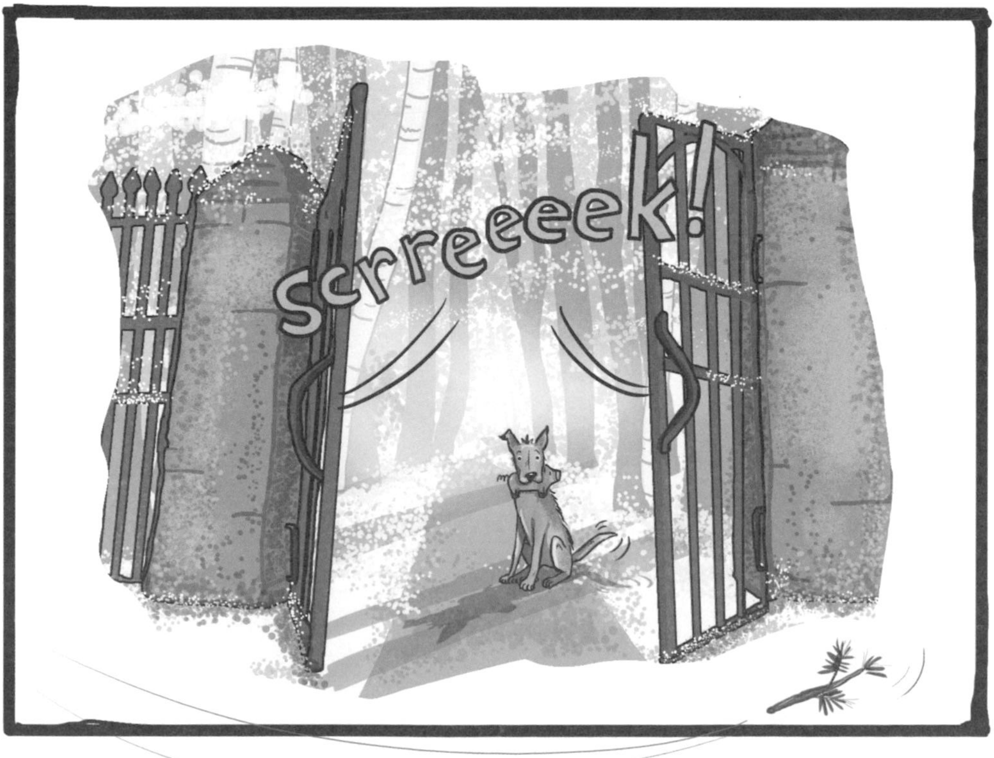
Scrreeeek!

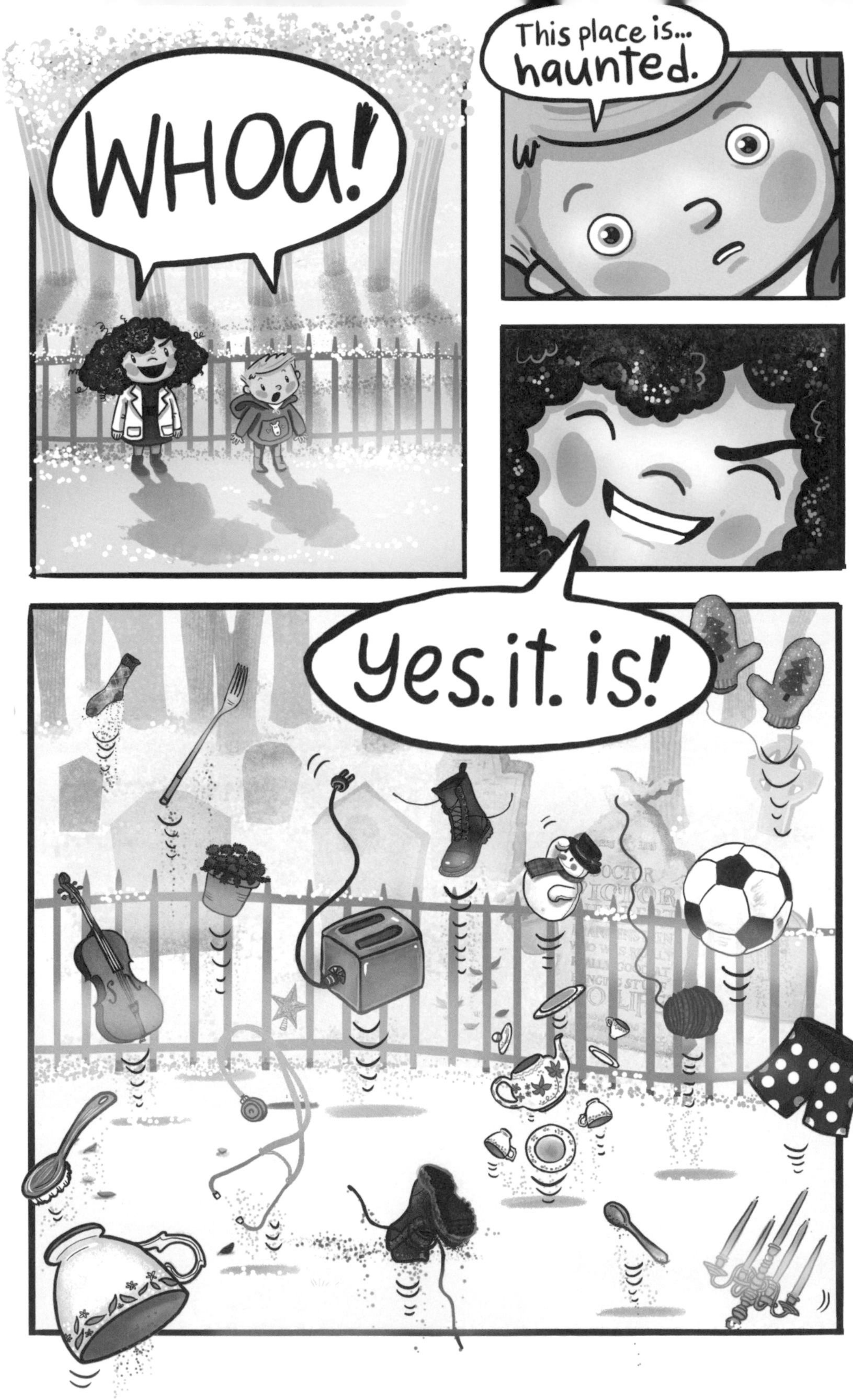
WHOA!
This place is...
haunted.
Yes. it. is!

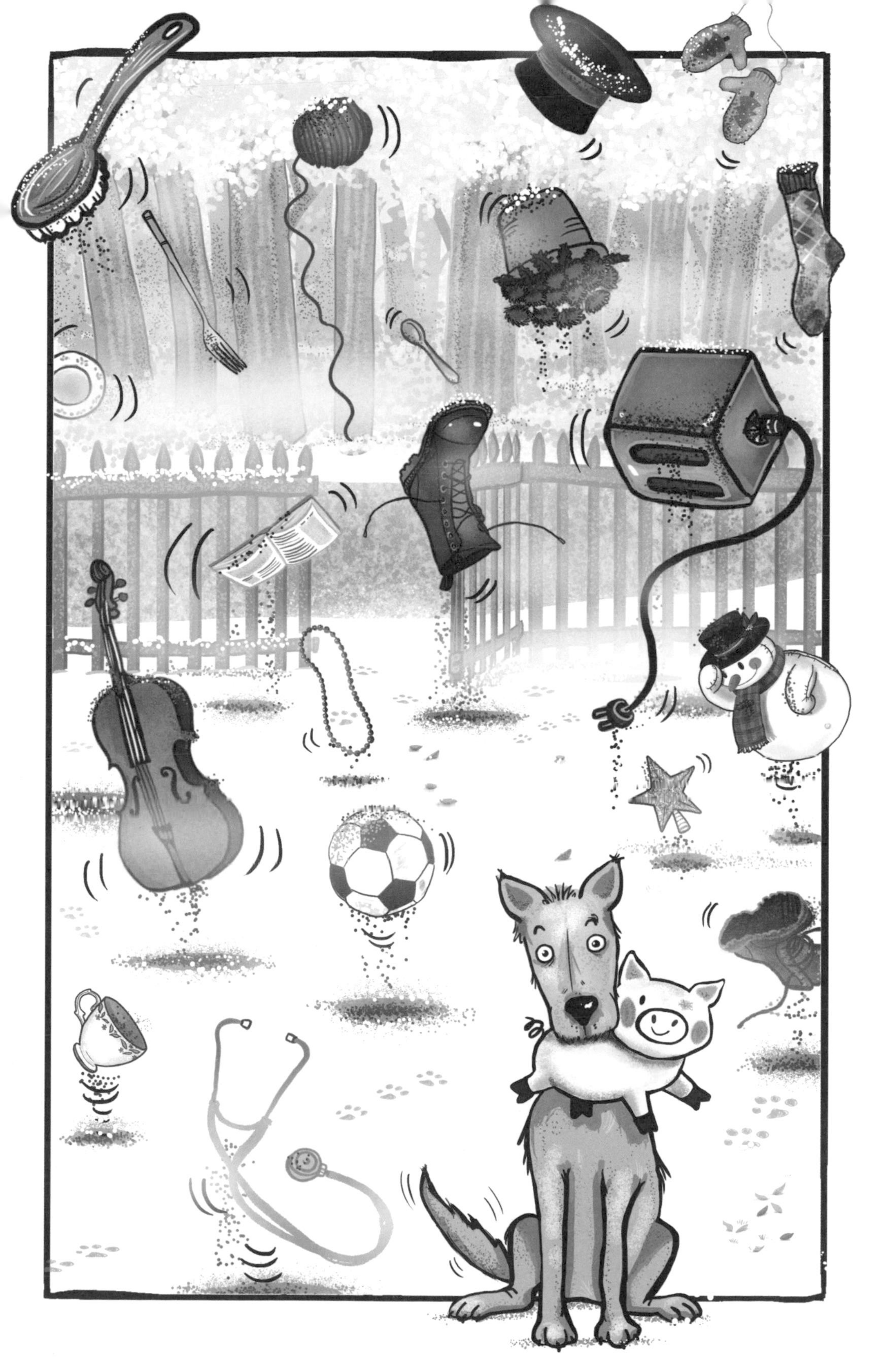

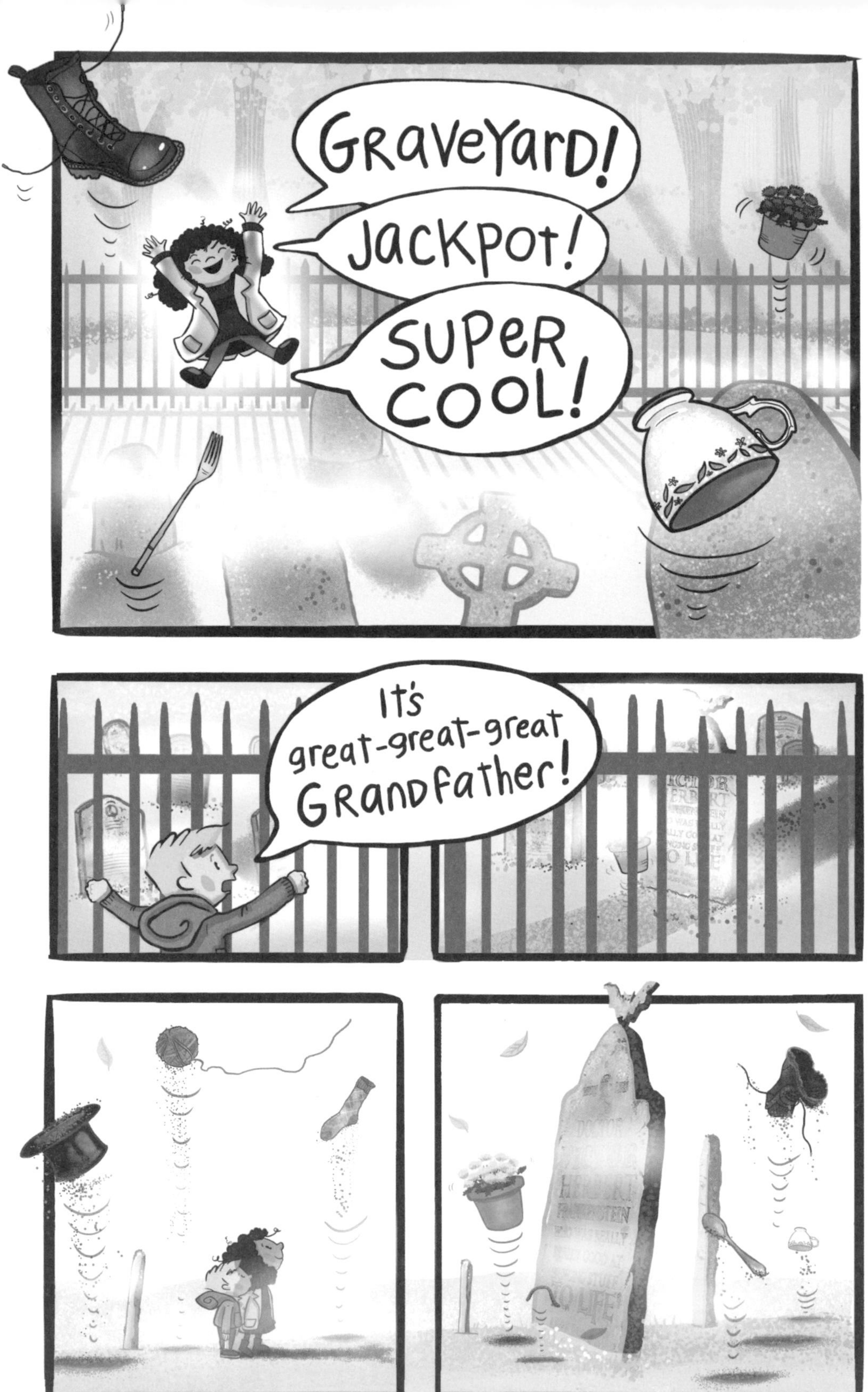
GRAVEYARD!
JACKPOT!
SUPER COOL!
It's great-great-great Grandfather!

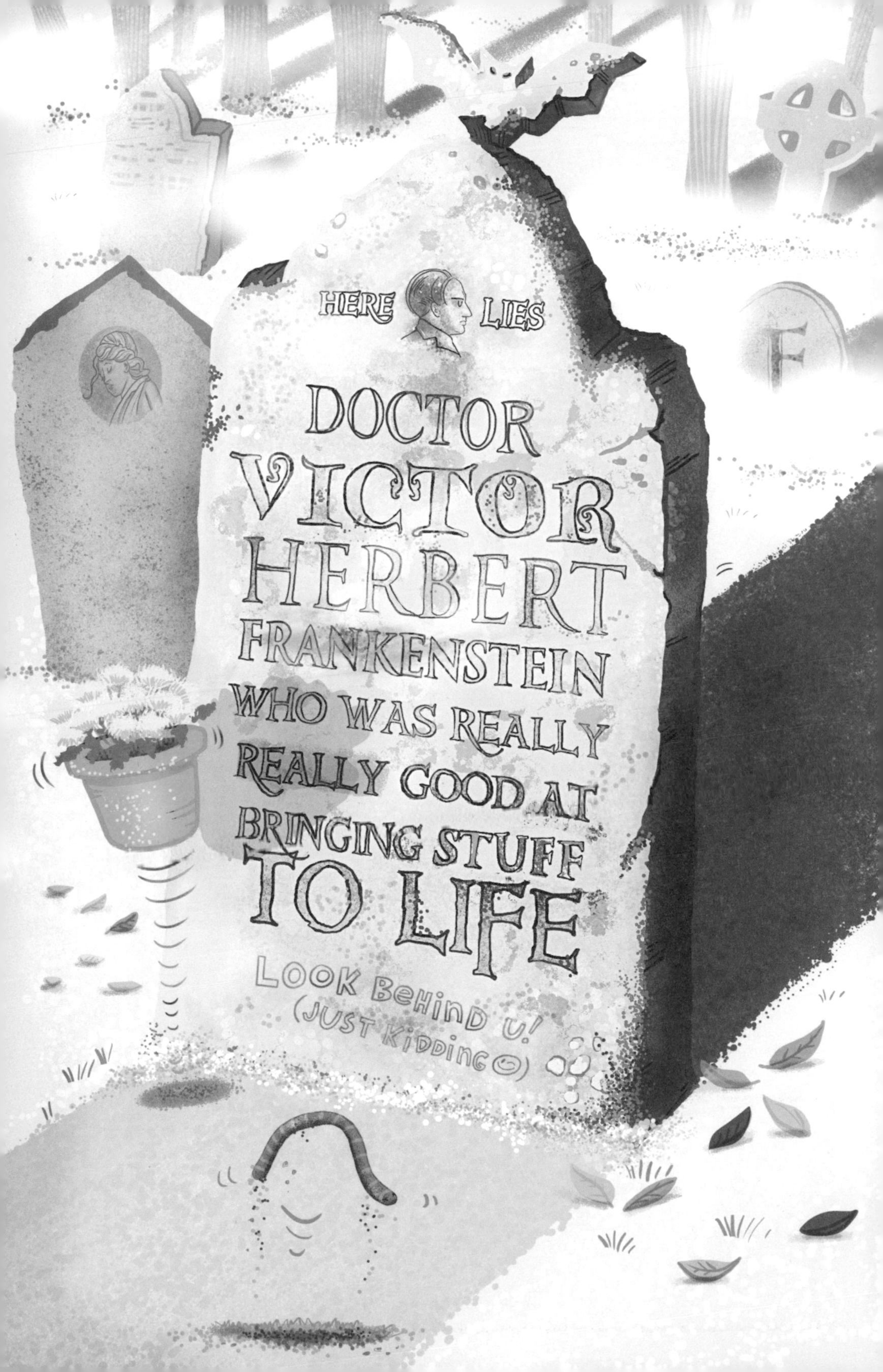
HERE LIES
DOCTOR VICTOR HERBERT FRANKENSTEIN WHO WAS REALLY REALLY GOOD AT BRINGING STUFF TO LIFE
LOOK BEHIND U! (JUST KIDDING ☺)
F

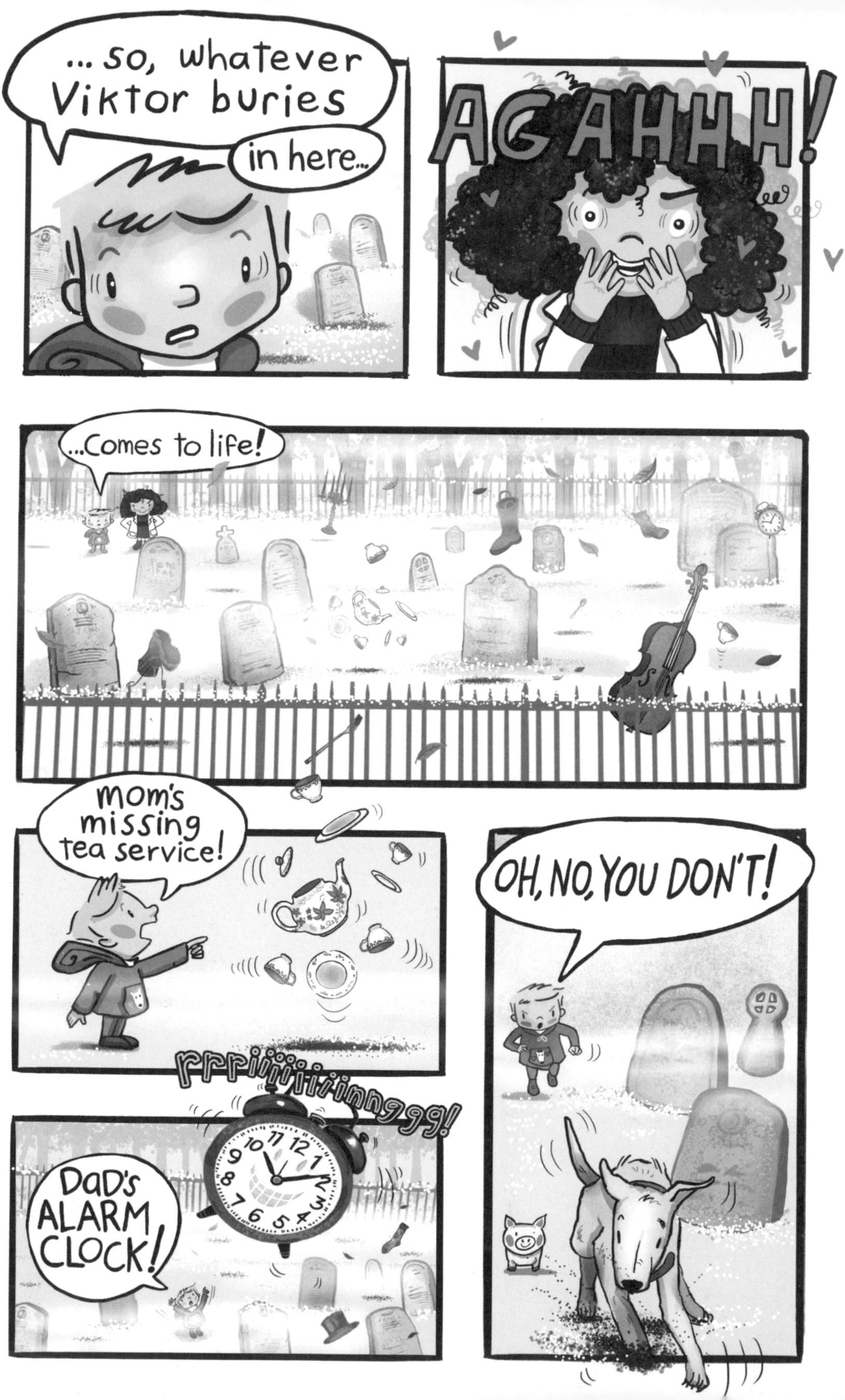
... so, whatever Viktor buries
in here...
AGAHHH!
...Comes to life!
mom's missing tea service!
OH, NO, YOU DON'T!
Dad's ALARM CLOCK!
rrriiiiiiiiinnggg!

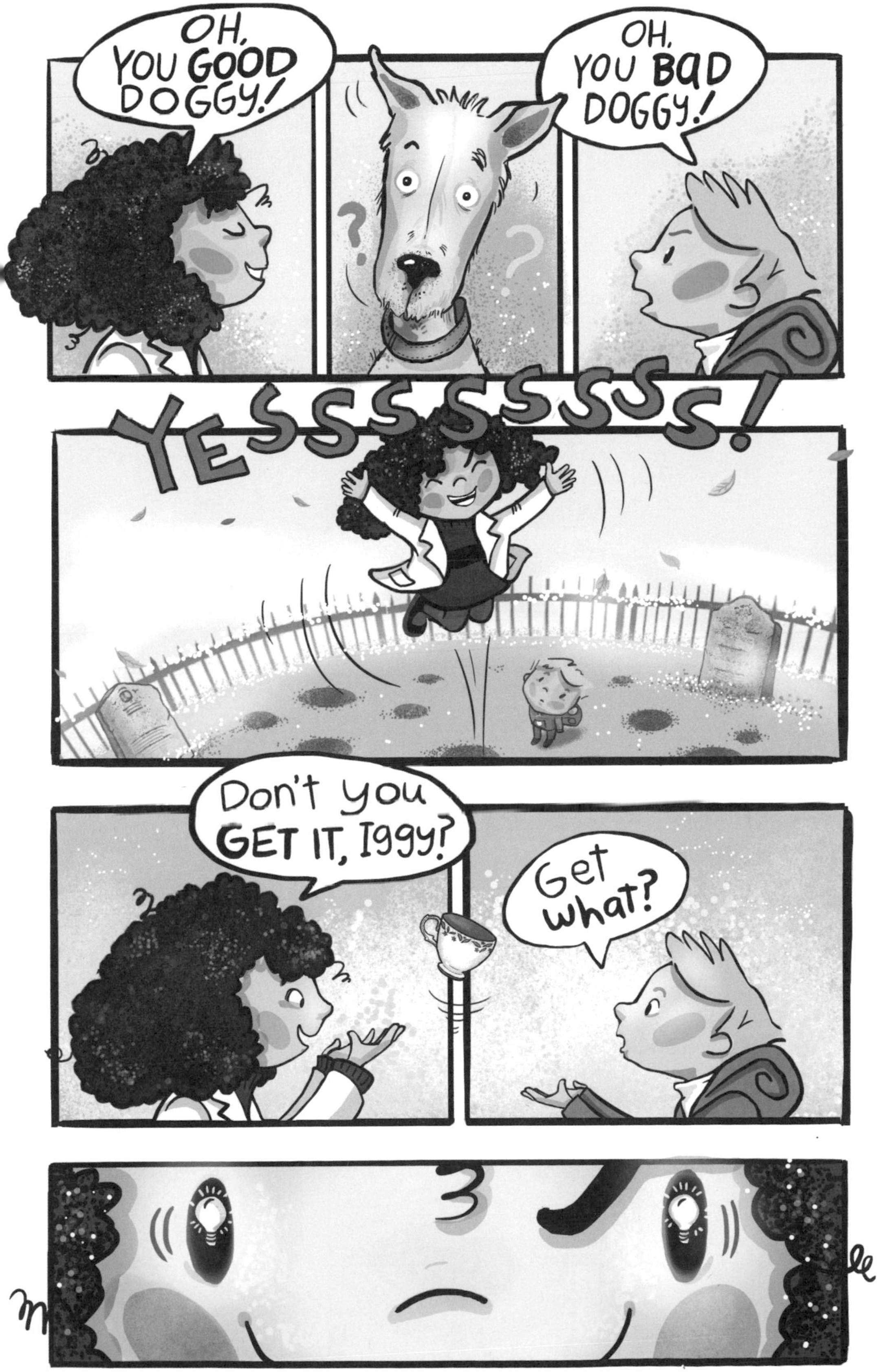
OH, YOU GOOD DOGGY!
OH, YOU BAD DOGGY!
YESSSSSSS!
Don't you GET IT, Iggy?
Get what?

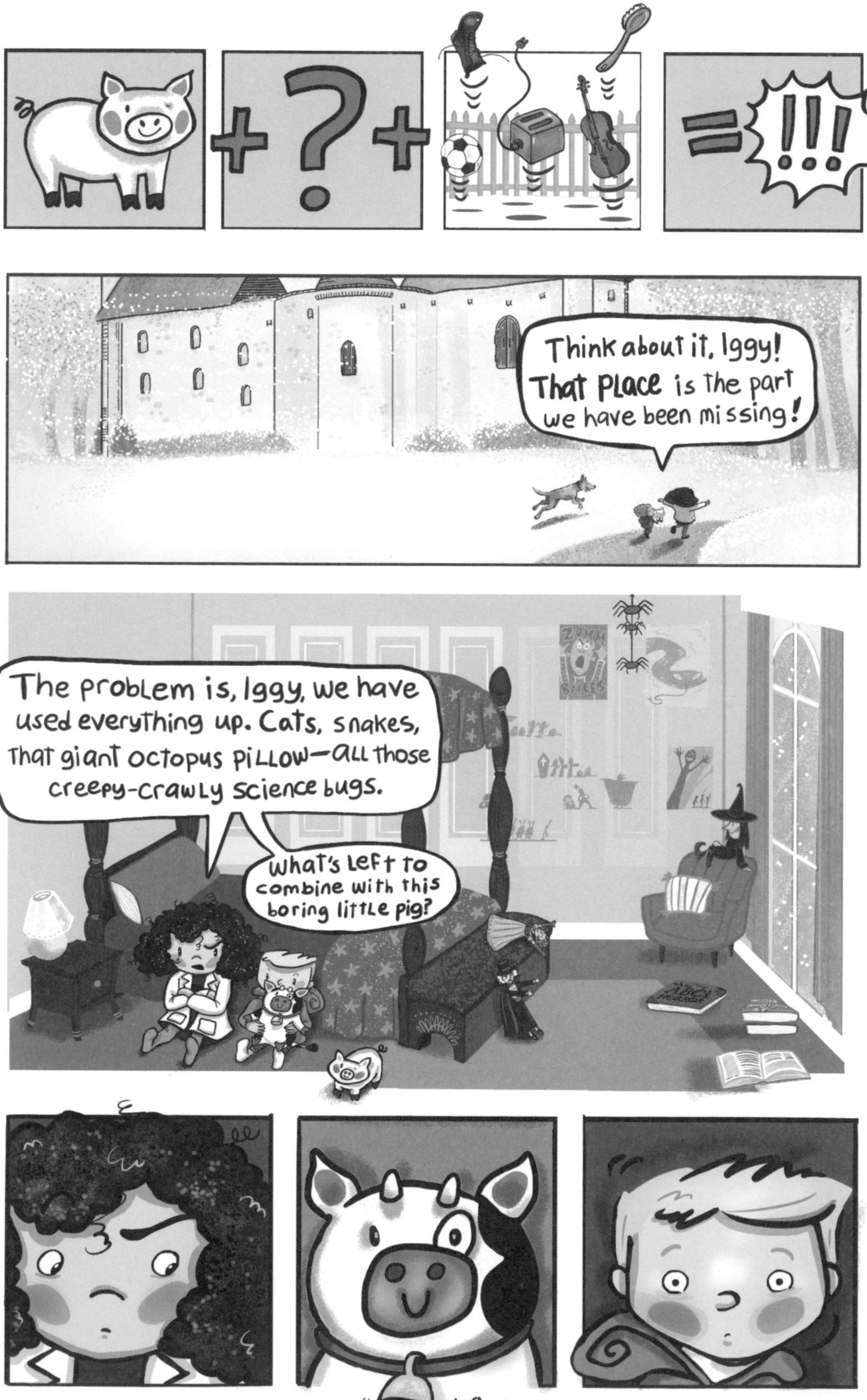
=!!!
Think about it, Iggy! That PLACE is the part we have been missing!
The problem is, Iggy, we have used everything up. Cats, snakes, that giant octopus pillow—all those creepy-crawly science bugs.
What's left to combine with this boring little pig?
ting ting!

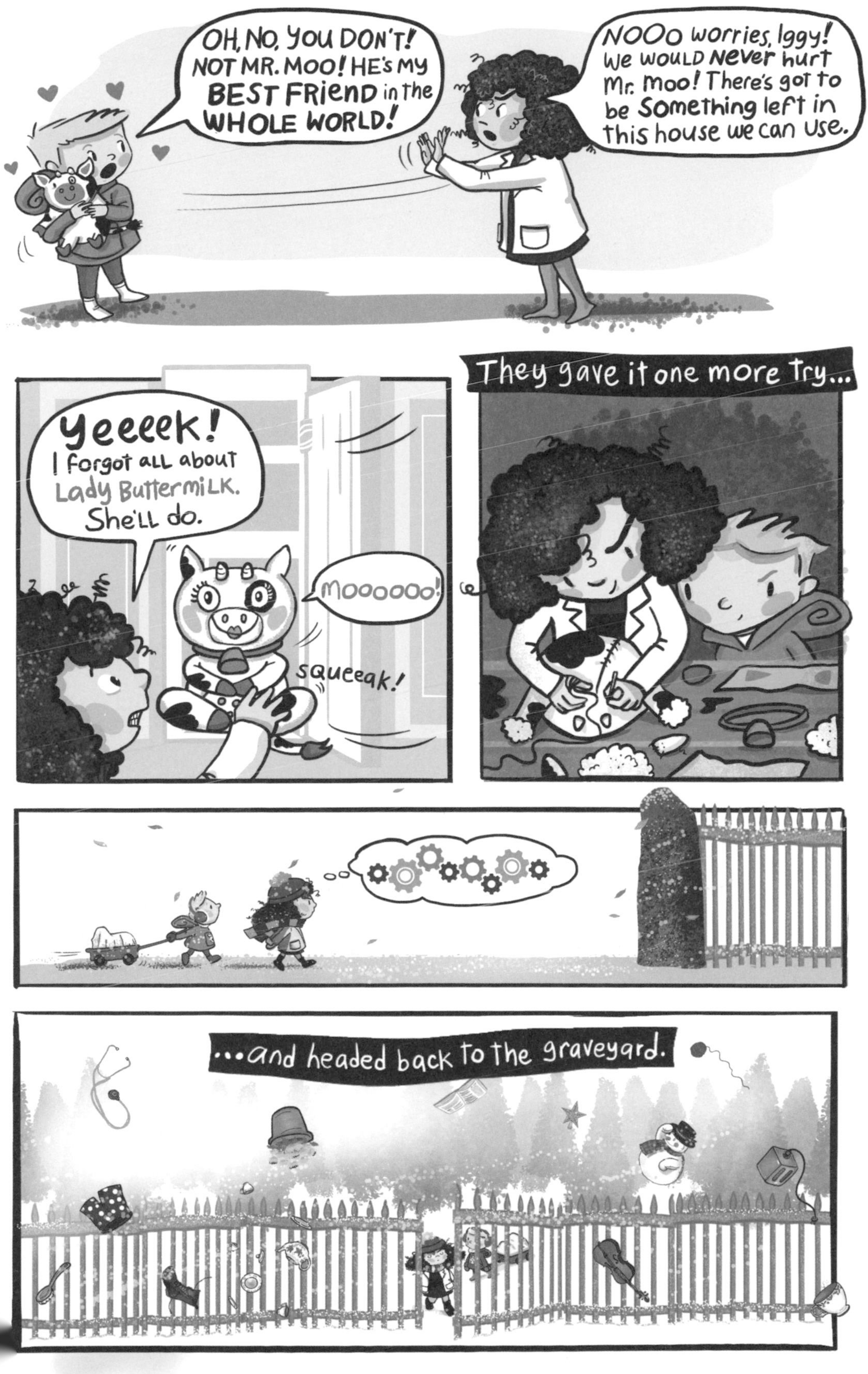

OH, NO, YOU DON'T! NOT MR. MOO! HE'S MY BEST FRIEND in the WHOLE WORLD!
NOOo worries, Iggy! We would Never hurt Mr. Moo! There's got to be Something left in this house we can use.
Yeeeek! I forgot all about Lady Buttermilk. She'll do.
Moooooo!
squeeak!
They gave it one more try...
...and headed back to the graveyard.

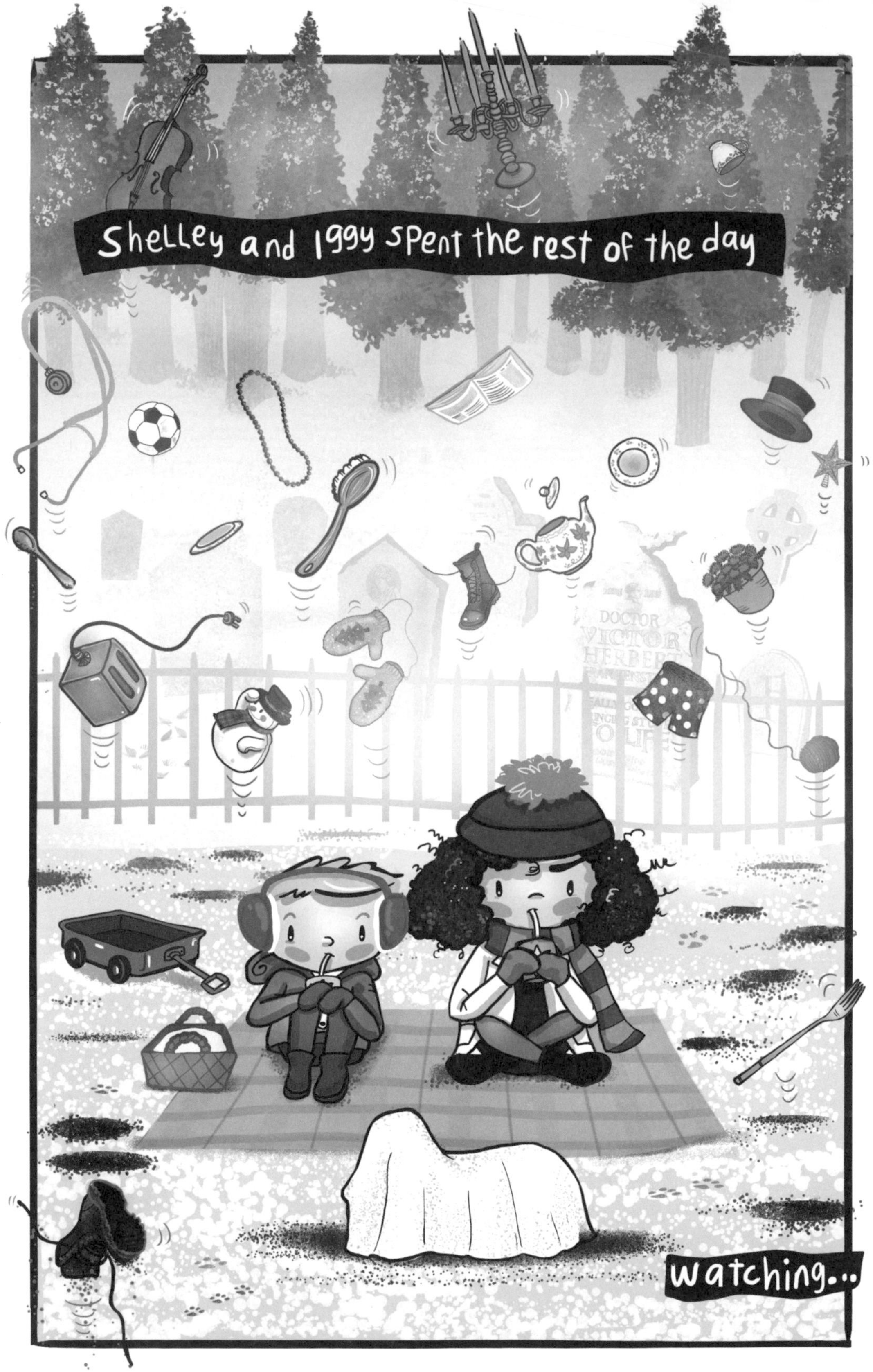
Shelley and Iggy spent the rest of the day
watching...

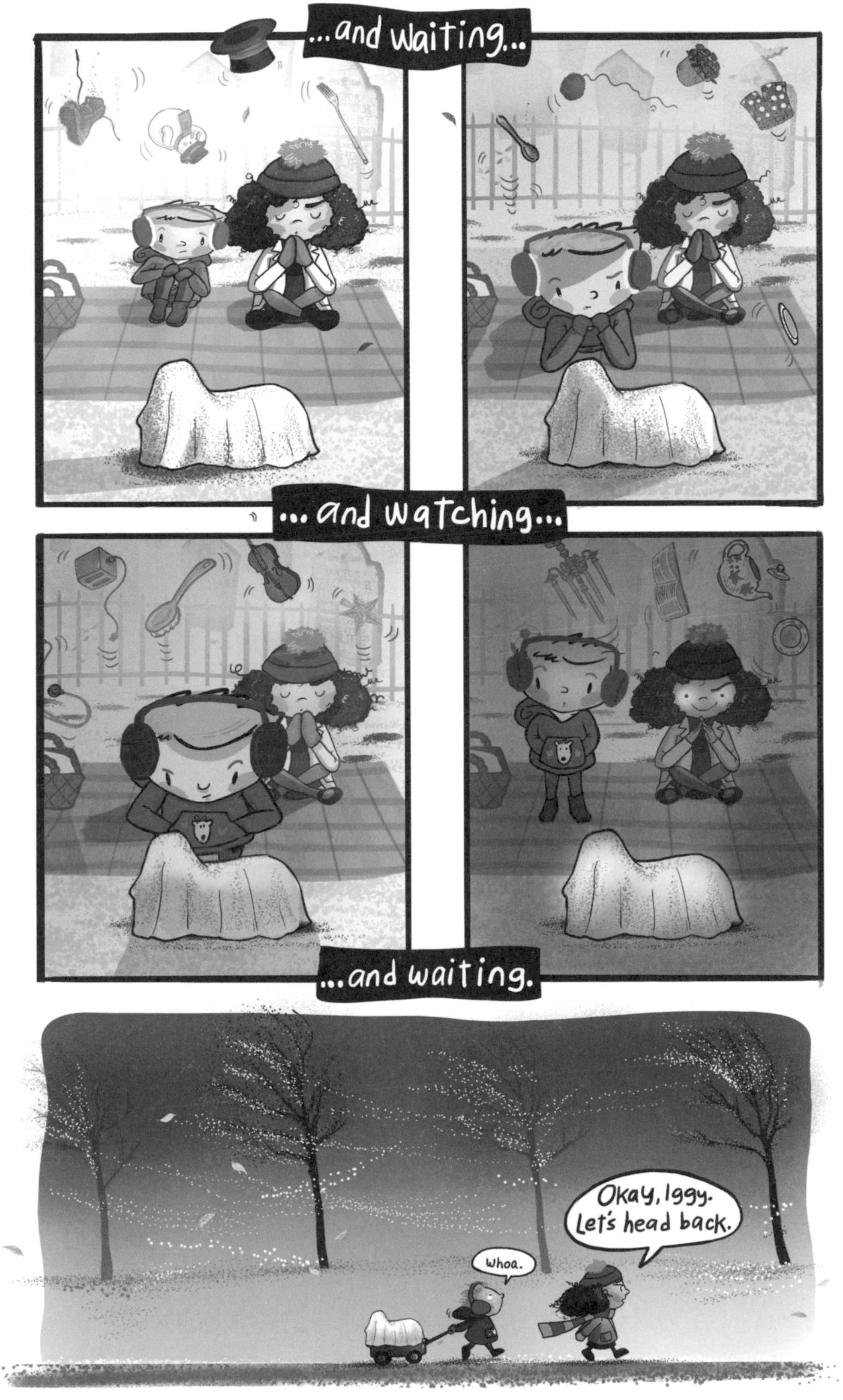
...and waiting...
...and watching...
...and waiting.
Whoa.
Okay, Iggy. Let's head back.

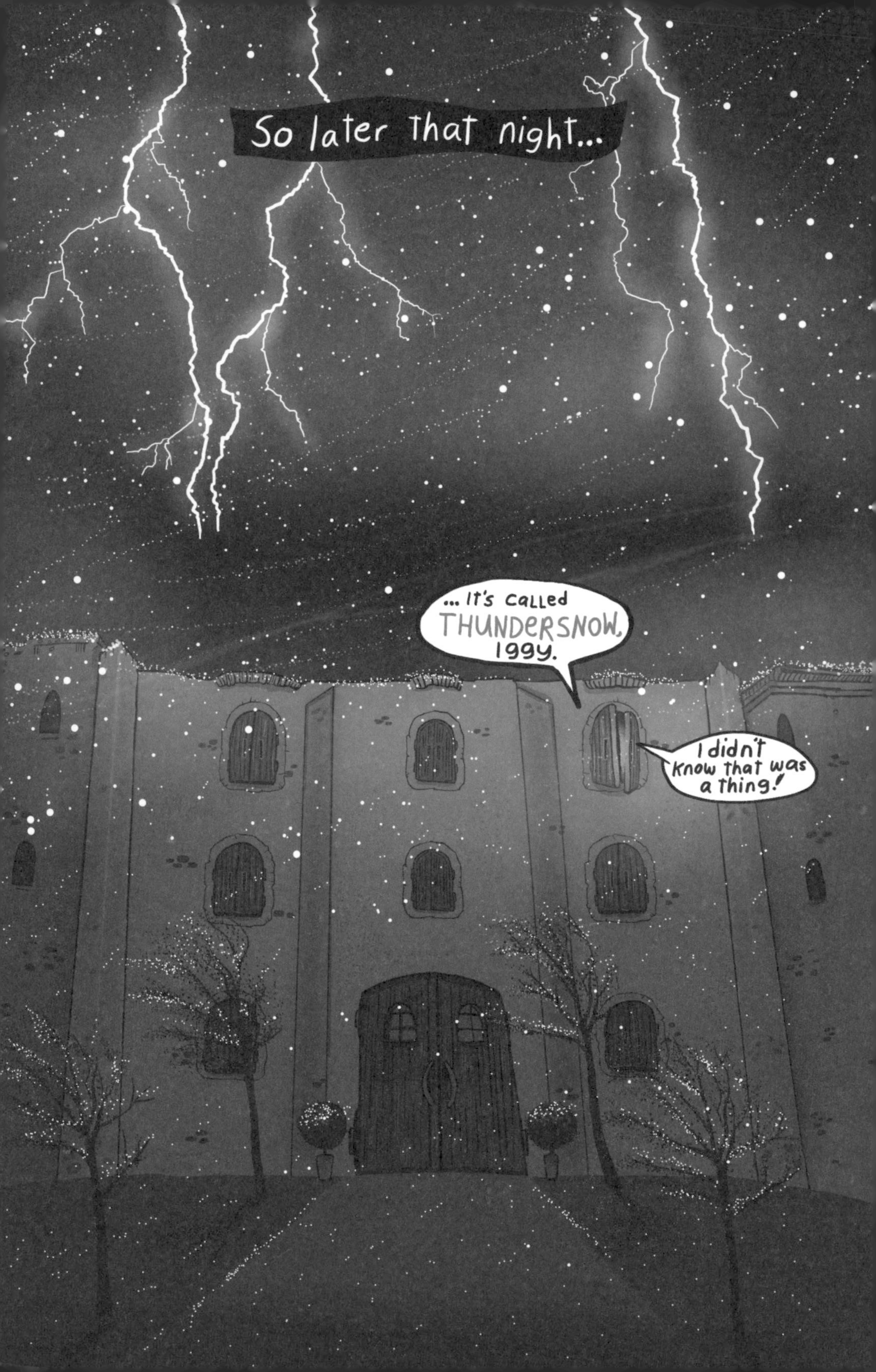
So later that night...
... It's called THUNDERSNOW, Iggy.
I didn't know that was a thing!

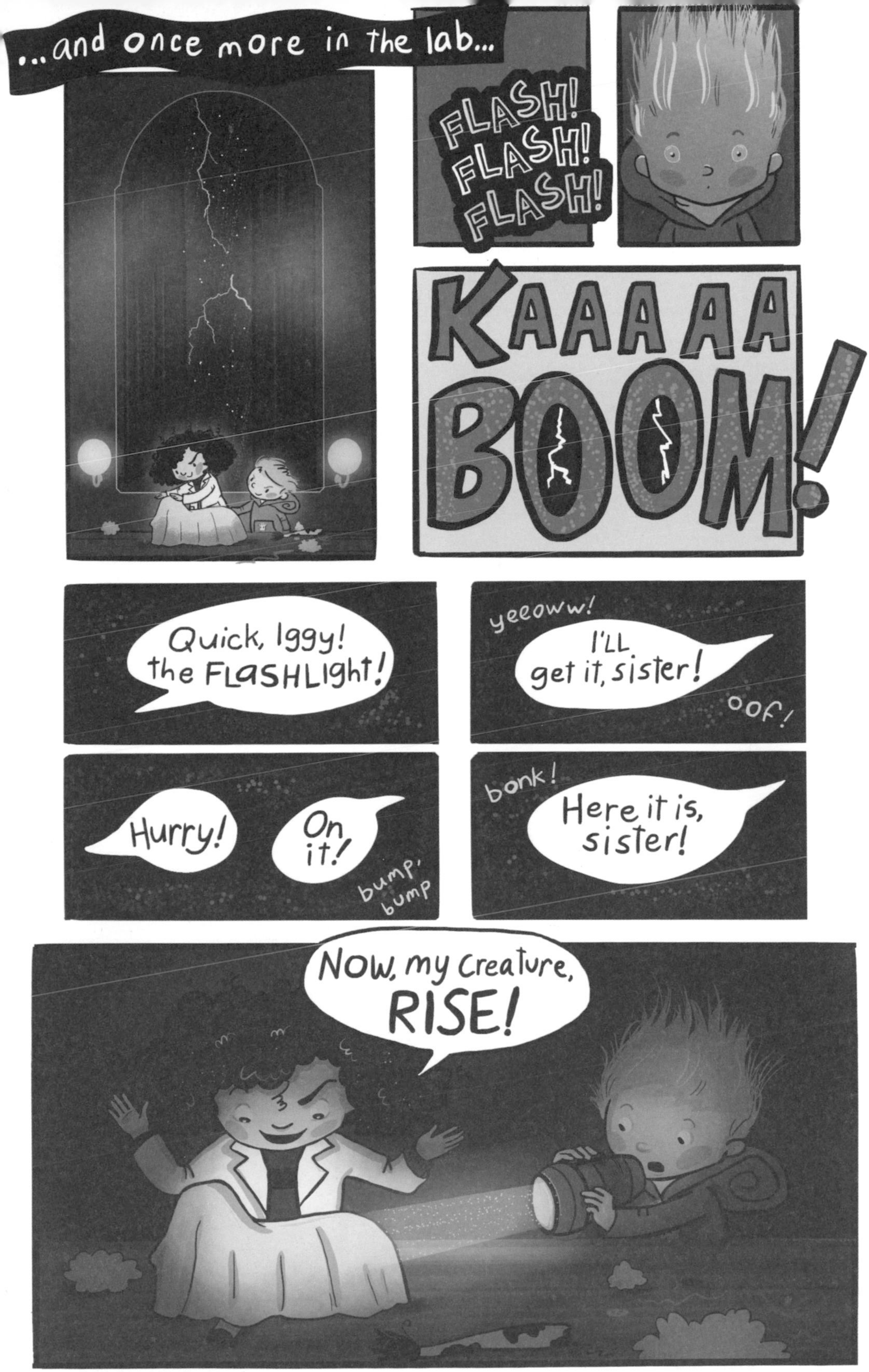
...and once more in the lab...
FLASH!
FLASH!
FLASH!
KAAAAA
BOOM!
Quick, Iggy! the FLASHLight!
yeeoww!
I'LL get it, sister!
oof!
Hurry!
On it!
bump, bump
bonk!
Here it is, sister!
Now, my Creature, RISE!

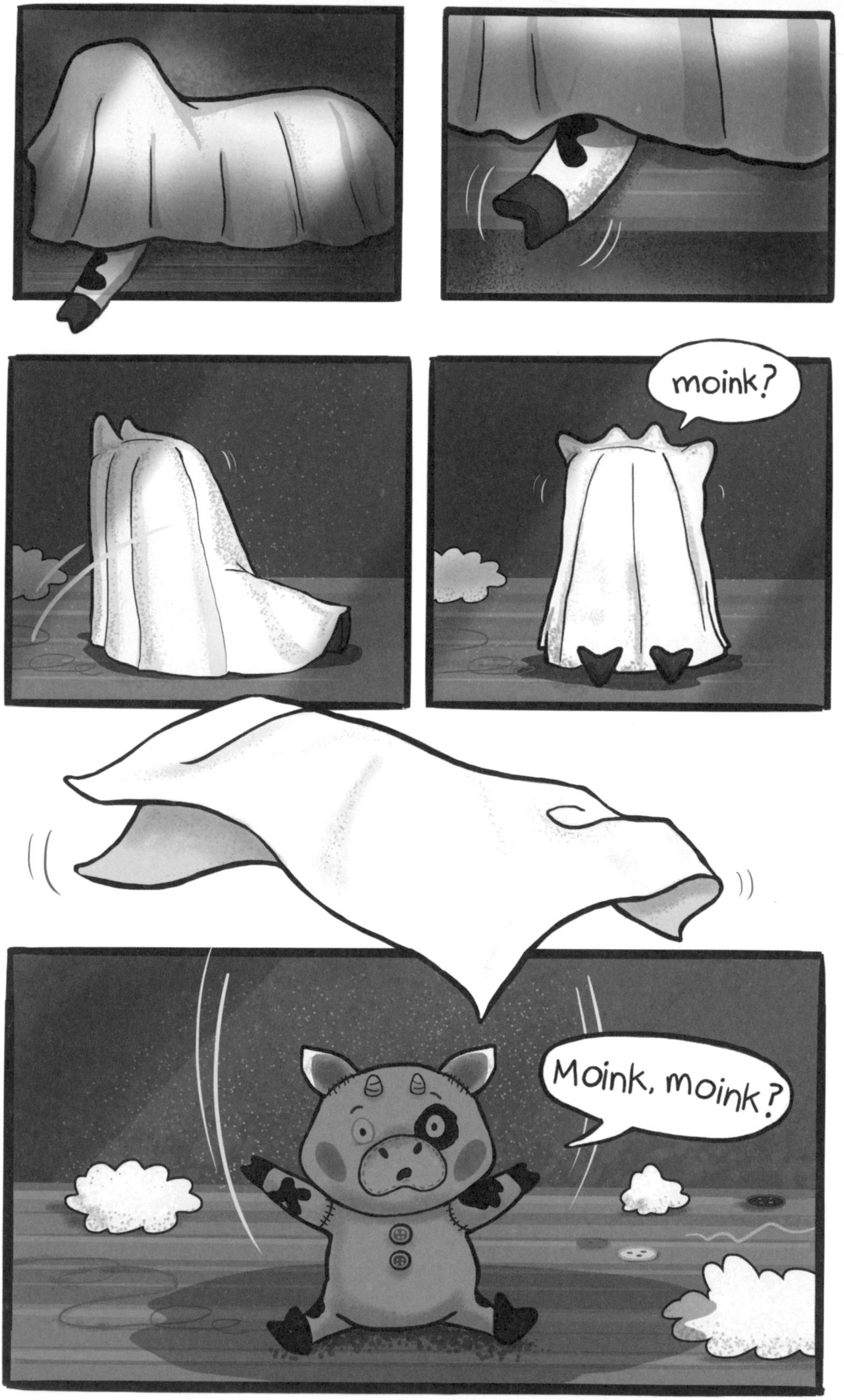
moink?
Moink, moink?

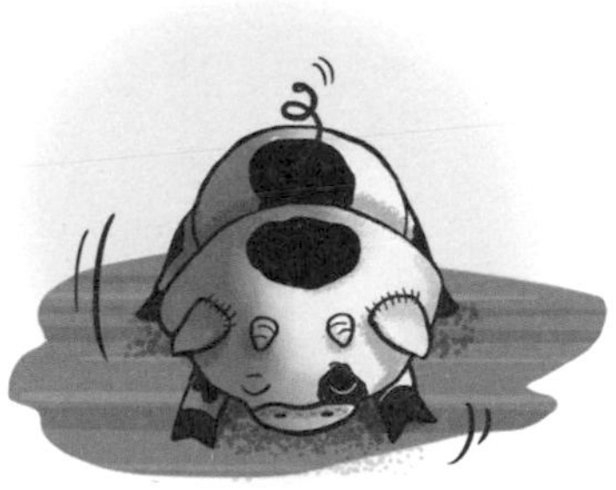

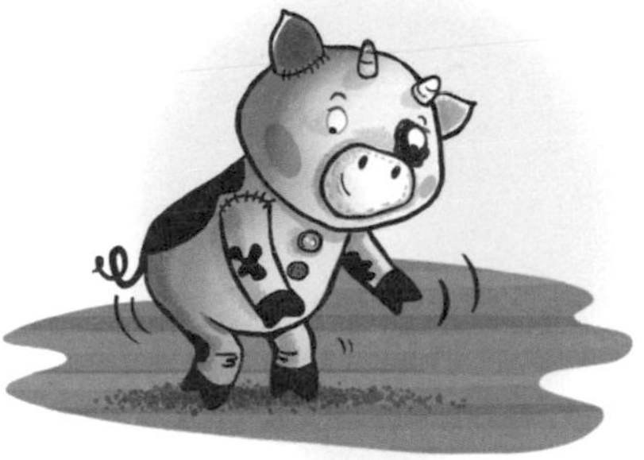

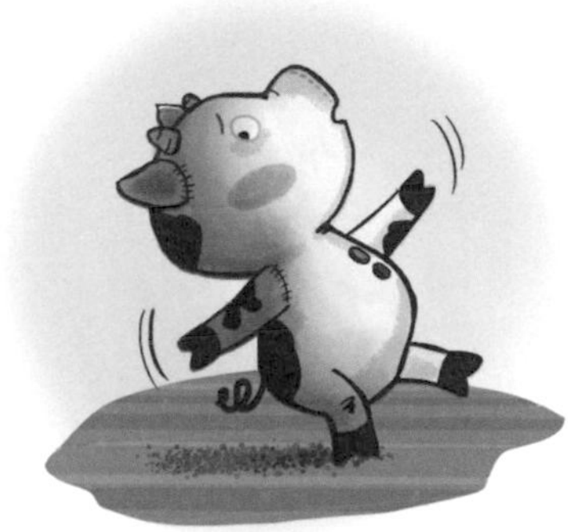

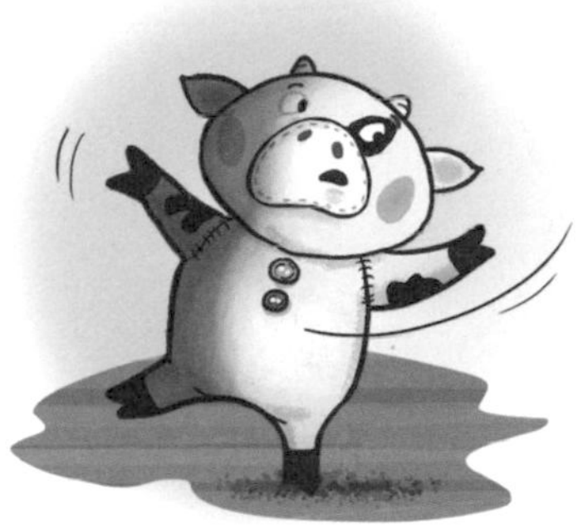

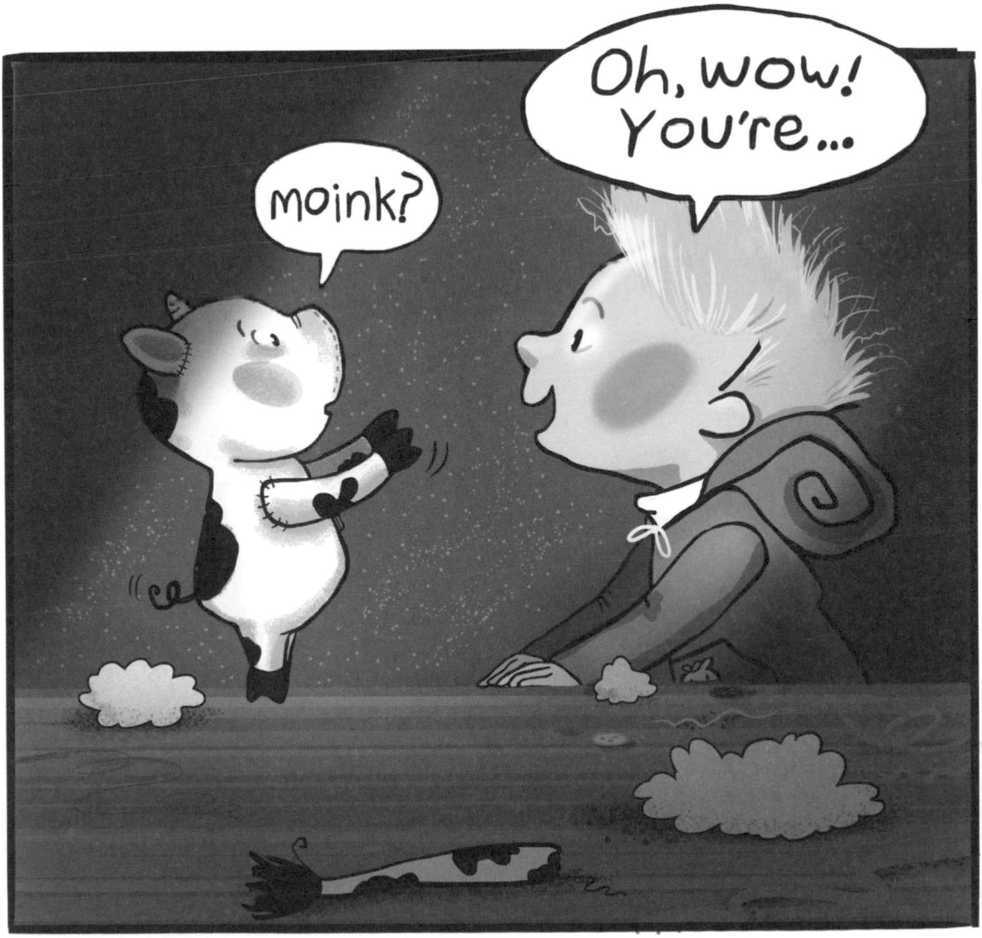
moink?
Oh, wow! You're...

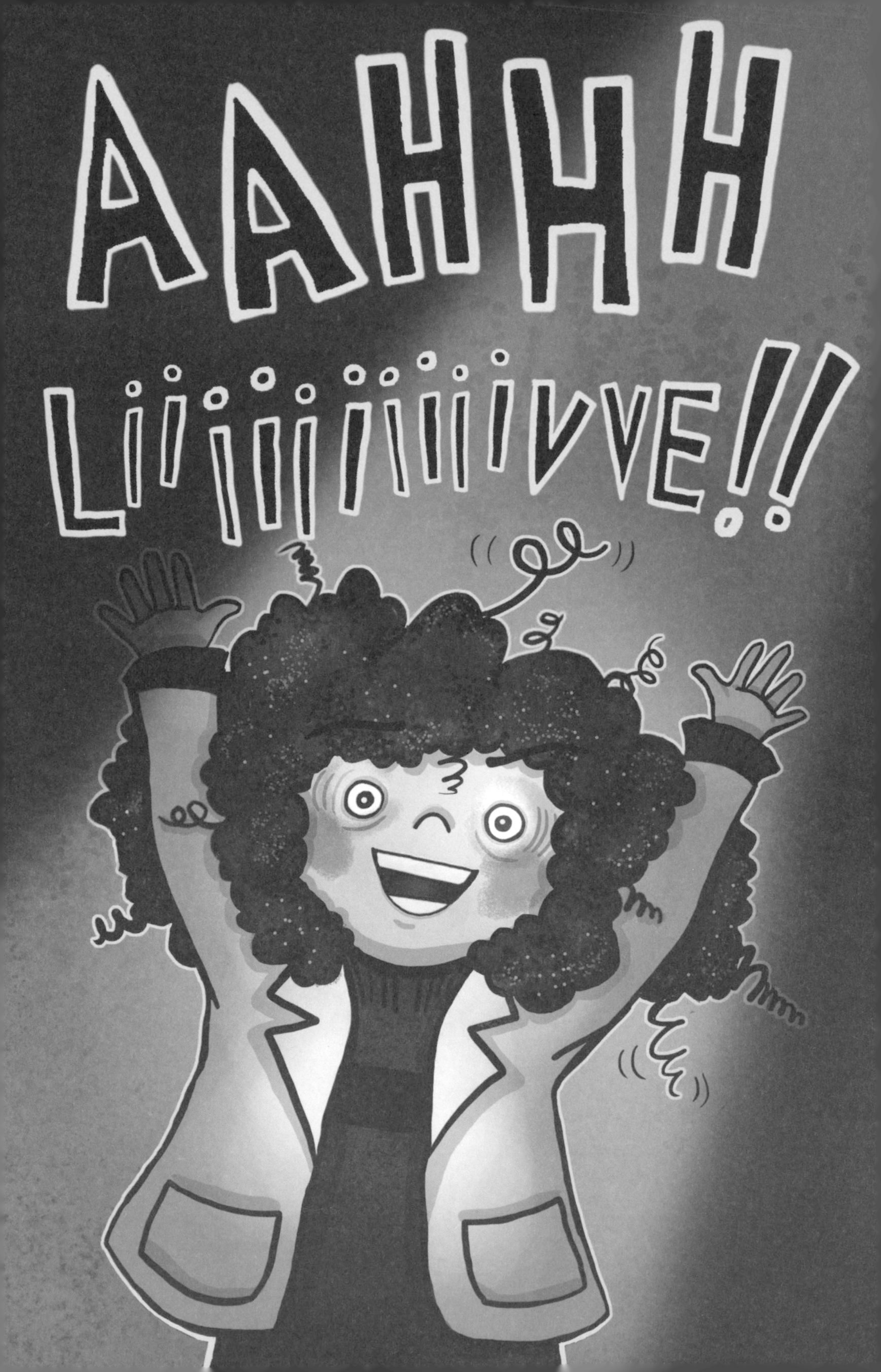
AAHHH
LIIIIIIIIIVVE!!

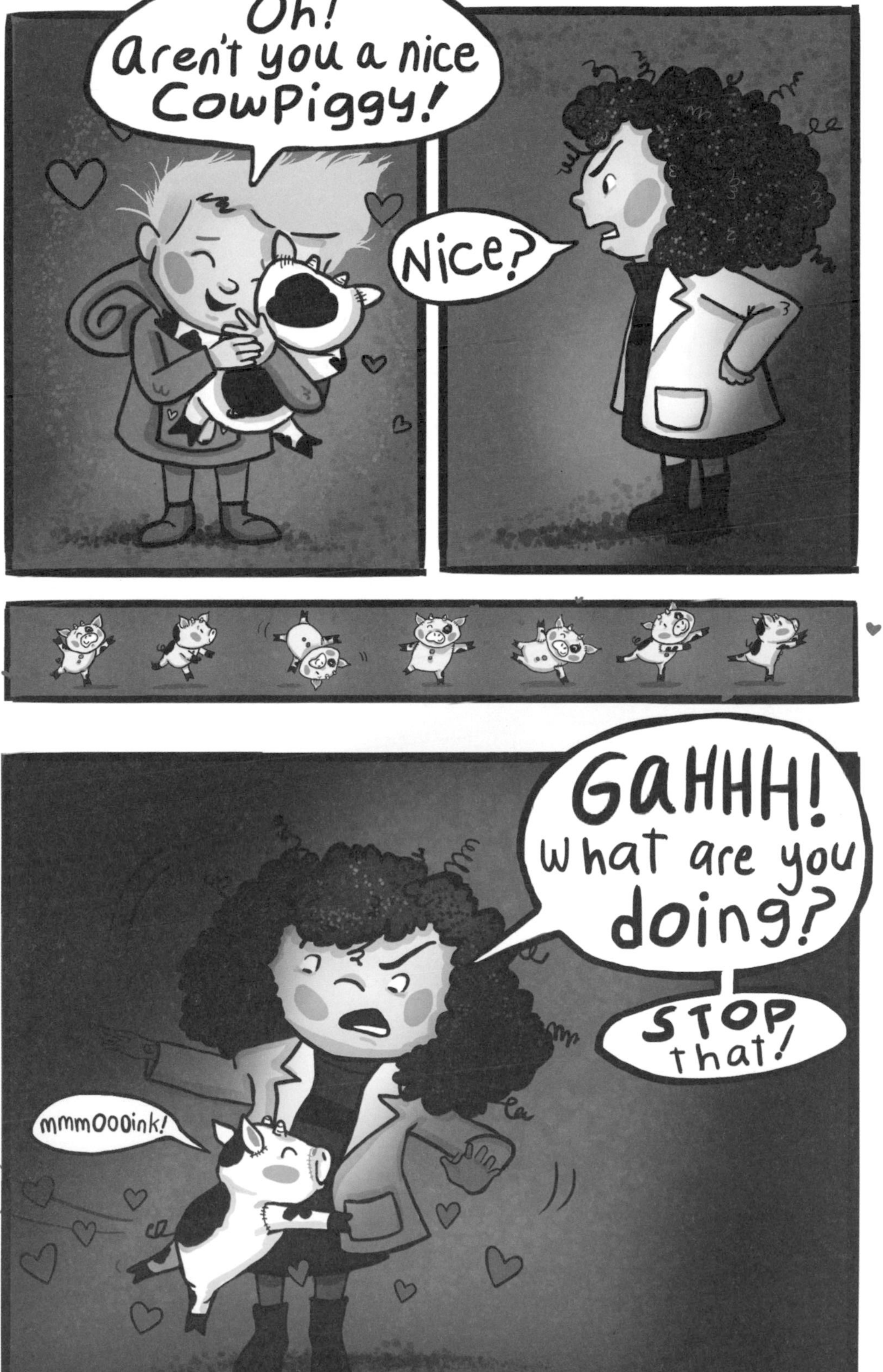
Oh!
Aren't you a nice
CowPiggy!
Nice?
GAHHH!
What are you
doing?
STOP
that!
mmmOOOink!

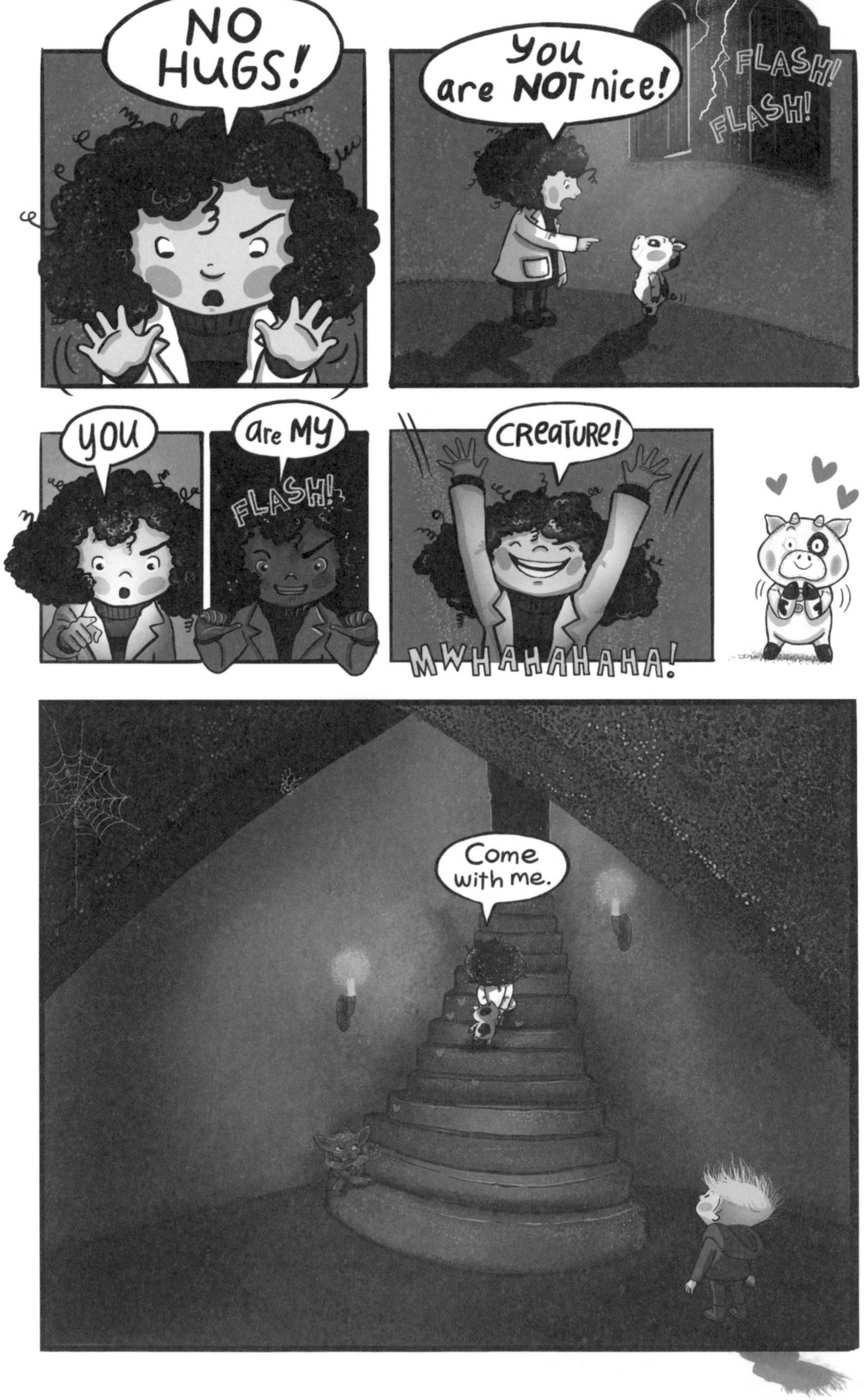

NO HUGS!
You are NOT nice!
FLASH!
FLASH!
YOU
are MY
FLASH!
CREATURE!
MWHAHAHAHAHA!
Come with me.

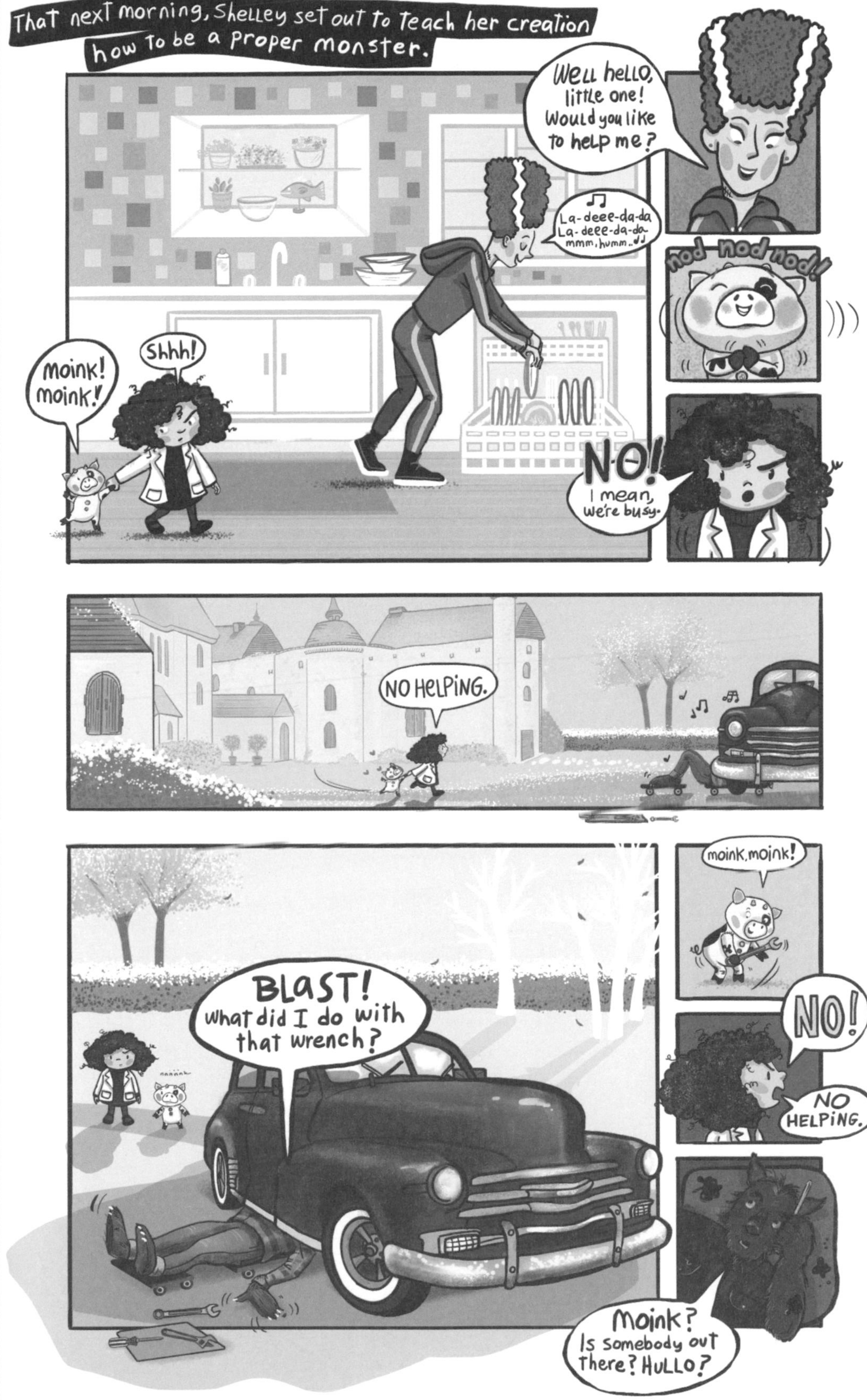

That next morning, Shelley set out to teach her creation how to be a proper monster.
Well hello, little one! Would you like to help me?
La-deee-da-da La-deee-da-da mmm, humm..
nod nod nod!
Shhh!
moink! moink!
NO! I mean, we're busy.
NO HELPING.
BLAST! What did I do with that wrench?
moink, moink!
NO!
NO HELPING.
Moink? Is somebody out there? HULLO?

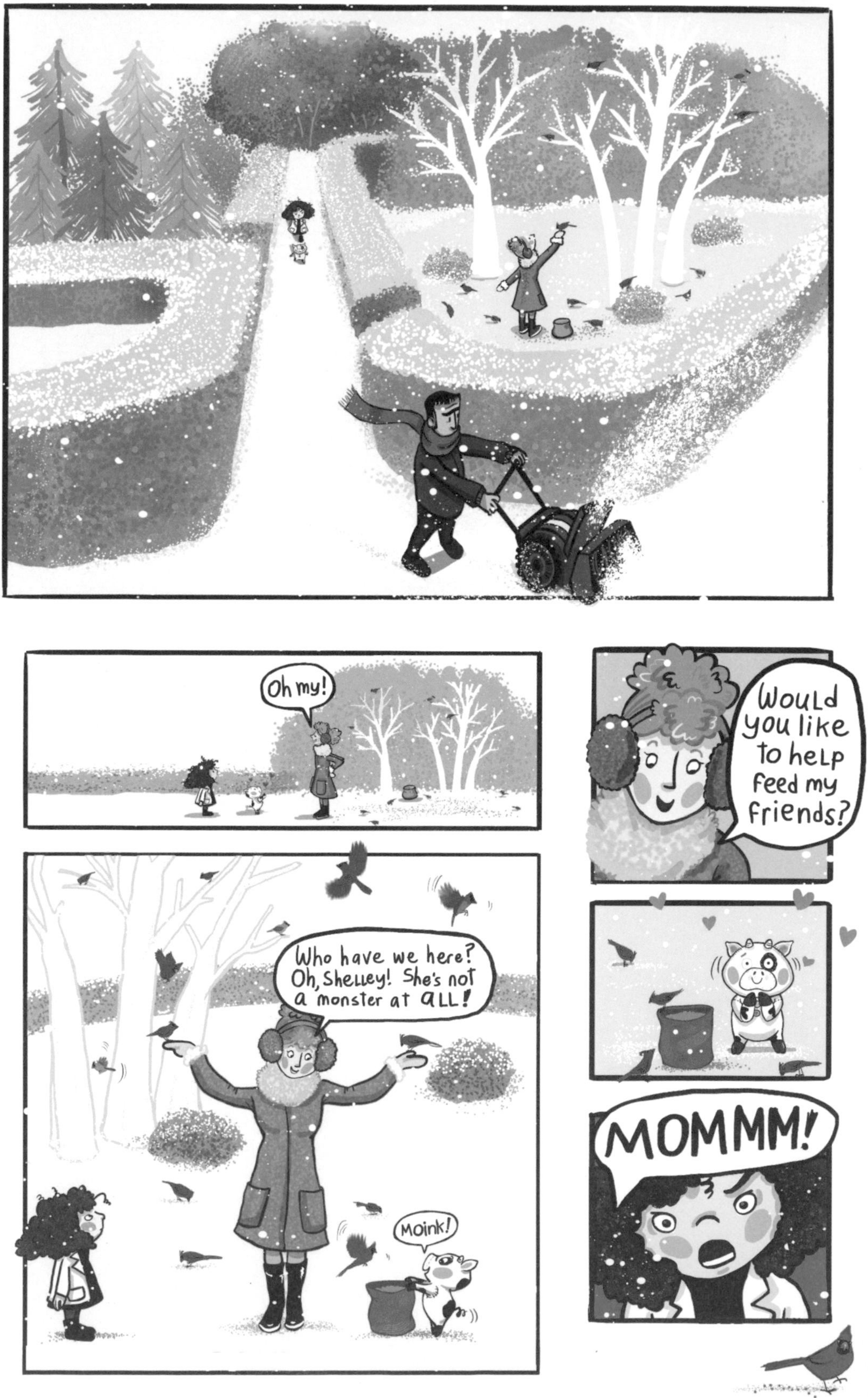
Oh my!
Would you like to help feed my friends?
Who have we here? Oh, Shelley! She's not a monster at ALL!
Moink!
MOMMM!

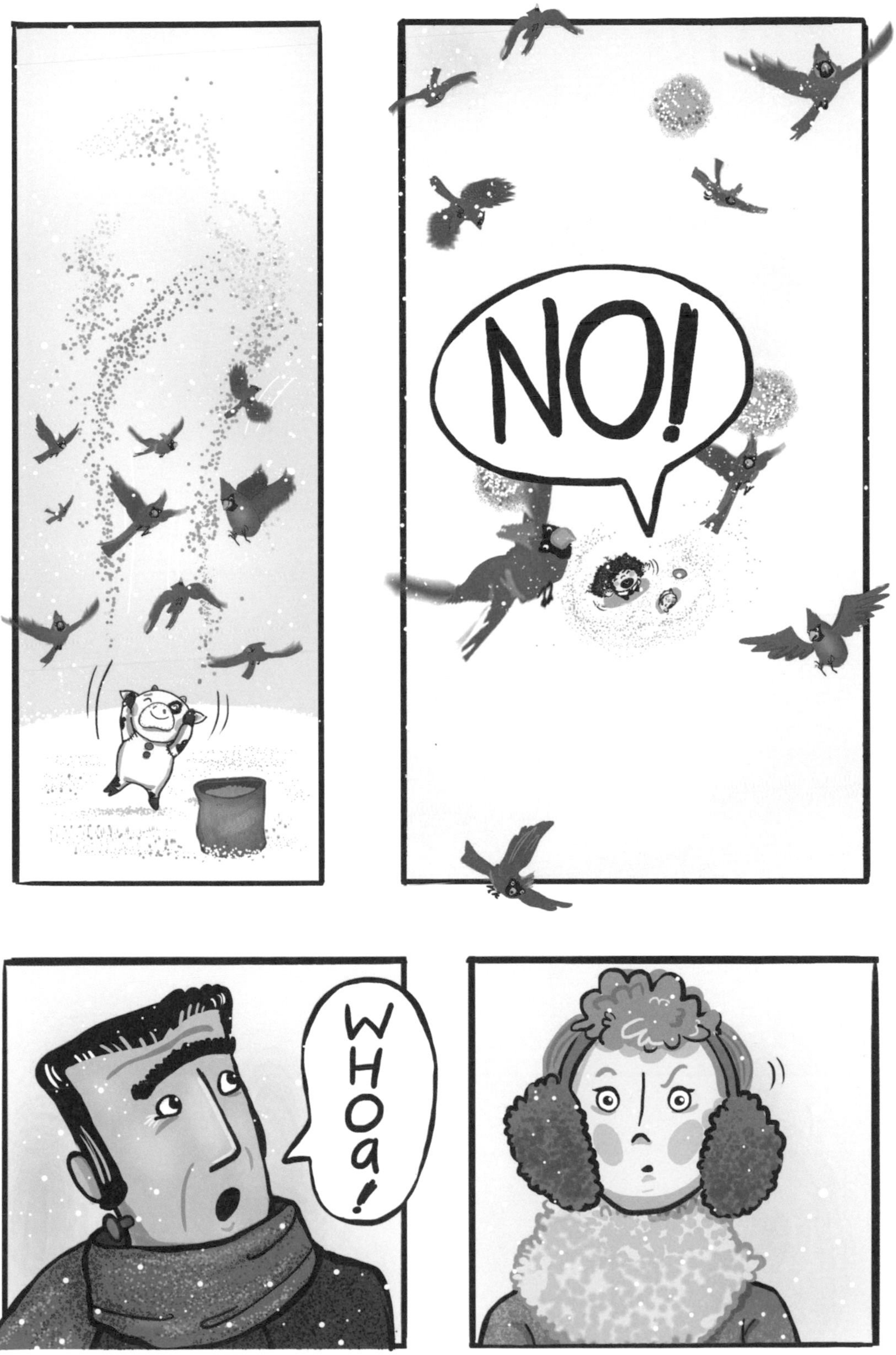
NO!
WHOa!

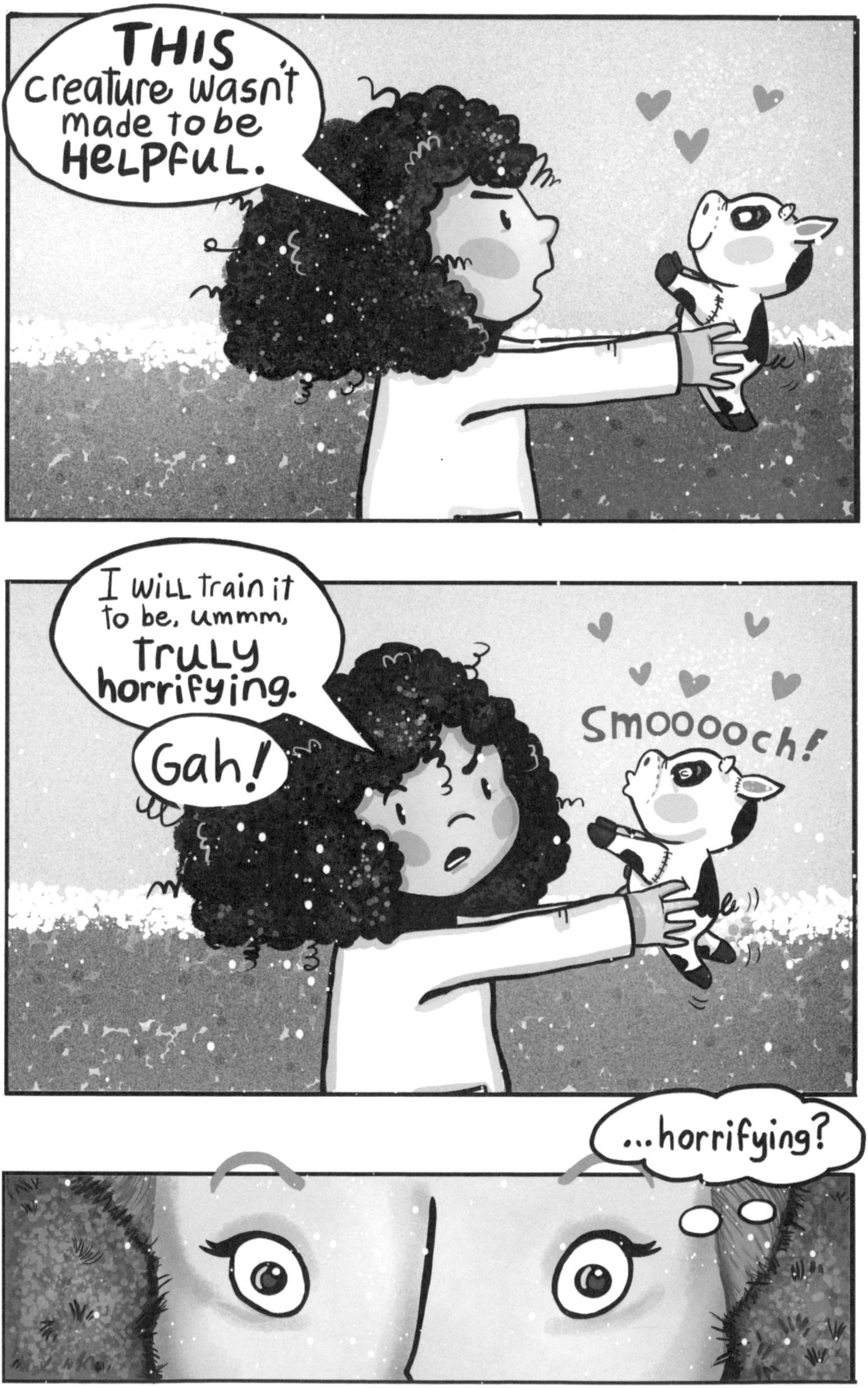
THIS creature wasn't made to be HELPFUL.
I WILL train it to be, ummm, TRULY horrifying.
Gah!
Smoooooch!
...horrifying?

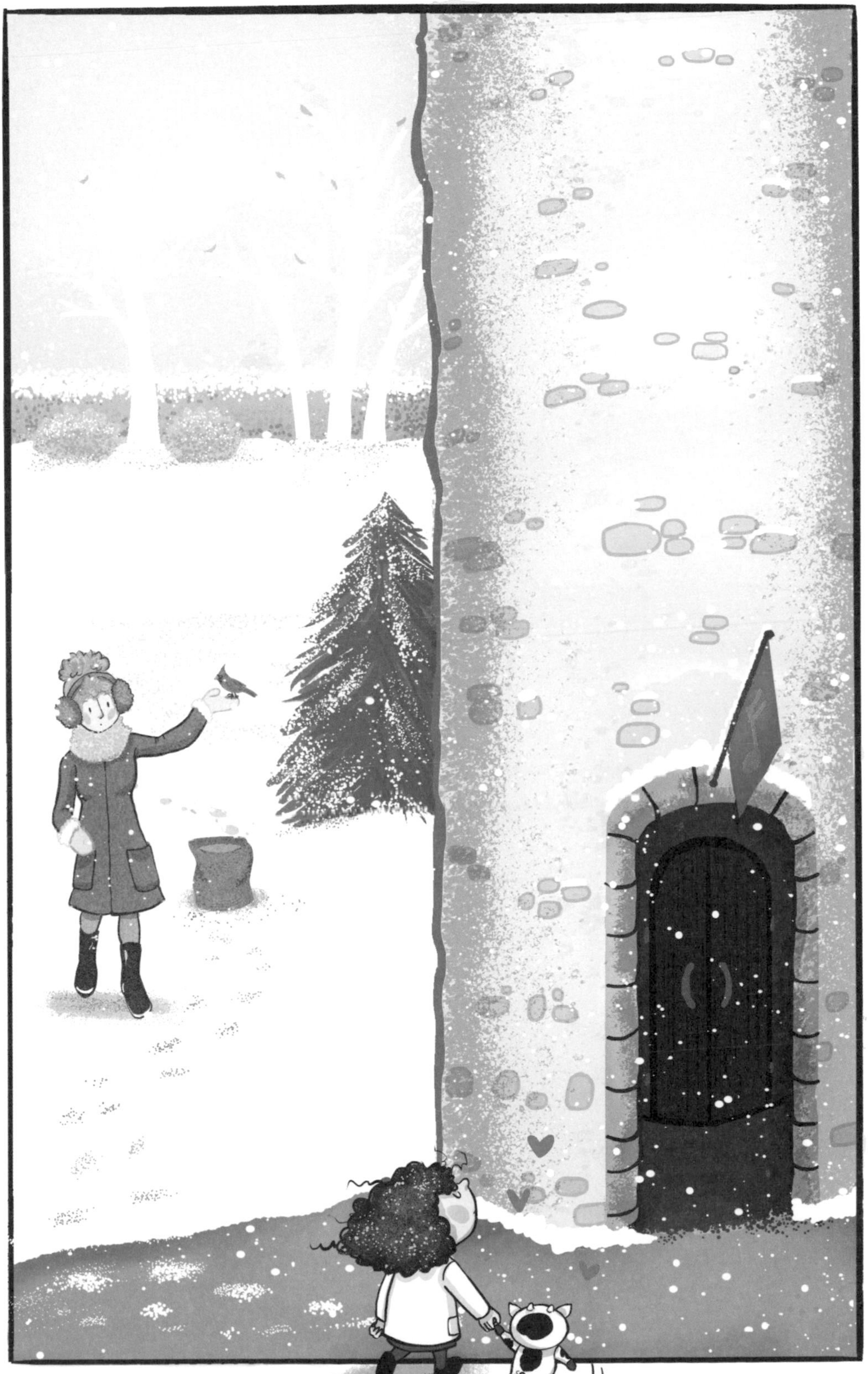

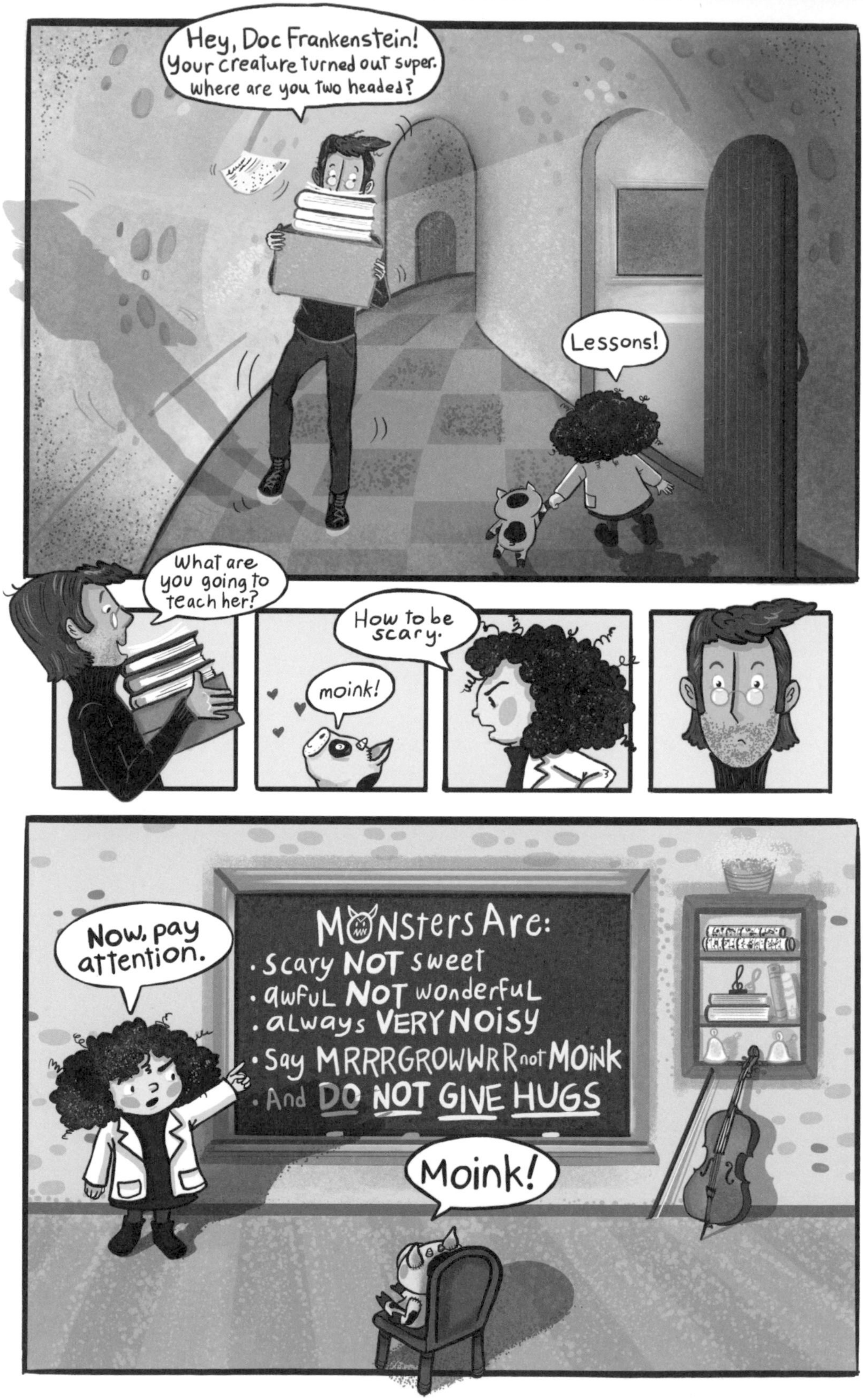
Hey, Doc Frankenstein! Your creature turned out super. Where are you two headed?
Lessons!
What are you going to teach her?
How to be scary.
moink!
MONSTERS ARE:
• Scary NOT sweet
• awful NOT wonderful
• always VERY NOISY
• Say MRRRGROWWRR not MOINK
• And DO NOT GIVE HUGS
Now, pay attention.
Moink!

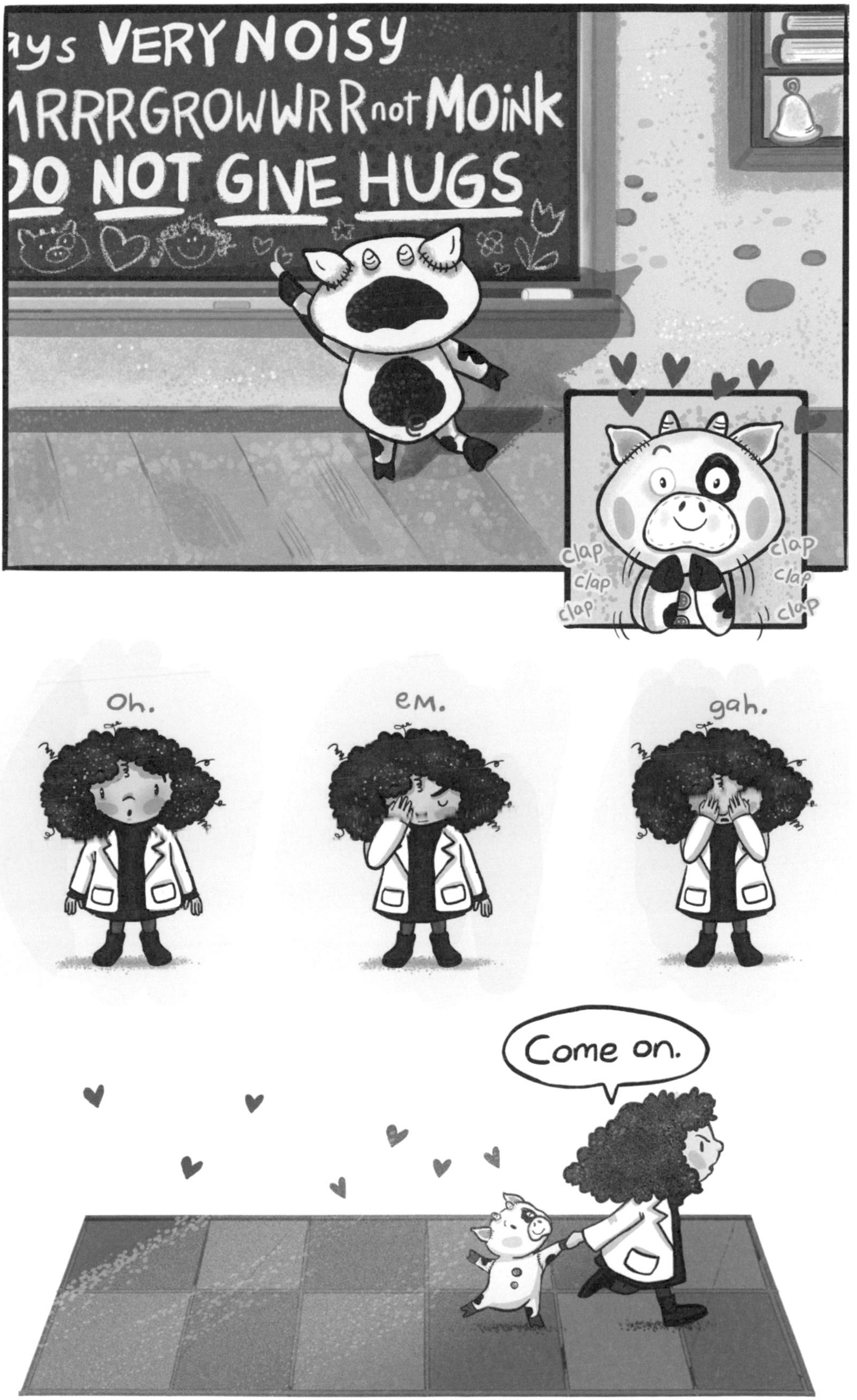

ays VERY NOiSY
MRRRGROWWRR not MOiNK
DO NOT GIVE HUGS
clap
clap
clap
clap
clap
clap
Oh.
em.
gah.
Come on.

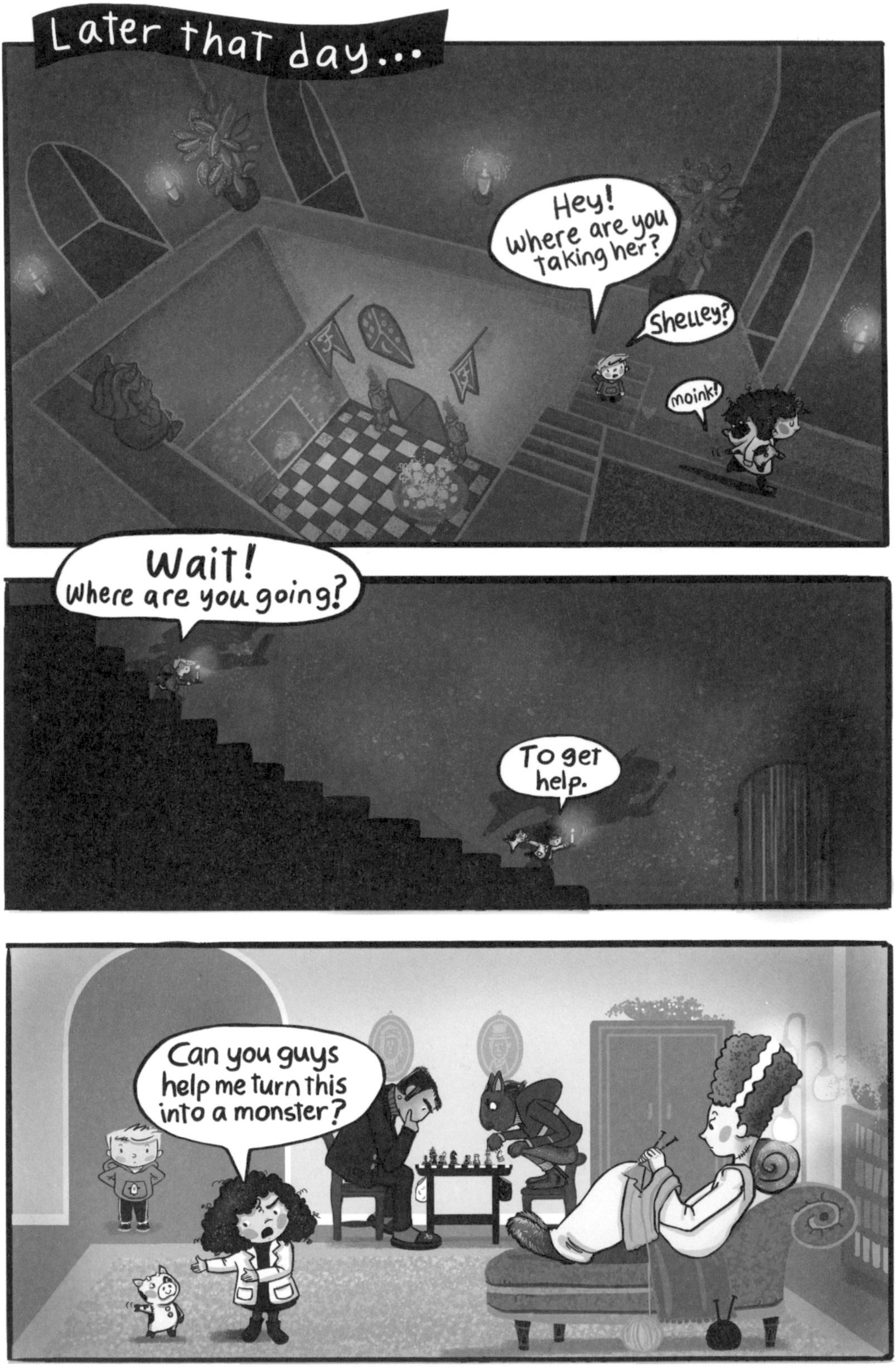
Later that day...
Hey! Where are you taking her?
Shelley?
moink!
Wait! Where are you going?
To get help.
Can you guys help me turn this into a monster?

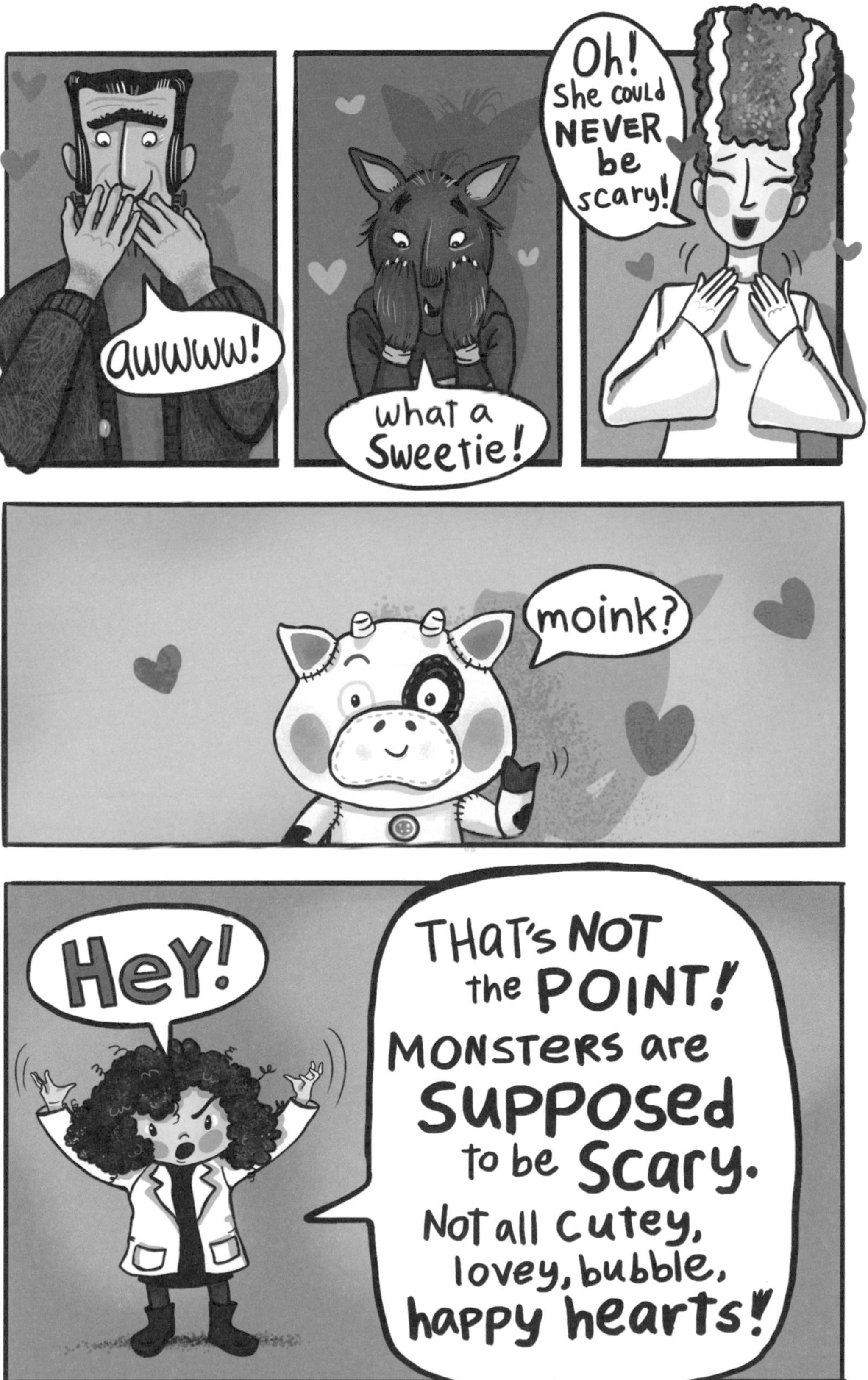
awwww!
what a Sweetie!
Oh! She could NEVER be scary!
moink?
Hey!
THAT's NOT the POINT! MONSTERS are SUPPOSED to be Scary. Not all cutey, lovey, bubble, happy hearts!

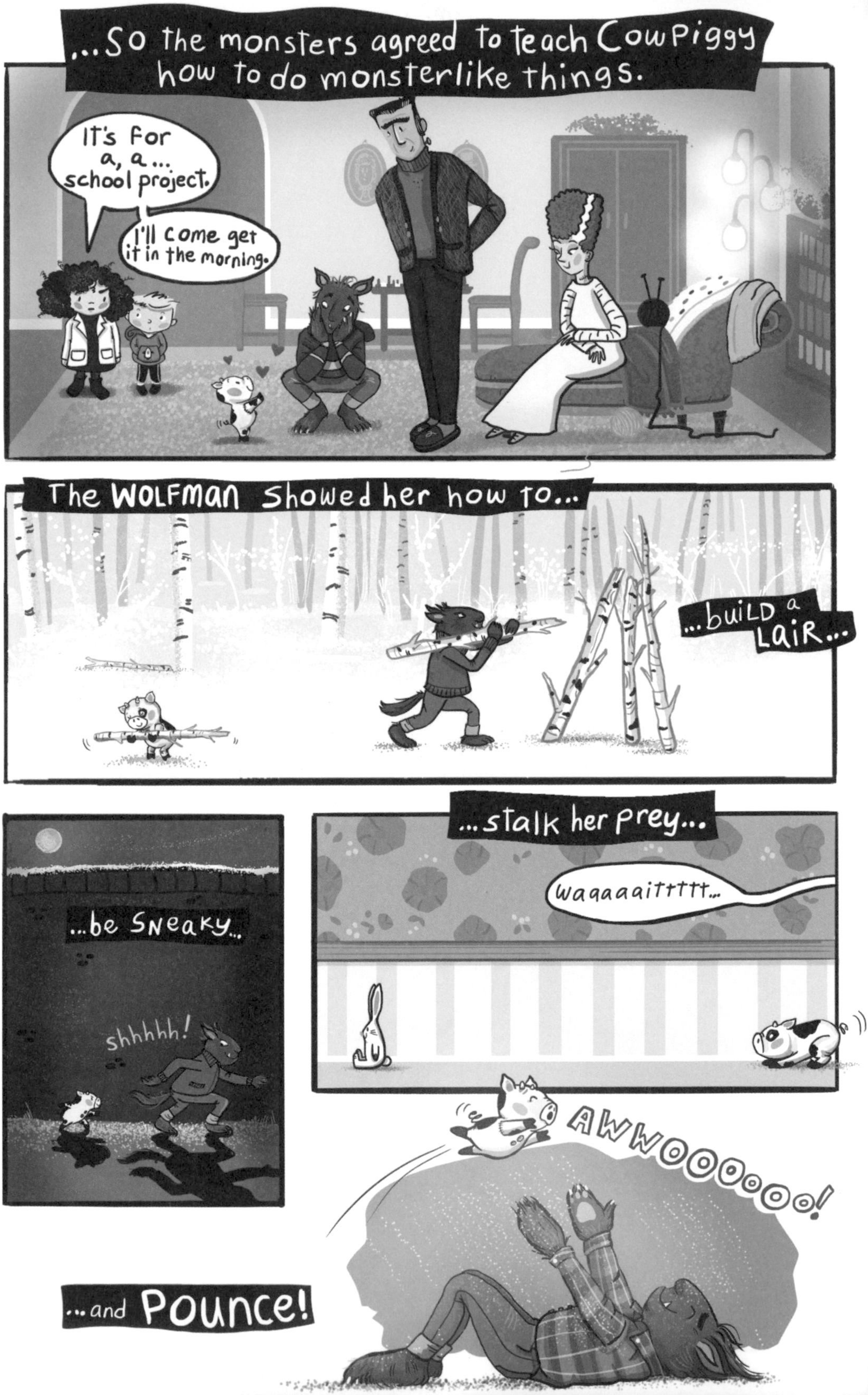
...So the monsters agreed to teach CowPiggy how to do monsterlike things.
It's for a, a... school project.
I'll come get it in the morning.
The WOLFMAN showed her how to...
...build a LAIR...
...be SNEAKY...
shhhhh!
...stalk her prey...
waaaaaitttttt...
AWWOOOOOOo!
...and POUNCE!

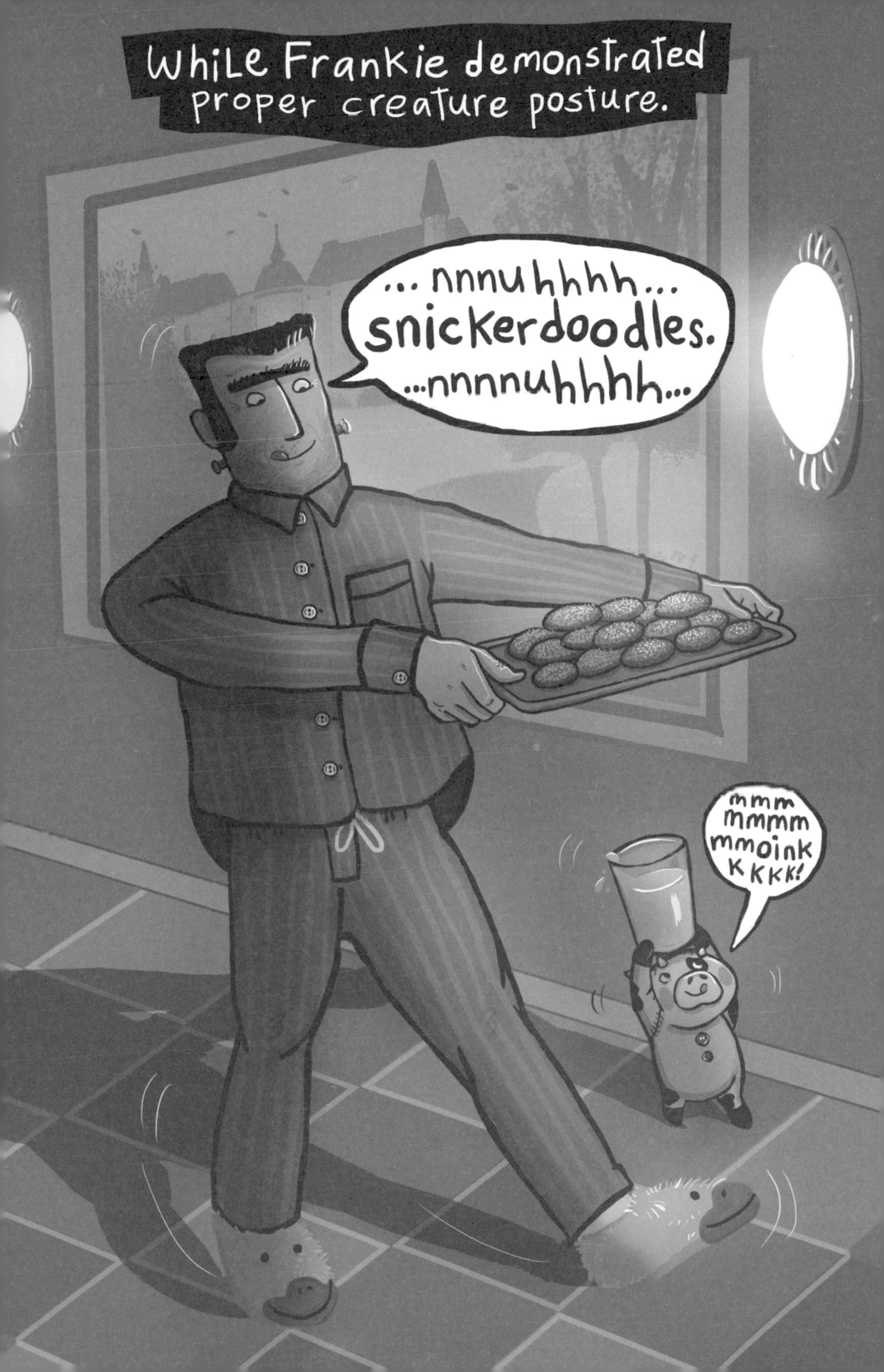
While Frankie demonstrated proper creature posture.
...nnnuhhhh... snickerdoodles. ...nnnnuhhhh...
mmm mmmm mmoink KKKK!

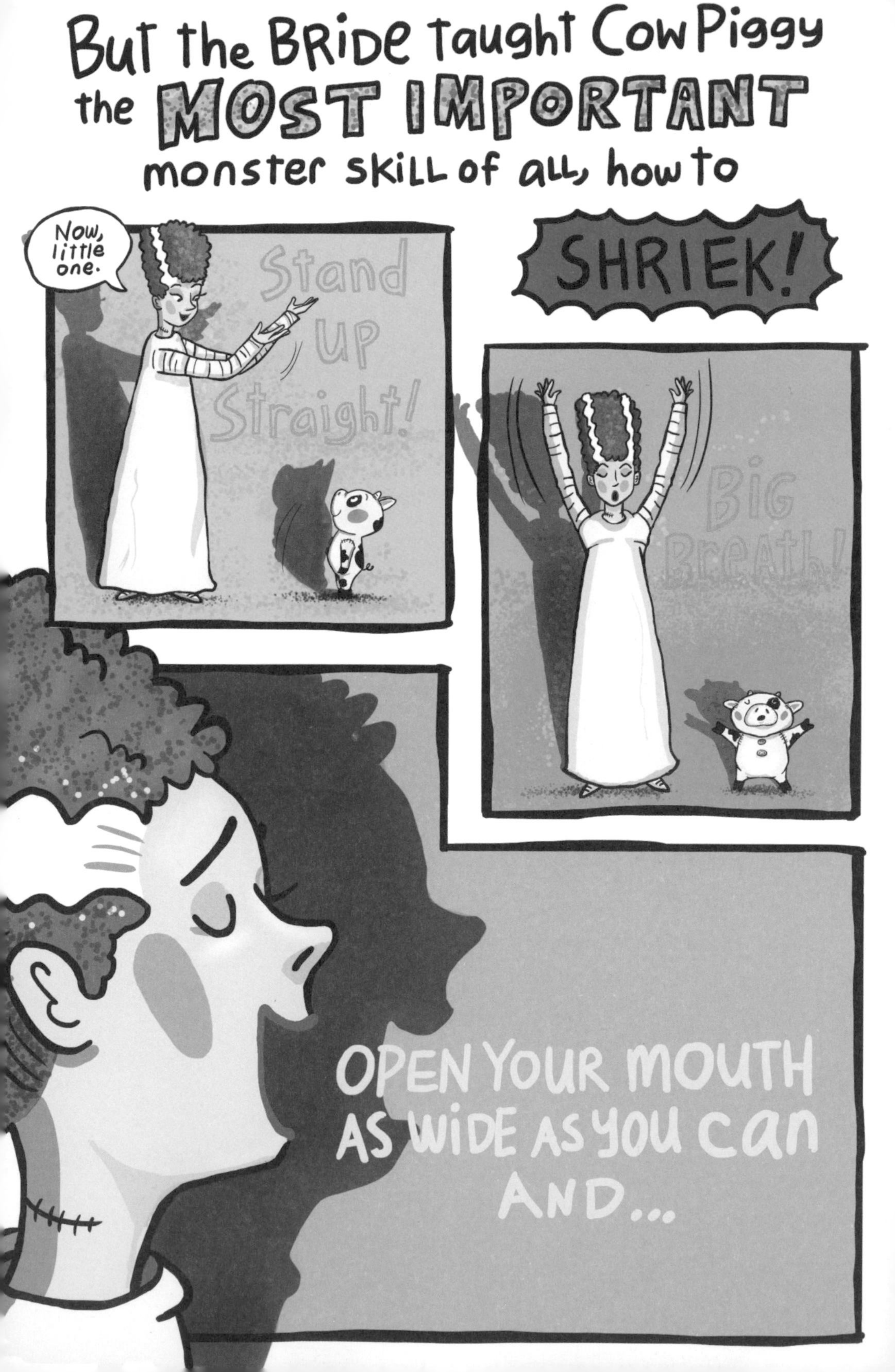
But the BRIDE taught Cow Piggy
the MOST IMPORTANT
monster SKILL of all, how to
SHRIEK!
Now, little one.
Stand up Straight!
Big Breath!
OPEN YOUR MOUTH
AS WIDE AS YOU CAN
AND...

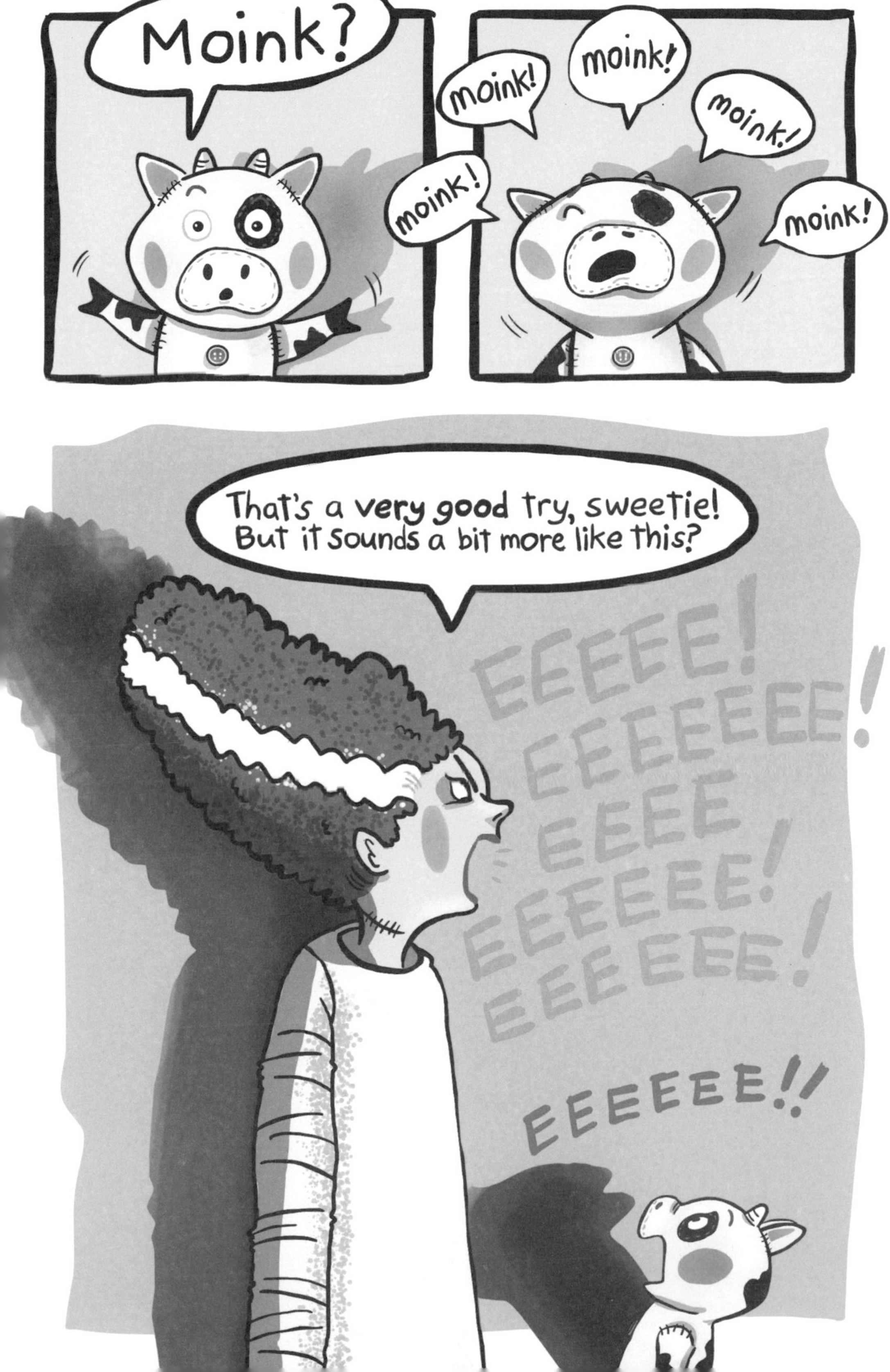

Moink?
moink!
moink!
moink!
moink!
moink!
That's a very good try, sweetie! But it sounds a bit more like this?
EEEEE! EEEEEEEE! EEEE EEEEEE! EEEEEE!
EEEEEE!!

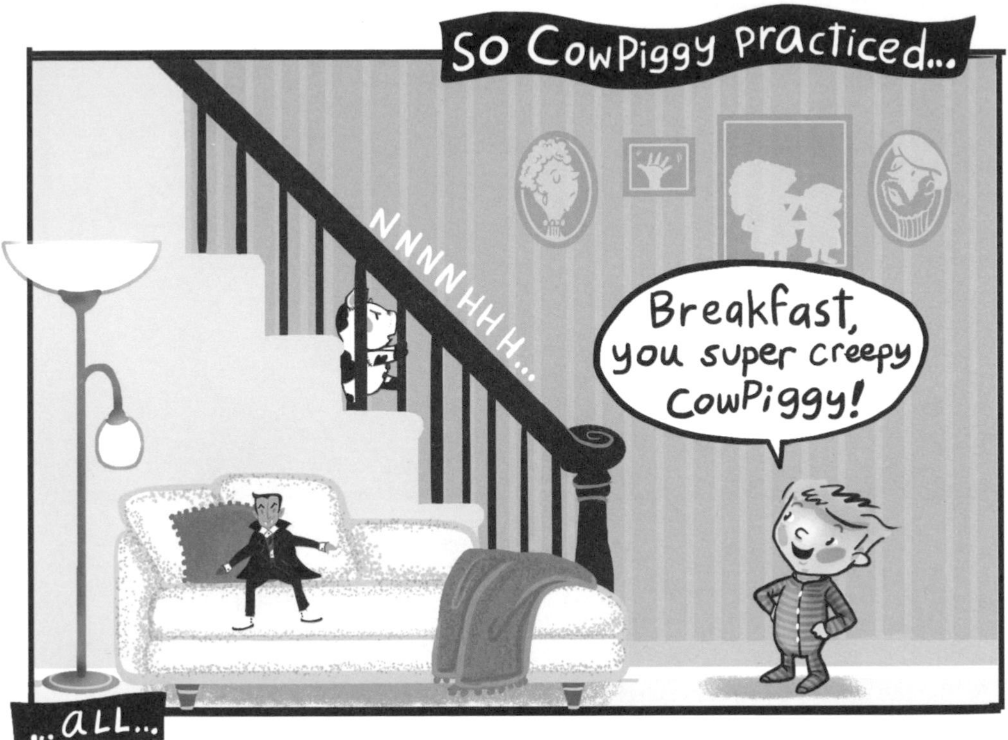
So CowPiggy practiced...
NNNNHHHH...
Breakfast, you super creepy CowPiggy!

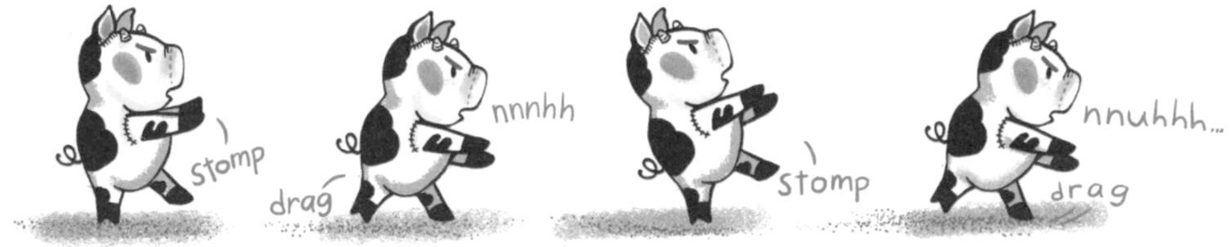
...all...
stomp
drag
nnnhh
stomp
nnuhhh...
drag

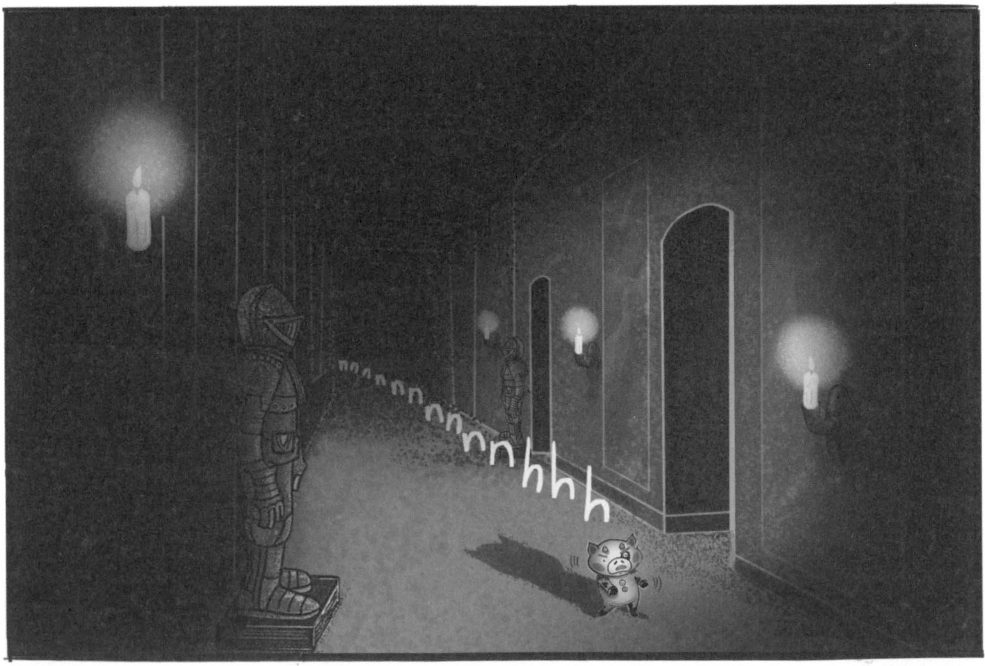
nnnnnnnnnhhh

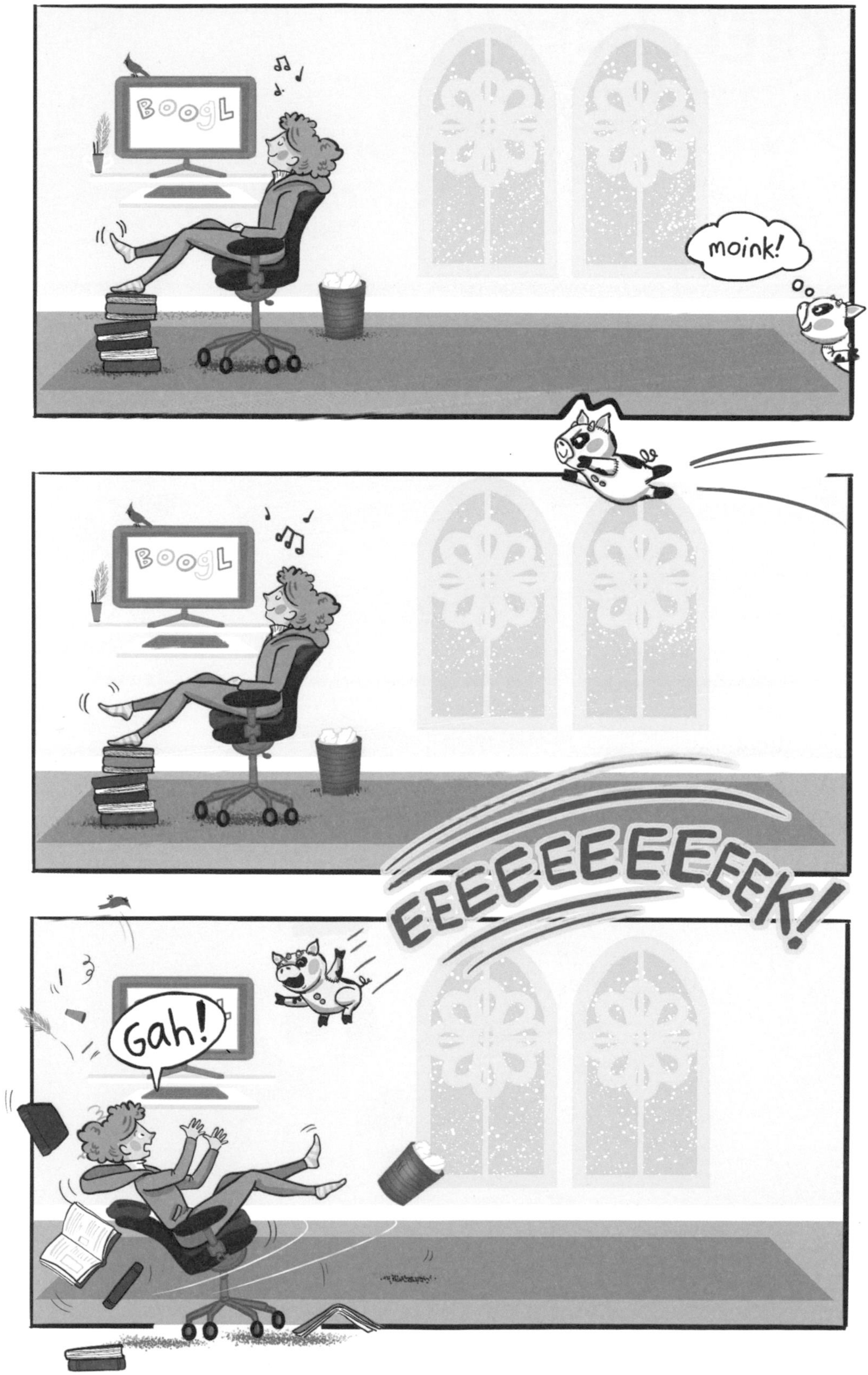
BOOGL
moink!
BOOGL
EEEEEEEEEK!
Gah!

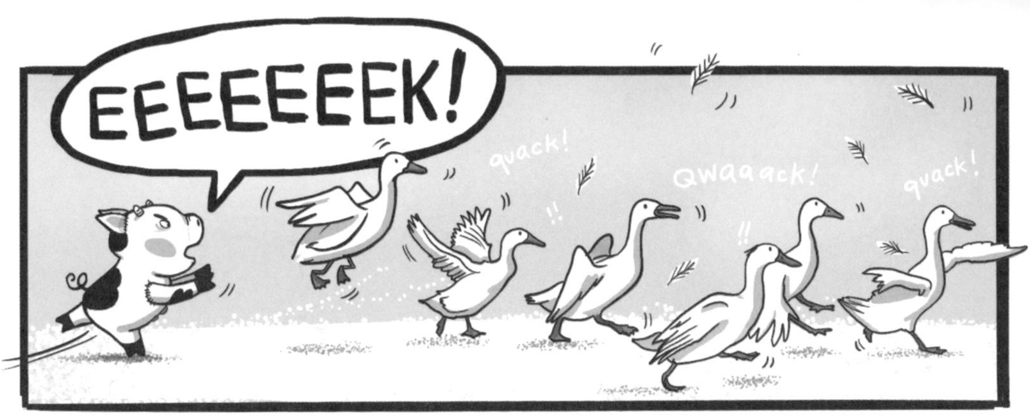
EEEEEEEK!
quack!
!!
Qwaaack!
!!
quack!

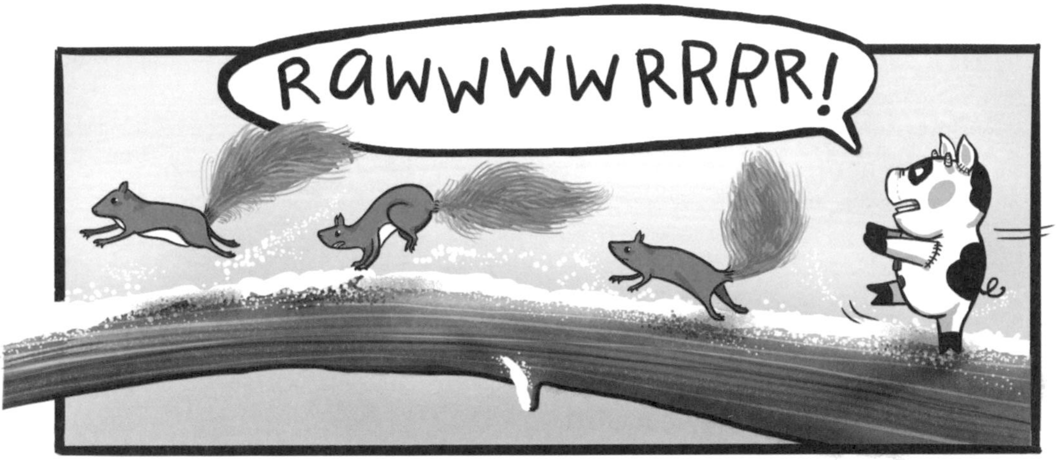
RAWWWWRRRR!

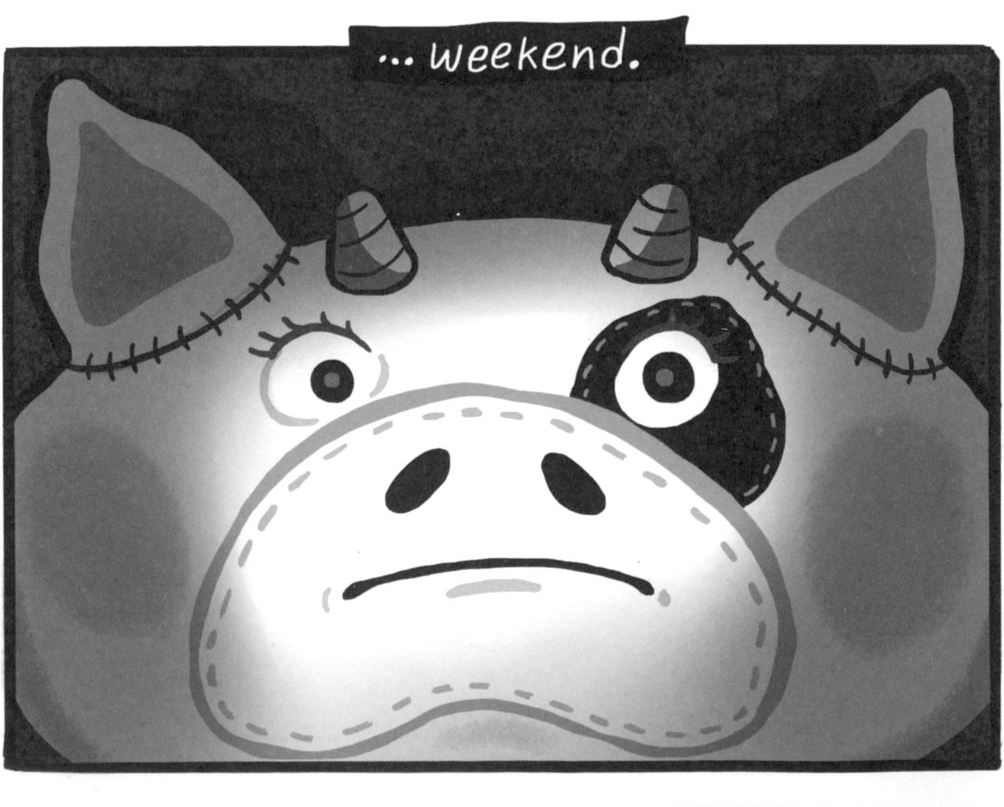
... weekend.

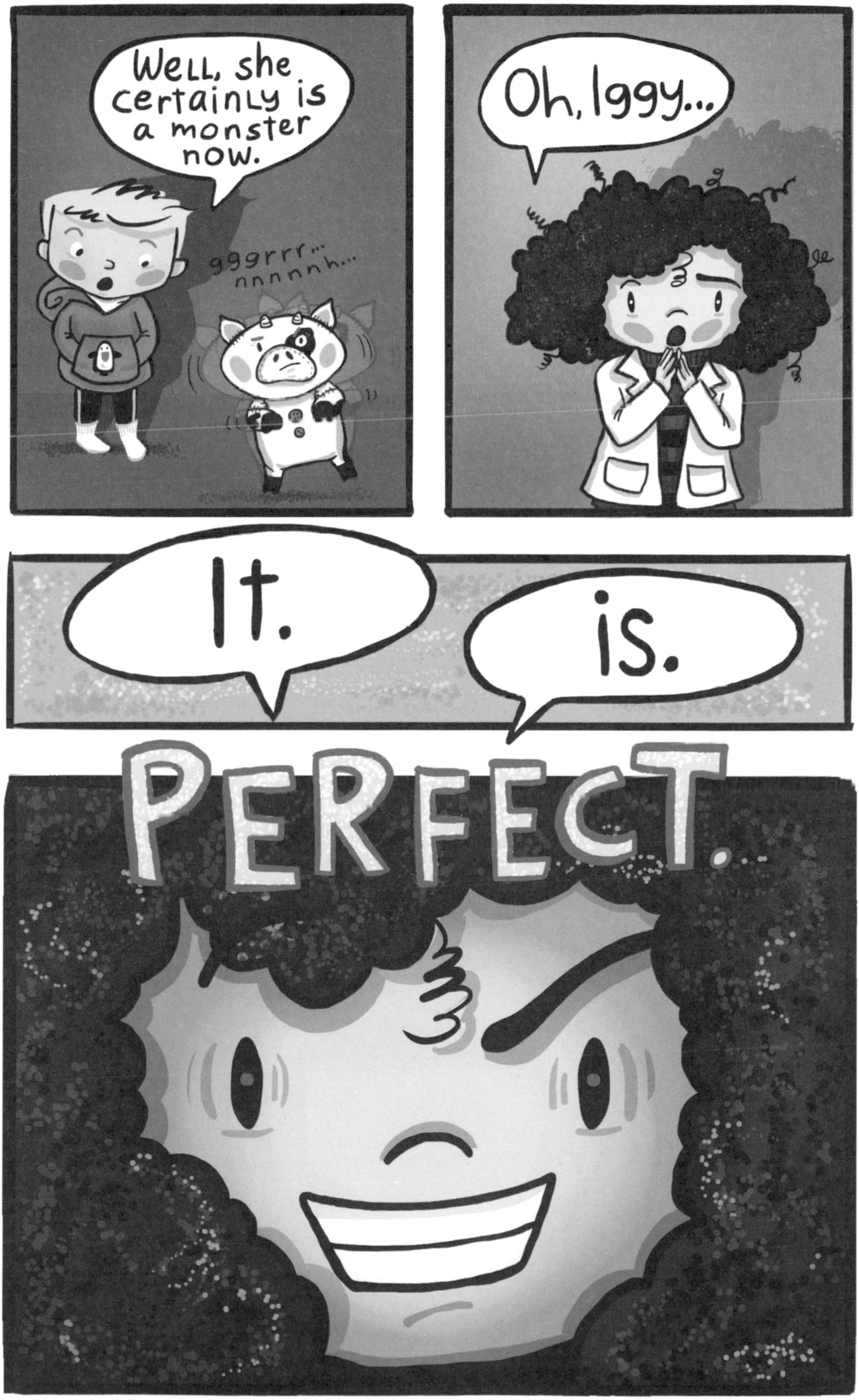

Well, she certainly is a monster now.
gggrrr... nnnnnh...
Oh, Iggy...
It.
is.
PERFECT.

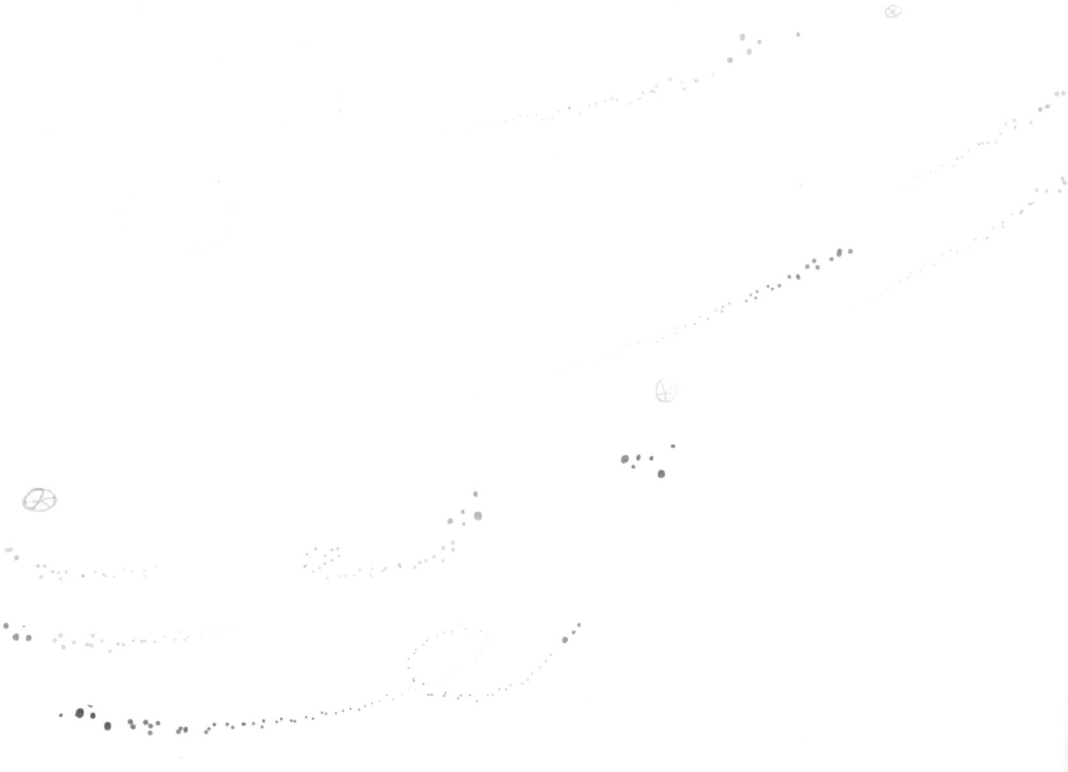

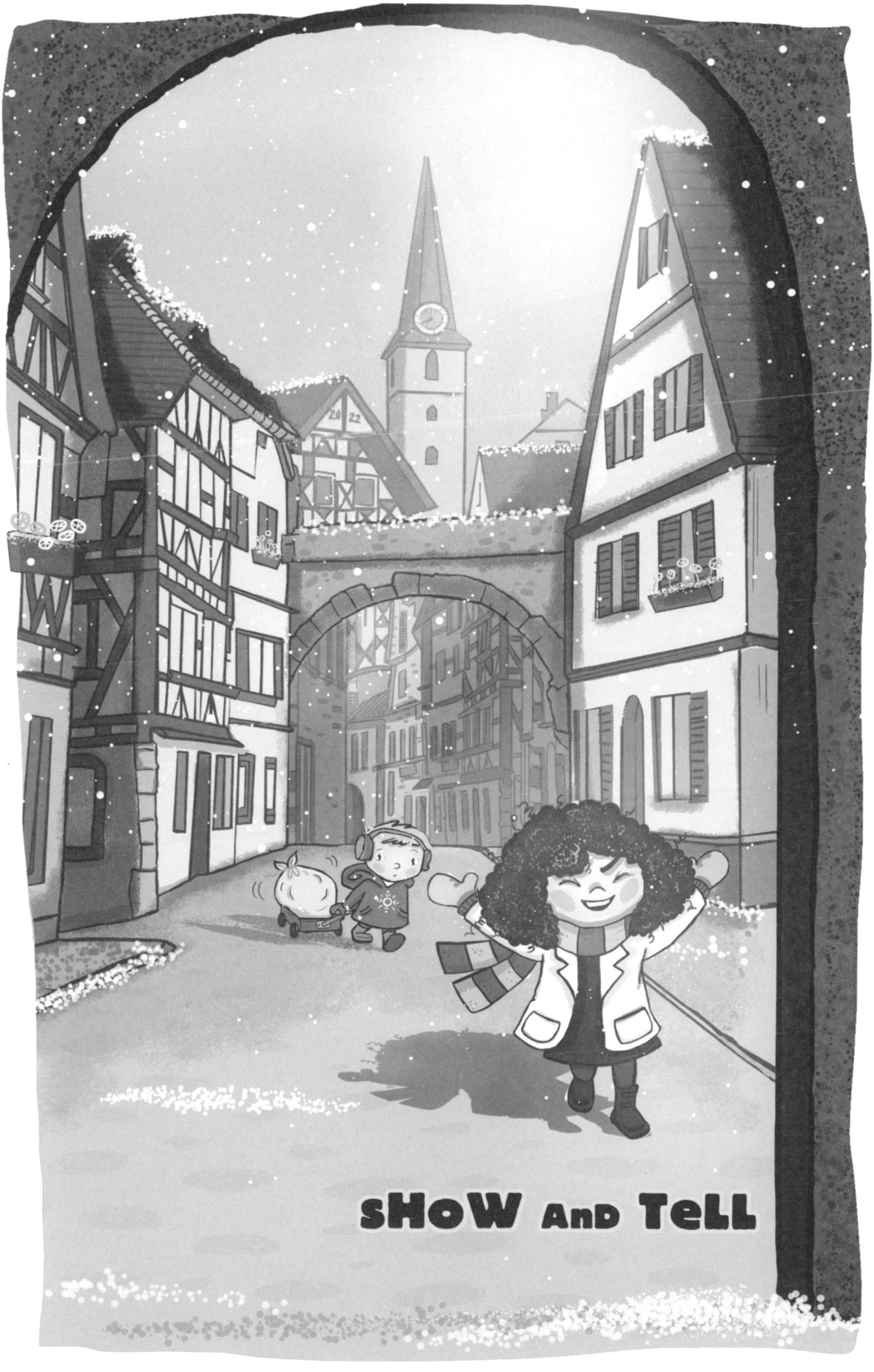
SHOW AND TELL

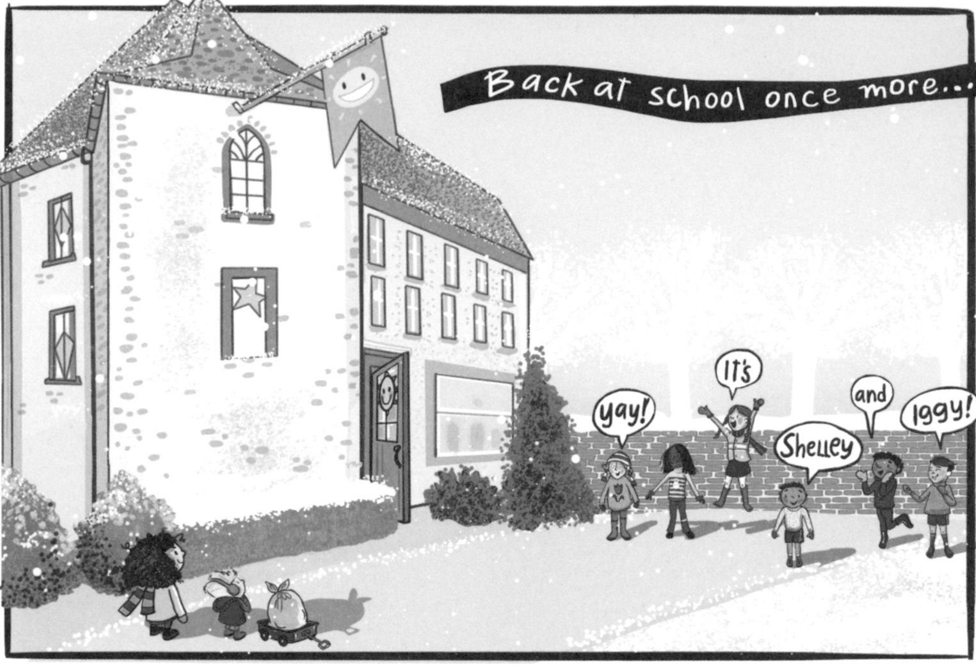
Back at school once more...
yay!
It's
Shelley
and
Iggy!

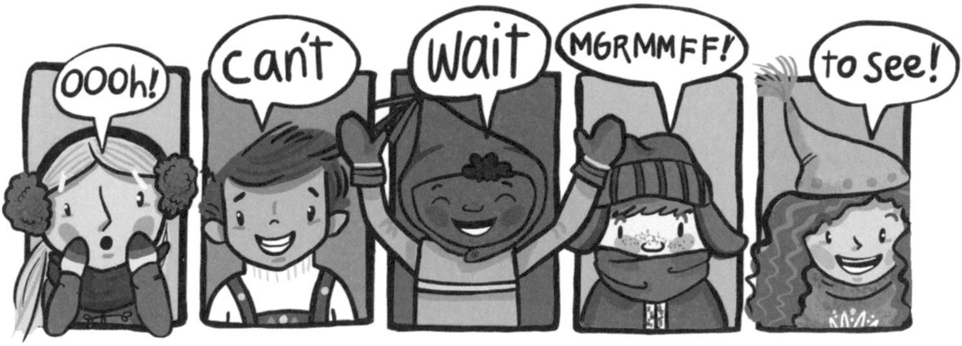
oooh!
can't
wait
MGRMMFF!
to see!

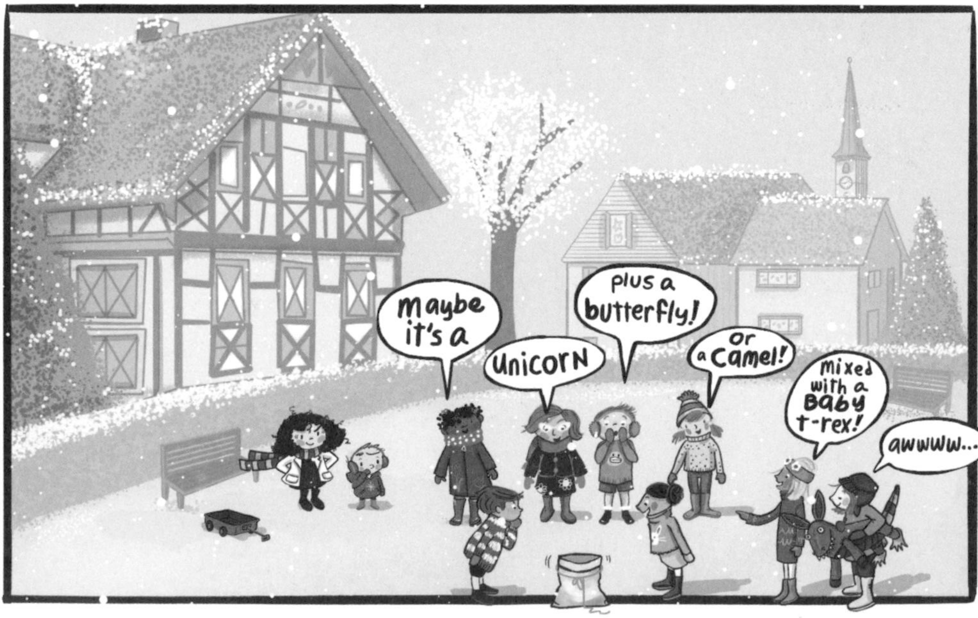
maybe it's a
unicorn
plus a butterfly!
or a camel!
mixed with a baby t-rex!
awwww...

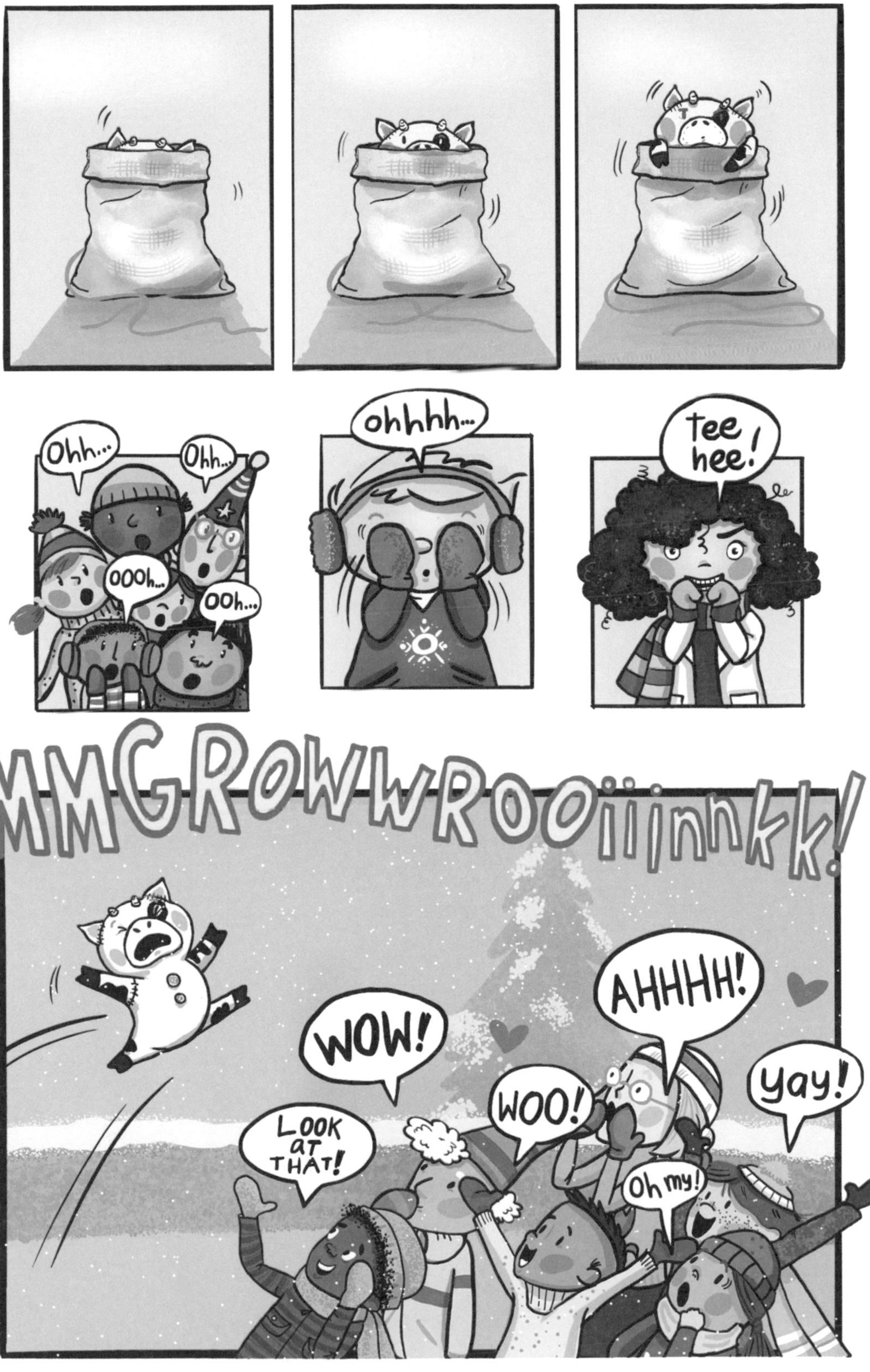
Ohh...
Ohh...
oooh...
ooh...
ohhhh...
tee hee!
MMGROWWROOiiinnkk!
LOOK at THAT!
WOW!
WOO!
AHHHH!
Oh my!
yay!

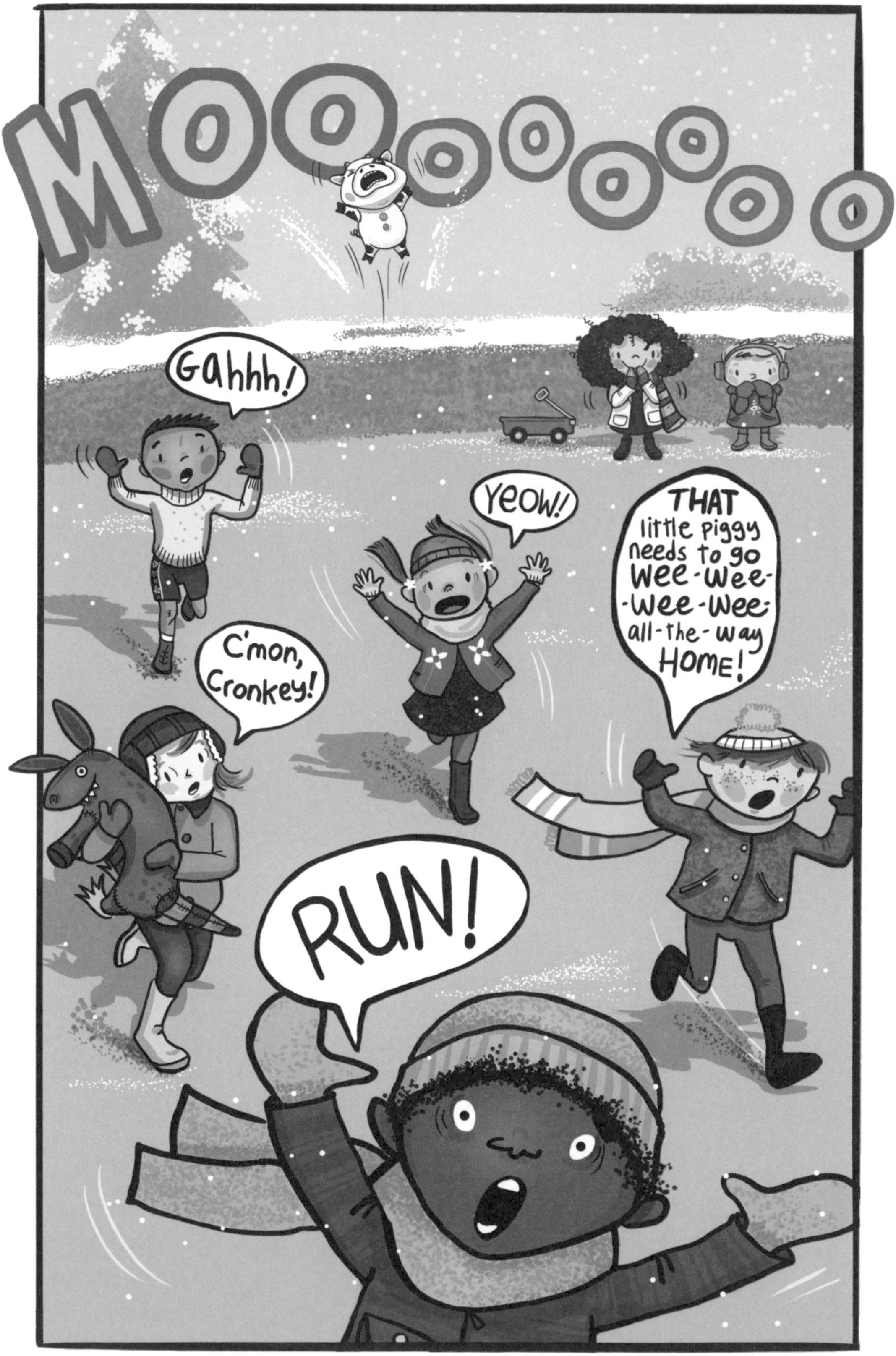
MOOOOOOOO
Gahhh!
YEOW!
THAT little piggy needs to go WEE-WEE-WEE-WEE all-the-way HOME!
C'mon, Cronkey!
RUN!

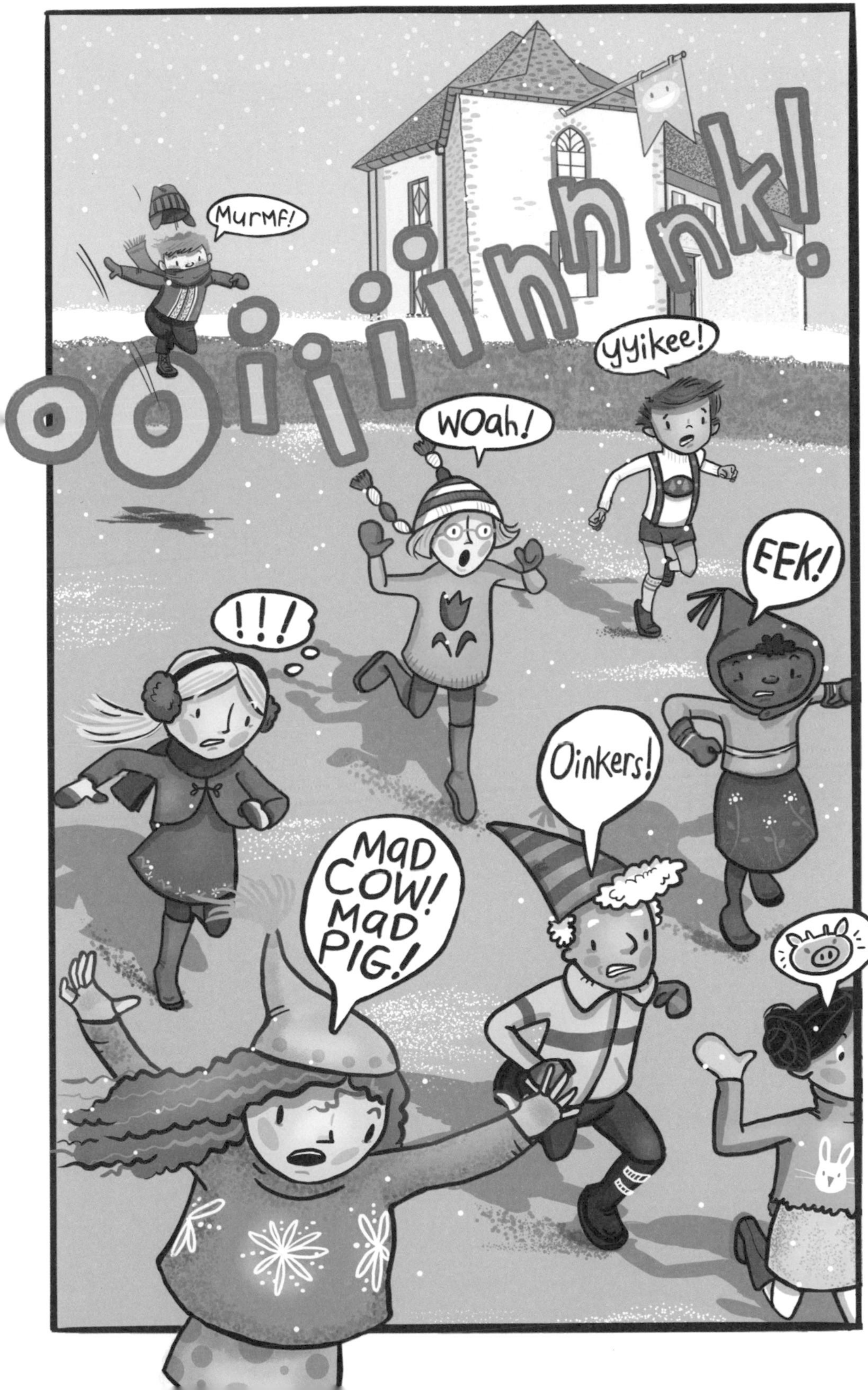
Murmf!
Ooiiiinhhnk!
yyikee!
WOah!
!!!
EEK!
Oinkers!
Mad COW! Mad PIG!

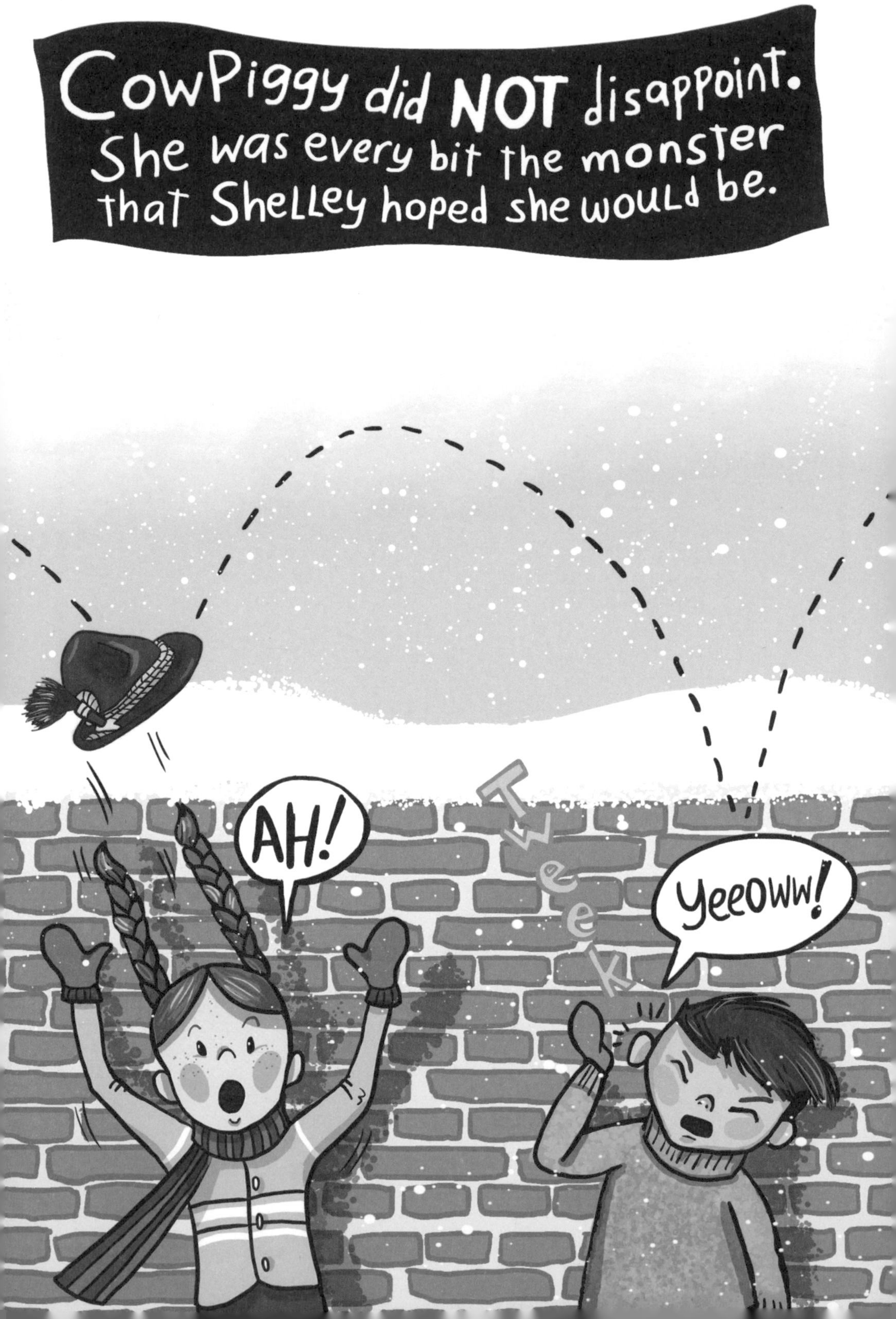
CowPiggy did NOT disappoint. She was every bit the monster that Shelley hoped she would be.
AH!
Tweek
Yeeoww!

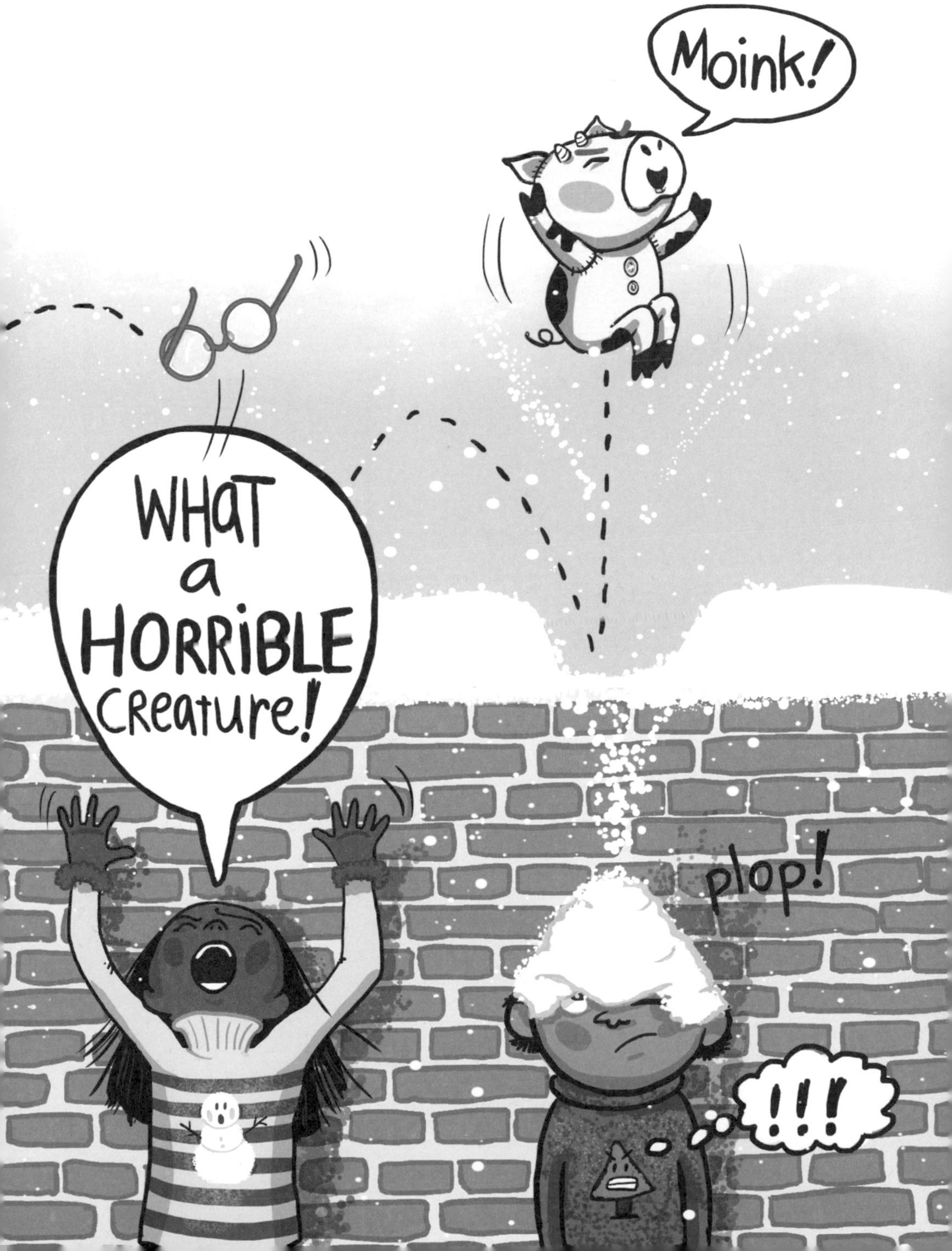
Moink!
WHAT a HORRIBLE Creature!
plop!
!!!

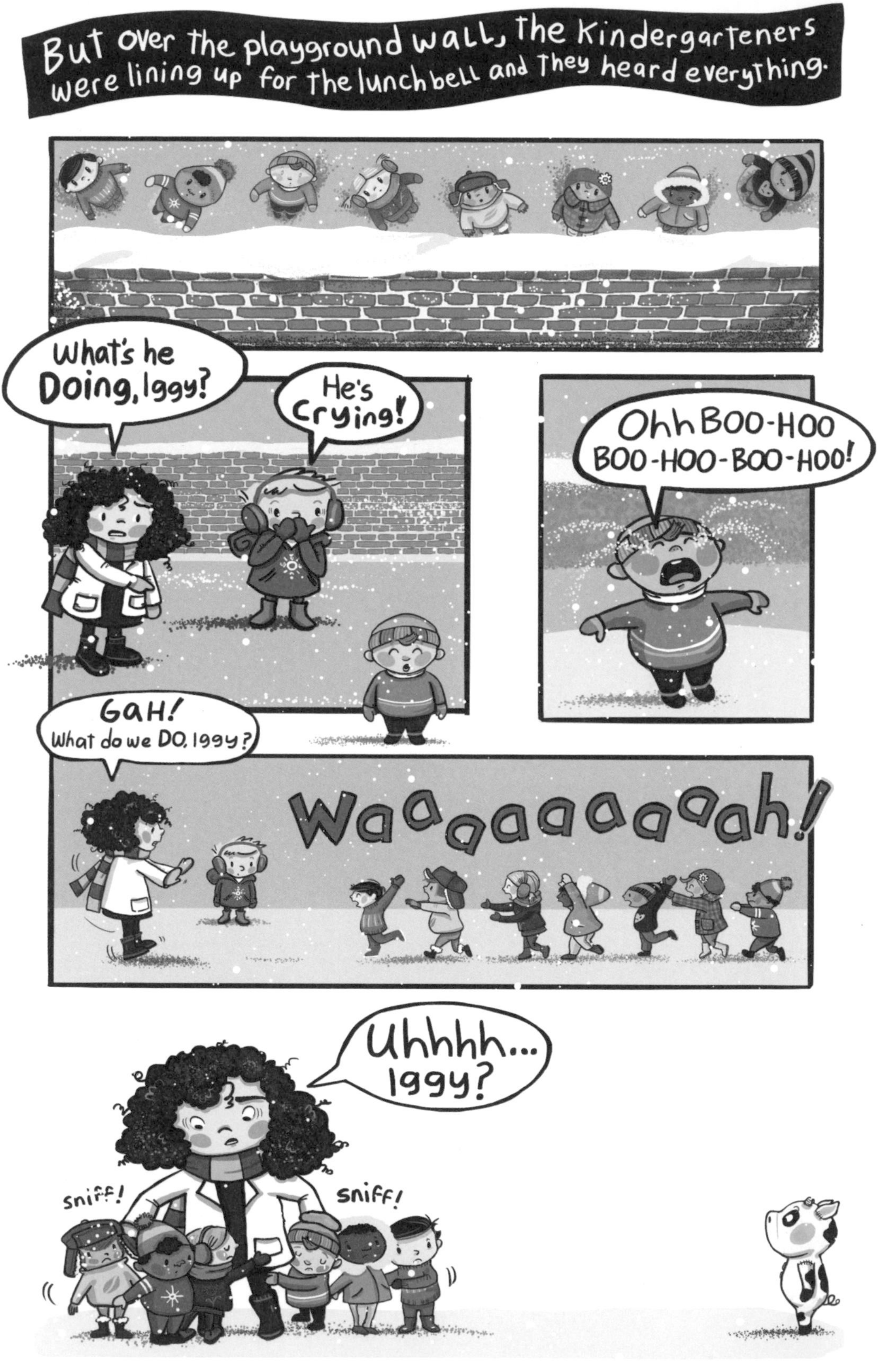

But over the playground wall, the Kindergarteners were lining up for the lunch bell and they heard everything.
What's he Doing, Iggy?
He's crying!
Ohh BOO-HOO BOO-HOO-BOO-HOO!
GAH! What do we DO, Iggy?
Waaaaaaaaah!
Uhhhh... Iggy?
sniff!
sniff!

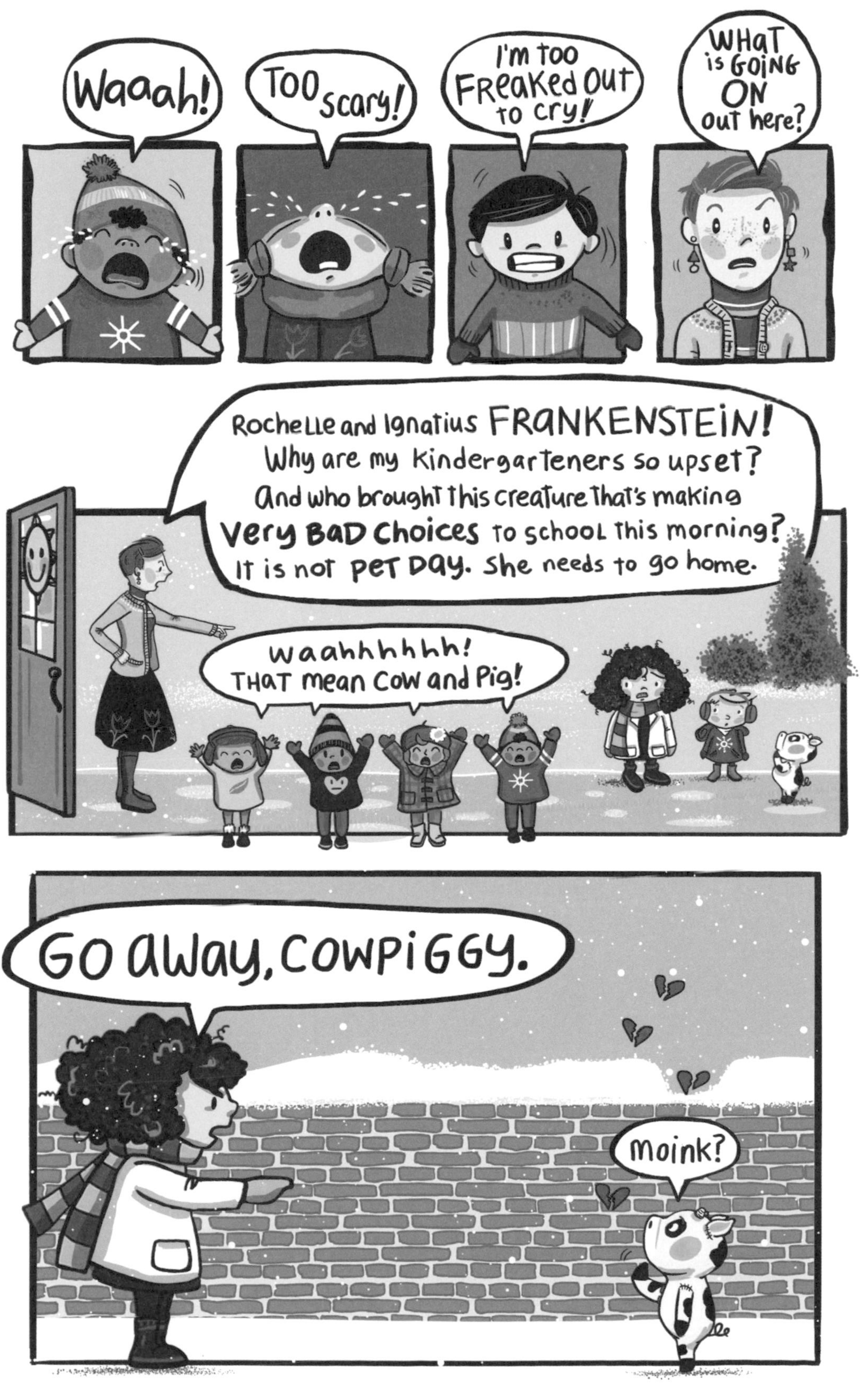
Waaah!
Too scary!
I'm too Freaked out to cry!
WHaT is GOING ON out here?
Rochelle and Ignatius FRANKENSTEIN! Why are my Kindergarteners so upset? And who brought this creature that's making VERY BAD CHOICES to school this morning? It is not PET DAY. She needs to go home.
Waahhhhhh! THAT mean Cow and Pig!
GO away, COWPIGGY.
Moink?

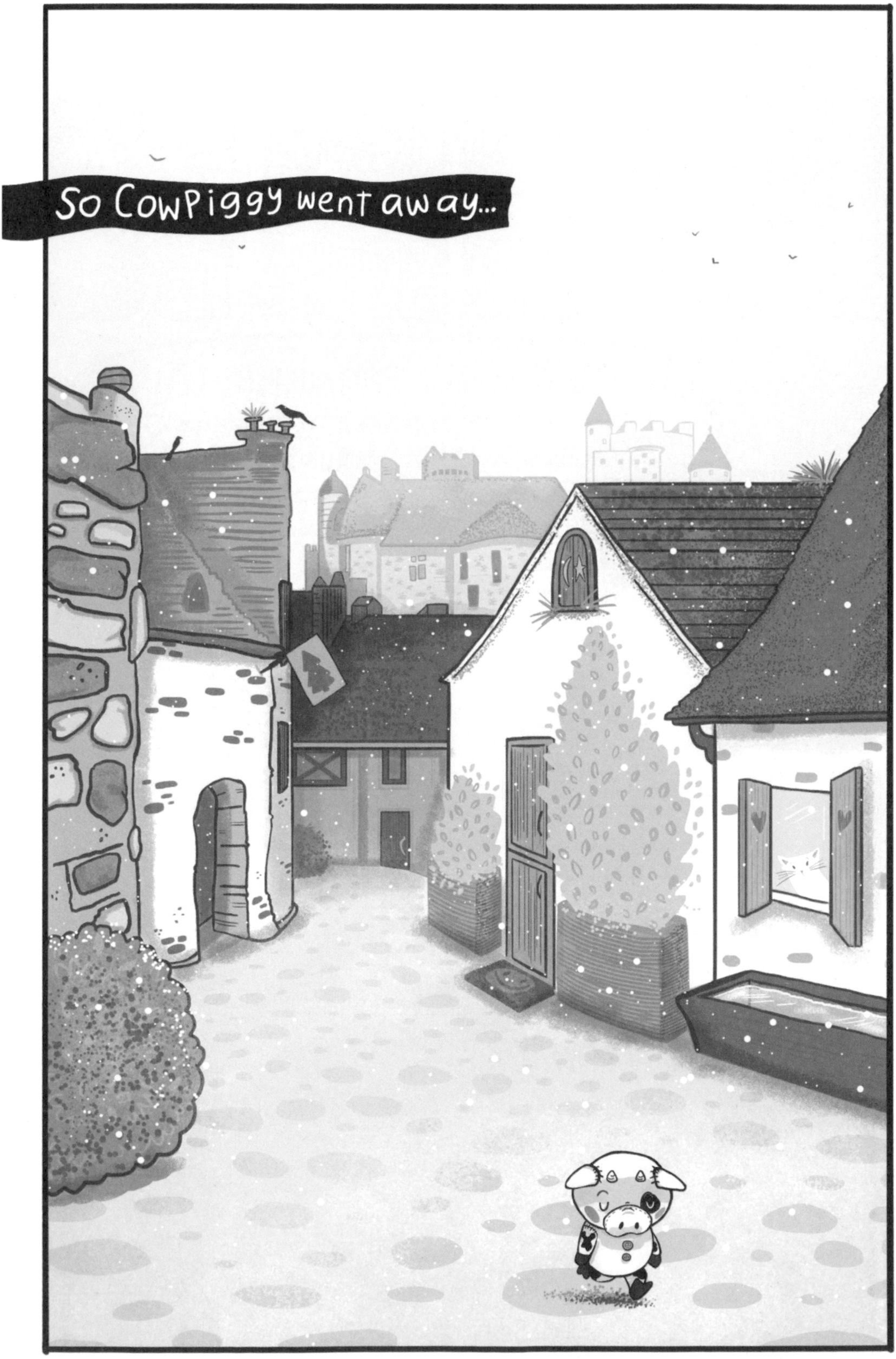
So CowPiggy went away...

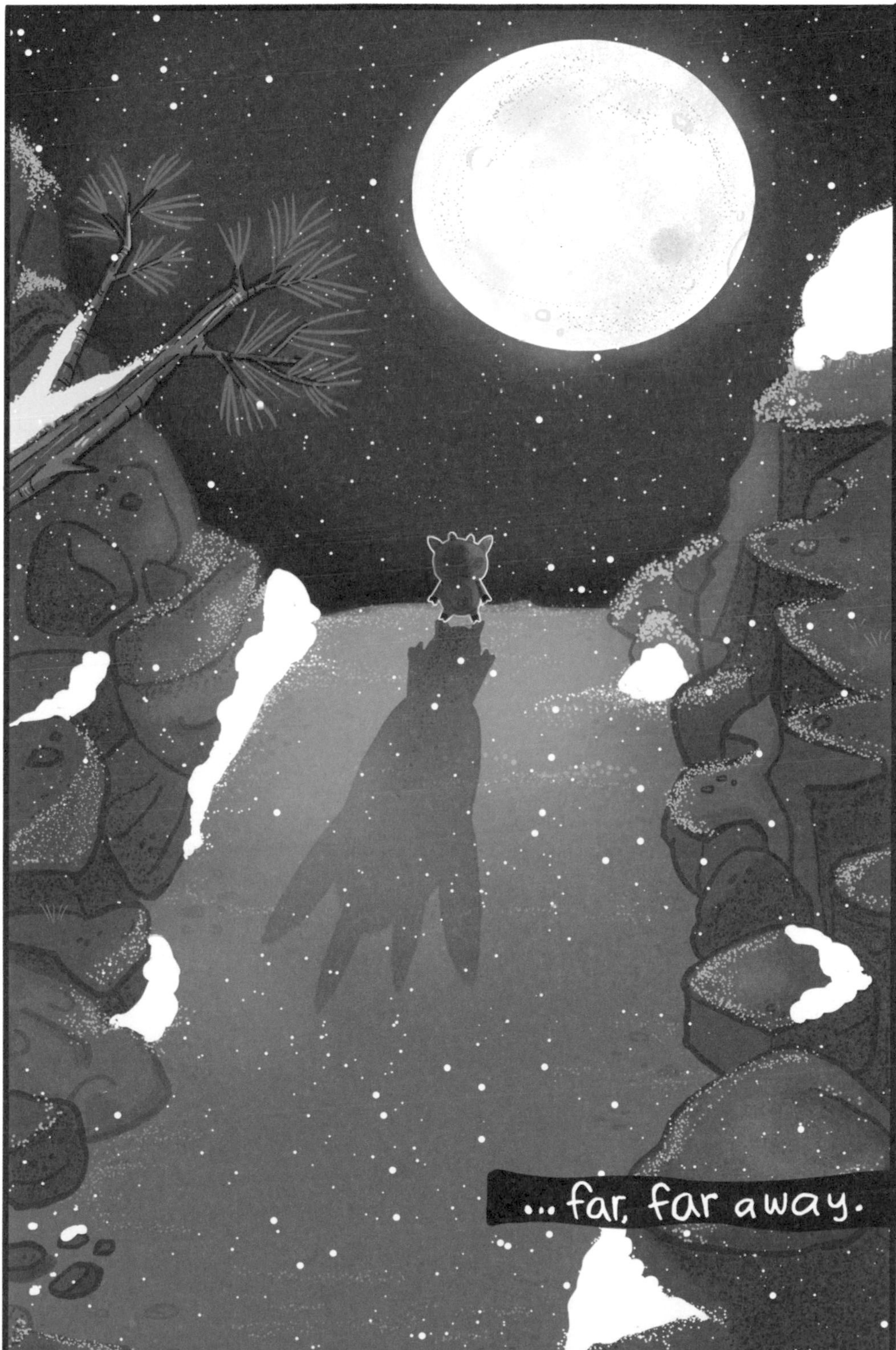
... far, far away.

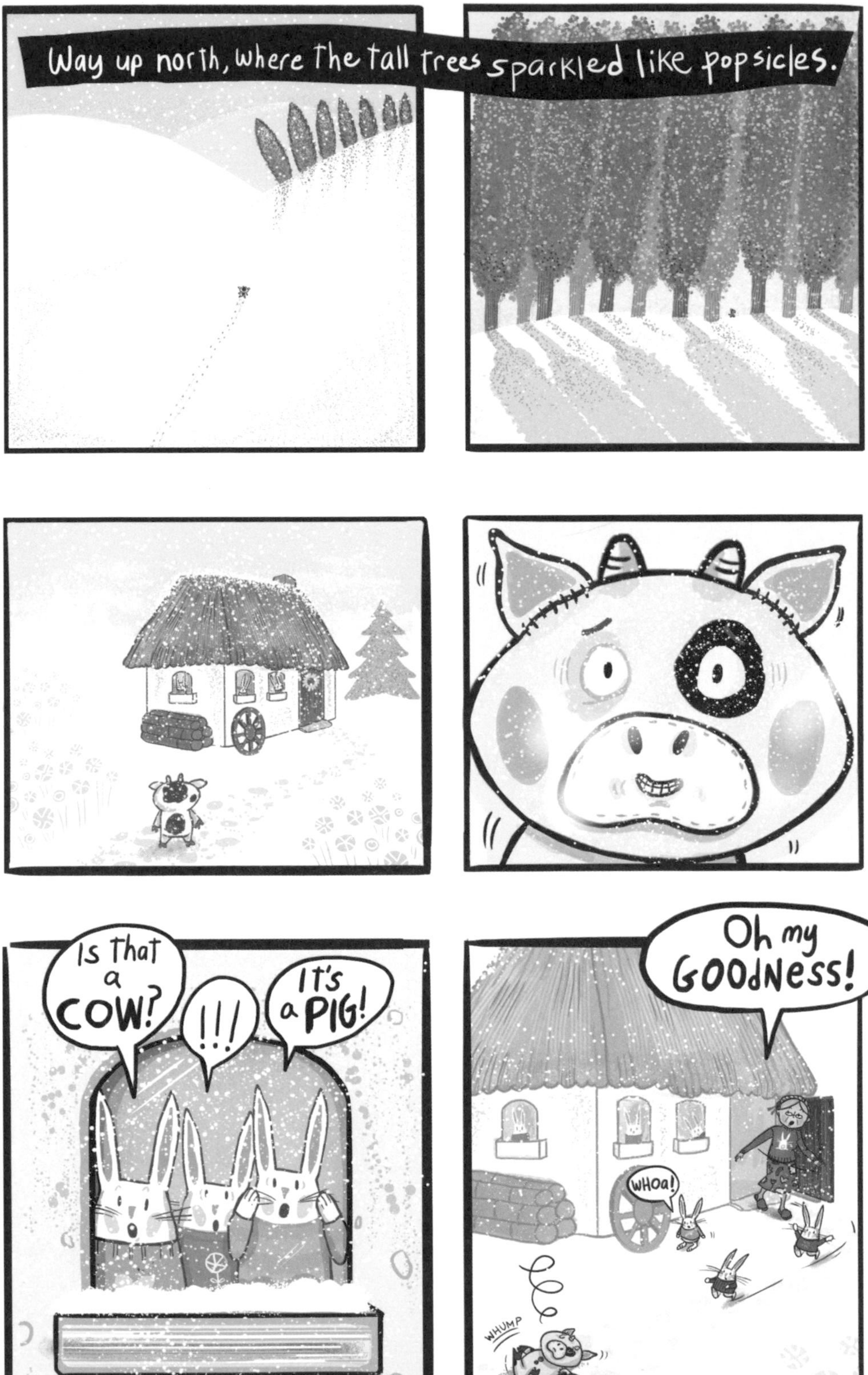
Way up north, where the tall trees sparkled like popsicles.
Is that a COW?
!!!
It's a PIG!
Oh my GOODNESS!
WHOa!
WHUMP

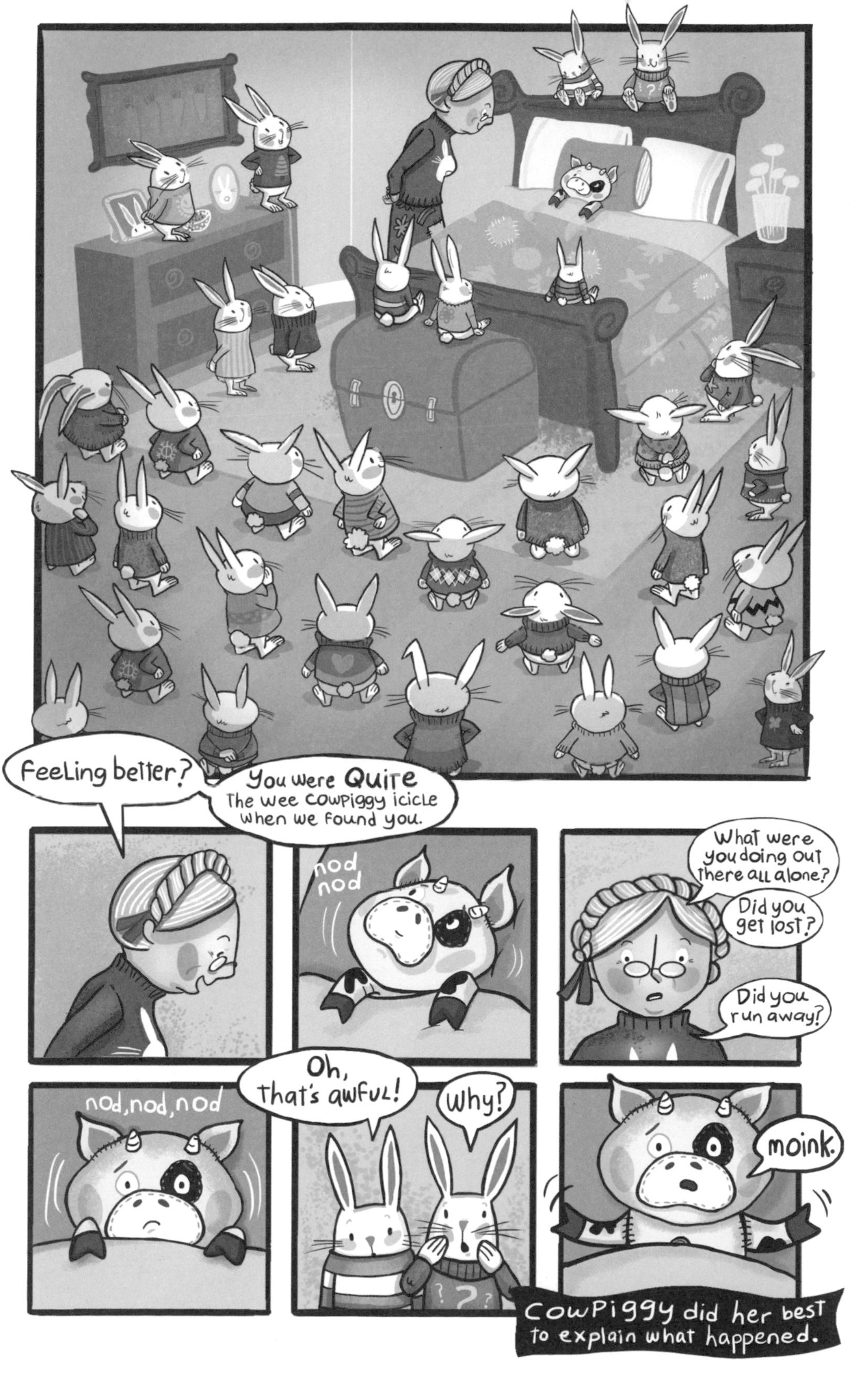
Feeling better?
You were QUITE The wee cowpiggy icicle when we found you.
nod nod
What were you doing out there all alone?
Did you get lost?
Did you run away?
nod, nod, nod
Oh, that's awful!
Why?
moink.
CowPiggy did her best to explain what happened.

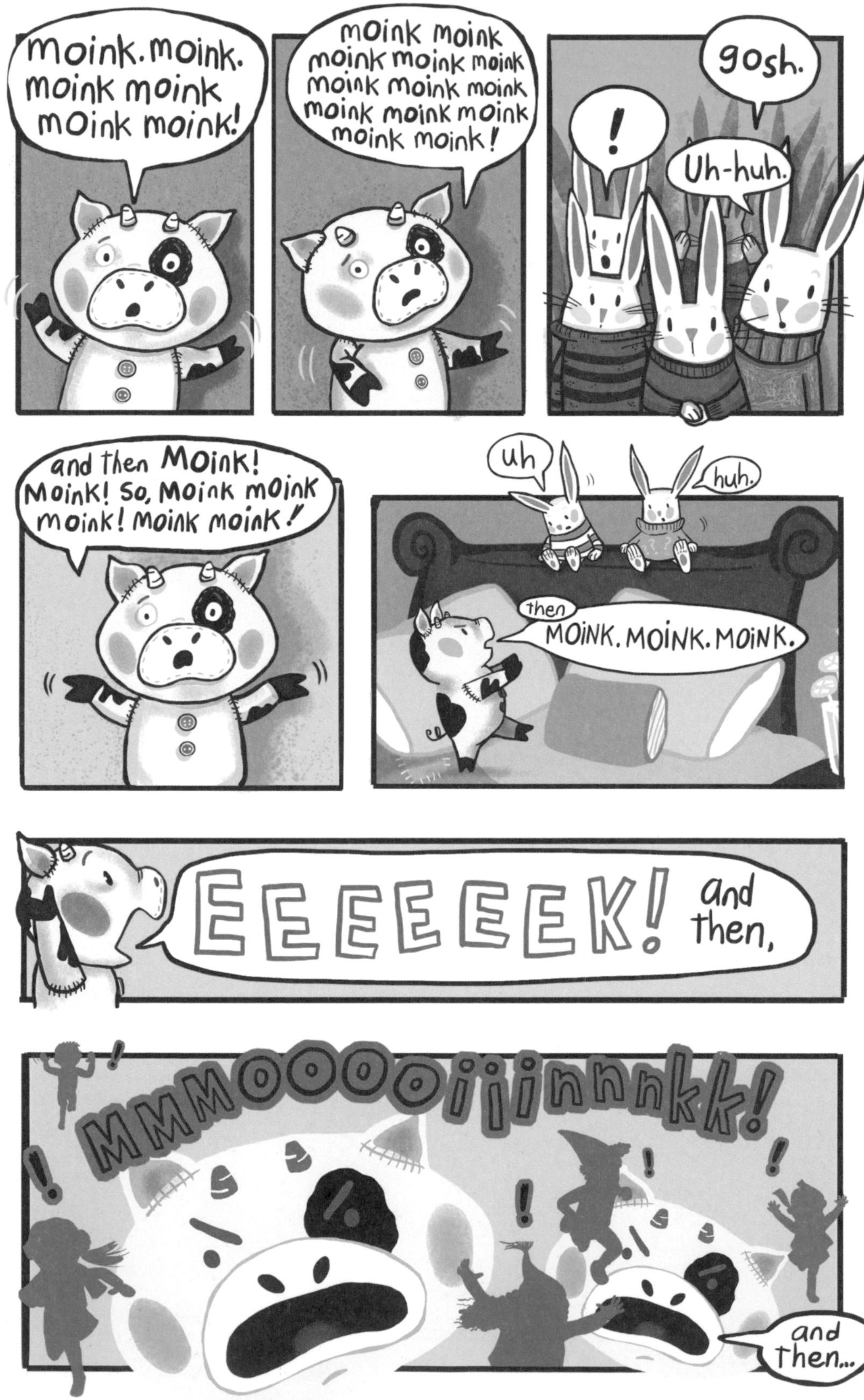
moink. moink. moink moink moink moink!
moink moink moink moink moink moink moink moink moink moink moink moink moink!
gosh.
!
Uh-huh.
and then Moink! Moink! So, Moink moink moink! Moink moink!
uh
huh.
then
MOINK. MOINK. MOINK.
EEEEEEK! and then,
MMMOOOOOiiinnnkk!
!
!
!
!
!
and then...

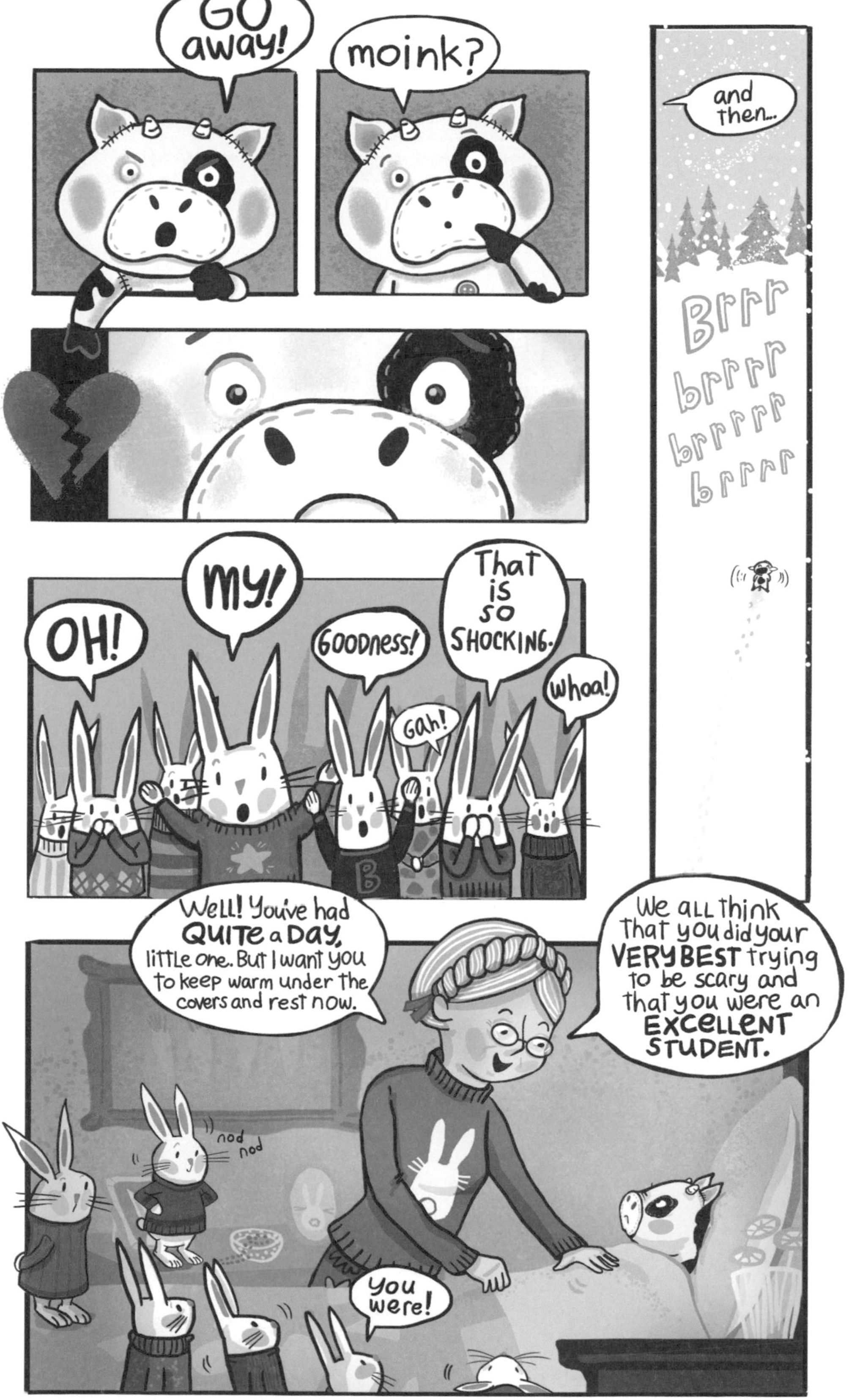

GO away!
moink?
and then...
Brrr
brrrr
brrrrr
brrrr
OH!
my!
Goodness!
That is so SHOCKING.
Gah!
Whoa!
Well! You've had QUITE a DAY, little one. But I want you to keep warm under the covers and rest now.
We all think that you did your VERY BEST trying to be scary and that you were an EXCELLENT STUDENT.
nod nod
You were!

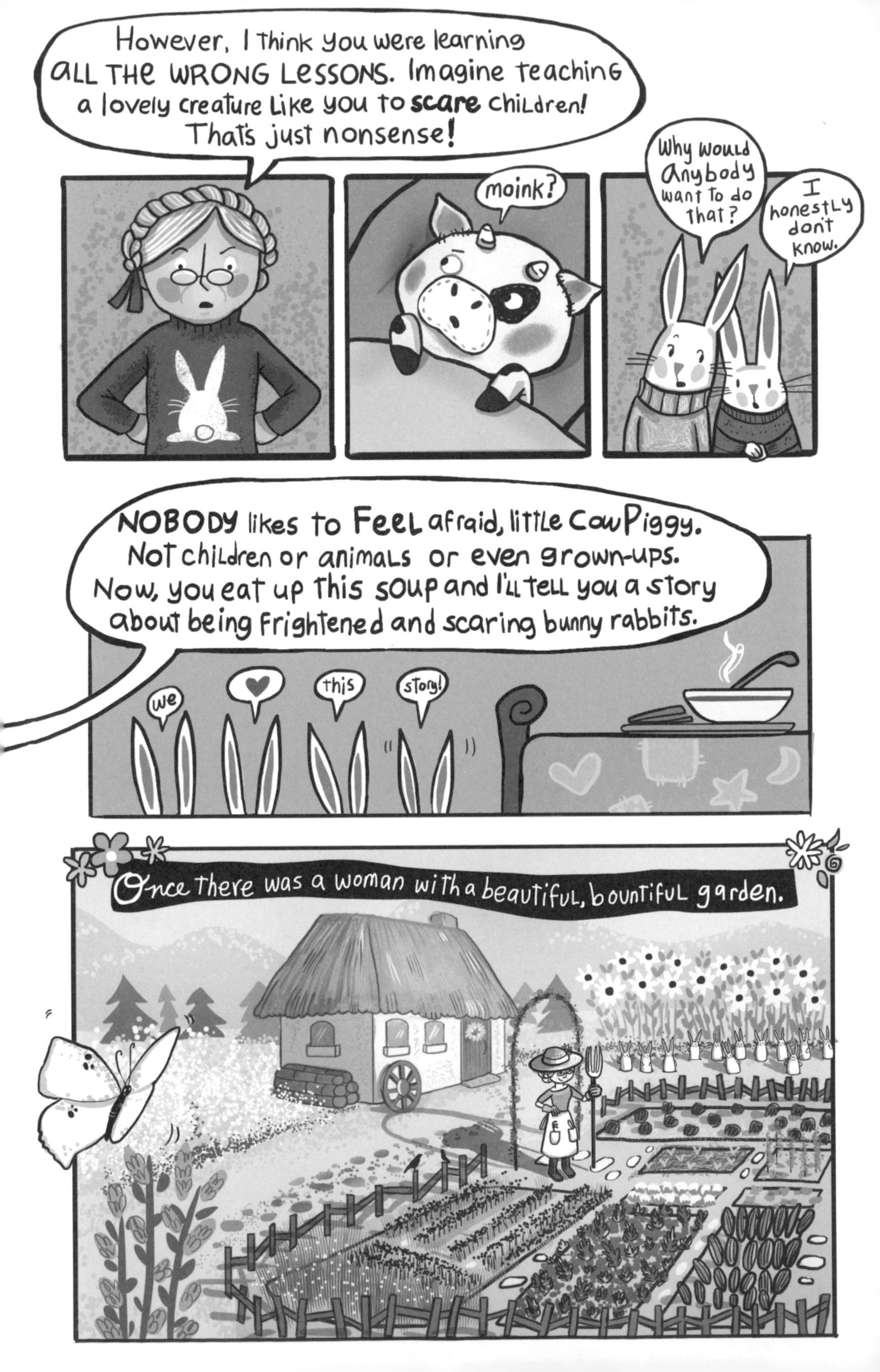
However, I think you were learning ALL THE WRONG LESSONS. Imagine teaching a lovely creature like you to scare children! That's just nonsense!
moink?
Why would anybody want to do that?
I honestly don't know.
NOBODY likes to FEEL afraid, little CowPiggy. Not children or animals or even grown-ups. Now, you eat up this soup and I'll tell you a story about being frightened and scaring bunny rabbits.
we
this
story!
Once there was a woman with a beautiful, bountiful garden.

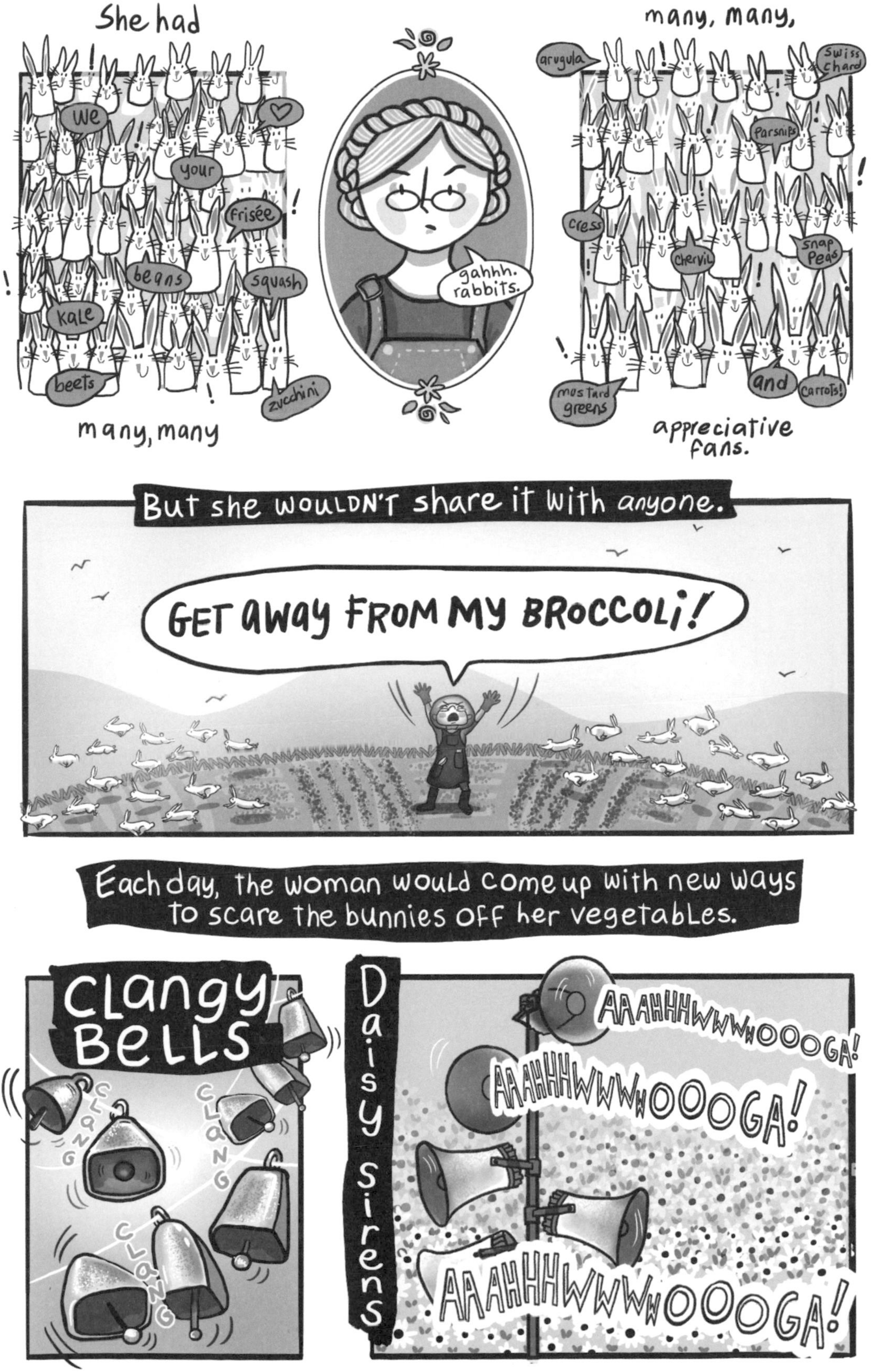
She had
We
♡
your
Frisée
beans
squash
kale
beets
zucchini
many, many
gahhh. rabbits.
many, many,
arugula
Swiss chard
Parsnips
cress
chervil
snap peas
mustard greens
and
carrots!
appreciative fans.
But she WOULDN'T share it with anyone.
GET away FROM MY BROCCOLi!
Each day, the woman would come up with new ways to scare the bunnies off her vegetables.
Clangy Bells
CLANG
CLANG
CLANG
CLANG
Daisy Sirens
AAAHHHWWWWOOOOGA!
AAAHHHWWWWOOOGA!
AAAHHHWWWWOOOOGA!

GUARD CHICKENS

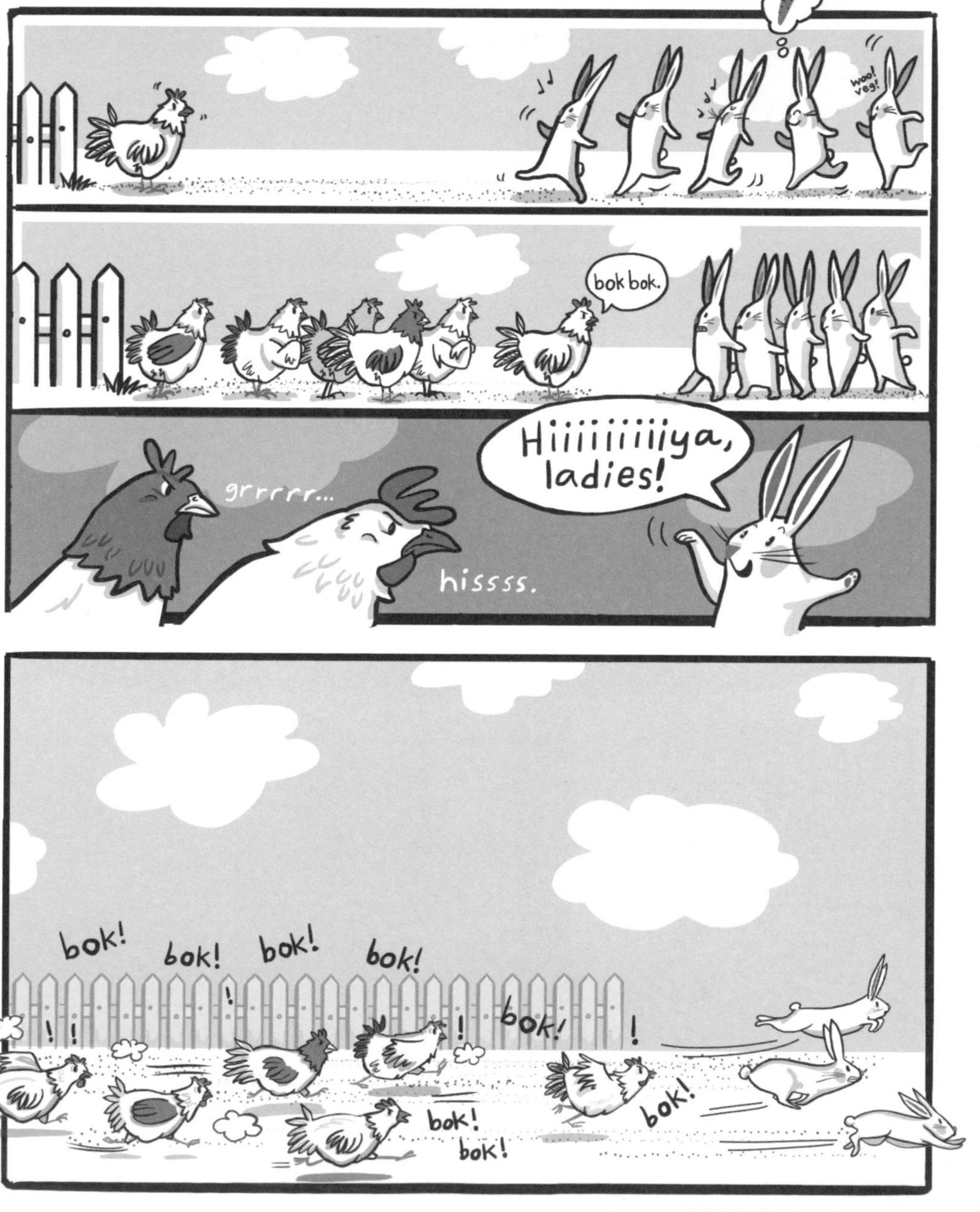
woo! veg!
bok bok.
grrrrr...
hissss.
Hiiiiiiiiiya, ladies!
bok!
bok!
bok!
bok!
bok!
bok!
bok!
bok!

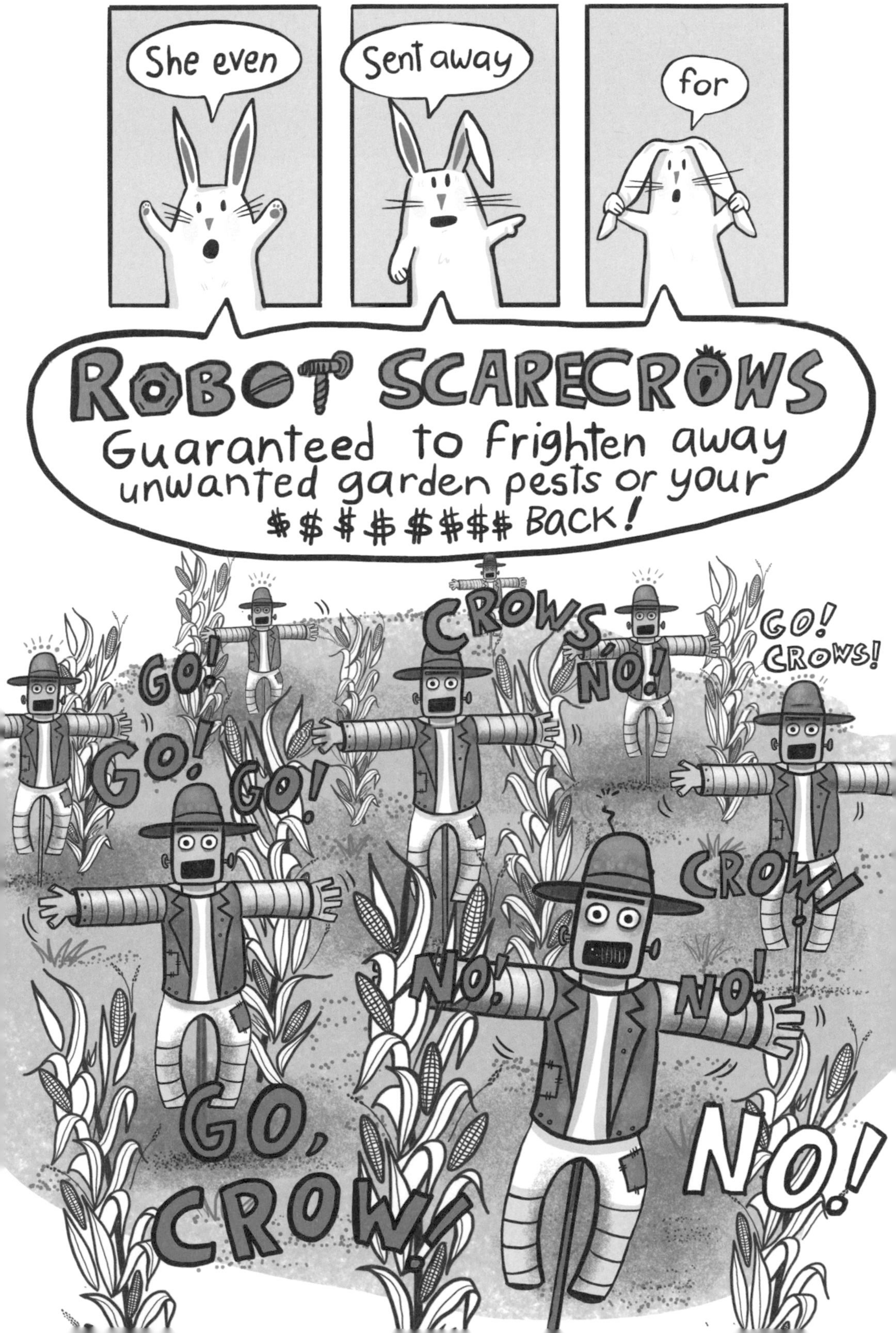
She even
Sent away
for
ROBOT SCARECROWS
Guaranteed to frighten away unwanted garden pests or your $$$$$$$ BACK!
GO!
GO!
GO!
CROWS, NO!
GO! CROWS!
CROW!
NO!
NO!
GO, CROW!
NO!

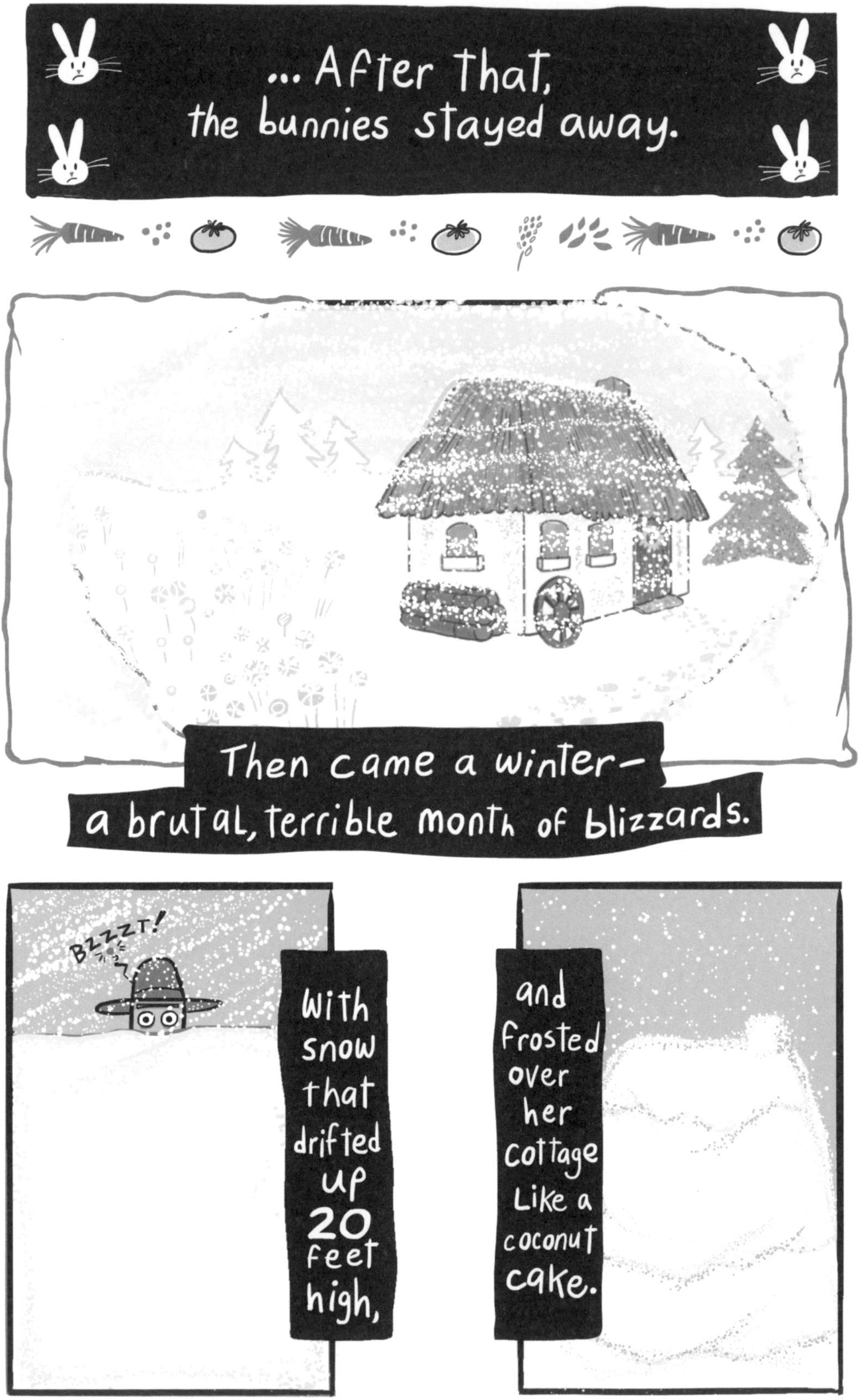
... After that, the bunnies stayed away.
Then came a winter—
a brutal, terrible month of blizzards.
BZZZT!
With snow that drifted up 20 feet high,
and frosted over her cottage like a coconut cake.

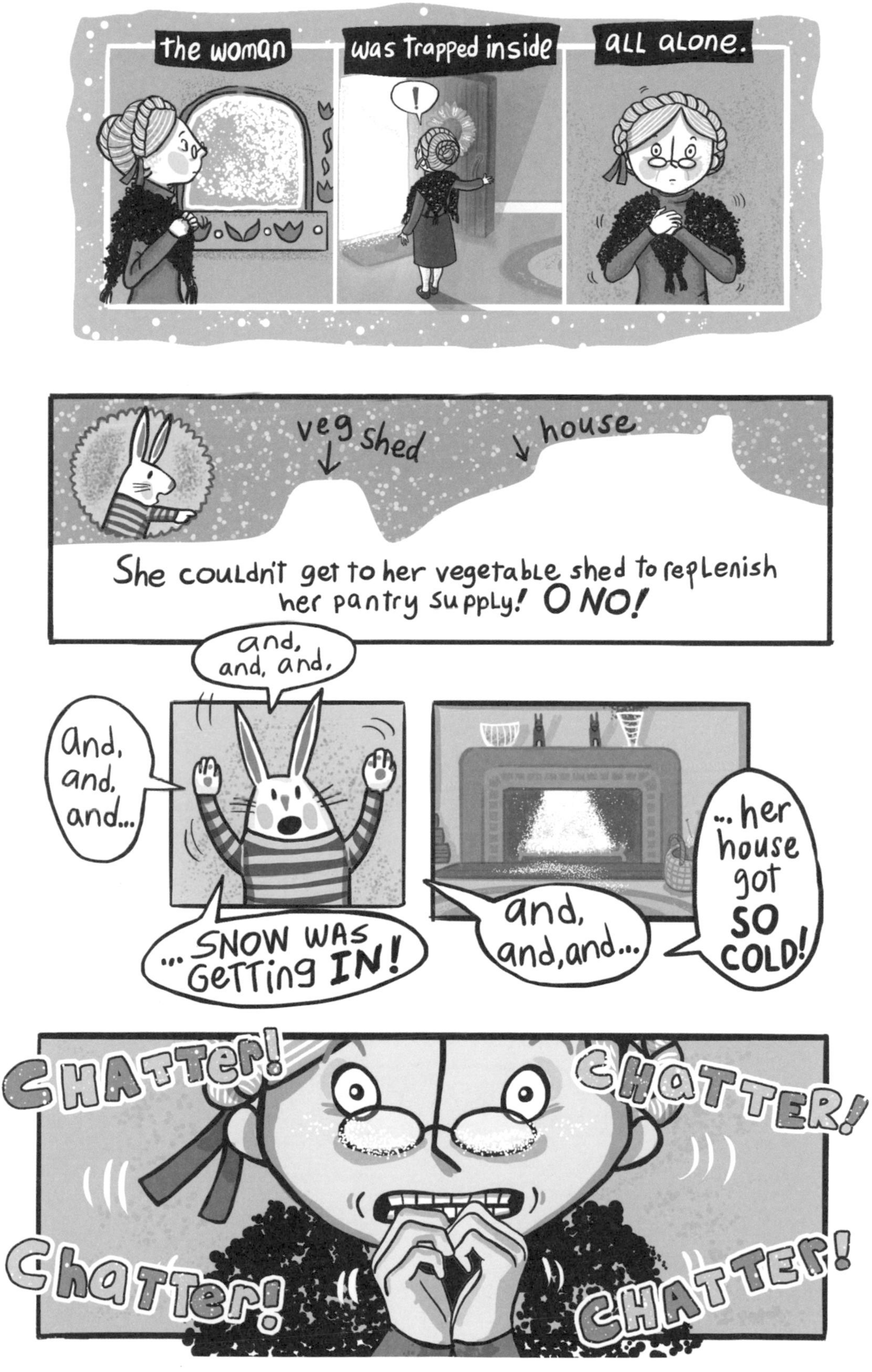
the woman
was trapped inside
ALL ALONE.
!
veg shed
house
She couldn't get to her vegetable shed to replenish her pantry supply! O NO!
and, and, and,
and, and, and...
...SNOW WAS GETTING IN!
and, and, and...
...her house got SO COLD!
CHATTER!
CHATTER!
Chatter!
CHATTER!

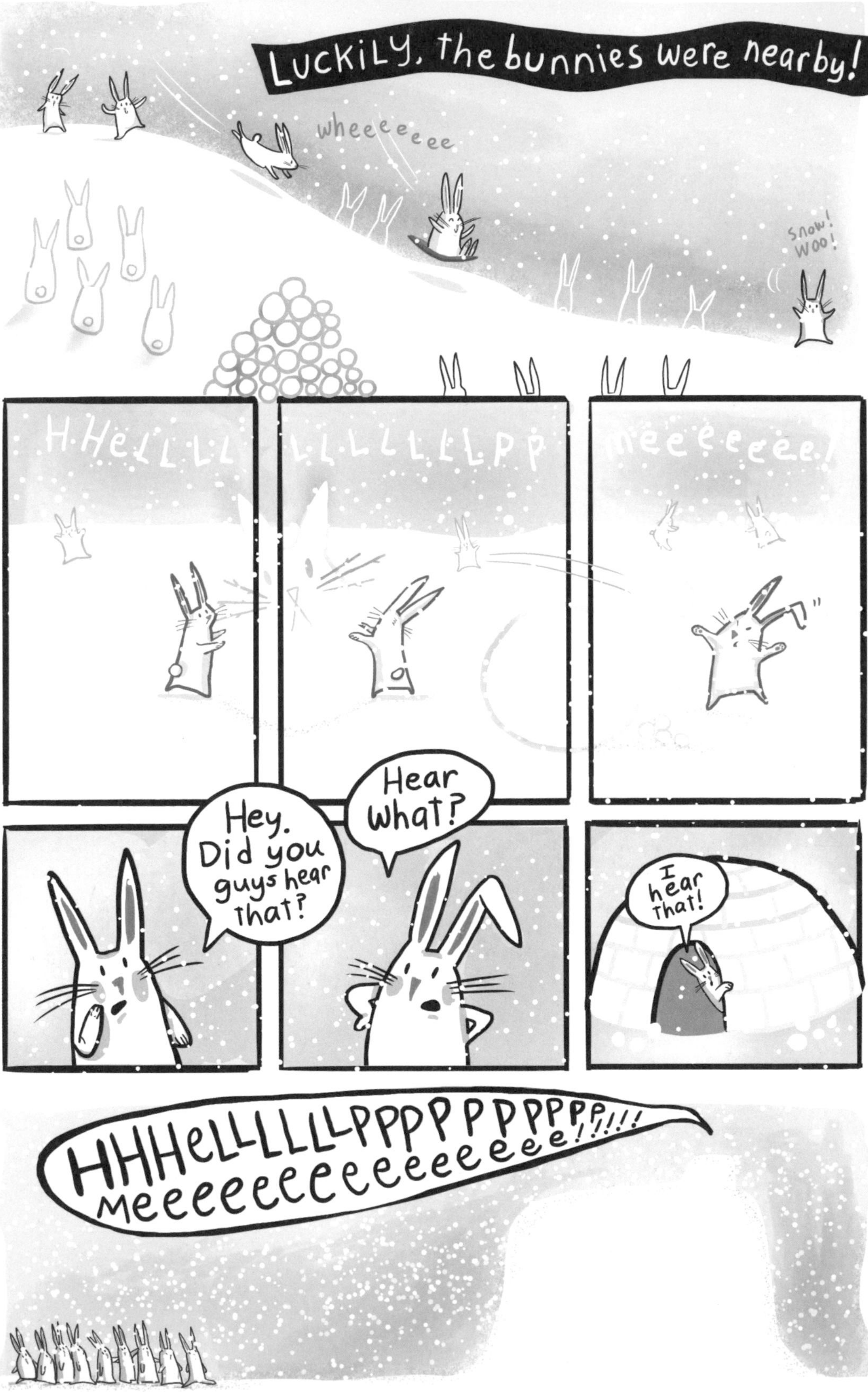

LUCKILY, the bunnies were nearby!
wheeeeeee
Snow! Woo!
HHeLLLL
LLLLLLLLPP
meeeeeee!
Hey. Did you guys hear that?
Hear what?
I hear that!
HHHeLLLLLLLPPPPPPPPP!!!!! Meeeeeeeeeeeeeeee!

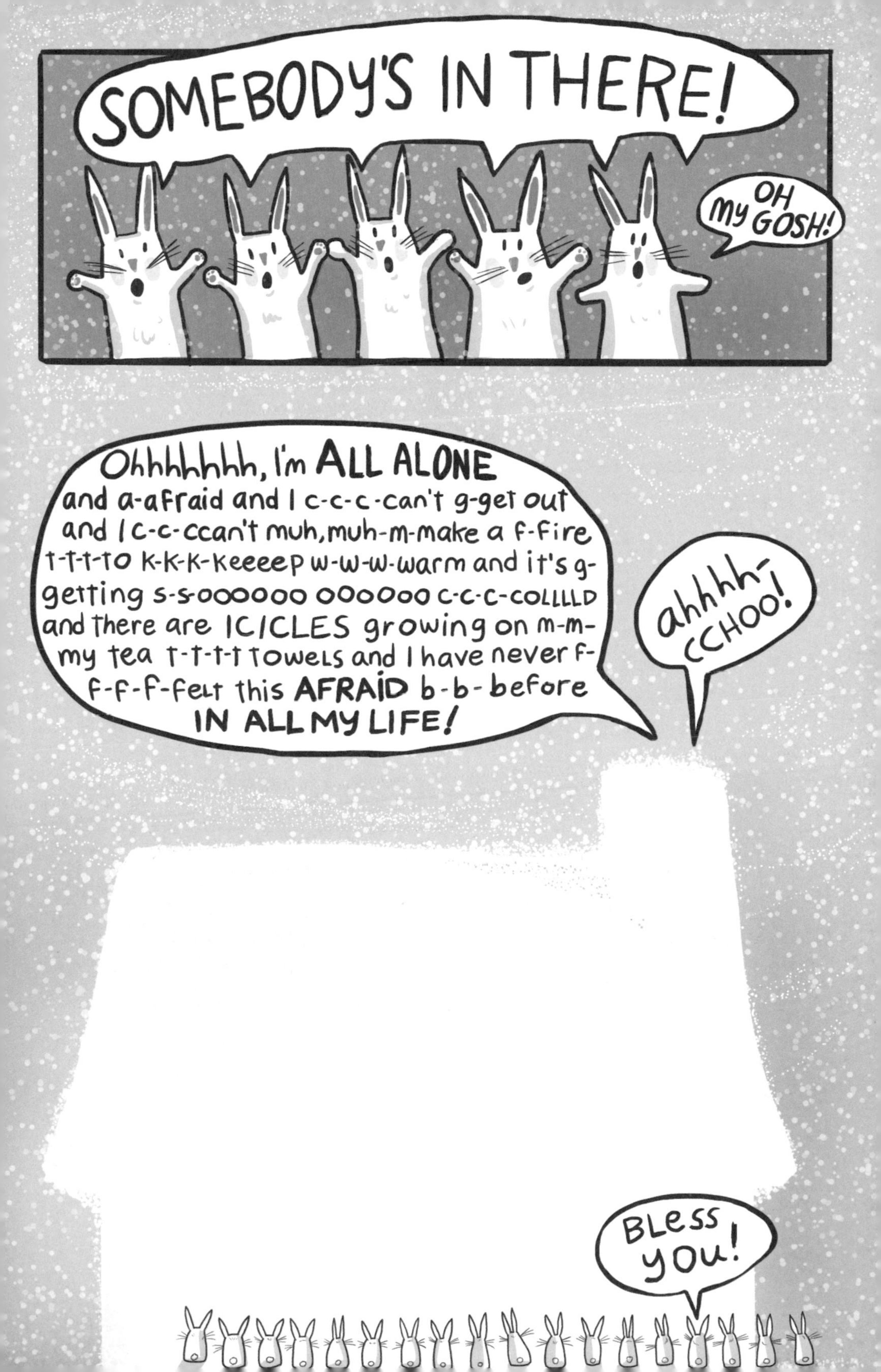
SOMEBODY'S IN THERE!
OH my GOSH!
Ohhhhhhh, I'm ALL ALONE and a-afraid and I c-c-c-can't g-get out and I c-c-ccan't muh, muh-m-make a f-fire t-t-t-to k-k-k-keeeep w-w-w-warm and it's g-getting s-s-oooooo oooooo c-c-c-COLLLLD and there are ICICLES growing on m-m-my tea t-t-t-t towels and I have never f-f-f-f-felt this AFRAID b-b-before IN ALL MY LIFE!
ahhhh-CCHOO!
BLESS YOU!

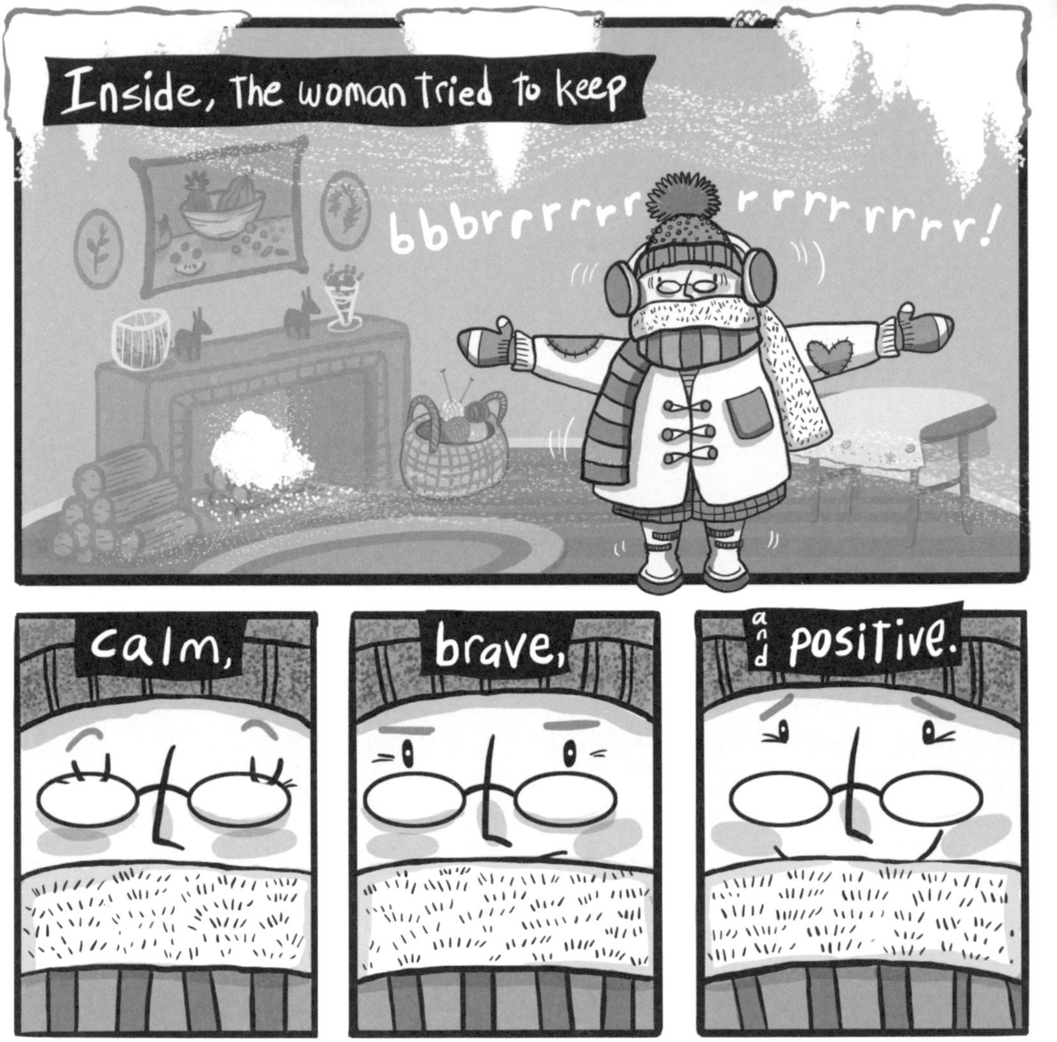
Inside, the woman tried to keep
bbbrrrrrrrrrrrrrrr!
calm,
brave,
and positive.

After a while, when the cold settled deep into her toes and it didn't seem like ANYONE was coming to help her, the woman began to feel afraid, really frightened that she would be trapped inside her own house until Spring.

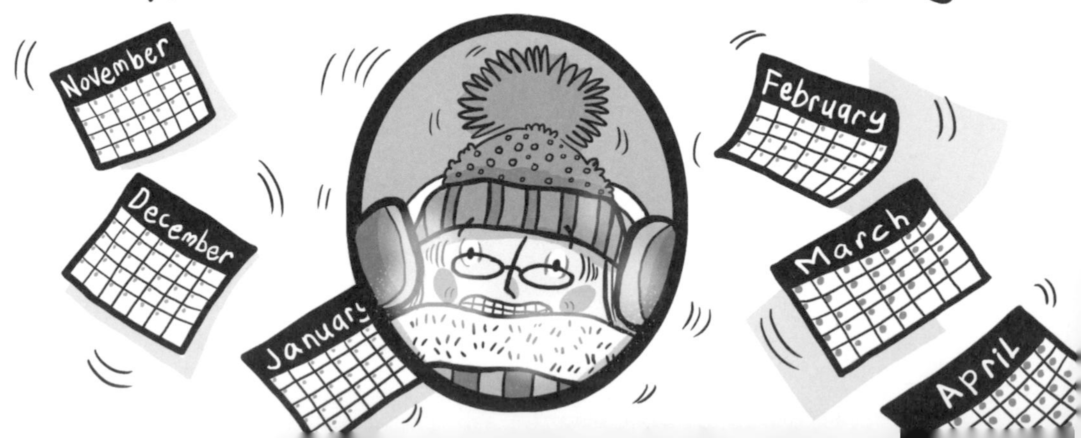
November
December
January
February
March
April

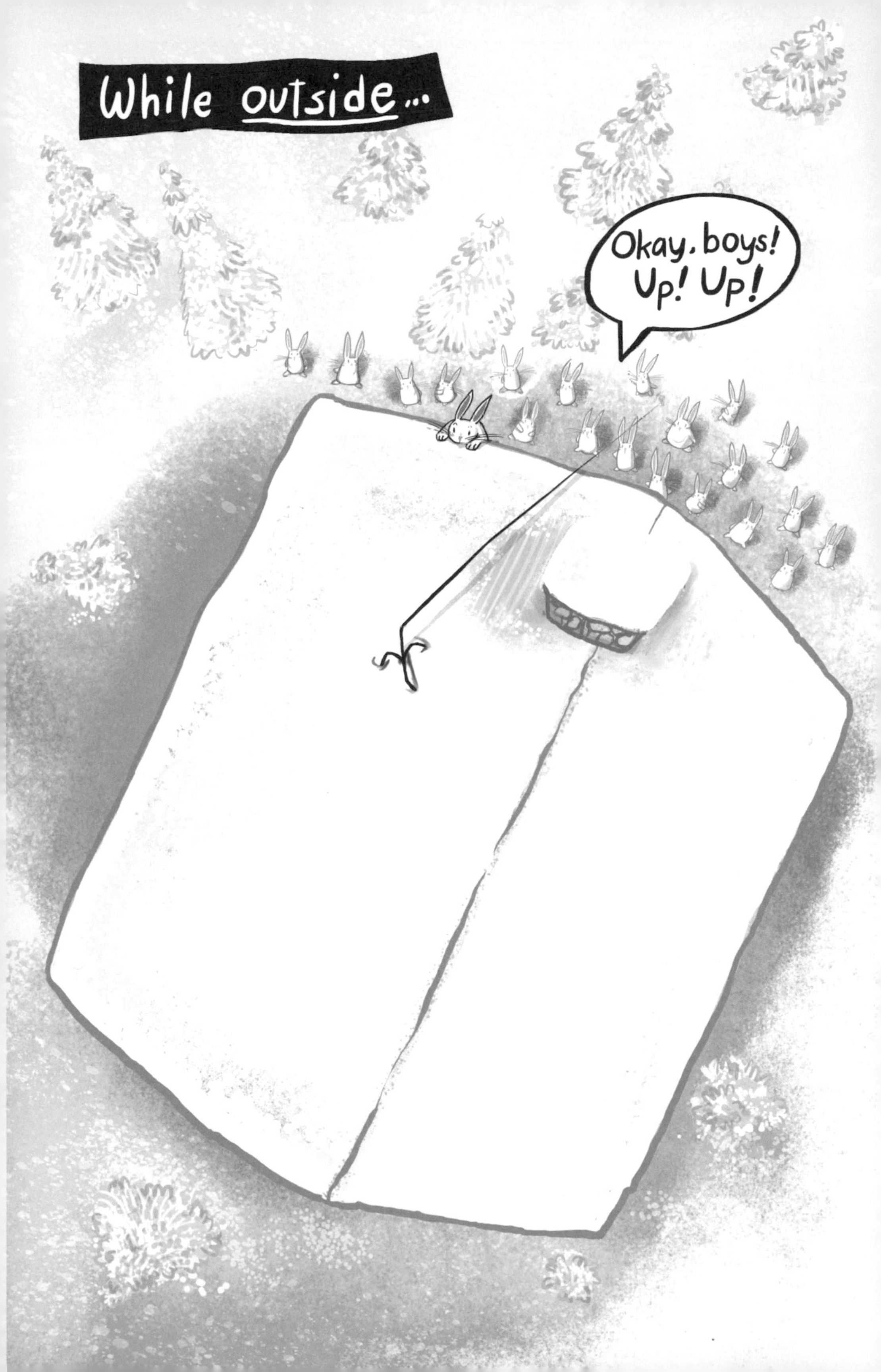
While outside...
Okay, boys! Up! Up!

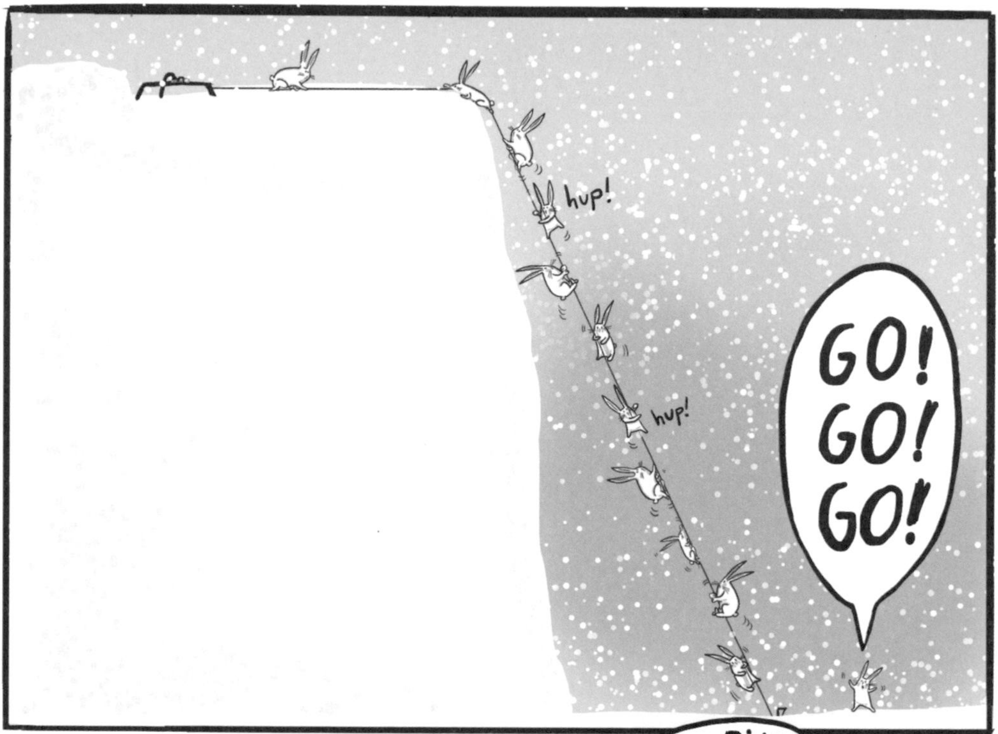
hup!
hup!
GO! GO! GO!

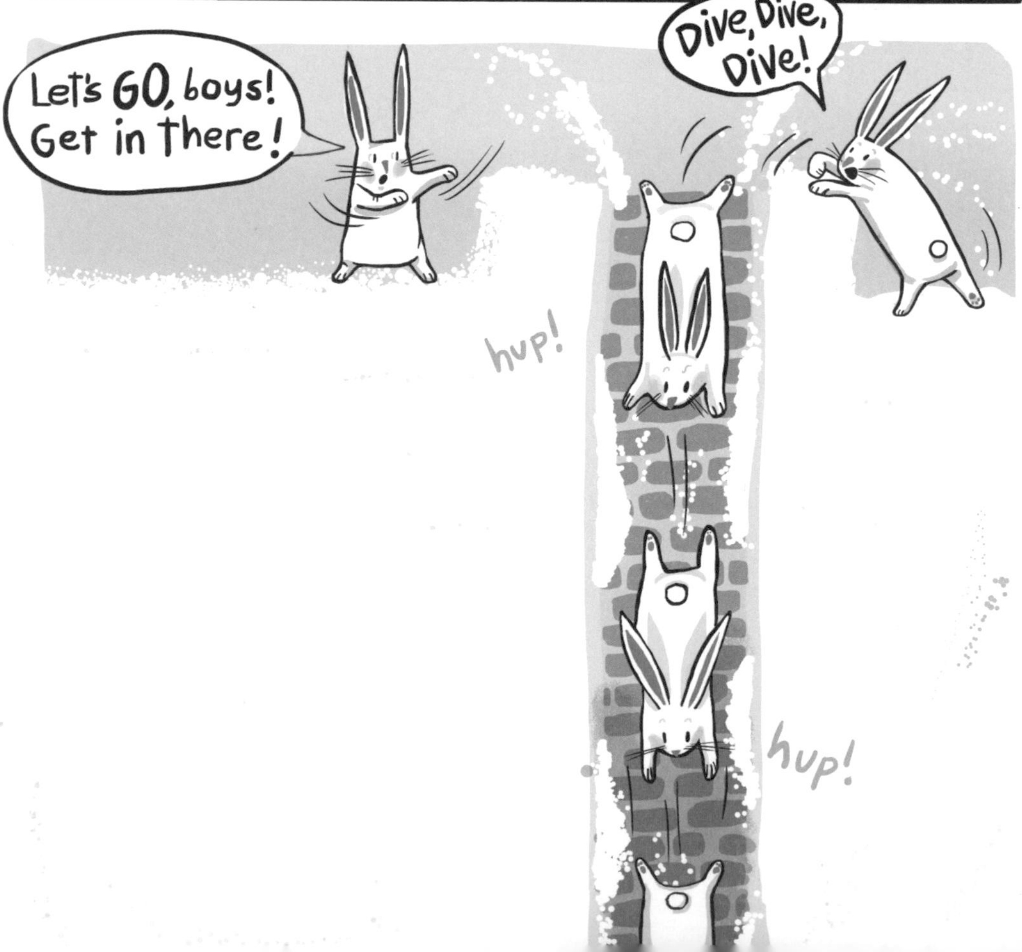
Let's GO, boys! Get in there!
Dive, Dive, Dive!
hup!
hup!

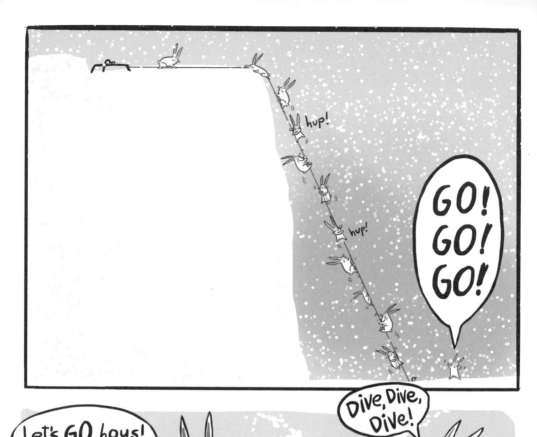

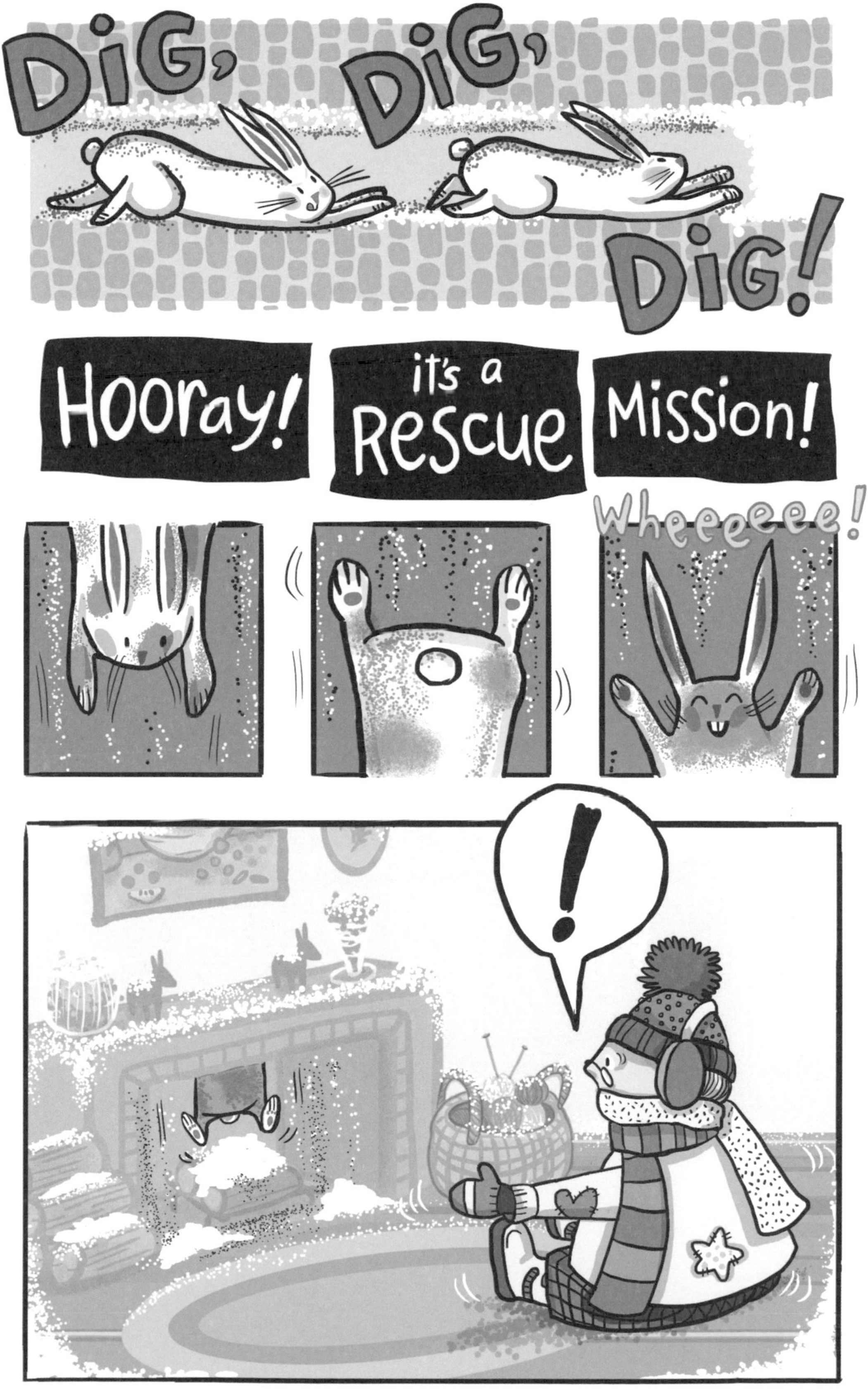
DIG, DIG, DIG!
HOORAY! IT'S A RESCUE MISSION!
Wheeeeee!
!

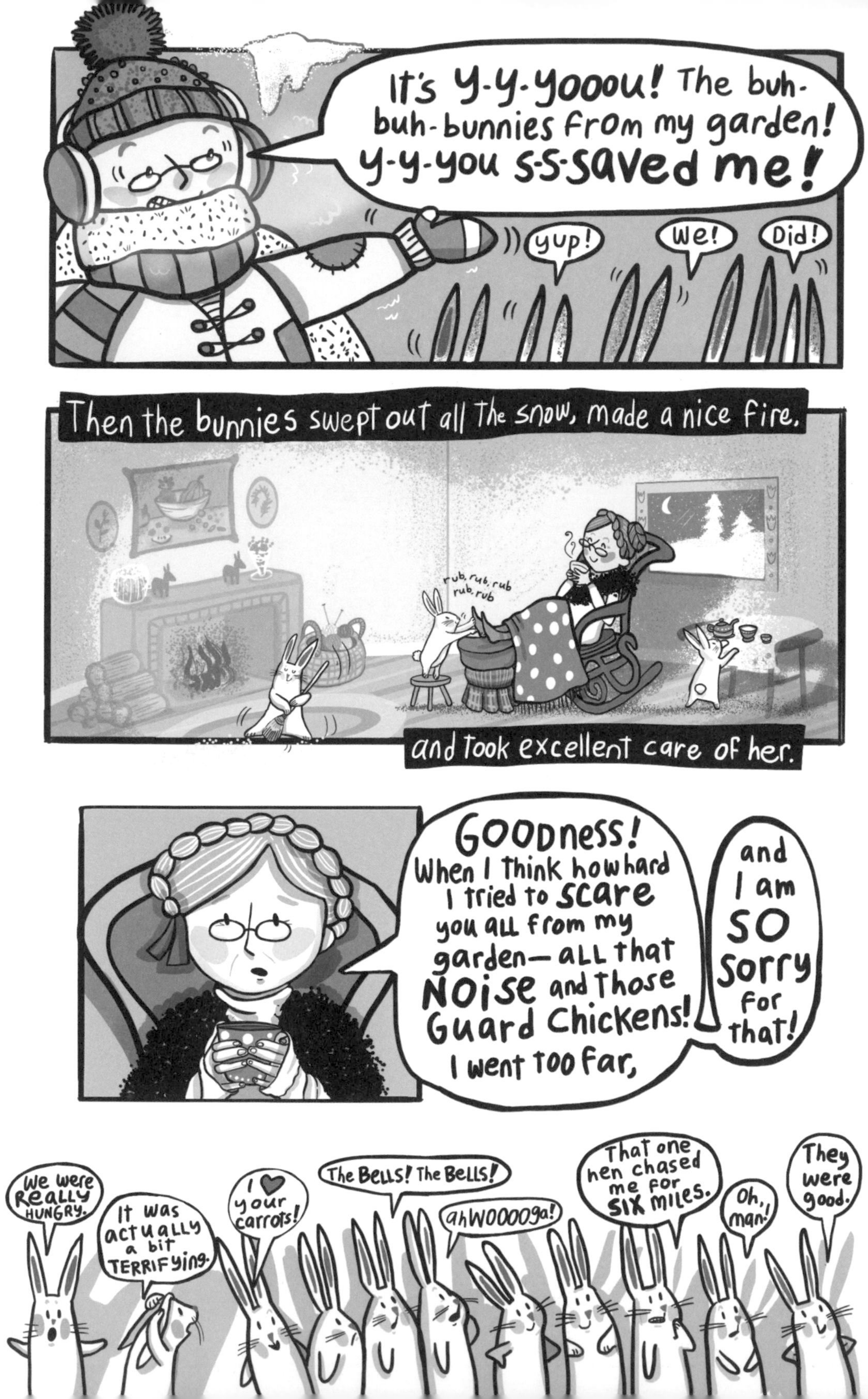
It's Y-Y-YOOOU! The buh-buh-bunnies from my garden! Y-Y-YOU S-S-SAVED ME!
Yup!
We!
Did!
Then the bunnies swept out all the snow, made a nice fire.
rub, rub, rub rub, rub
and took excellent care of her.
GOODNESS! When I think how hard I tried to scare you all from my garden—ALL that NOISE and those Guard Chickens! I went too far,
and I am SO sorry for that!
We were REALLY HUNGRY.
It was actually a bit TERRIFYING.
I ♥ your carrots!
The BELLS! The BELLS!
ahWOOOOga!
That one hen chased me for SIX MILES.
Oh, man!
They were good.

For the rest of that winter and all the winters after,

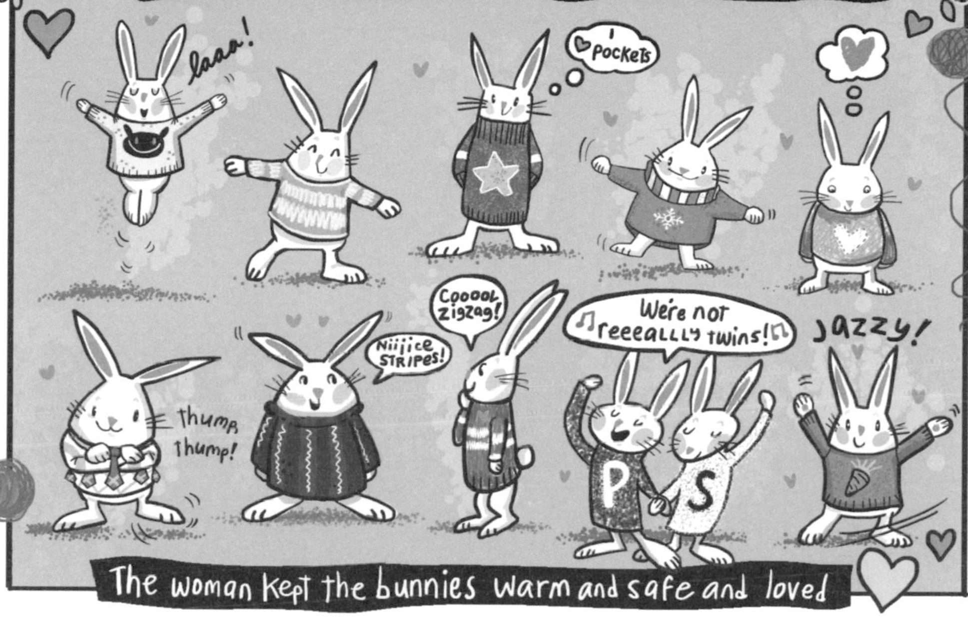

laaa!
I ♡ pockets
Cooool zigzag!
Niiiice stripes!
We're not reeeallly twins!
jazzy!
thump thump!

The woman kept the bunnies warm and safe and loved

and never tried to scare them again.

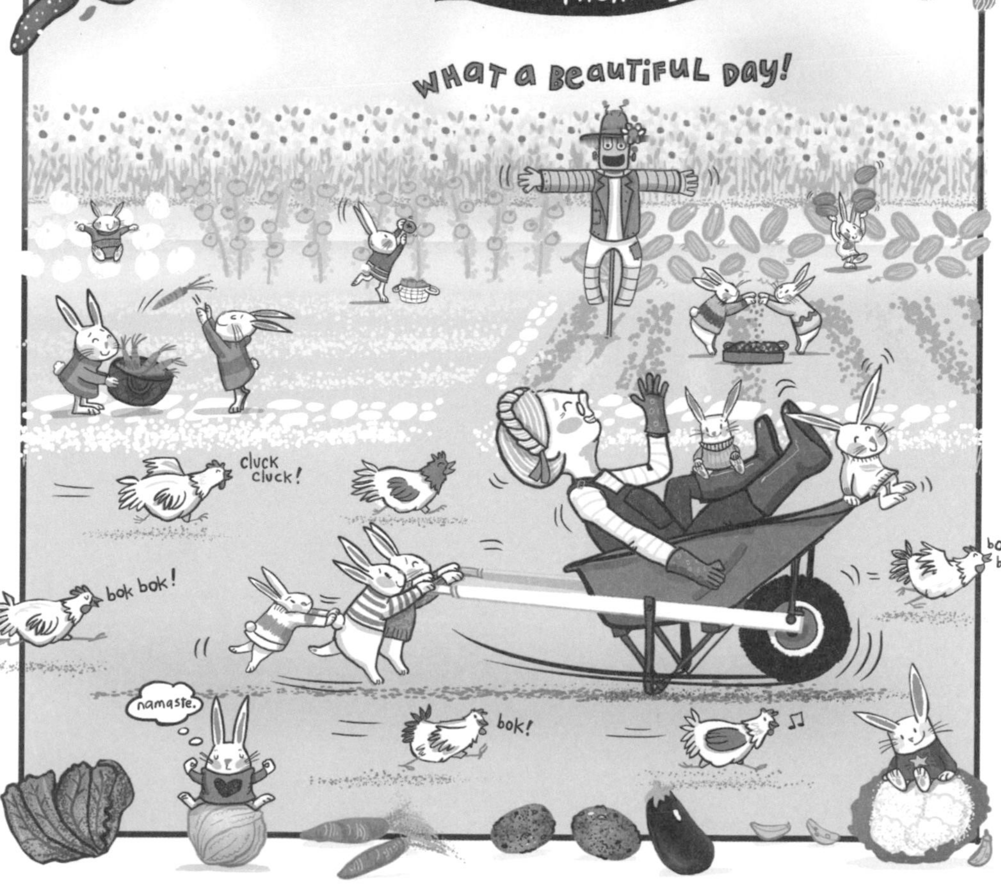

WHAT A BEAUTIFUL DAY!
cluck cluck!
bok bok!
bok bok!
namaste.
bok!

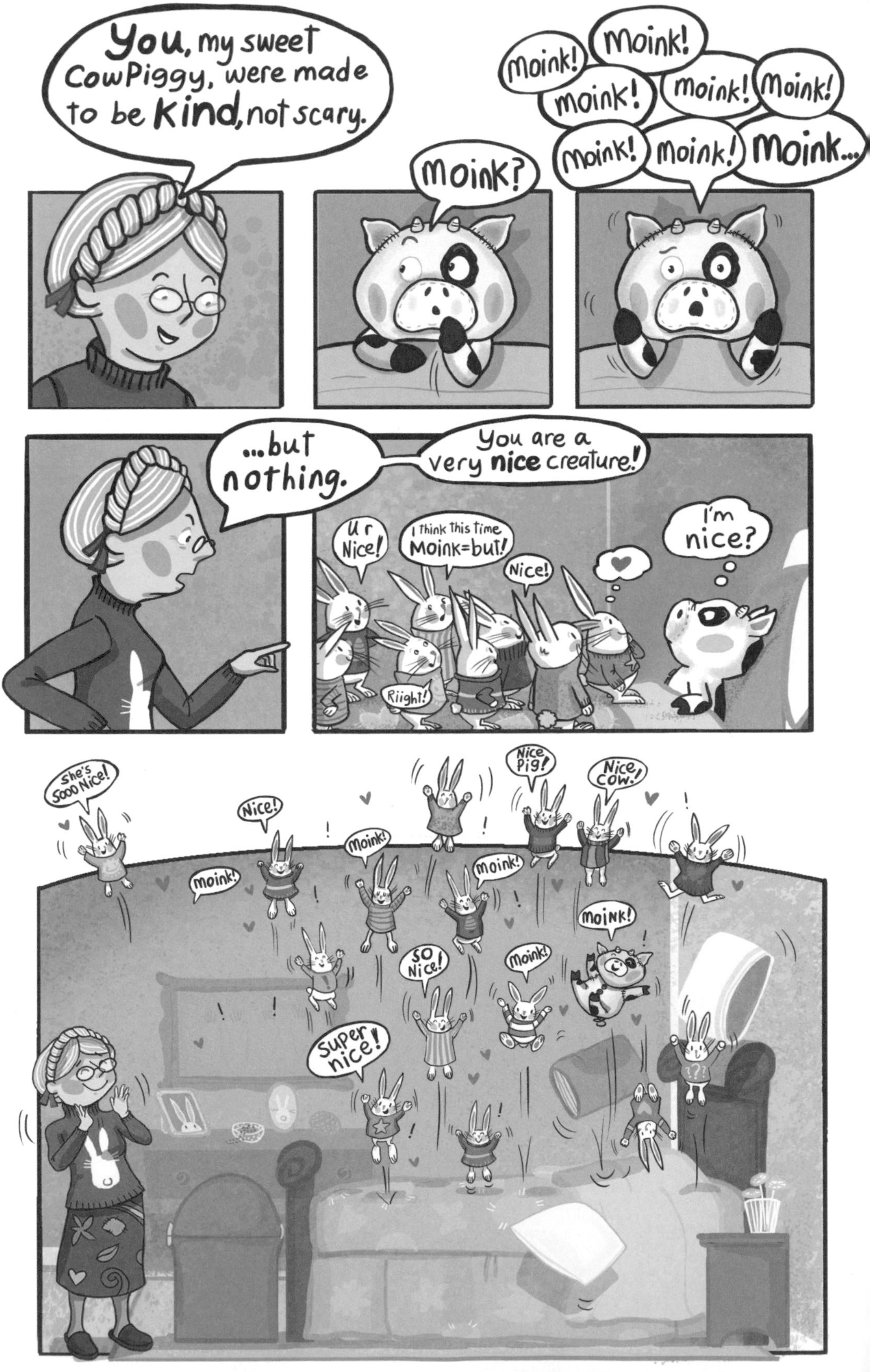

You, my sweet CowPiggy, were made to be kind, not scary.
Moink?
Moink!
Moink!
Moink!
Moink!
Moink!
Moink!
Moink!
Moink...
...but nothing.
You are a very nice creature!
Ur Nice!
I think this time Moink=but!
Nice!
Riight!
I'm nice?
She's Sooo Nice!
Nice!
Moink!
Nice Pig!
Nice Cow!
Moink!
Moink!
Moink!
Moink!
SO Nice!
Moink!
Super nice!

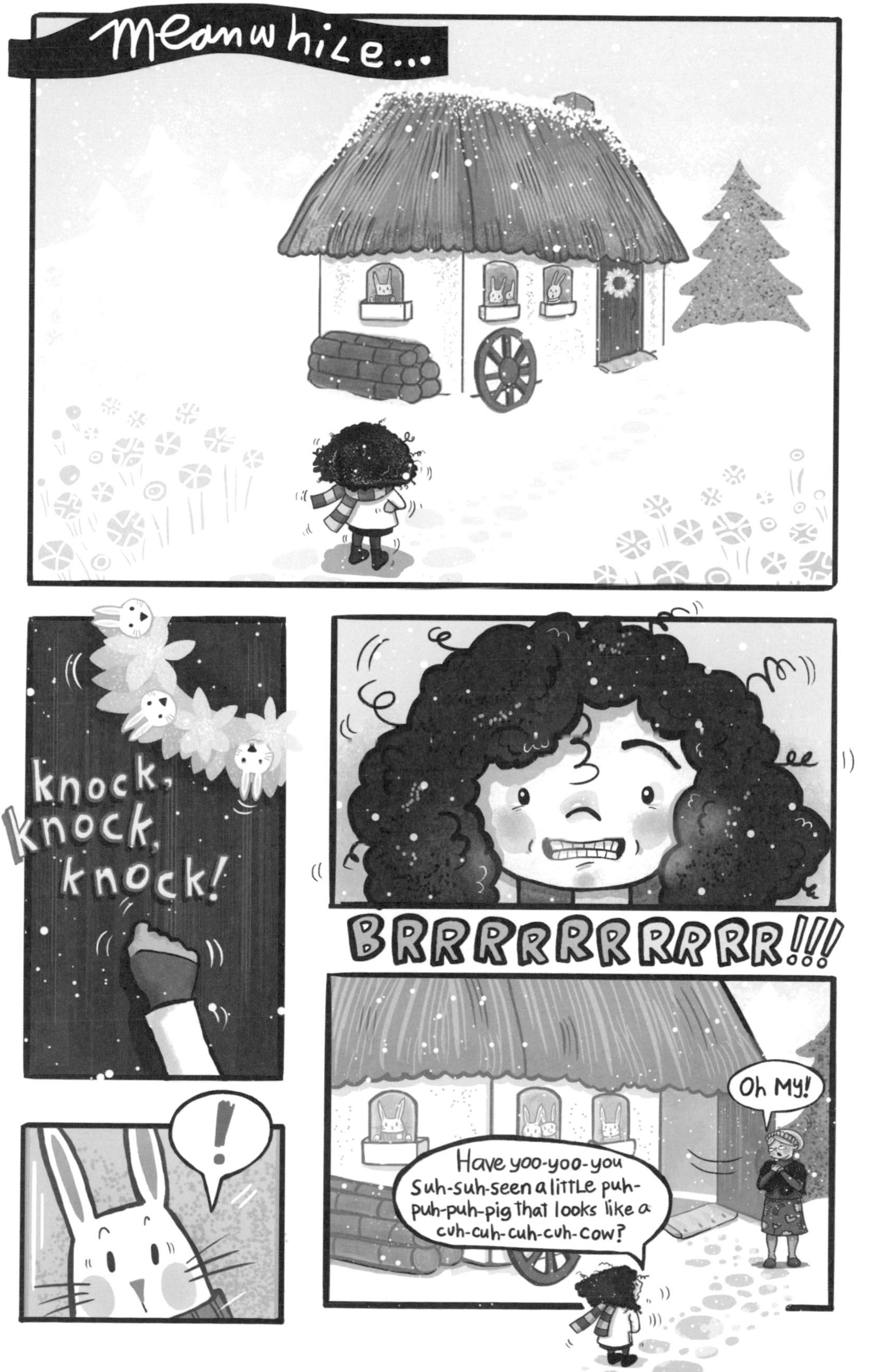
Meanwhile...
knock, knock, knock!
!
BRRRRRRRRRRR!!!
Have yoo-yoo-you suh-suh-seen a little puh-puh-puh-pig that looks like a cuh-cuh-cuh-cuh-cow?
Oh My!

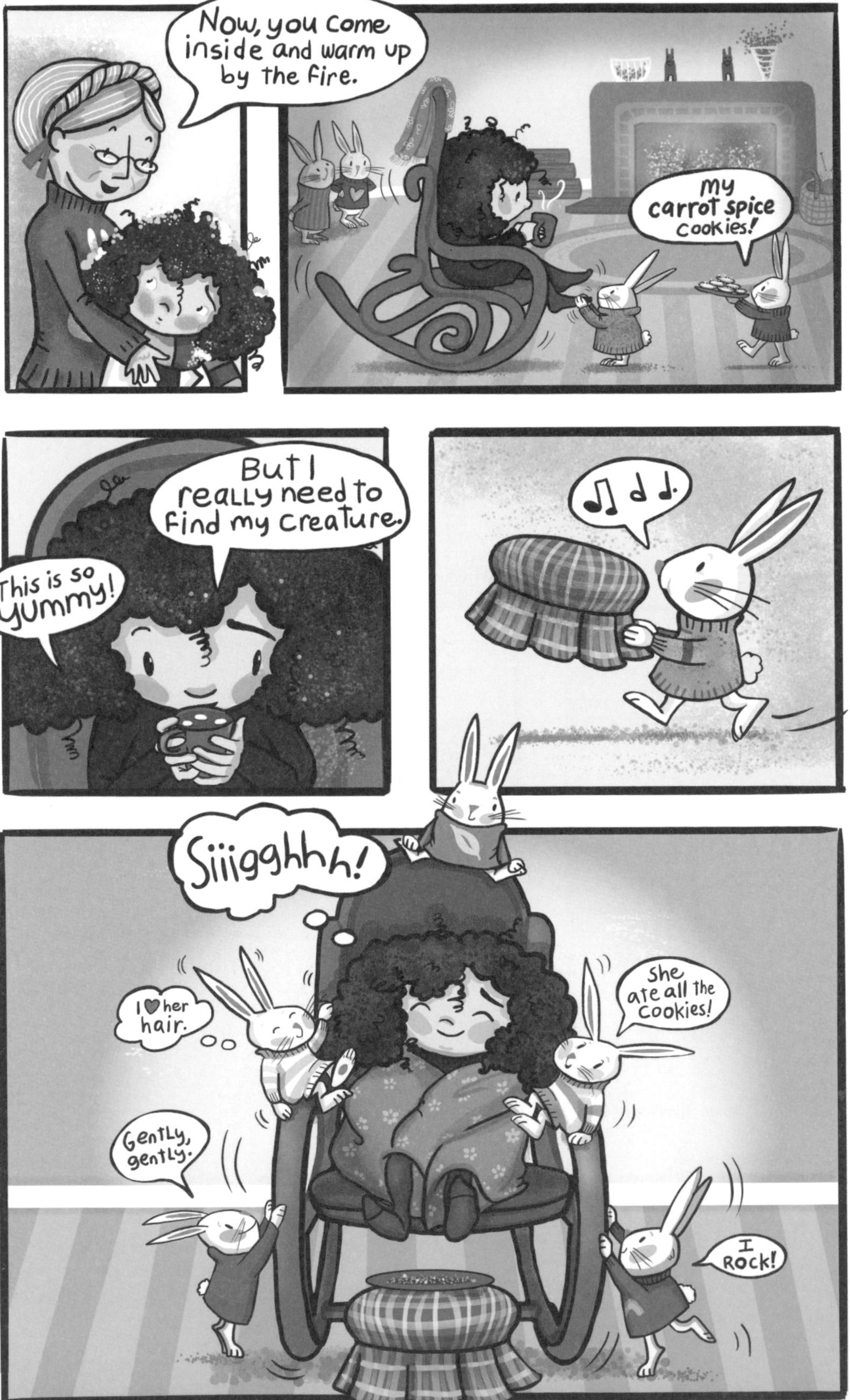

Now, you come inside and warm up by the fire.
My carrot spice cookies!
This is so yummy!
But I really need to find my creature.
Siiigghhh!
I ♥ her hair.
She ate all the cookies!
Gently, gently.
I ROCK!

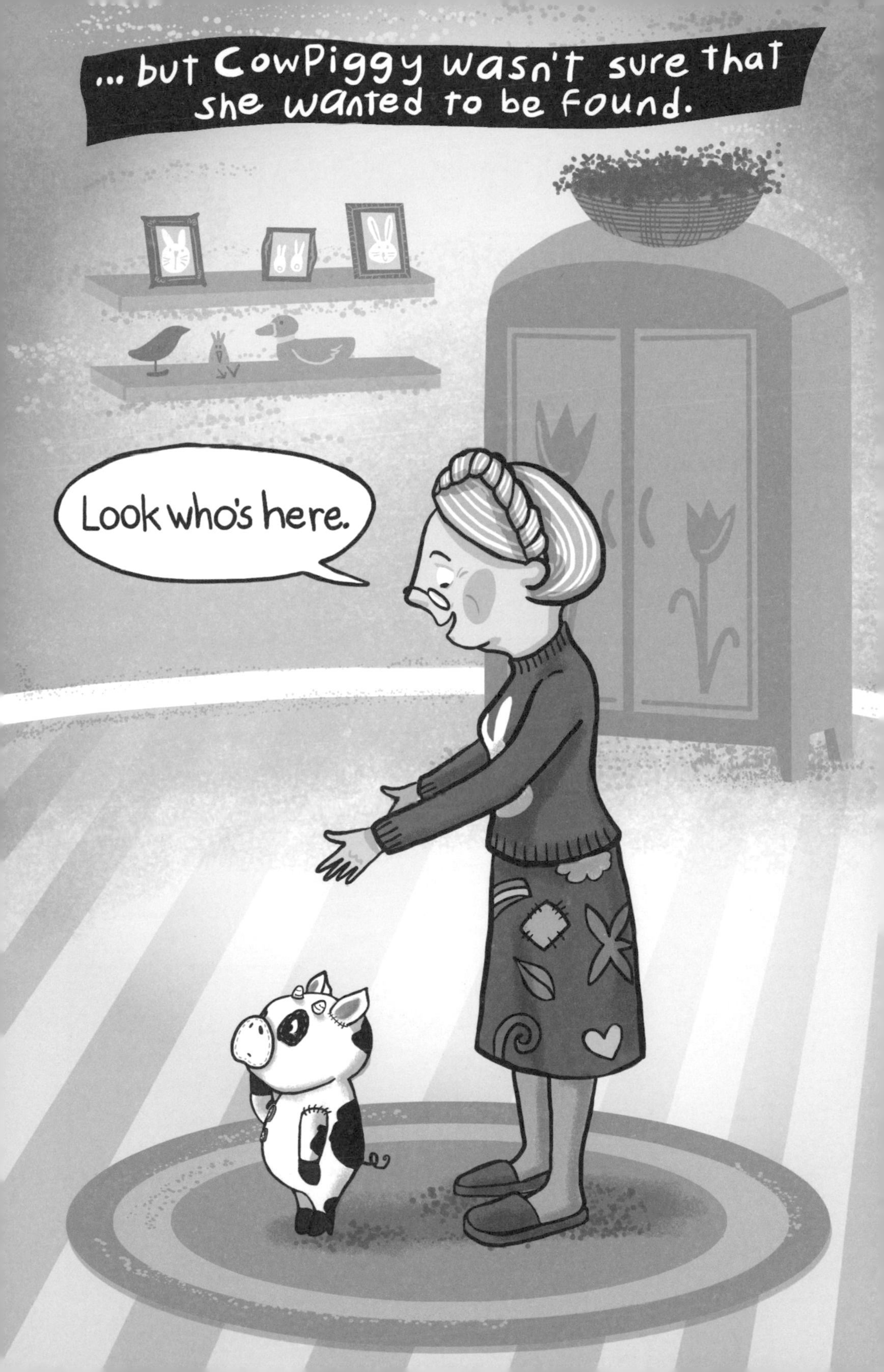
... but CowPiggy wasn't sure that she wanted to be found.
Look who's here.

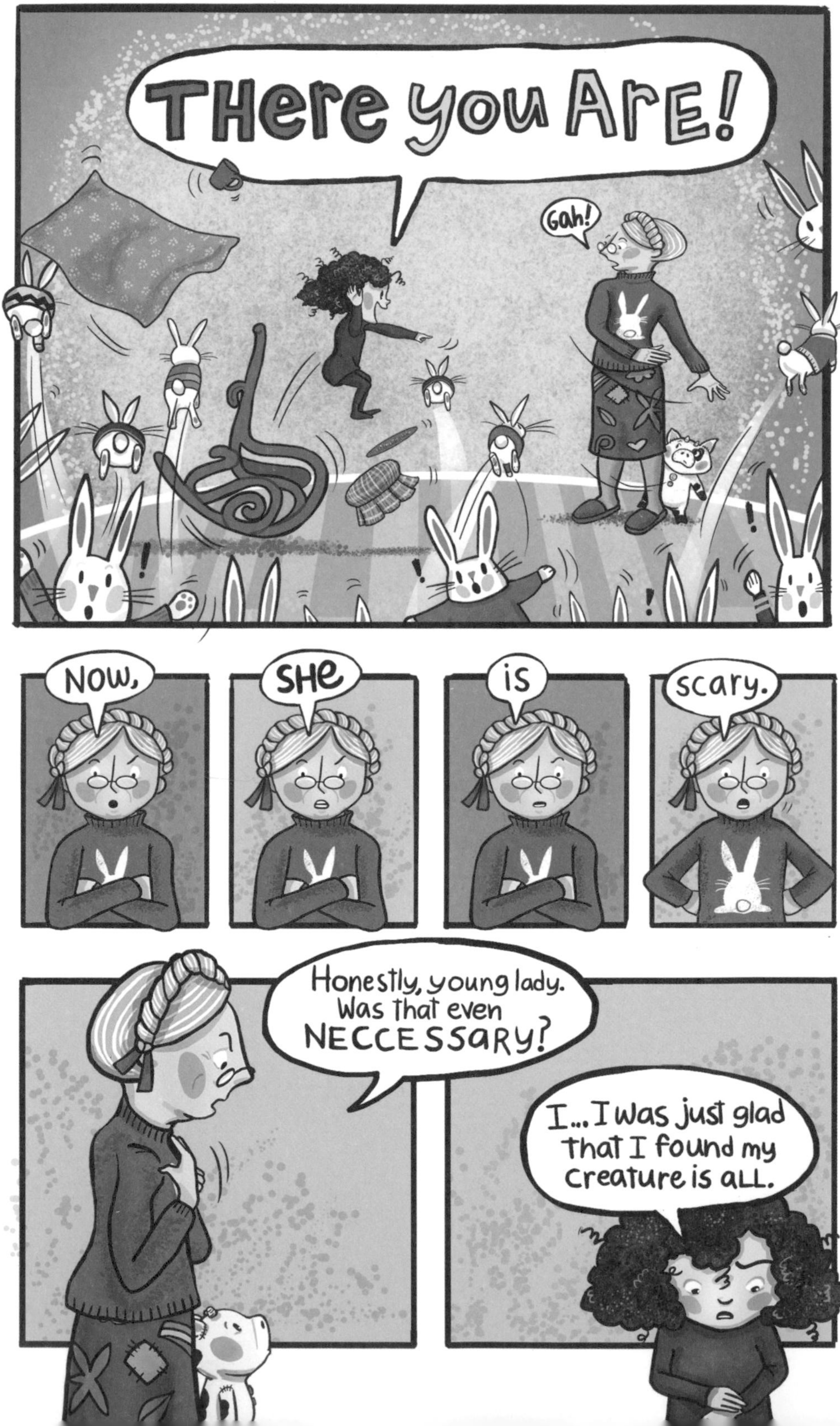
There you ARE!
Gah!
Now,
SHE
is
scary.
Honestly, young lady.
Was that even
NECCESSARY?
I... I was just glad
that I found my
creature is ALL.

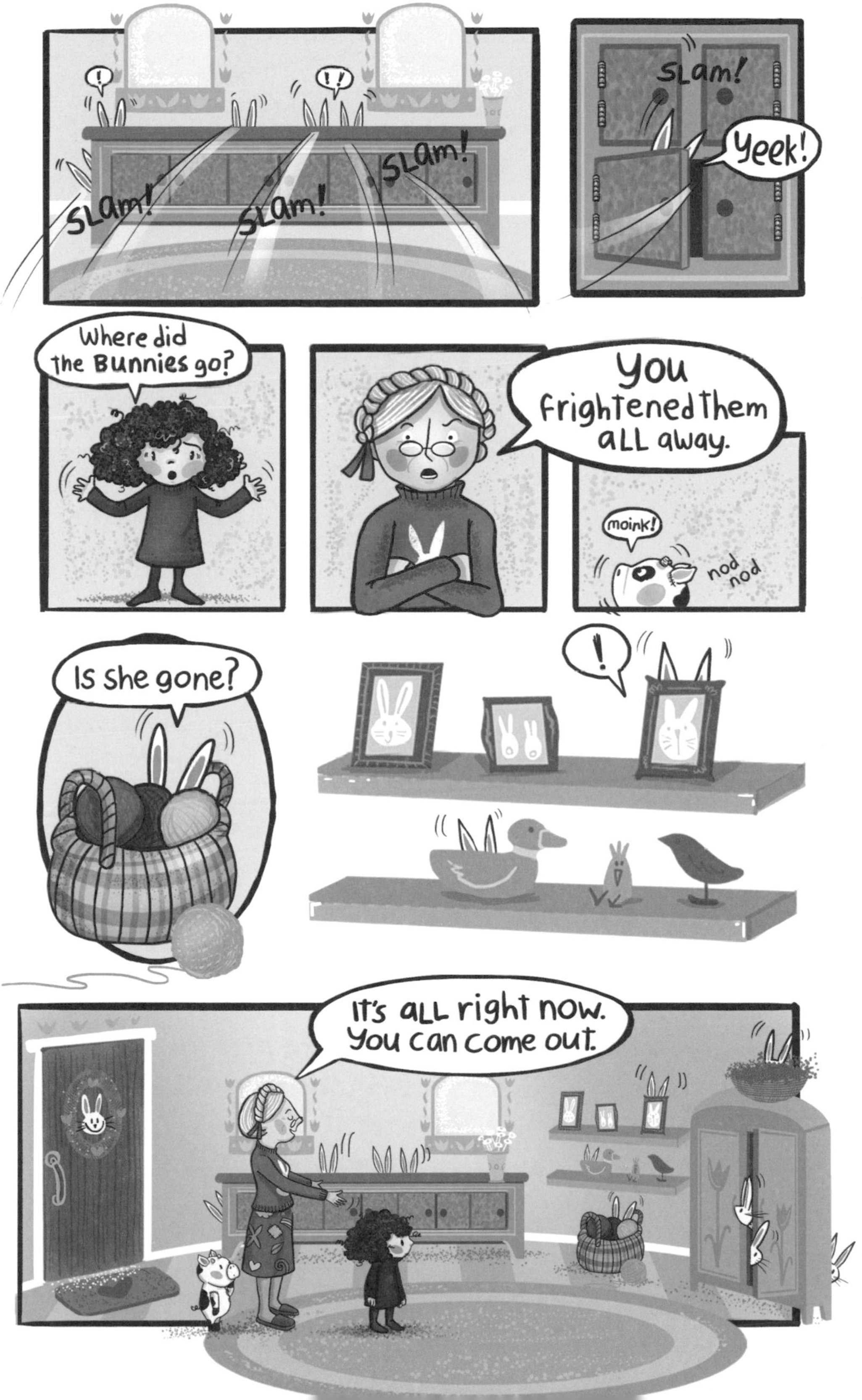
!
!!
SLAM!
SLAM!
SLAM!
SLAM!
Yeek!
Where did the Bunnies go?
You frightened them all away.
moink!
nod nod
Is she gone?
!
It's all right now. You can come out.

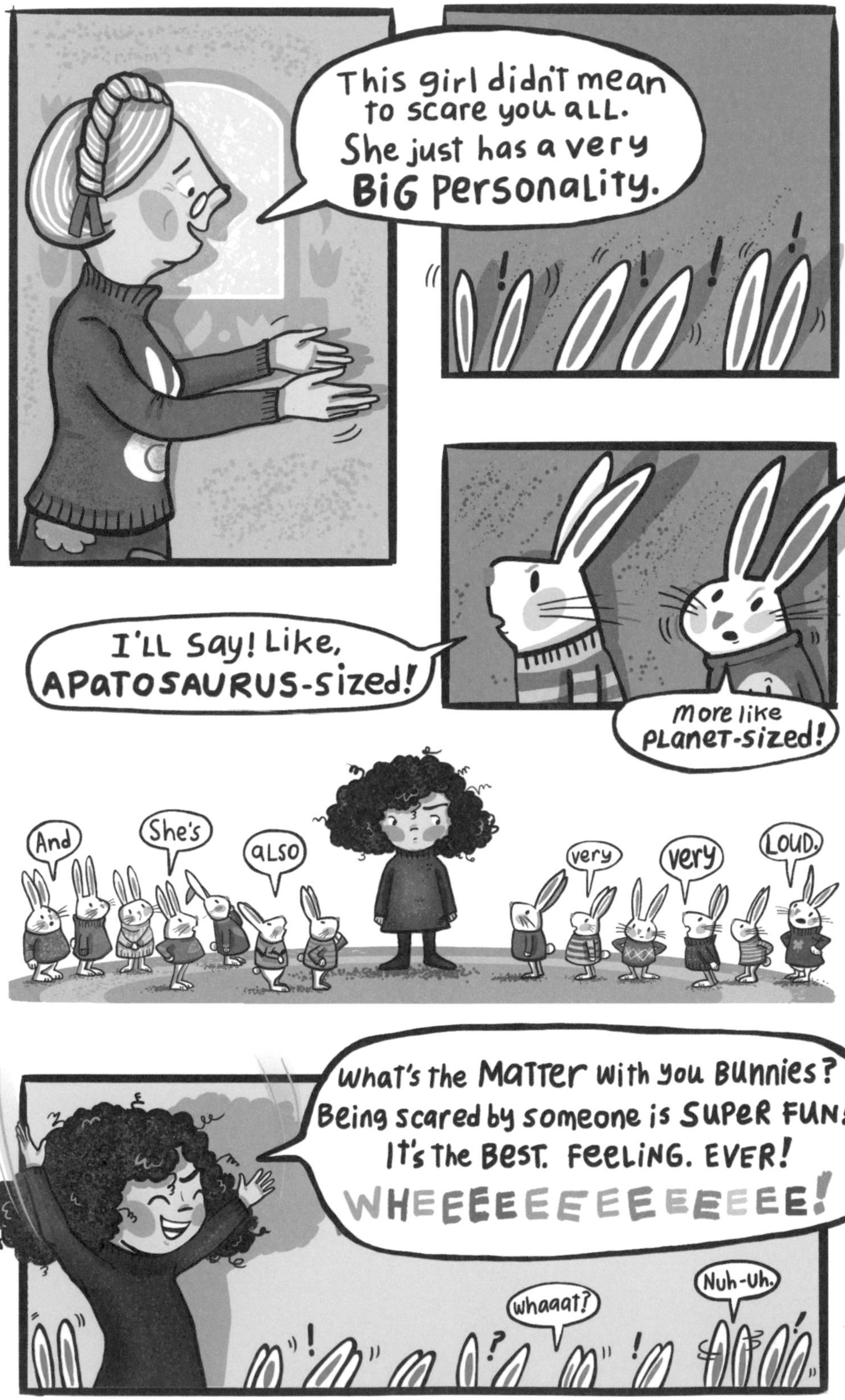

This girl didn't mean to scare you all. She just has a very BIG Personality.
I'll say! Like, APATOSAURUS-sized!
more like PLANET-sized!
And
She's
also
very
very
LOUD.
What's the MATTER with you BUNNIES? Being scared by someone is SUPER FUN! It's the BEST. FEELING. EVER!
WHEEEEEEEEEEEEE!
whaaat?
Nuh-uh.

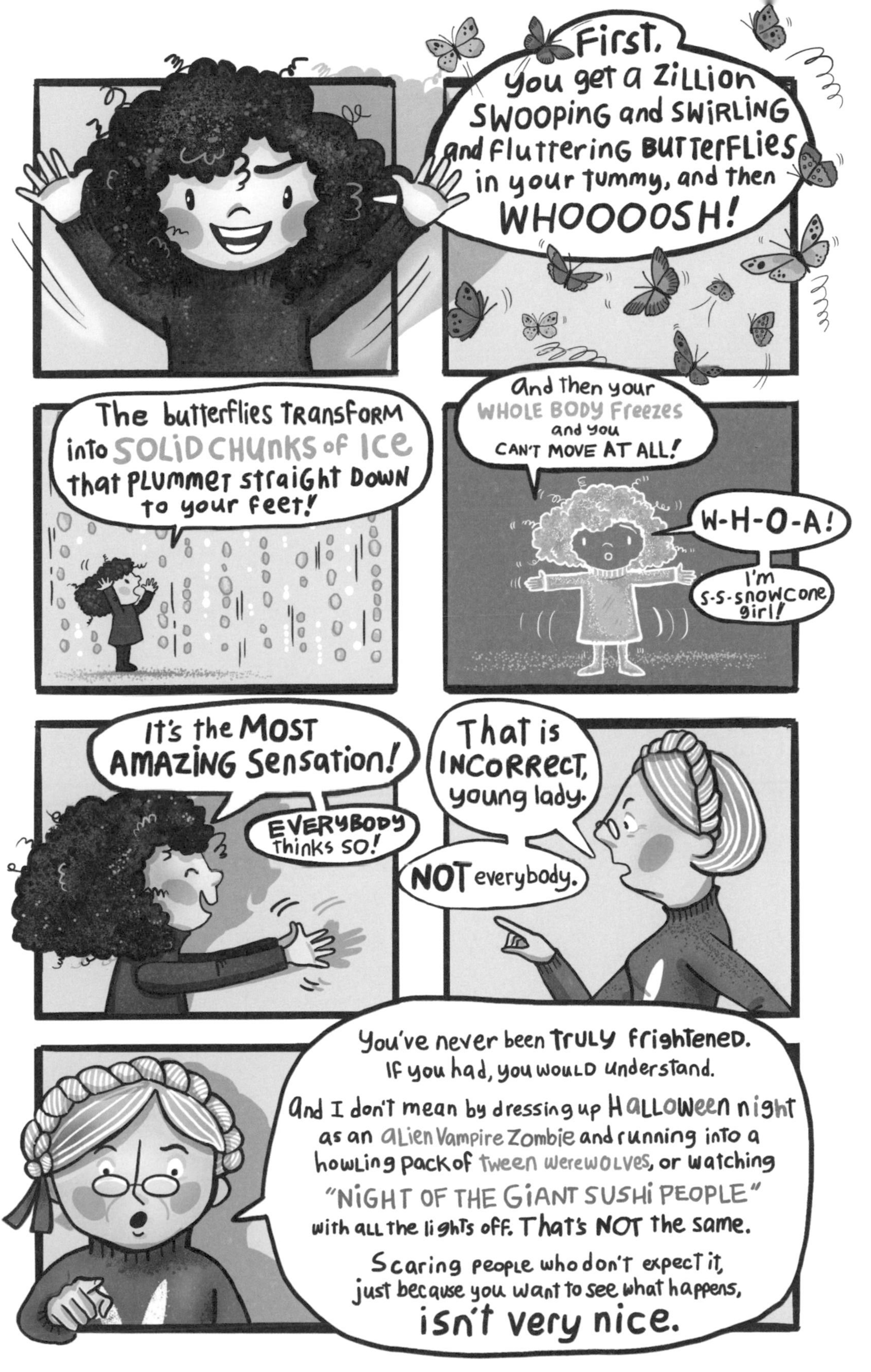
First, you get a ZILLION SWOOPING and SWIRLING and fluttering BUTTERFLIES in your tummy, and then WHOOOOSH!
The butterflies transform into SOLID CHUNKS of ICE that plummet straight down to your feet!
And then your WHOLE BODY Freezes and you CAN'T MOVE AT ALL!
W-H-O-A!
I'm S-S-SNOWCONE girl!
It's the MOST AMAZING Sensation!
EVERYBODY thinks so!
That is INCORRECT, young lady.
NOT everybody.
You've never been TRULY frightened. If you had, you would understand.
And I don't mean by dressing up HALLOWEEN night as an ALien Vampire Zombie and running into a howling pack of tween werewolves, or watching "NIGHT OF THE GIANT SUSHI PEOPLE" with all the lights off. That's NOT the same.
Scaring people who don't expect it, just because you want to see what happens, isn't very nice.

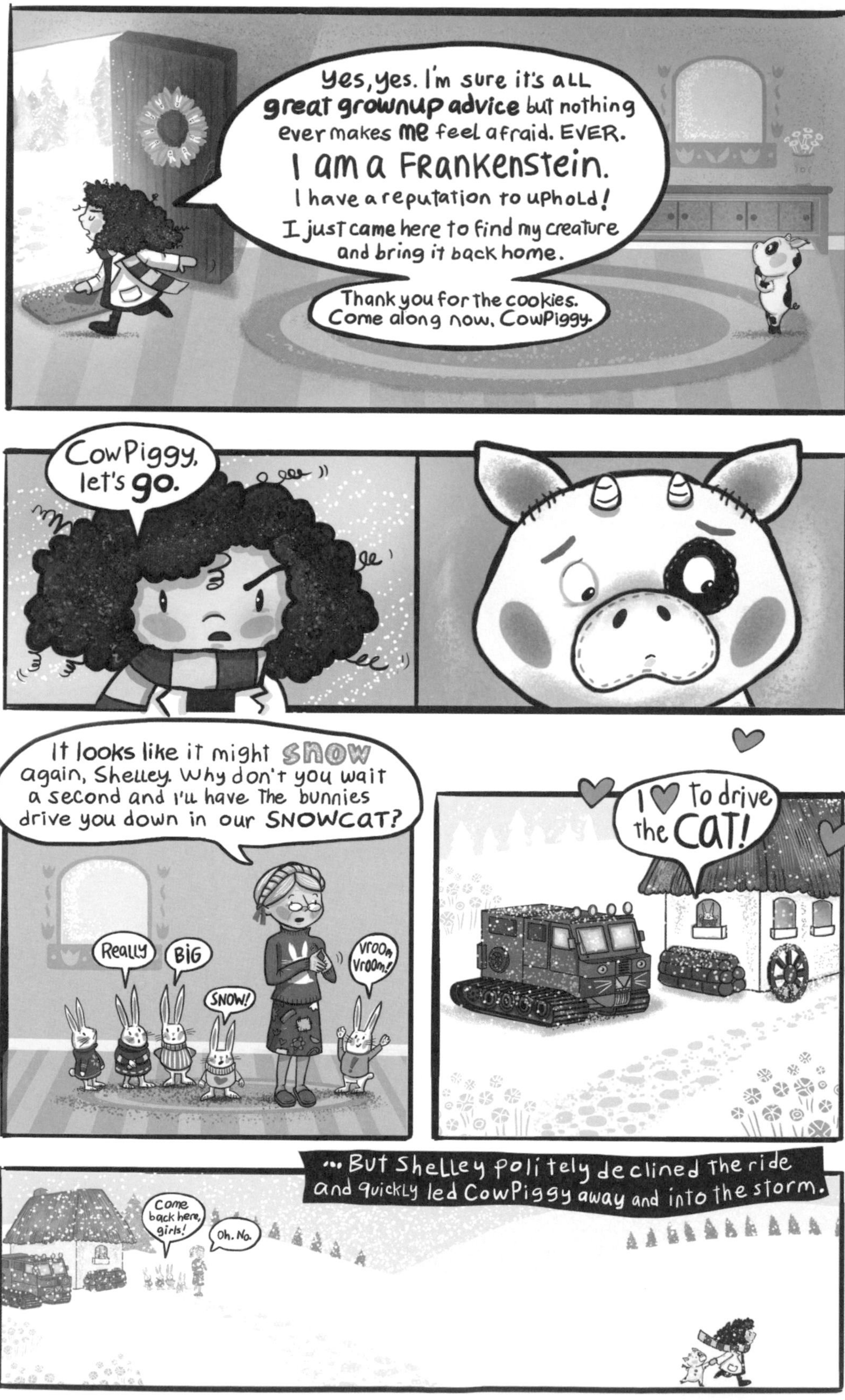
Yes, yes. I'm sure it's ALL great grownup advice but nothing ever makes me feel afraid. EVER. I am a Frankenstein. I have a reputation to uphold! I just came here to find my creature and bring it back home.
Thank you for the cookies. Come along now, CowPiggy.
CowPiggy, let's go.
It looks like it might SNOW again, Shelley. Why don't you wait a second and I'll have the bunnies drive you down in our SNOWCAT?
Really
BIG
SNOW!
Vroom, Vroom!
I ♥ to drive the CAT!
... But Shelley politely declined the ride and quickly led CowPiggy away and into the storm.
Come back here, girls!
Oh. No.

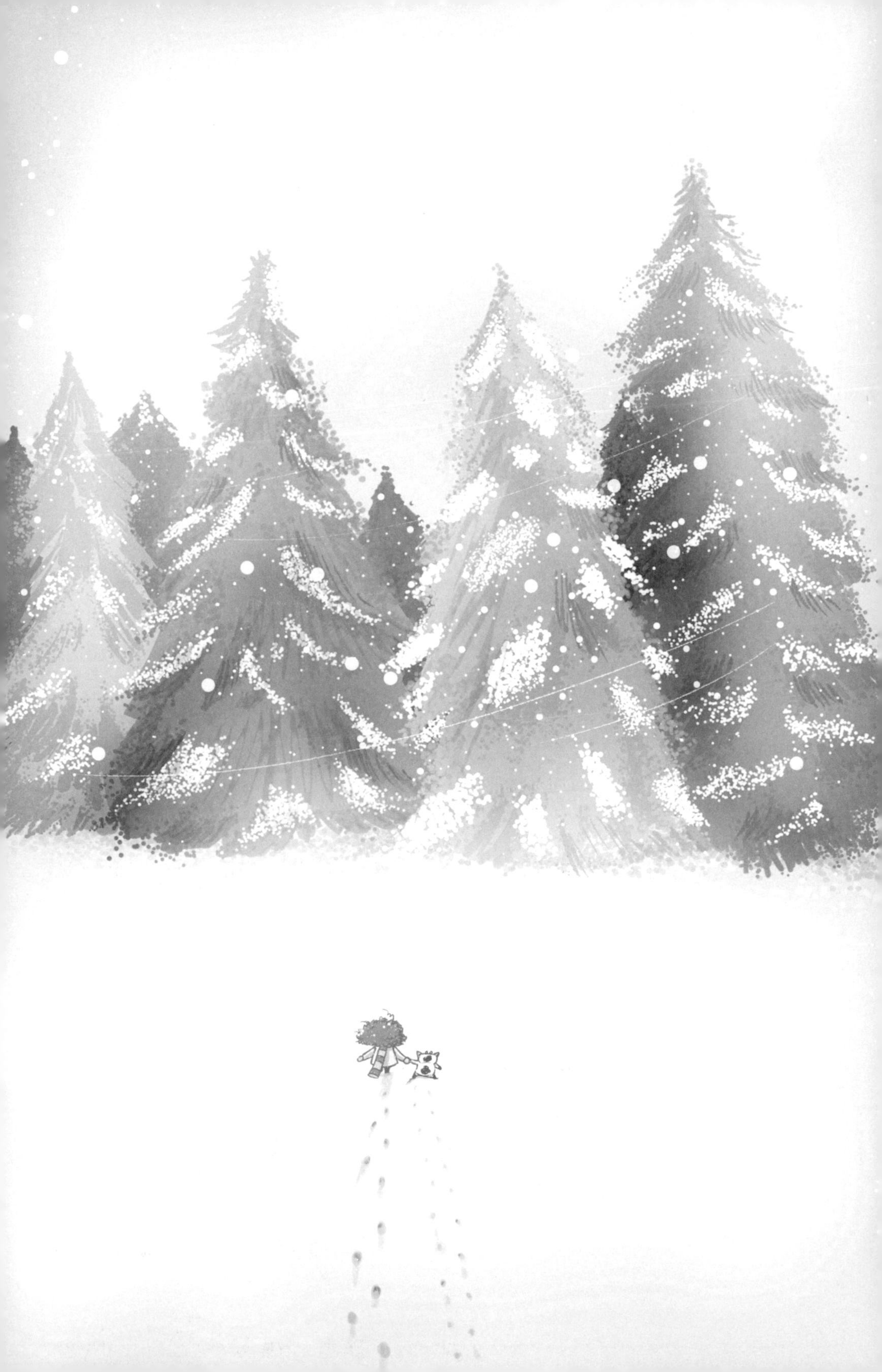

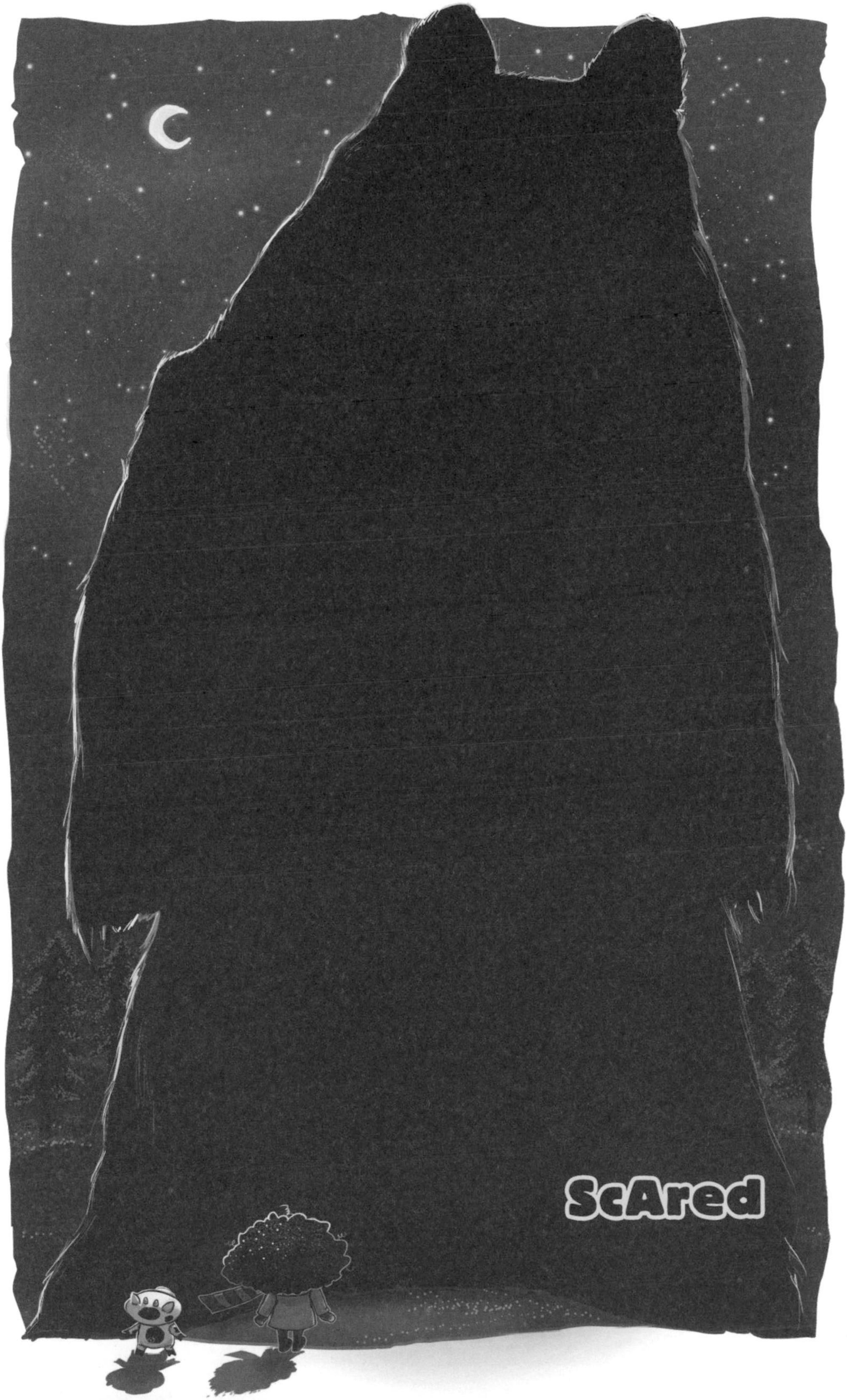

ScAred

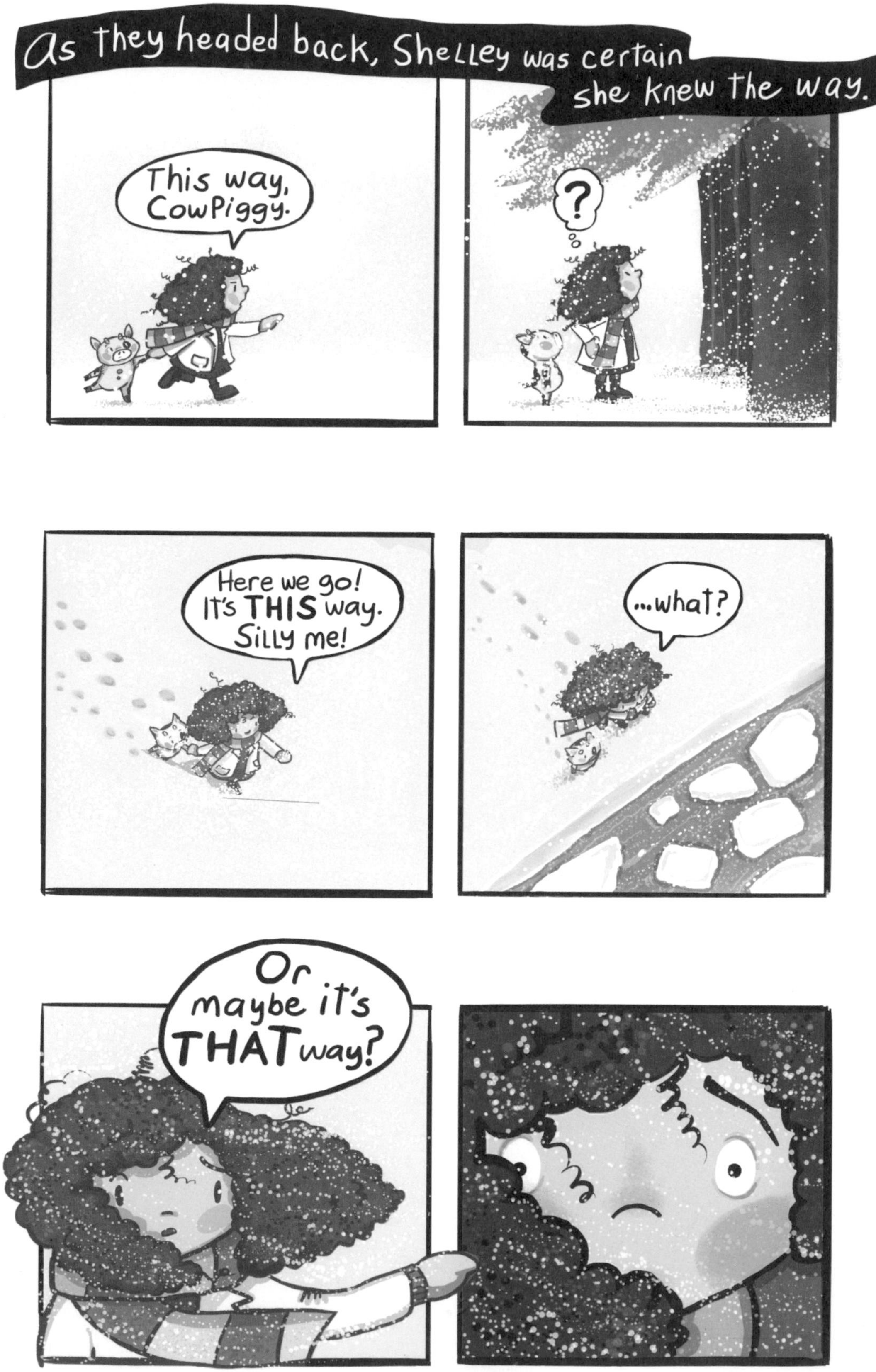
As they headed back, Shelley was certain she knew the way.
This way, CowPiggy.
?
Here we go! It's THIS way. Silly me!
...what?
Or maybe it's THAT way?

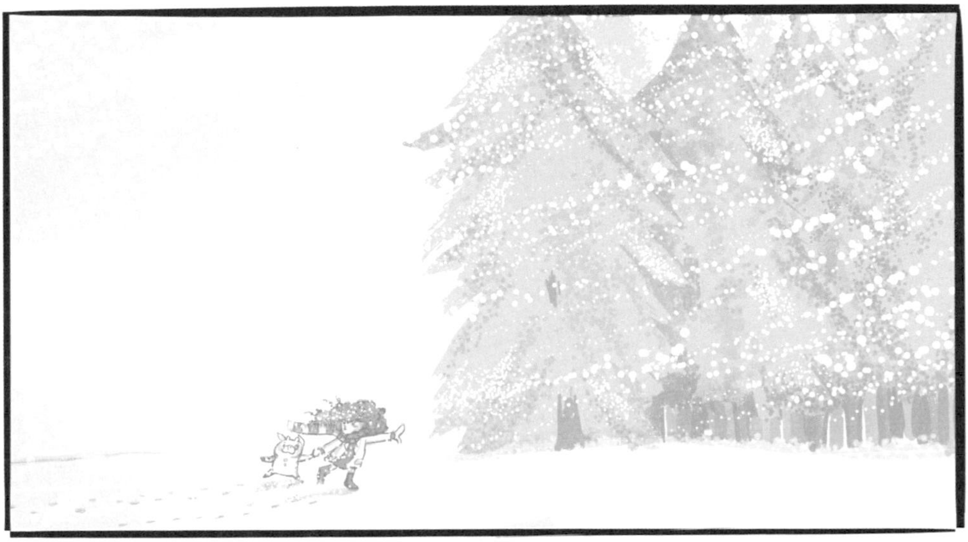
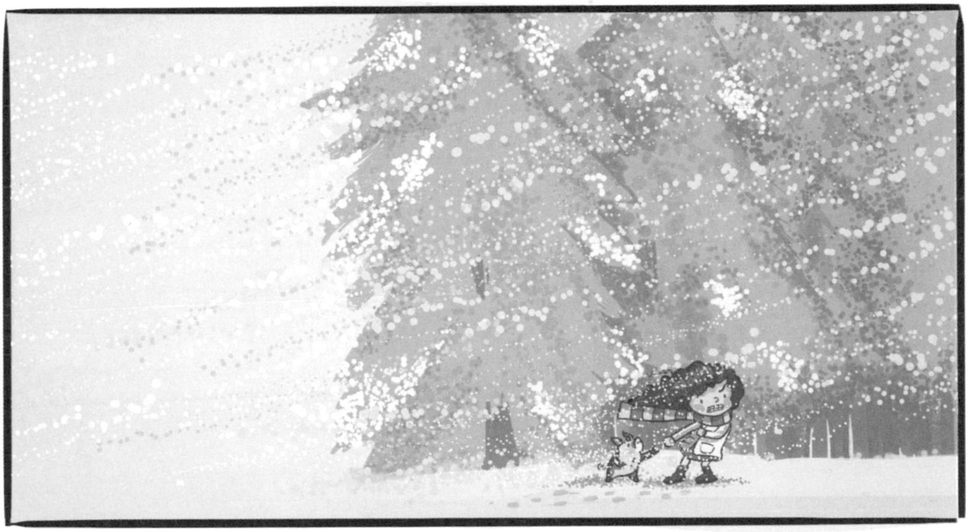
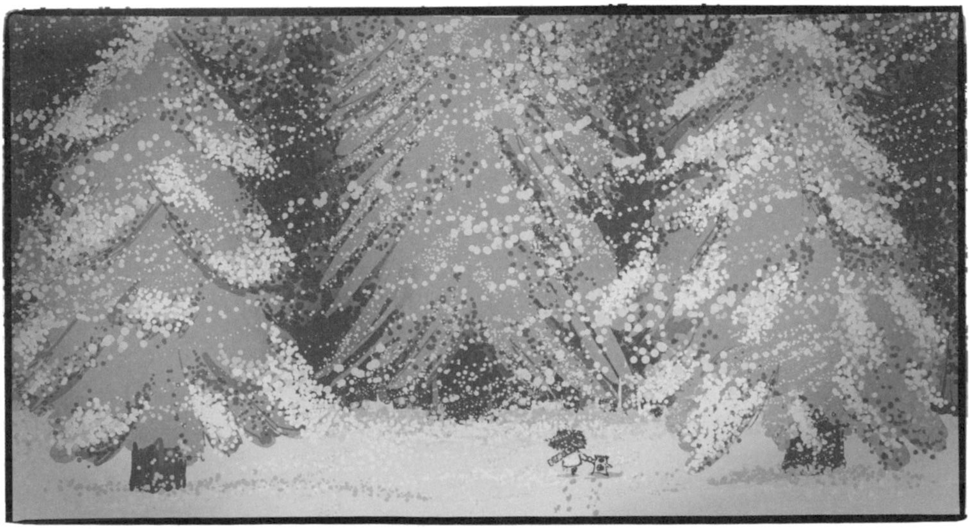

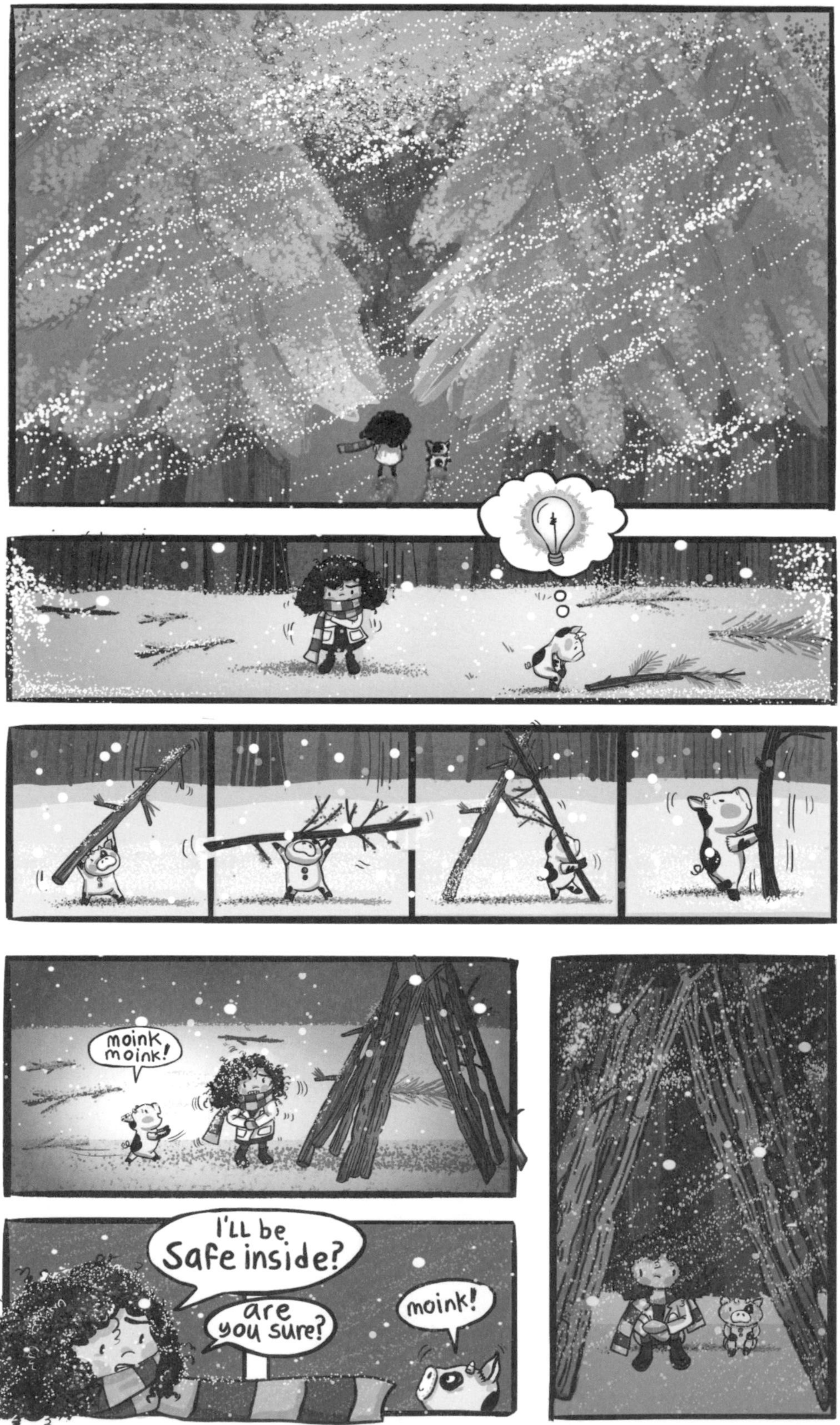
moink moink!
I'LL be Safe inside?
are you sure?
moink!

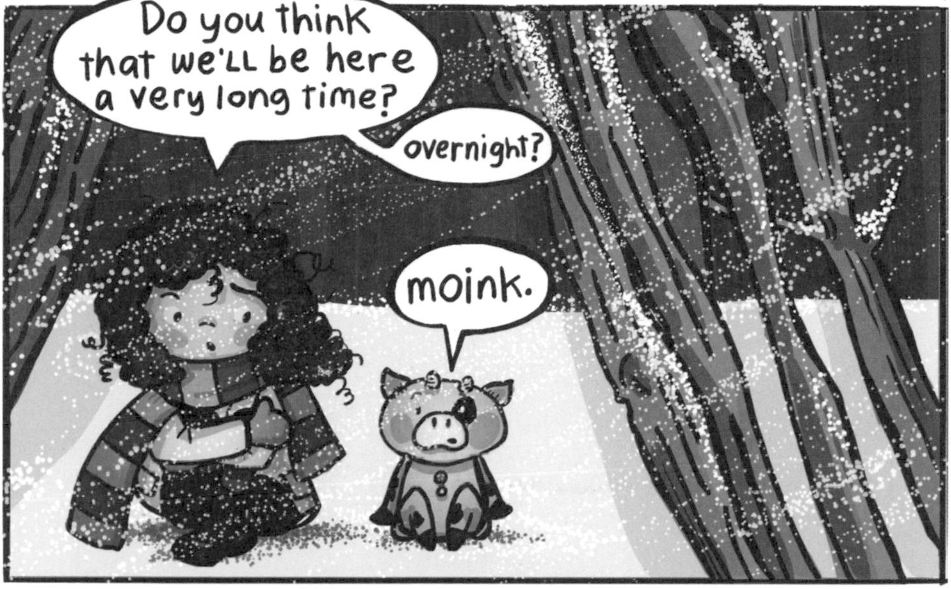
Do you think that we'll be here a very long time?
overnight?
moink.

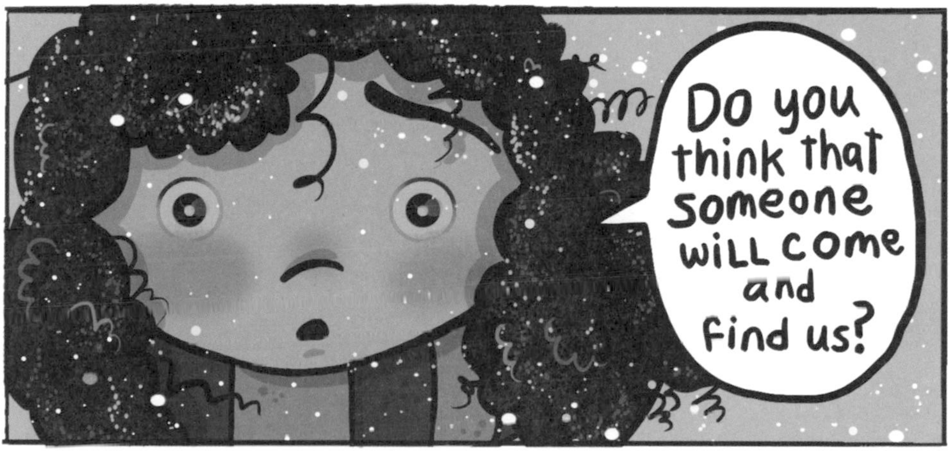
Do you think that someone will come and find us?

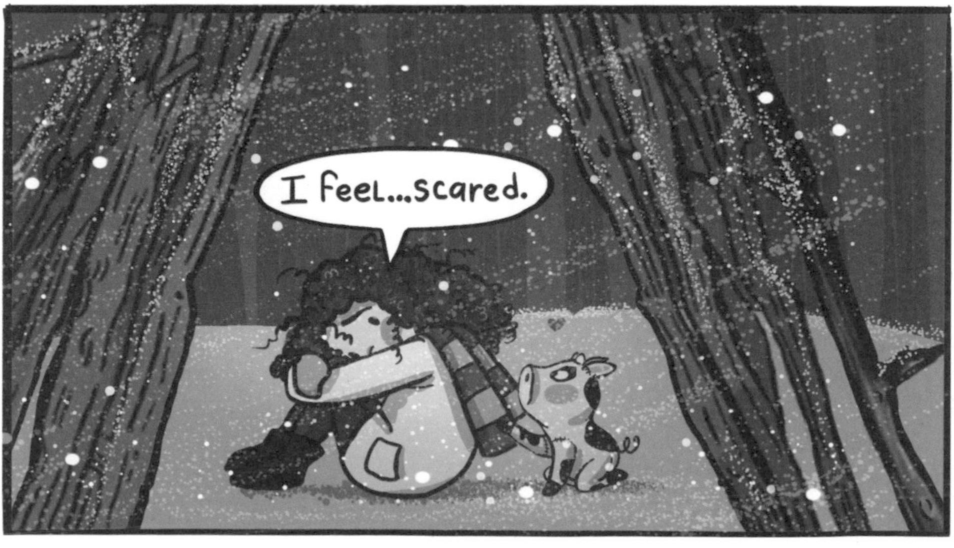
I feel...scared.

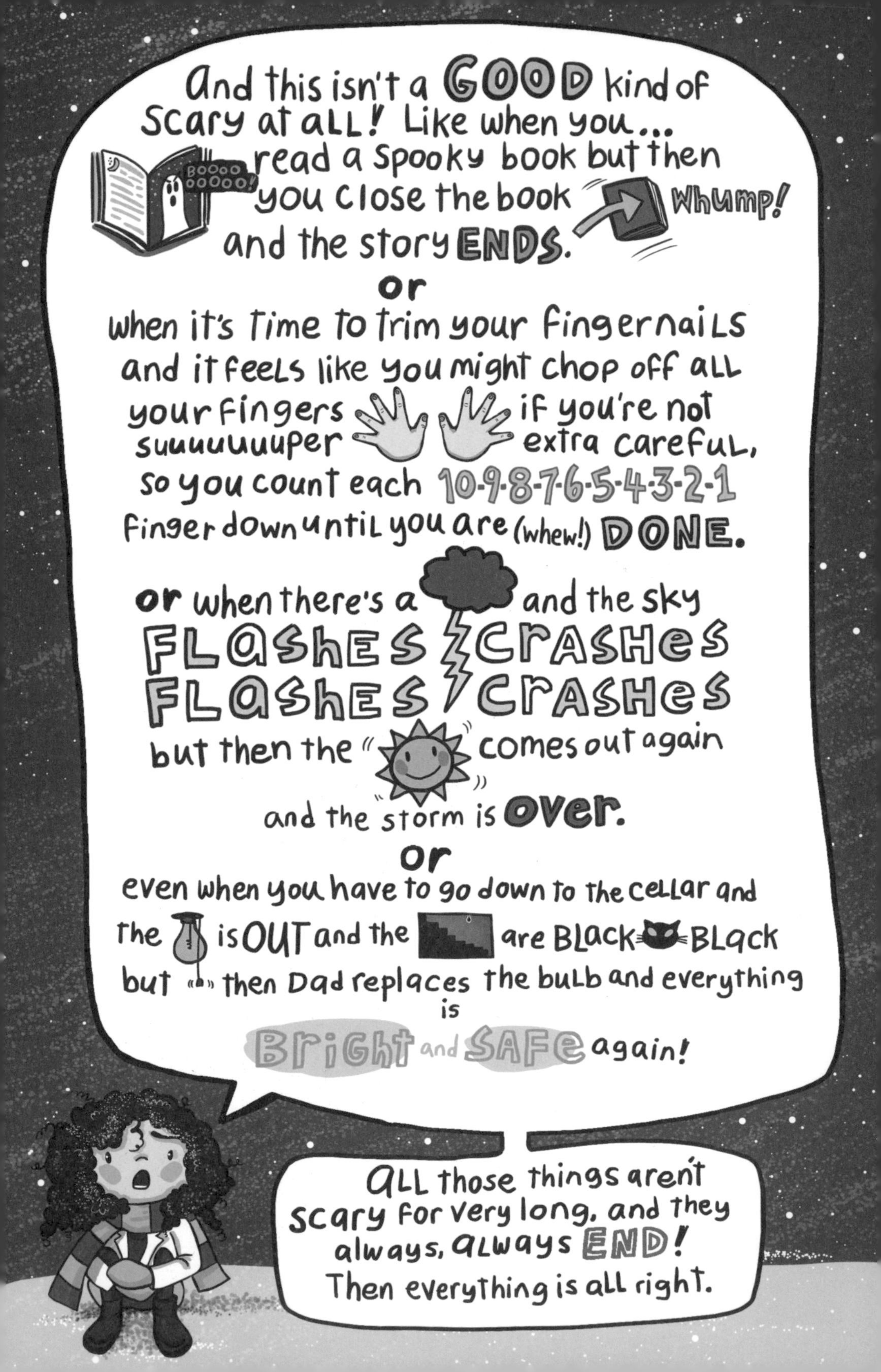
And this isn't a GOOD kind of scary at ALL! Like when you... read a spooky book but then you close the book and the story ENDS.
BOOOOOOOOO!
Whump!
or
when it's time to trim your fingernails and it feels like you might chop off all your fingers if you're not suuuuuuuper extra careful, so you count each 10-9-8-7-6-5-4-3-2-1 finger down until you are (whew!) DONE.
or when there's a and the sky FLASHES CRASHES FLASHES CRASHES but then the comes out again and the storm is over.
or
even when you have to go down to the cellar and the is OUT and the are BLACK BLACK but then Dad replaces the bulb and everything is BRIGHT and SAFE again!
ALL those things aren't scary for very long, and they always, always END! Then everything is all right.

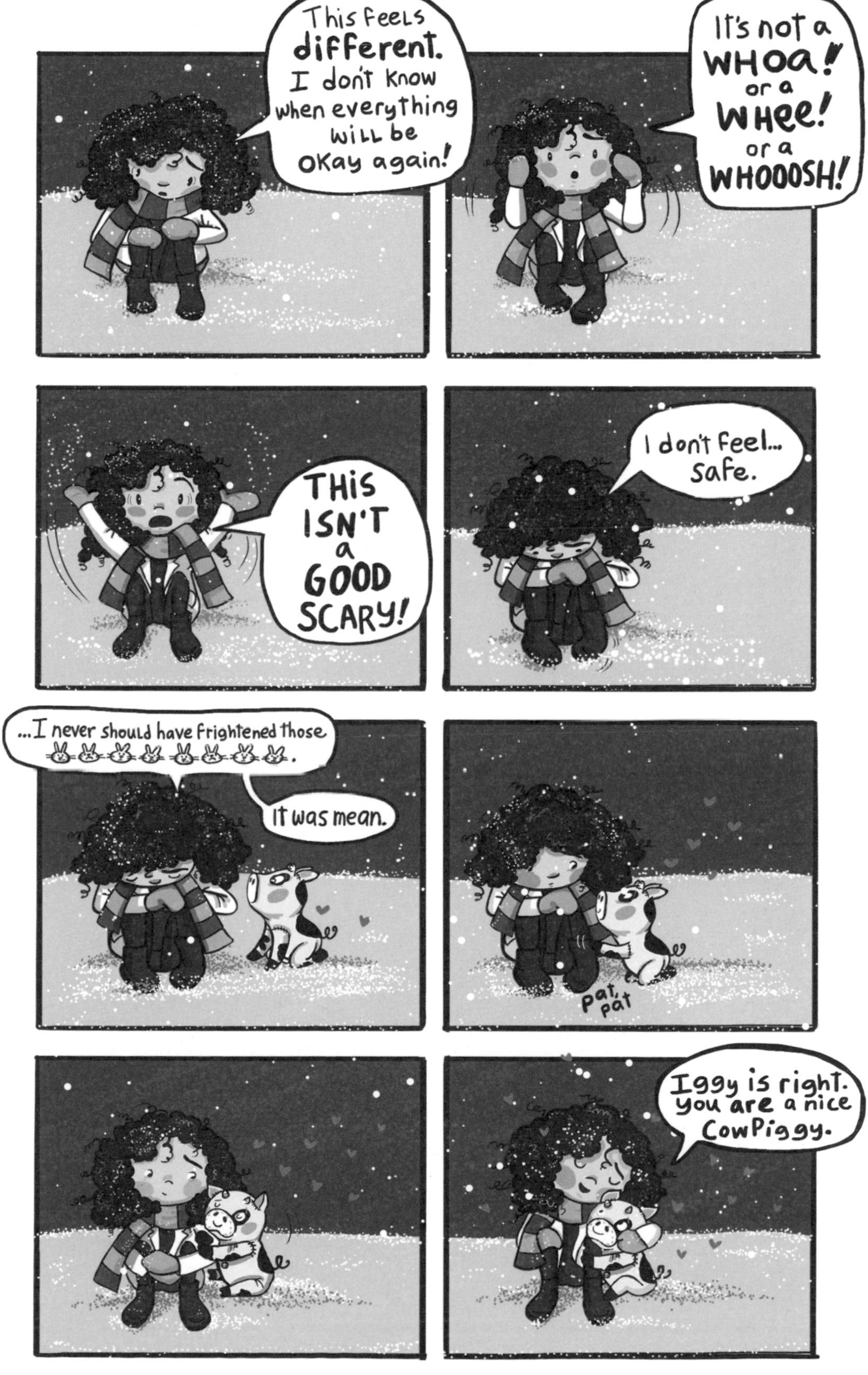
This feels different. I don't know when everything will be okay again!
It's not a WHOA! or a WHEE! or a WHOOOSH!
THIS ISN'T a GOOD SCARY!
I don't feel... safe.
...I never should have frightened those
It was mean.
pat, pat
Iggy is right. You are a nice CowPiggy.

RUMBLE ROAR GROWWWLLL!

What is that?

moink?

RUMBLE ROAR GROWWWWLLL!

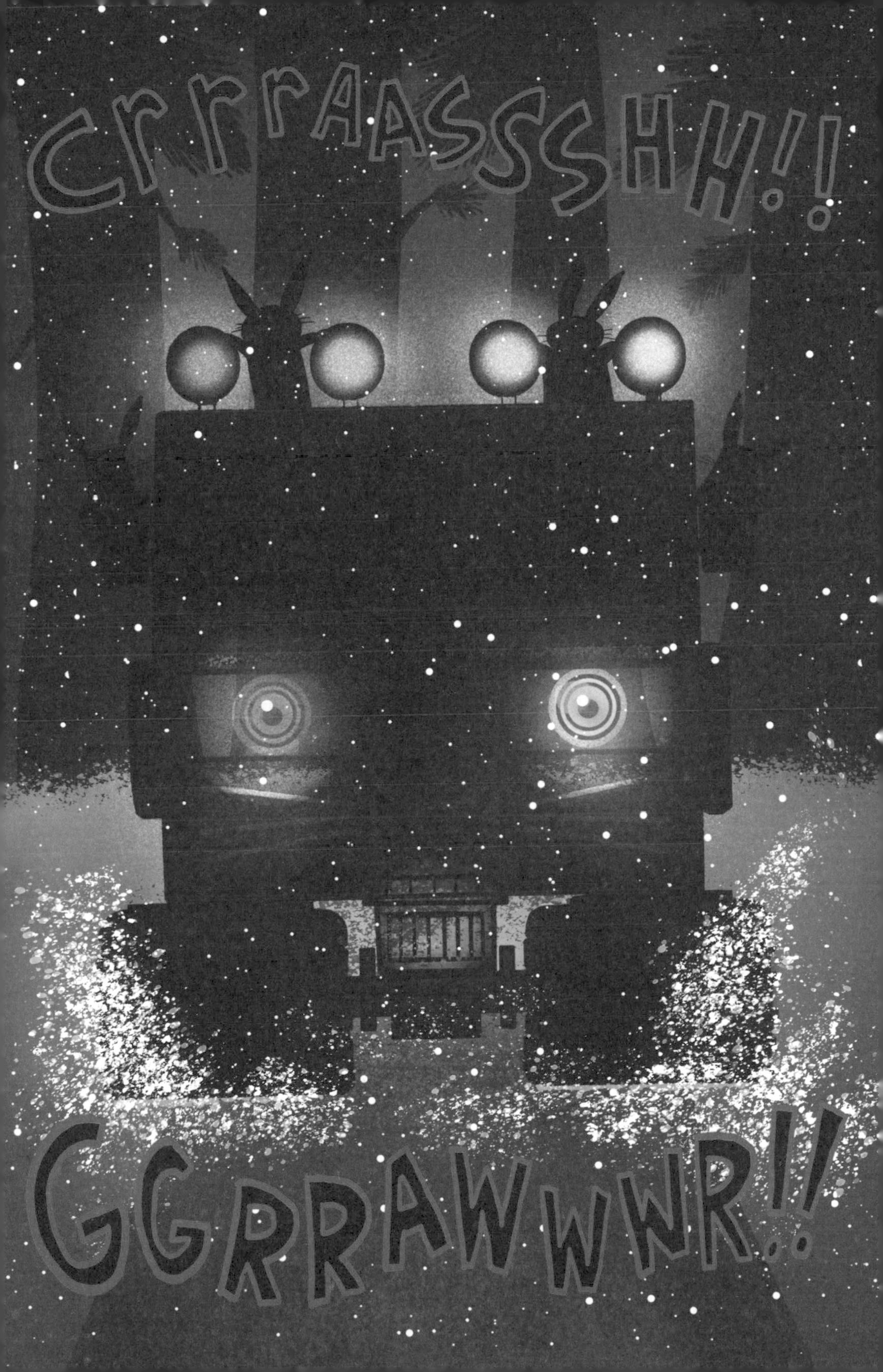
CRRRAASSSHH!!
GGRRAWWNR!!

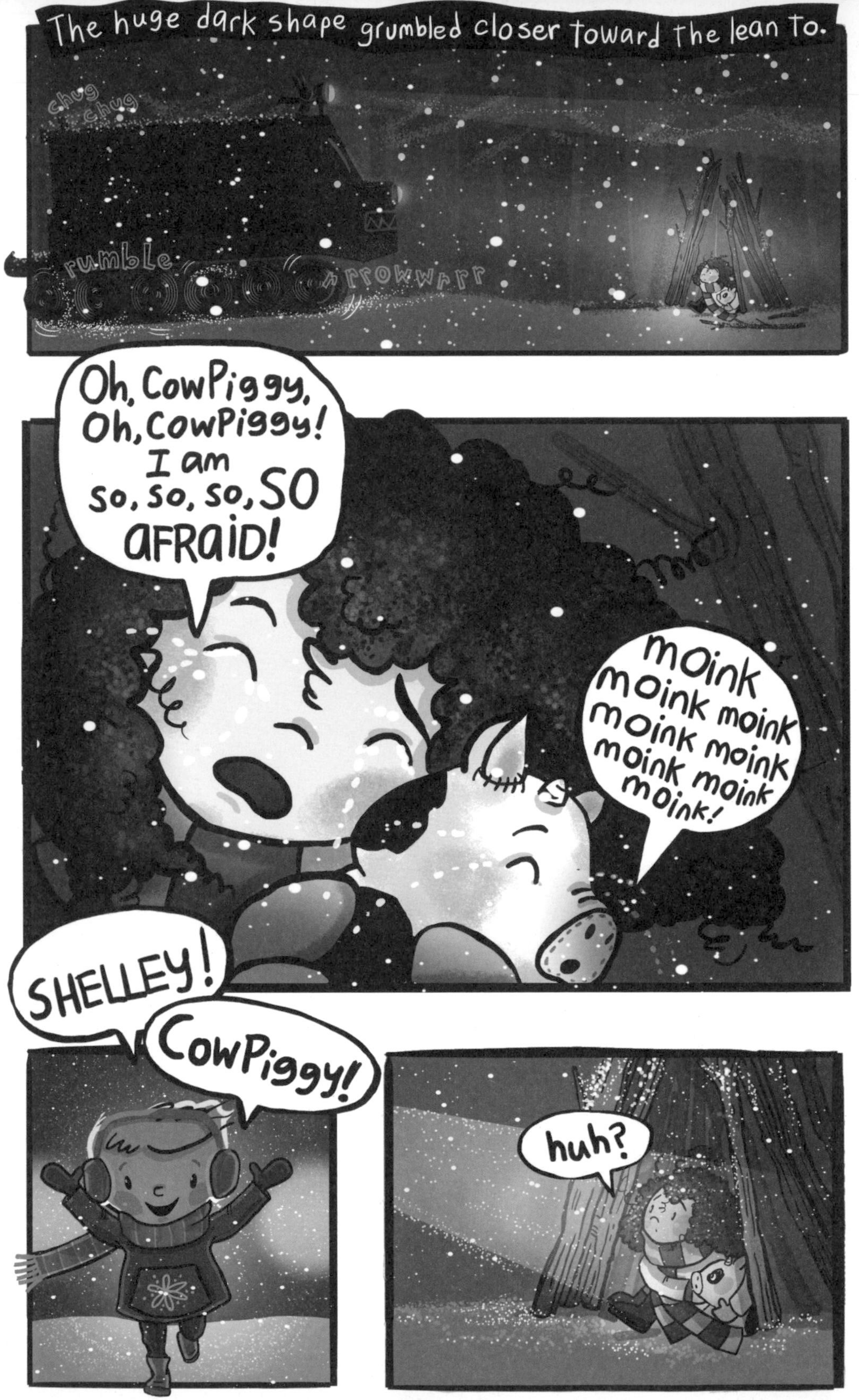
The huge dark shape grumbled closer toward the lean to.
chug chug
rumble
rrowwrrr
Oh, CowPiggy, Oh, CowPiggy! I am so, so, so, SO afraid!
moink moink moink moink moink moink moink moink!
SHELLEY!
CowPiggy!
huh?

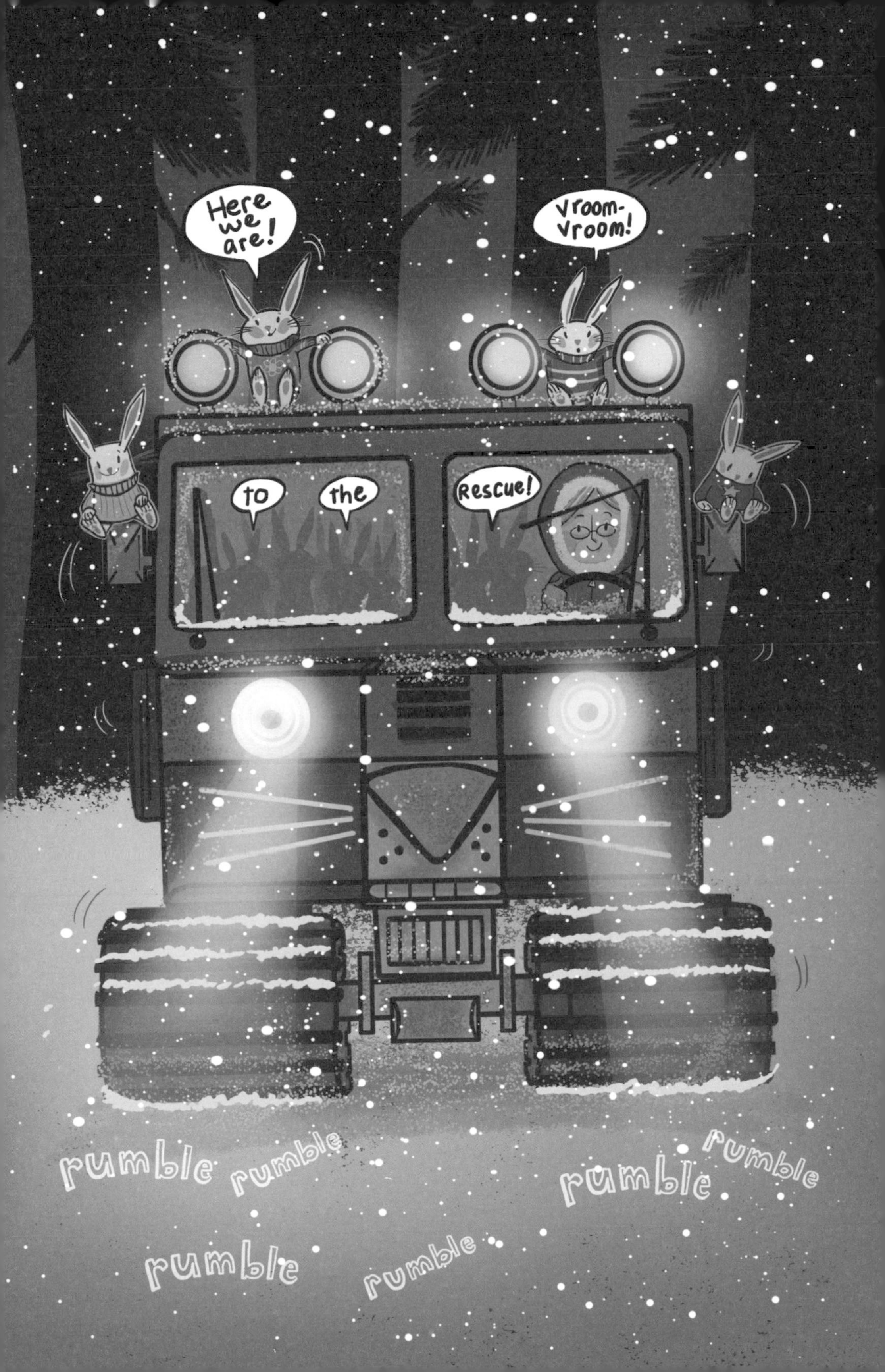
Here we are!
Vroom-Vroom!
to
the
Rescue!
rumble
rumble
rumble
rumble
rumble
rumble

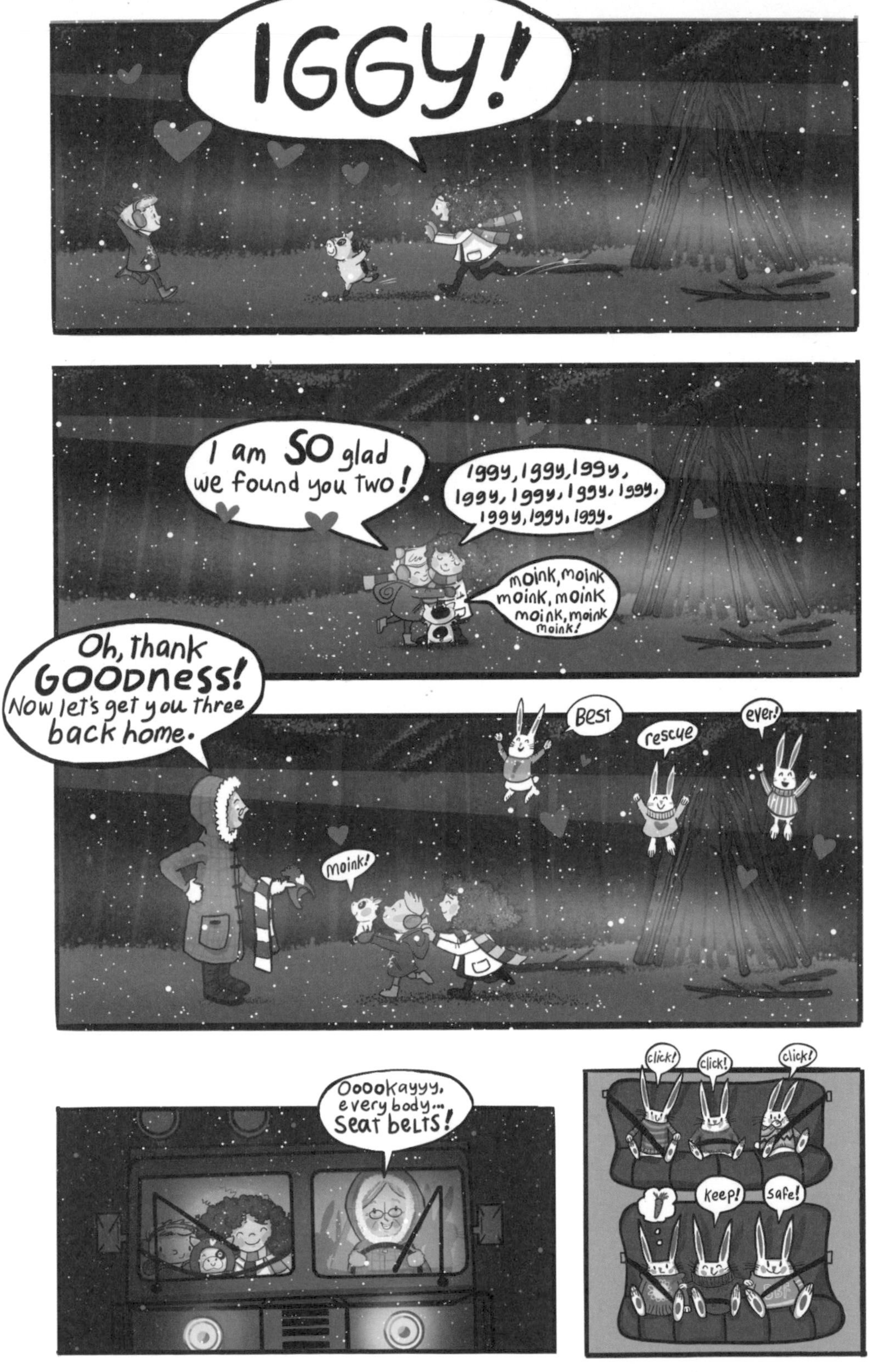
IGGY!
I am SO glad we found you two!
Iggy, Iggy, Iggy, Iggy, Iggy, Iggy, Iggy, Iggy, Iggy, Iggy.
moink, moink moink, moink moink, moink moink!
Oh, thank GOODNESS! Now let's get you three back home.
Best
rescue
ever!
moink!
Ooookayyy, every body... Seat belts!
click!
click!
click!
Keep!
safe!

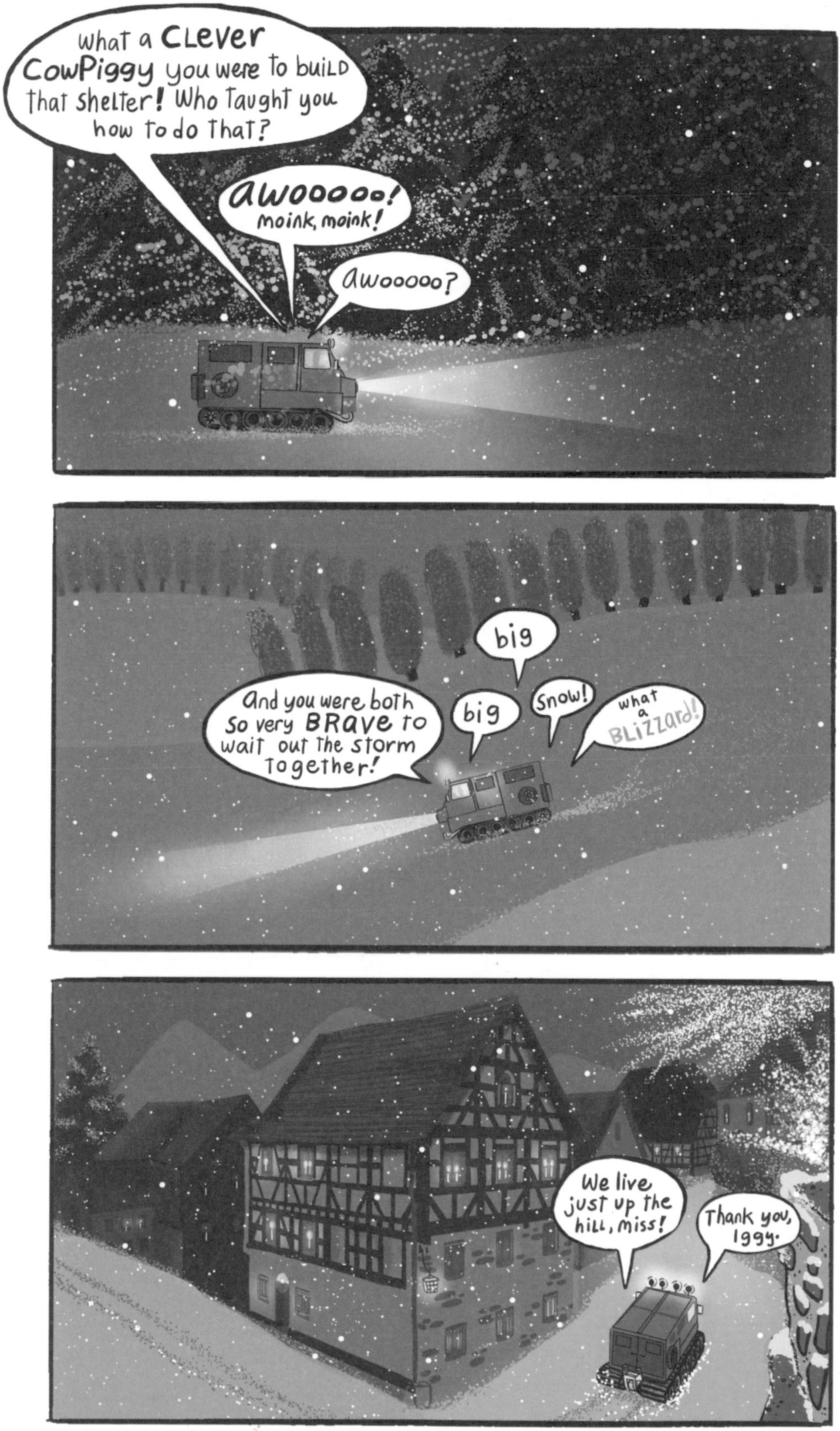
What a CLEVER CowPiggy you were to build that shelter! Who taught you how to do that?
Awooooo! moink, moink!
Awooooo?
And you were both so very BRAVE to wait out the storm together!
big
big
snow!
what a BLIZZARD!
We live just up the hill, miss!
Thank you, Iggy.

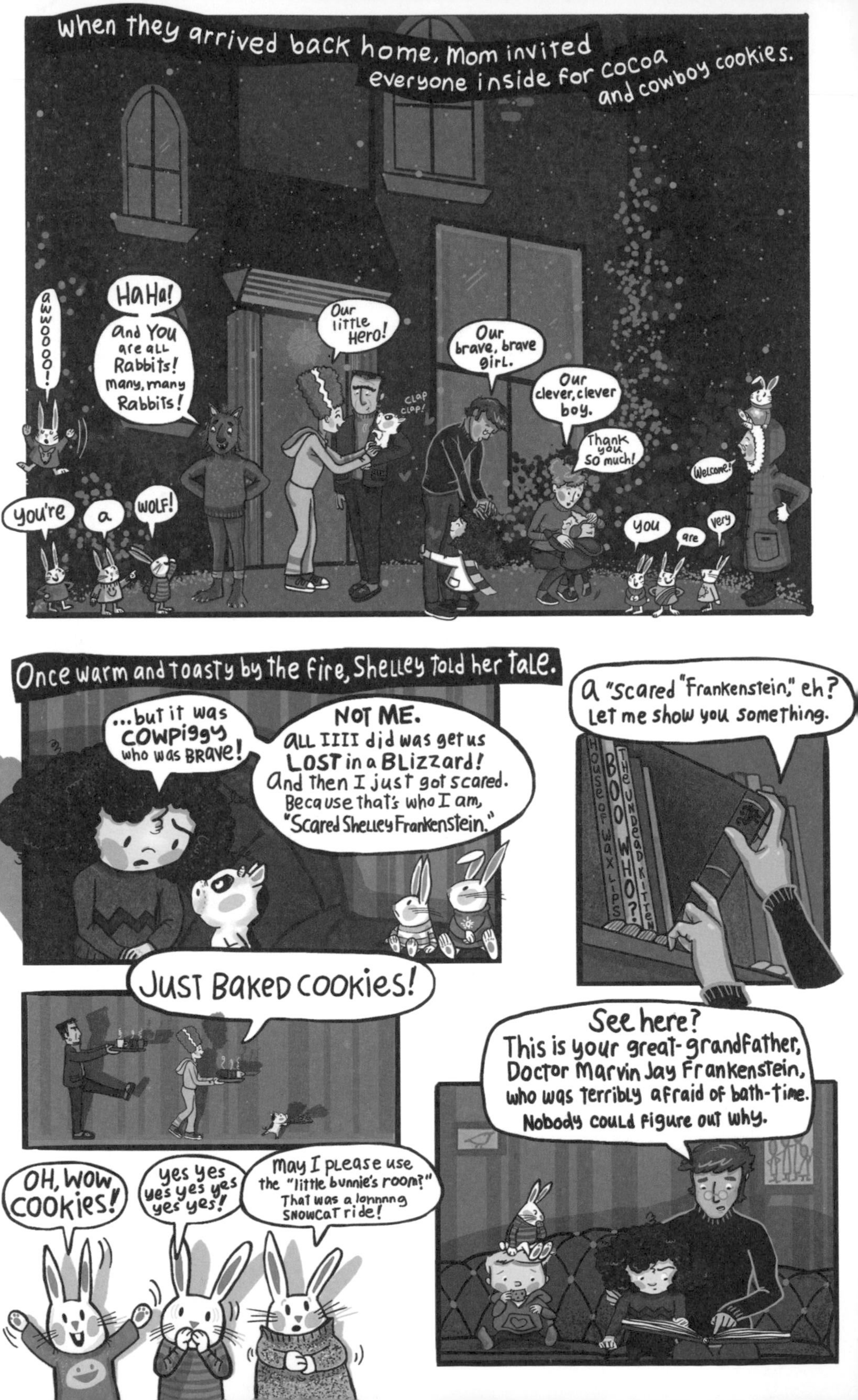
When they arrived back home, Mom invited everyone inside for cocoa and cowboy cookies.
awwooooo!
HaHa! And You are all Rabbits! many, many Rabbits!
Our little Hero!
Clap clap!
Our brave, brave girl.
Our clever, clever boy.
Thank you so much!
Welcome!
You're
a
WOLF!
You
are
very
Once warm and toasty by the fire, Shelley told her tale.
...but it was COWPIGGY who was BRAVE!
NOT ME. ALL IIII did was get us LOST in a BLIZZARD! And then I just got scared. Because that's who I am, "Scared Shelley Frankenstein."
A "scared" Frankenstein," eh? Let me show you something.
HOUSE OF WAX LIPS
BOO WHO?
THE UNDEAD KITTEN
JUST BAKED COOKIES!
See here? This is your great-grandfather, Doctor Marvin Jay Frankenstein, who was terribly afraid of bath-time. Nobody could figure out why.
OH, WOW COOKIES!
yes yes yes yes yes yes yes!
May I please use the "little bunnie's room?" That was a lonnnng snowcat ride!

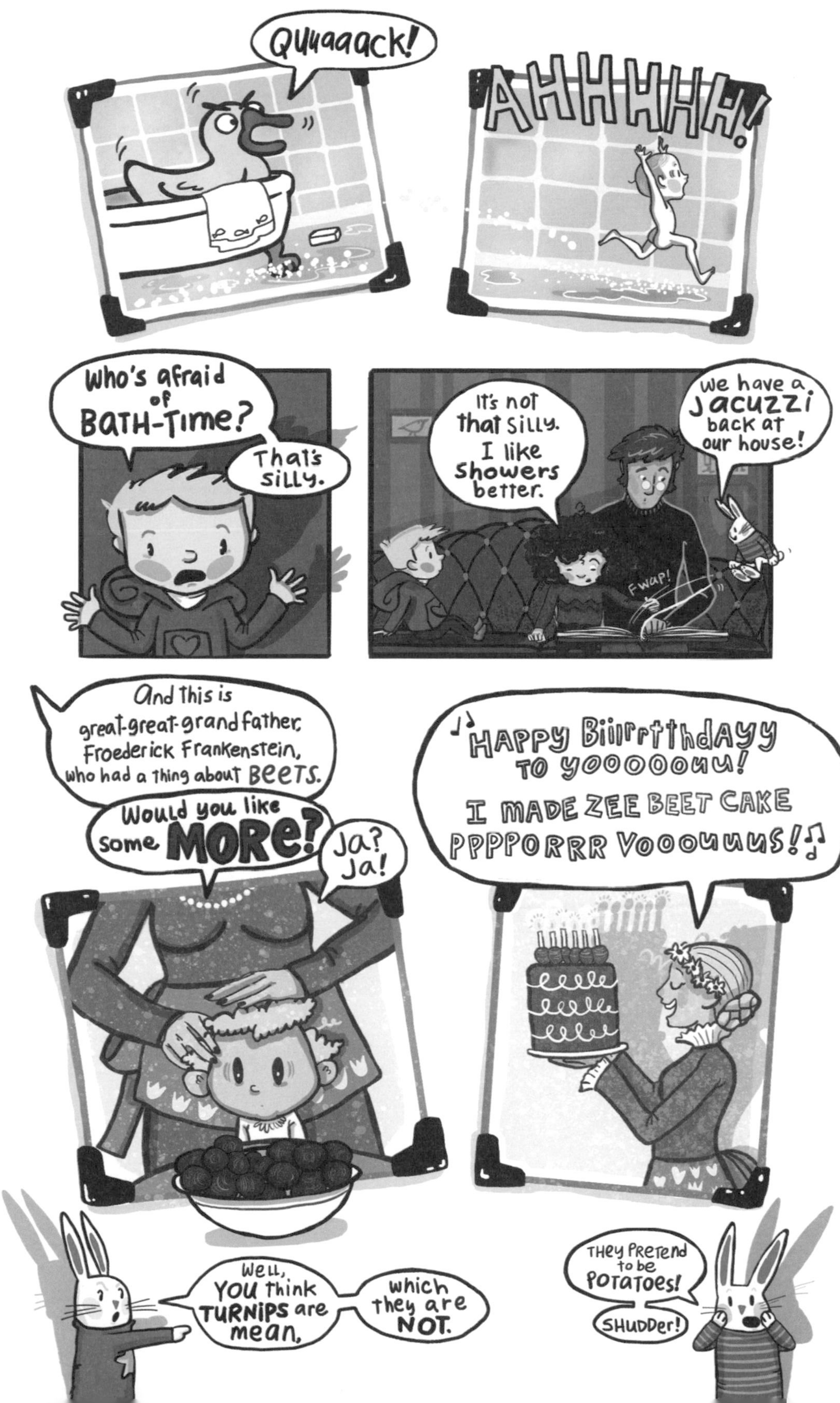
Quuaaack!
AHHHHHH!
Who's afraid of BATH-TIME?
That's silly.
It's not that silly. I like showers better.
We have a JACUZZI back at our house!
FWAP!
And this is great-great-grandfather, Froederick Frankenstein, who had a thing about BEETS.
Would you like some MORE?
Ja? Ja!
HAPPY Biiirrtthdayy TO YOOOOOOUU!
I MADE ZEE BEET CAKE PPPPORRR VOOOOUUUS!
Well, YOU think TURNIPS are mean,
which they are NOT.
THEY PRETEND to be POTATOES!
SHUDDER!

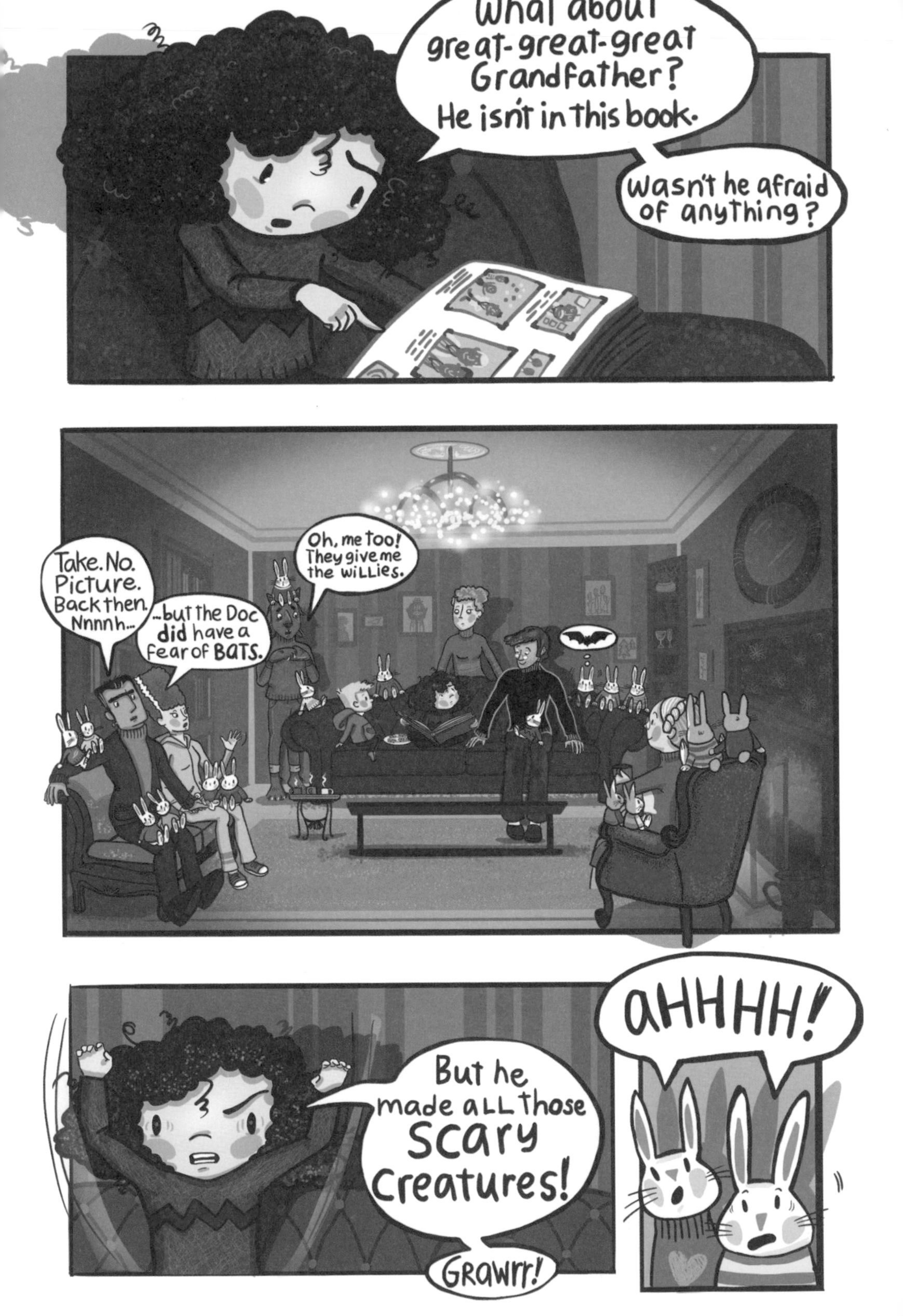
What about great-great-great Grandfather? He isn't in this book.
Wasn't he afraid of anything?
Take. No. Picture. Back then. Nnnnh...
...but the Doc did have a fear of BATS.
Oh, me too! They give me the willies.
But he made all those scary creatures!
Grawrr!
aHHHH!

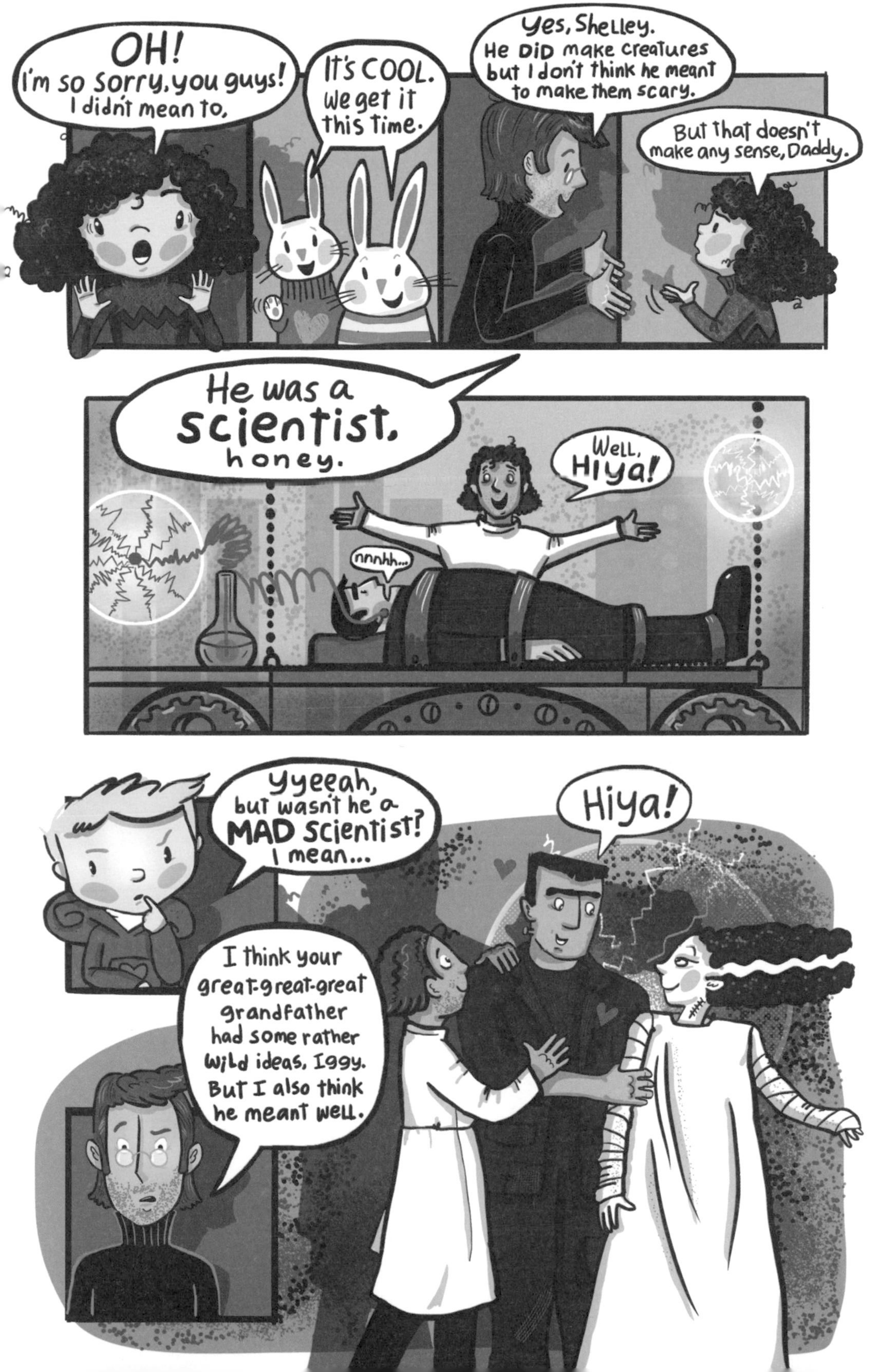
OH! I'm so sorry, you guys! I didn't mean to,
It's COOL. We get it this time.
Yes, Shelley. He DID make creatures but I don't think he meant to make them scary.
But that doesn't make any sense, Daddy.
He was a scientist, honey.
Well, Hiya!
nnnhh...
Yyeeah, but wasn't he a MAD scientist? I mean...
Hiya!
I think your great-great-great grandfather had some rather wild ideas, Iggy. But I also think he meant well.

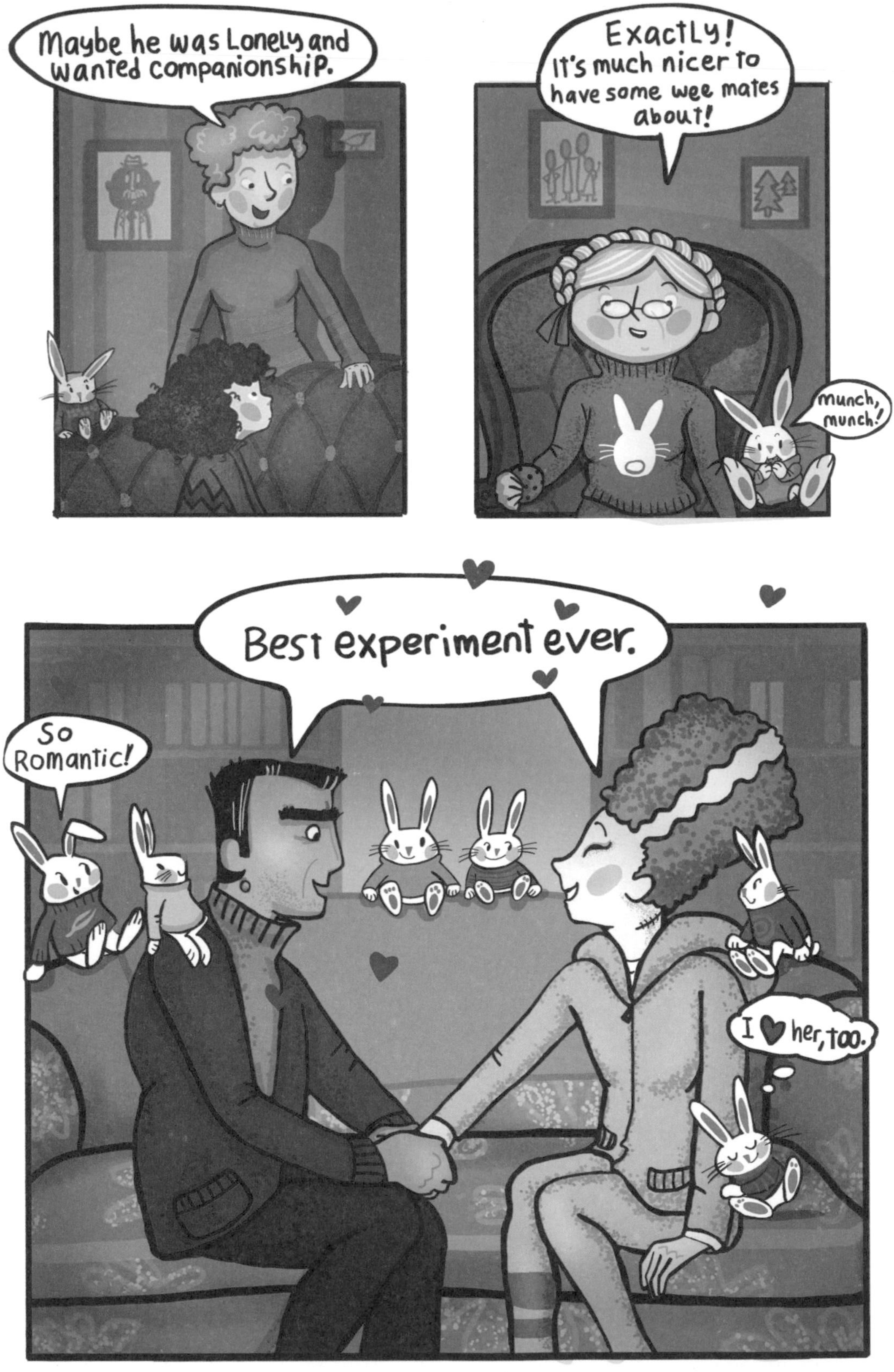
Maybe he was Lonely and wanted companionship.
Exactly! It's much nicer to have some wee mates about!
munch, munch!
Best experiment ever.
So Romantic!
I ♥ her, too.

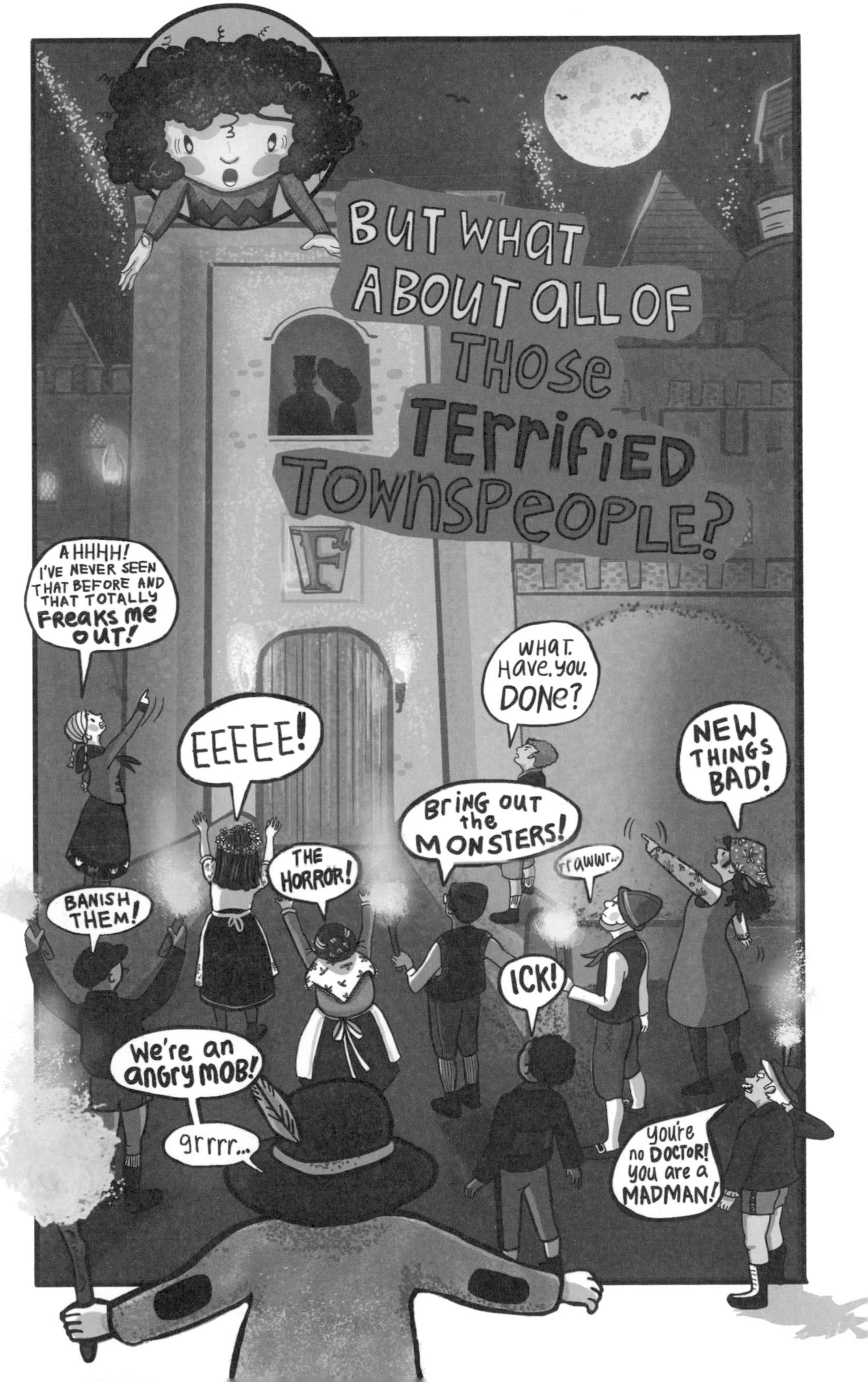
BUT WHAT ABOUT ALL OF THOSE TERRIFIED TOWNSPEOPLE?
F
AHHHH! I'VE NEVER SEEN THAT BEFORE AND THAT TOTALLY FREAKS ME OUT!
EEEEE!
WHAT. Have. you. DONE?
NEW THINGS BAD!
Bring out the MONSTERS!
THE HORROR!
rawwr...
BANISH THEM!
ICK!
We're an angry MOB!
grrrr...
you're no DOCTOR! you are a MADMAN!

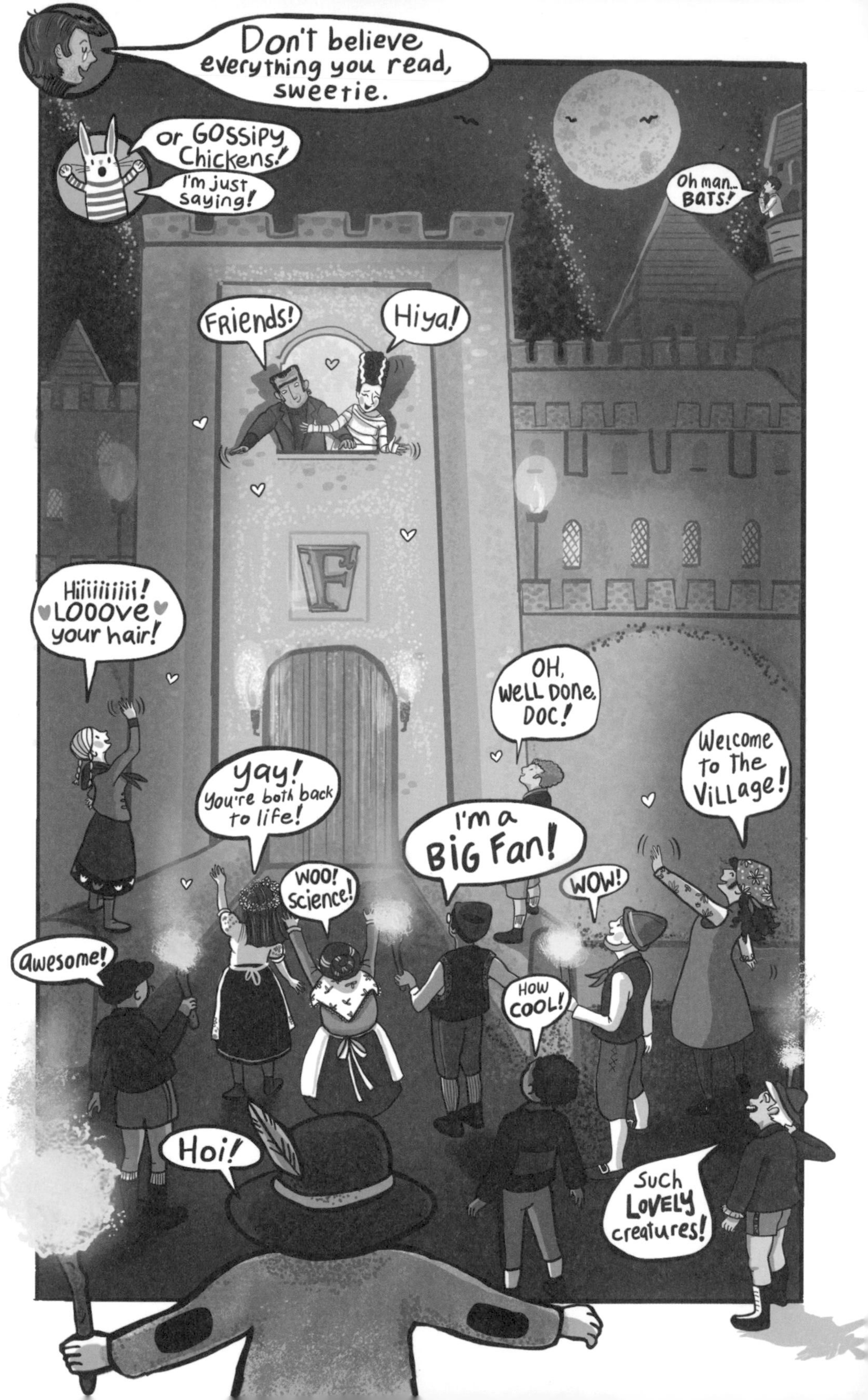
Don't believe everything you read, sweetie.
Or GOSSIPY Chickens!
I'm just saying!
Oh man... BATS!
Friends!
Hiya!
Hiiiiiiiii! LOOOVE your hair!
OH, WELL DONE, DOC!
Welcome to the VILLAGE!
Yay! You're both back to life!
I'm a BIG Fan!
WOO! Science!
WOW!
awesome!
HOW COOL!
Hoi!
Such LOVELY creatures!

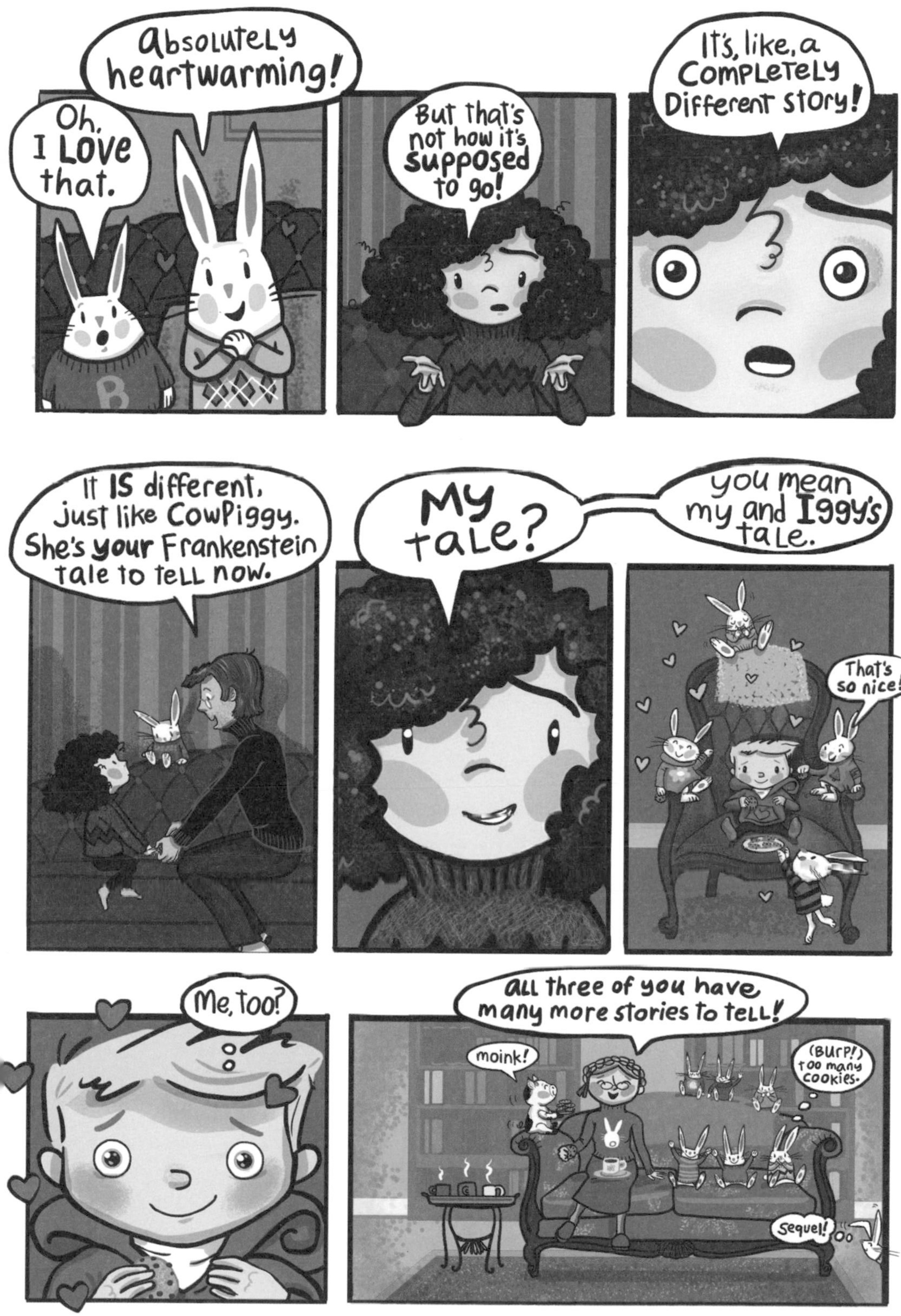
Oh, I LOVE that.
Absolutely heartwarming!
But that's not how it's supposed to go!
It's, like, a COMPLETELY Different story!
It IS different, just like CowPiggy. She's your Frankenstein tale to tell now.
My tale?
You mean my and Iggy's tale.
That's so nice!
Me, too?
All three of you have many more stories to tell!
moink!
(BURP!) Too many cookies.
Sequel!

Oh! **OH!**
I HAVE A STORY, TOO!
I WROTE IT ON THE WAY HERE!
I'LL STOP YELLING AND
TELL IT TO YOU!

nce upon a time, a retired fairy godmother called Carole was driving a shuttlebus of grannies to their weekly "tai chi & tea" class when a frantic red squirrel flagged the bus down shouting, "AHH! HELP! HELP! THEY ARE COMING AFTER ME!" Carole opened the door, and the squirrel hopped on board. He introduced himself as Murray and immediately apologized for any inconvenience but explained that a flock of evil robot seagulls had swooped down and chased him all around the park, demanding that he order them a pizza with anchovies.

But Murray told them, "I can't get you guys a pizza! I'm allergic to fish and cheese and wheat! Now fly away!"

BUT the robot seagulls wouldn't take no for an answer and dive-bombed Murray anyway, who managed to escape out of the park and into the busy street. "Then I saw your bus and I waved my arms like this," pantomimed Murray, "and then you stopped for me!"

Then one of the grannies who was looking out a window shrieked,

"Here THEY COME! **DO STEP ON IT, CAROLE!**"

Carole hit the gas and sped away down the road, temporarily leaving the pizza-crazy robot seagulls flapping in their wake like tube socks on a windy washing line. Back on the bus, Murray and the grannies all tightened their seat belts, and, and, annnnn and...

Annnnnd, that's quite enough **BUNNY TALES** for today, Kevin.

Time for us to be heading home.

But wait! There's more!

Chomp chomp chomp chomp

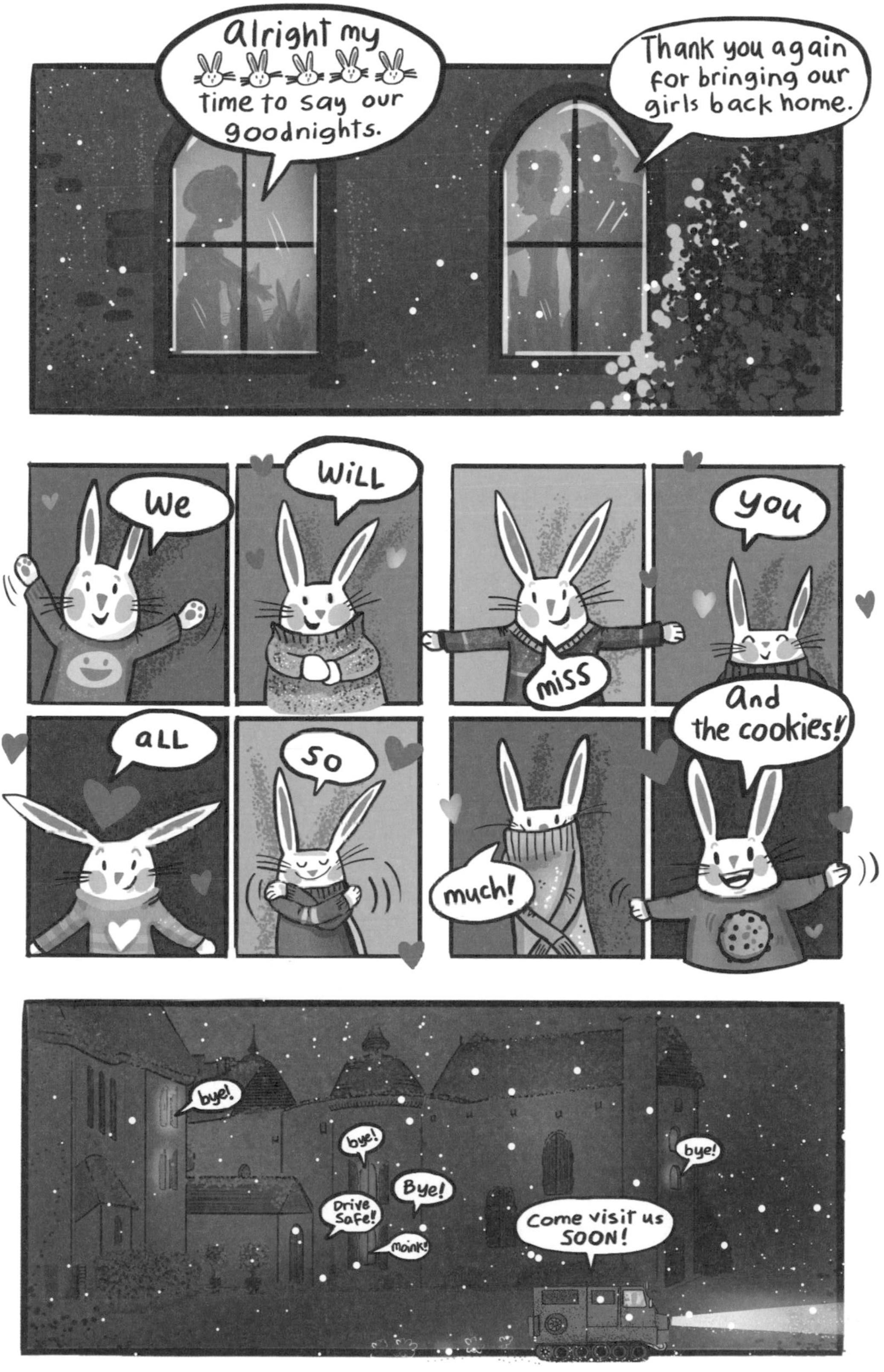

alright my [bunny icons] time to say our goodnights.
Thank you again for bringing our girls back home.
We
WiLL
miss
you
aLL
so
much!
and the cookies!
bye!
bye!
Bye!
Drive Safe!
moink!
bye!
Come visit us SOON!

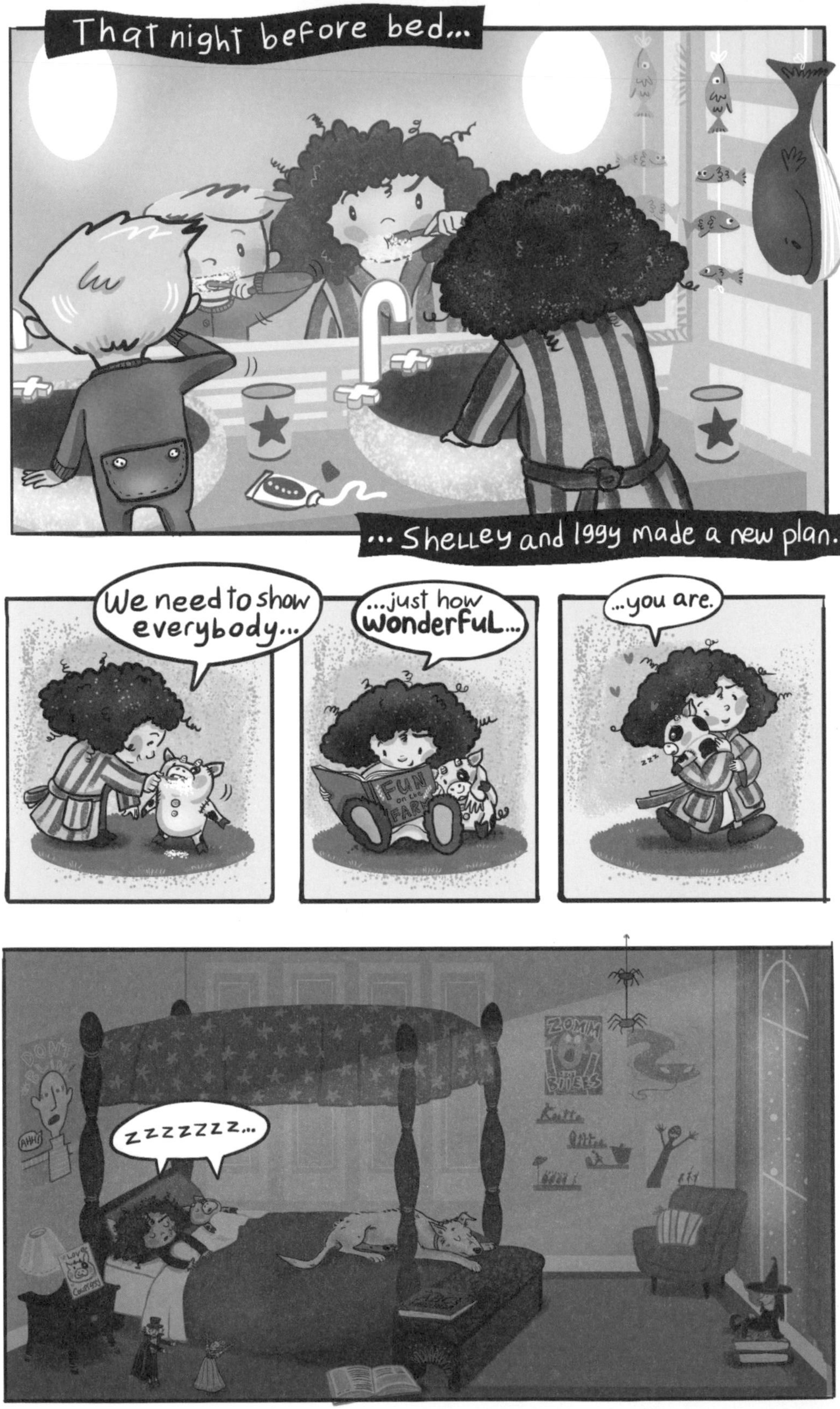
That night before bed...
... Shelley and Iggy made a new plan.
We need to show everybody...
...just how wonderful...
FUN on the FARM
...you are.
zzzzzzz...

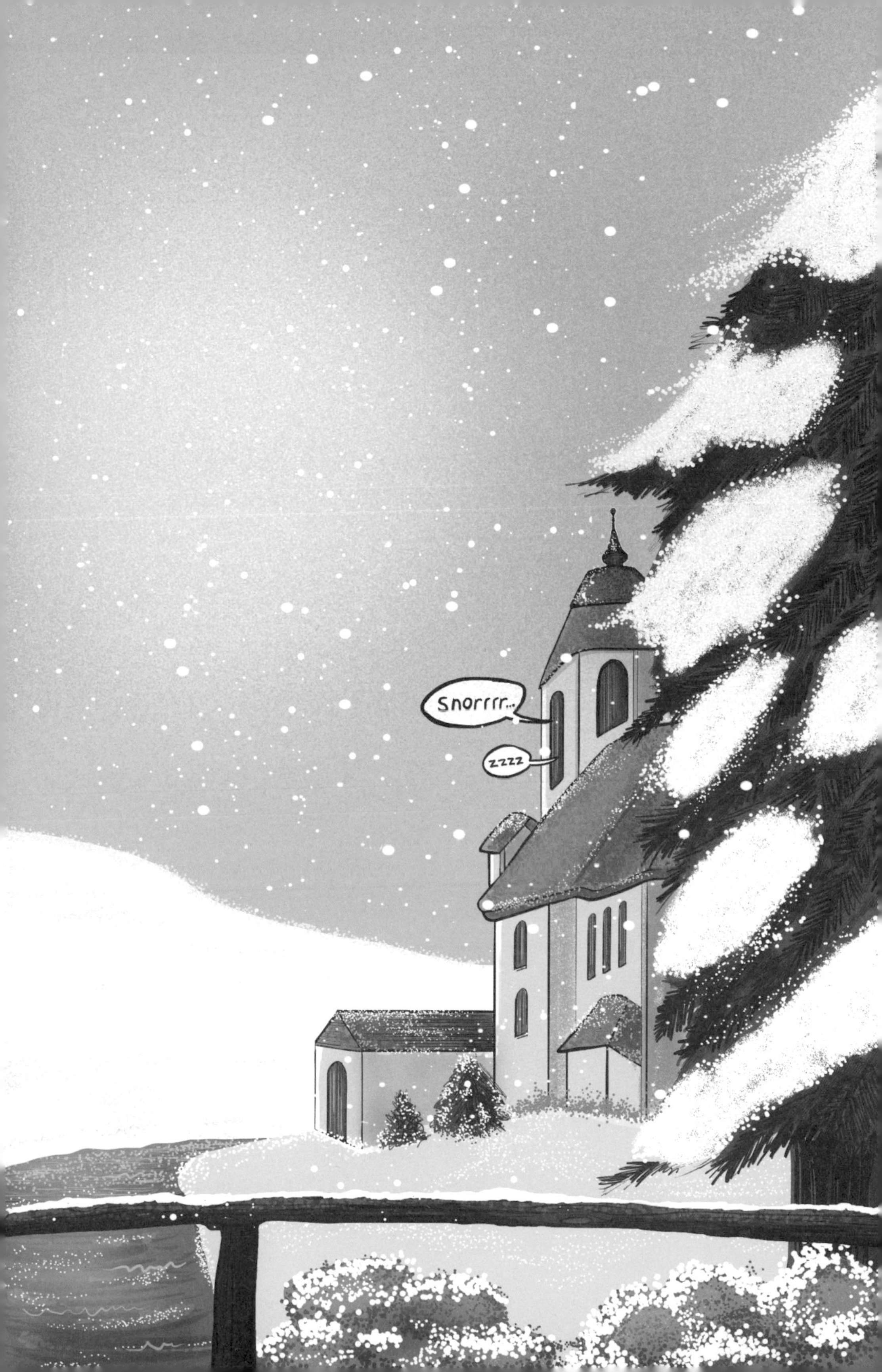
Snorrrr...
zzzz

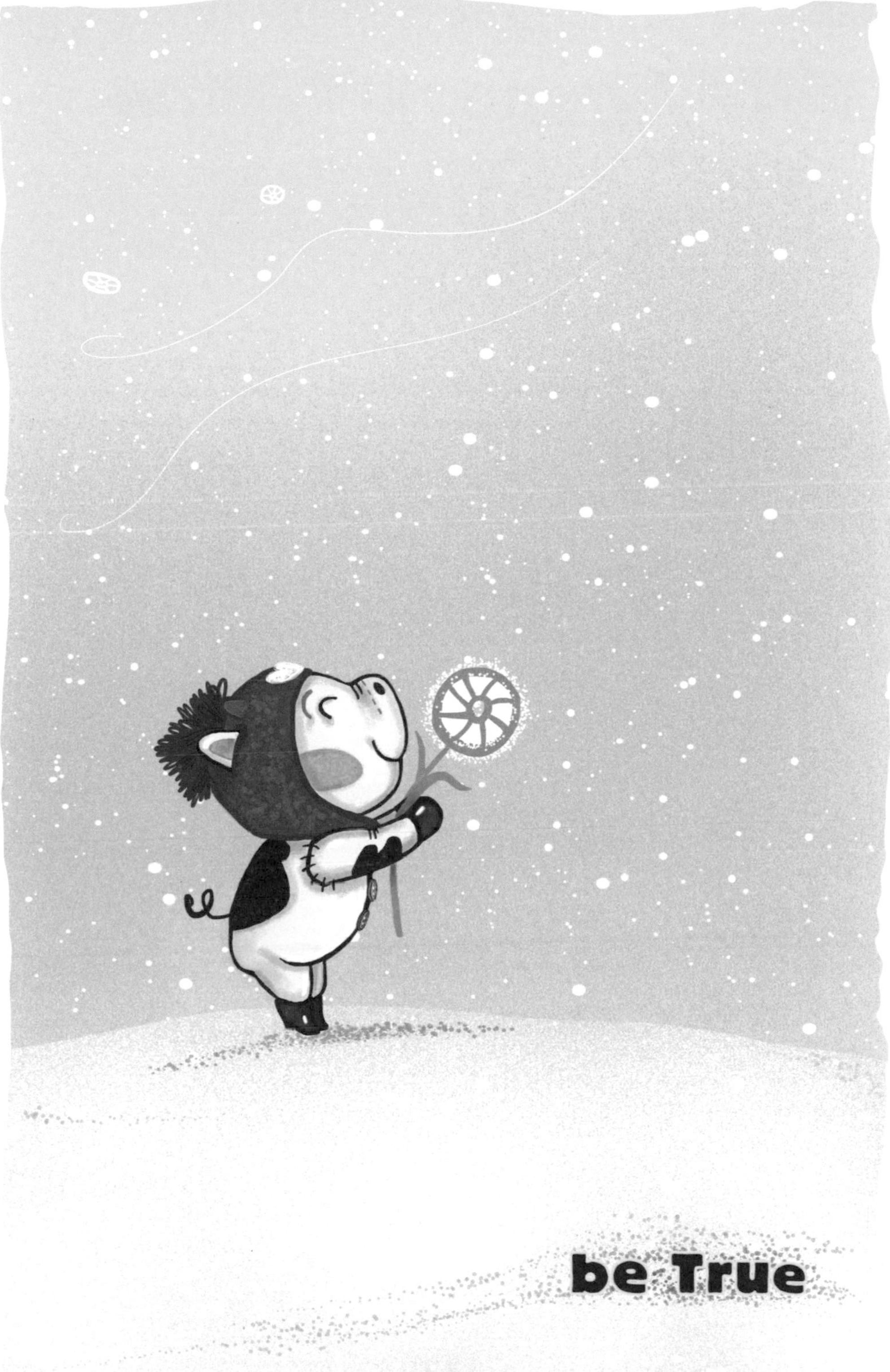
be True

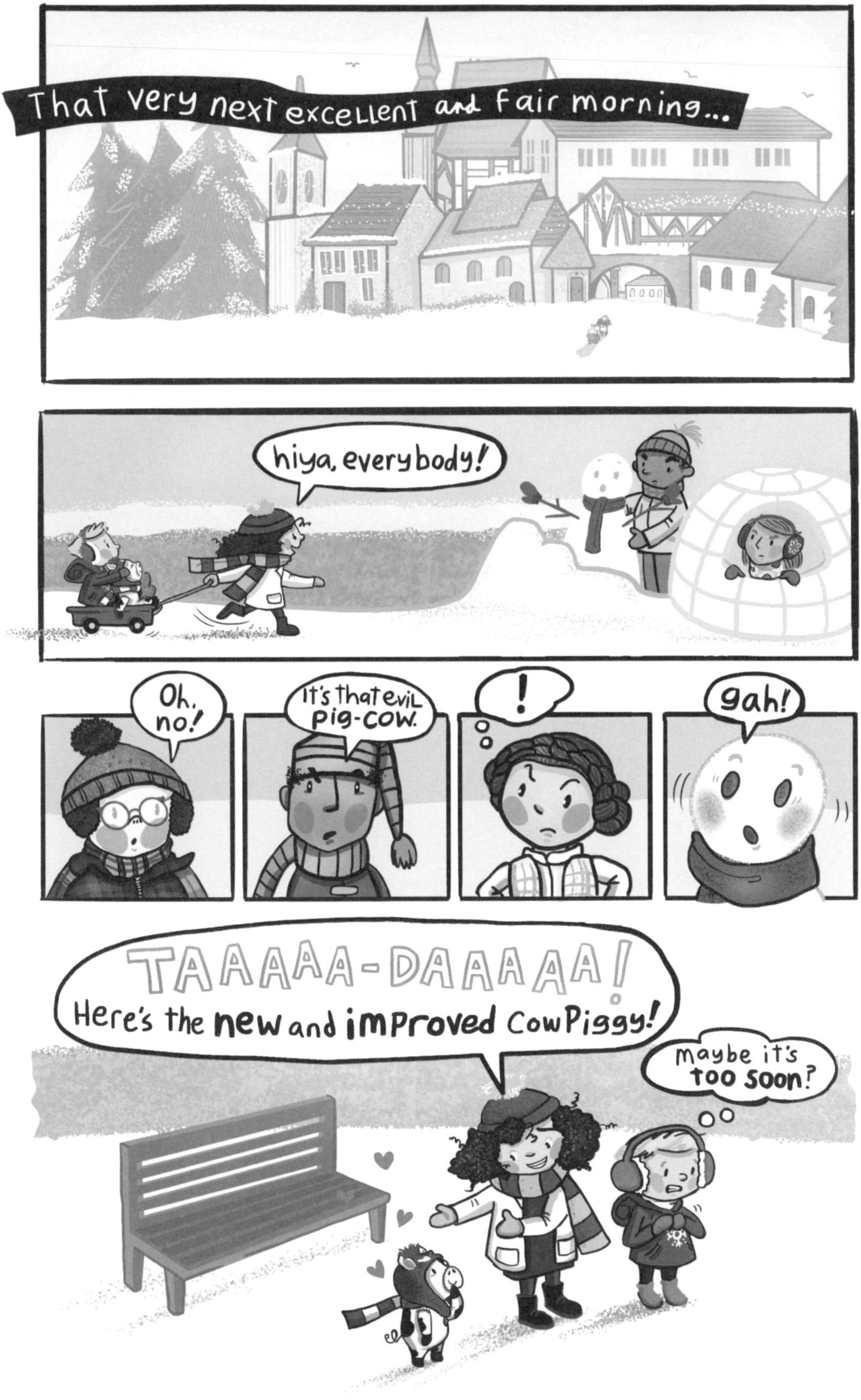
That very next excellent and fair morning...
hiya, everybody!
Oh, no!
It's that evil pig-cow.
!
gah!
TAAAAA-DAAAAA!
Here's the new and improved CowPiggy!
maybe it's too soon?

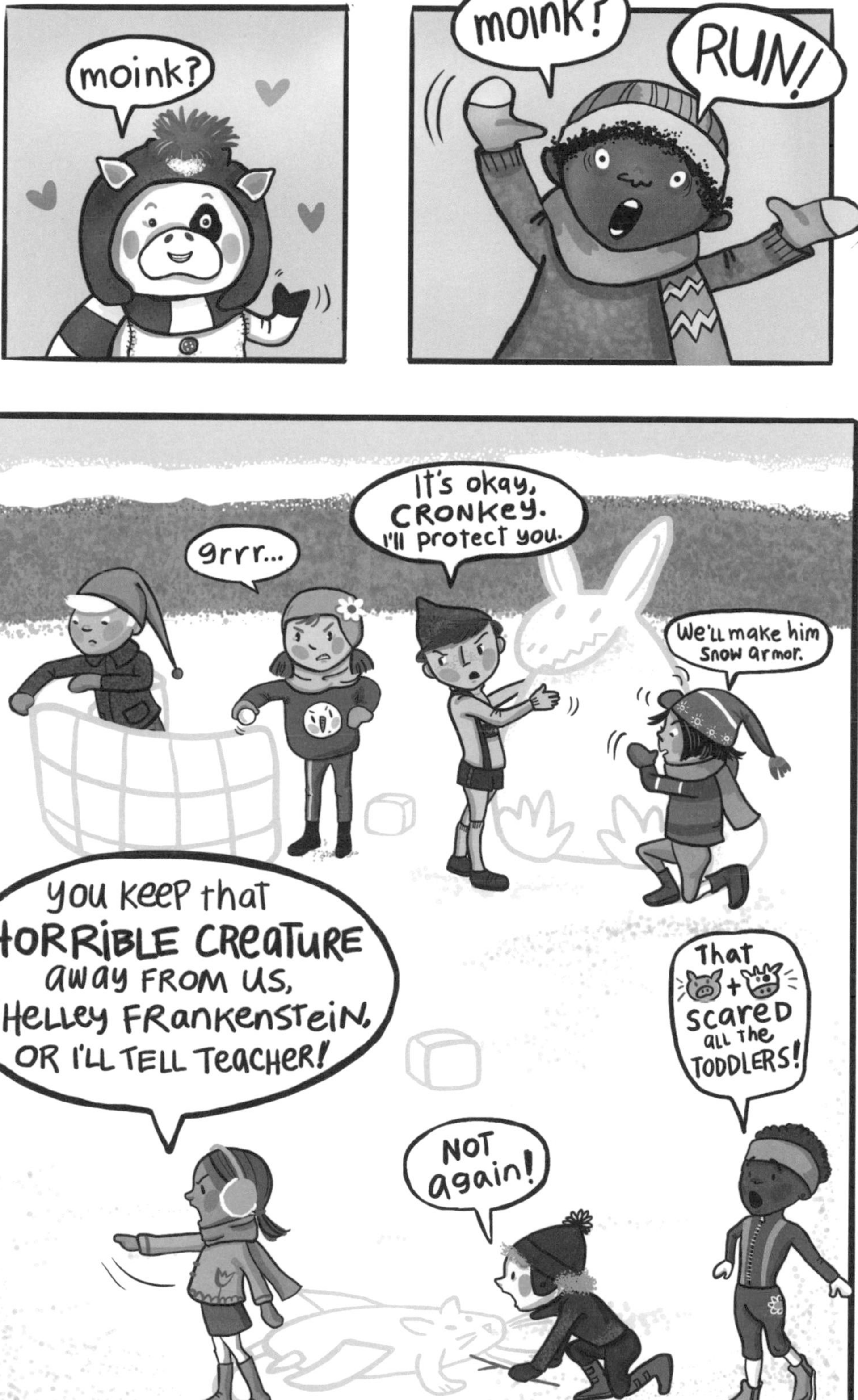
moink?
moink?
RUN!
grrr...
It's okay, CRONKey. I'll protect you.
We'll make him snow armor.
you keep that HORRIBLE CReaTURE away FROM US, SHelley FRankensTeiN, OR I'LL TELL TeacHeR!
NOT again!
That + scared all the TODDLERS!

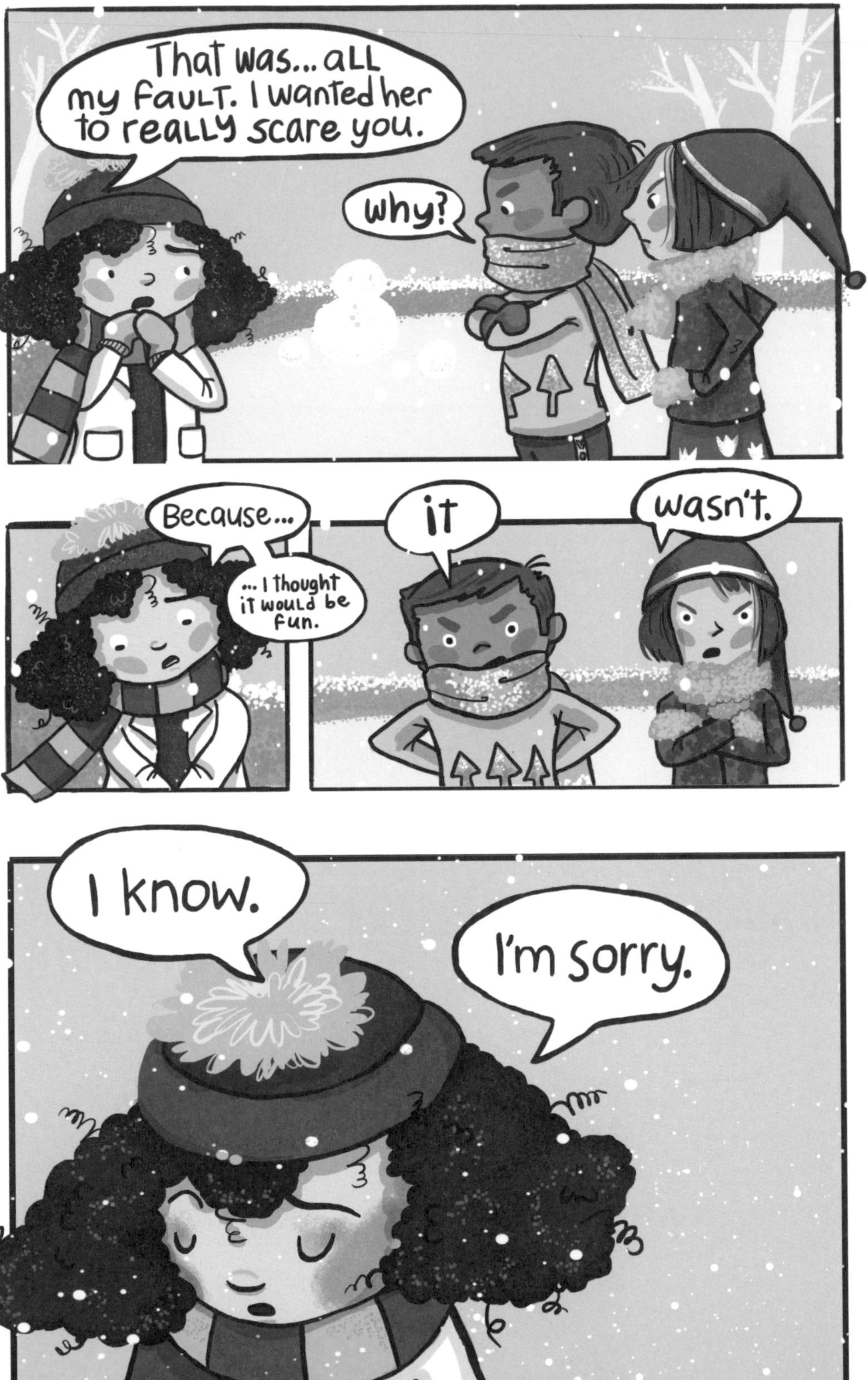
That was... all my fault. I wanted her to really scare you.
Why?
Because...
...I thought it would be fun.
it
wasn't.
I know.
I'm sorry.

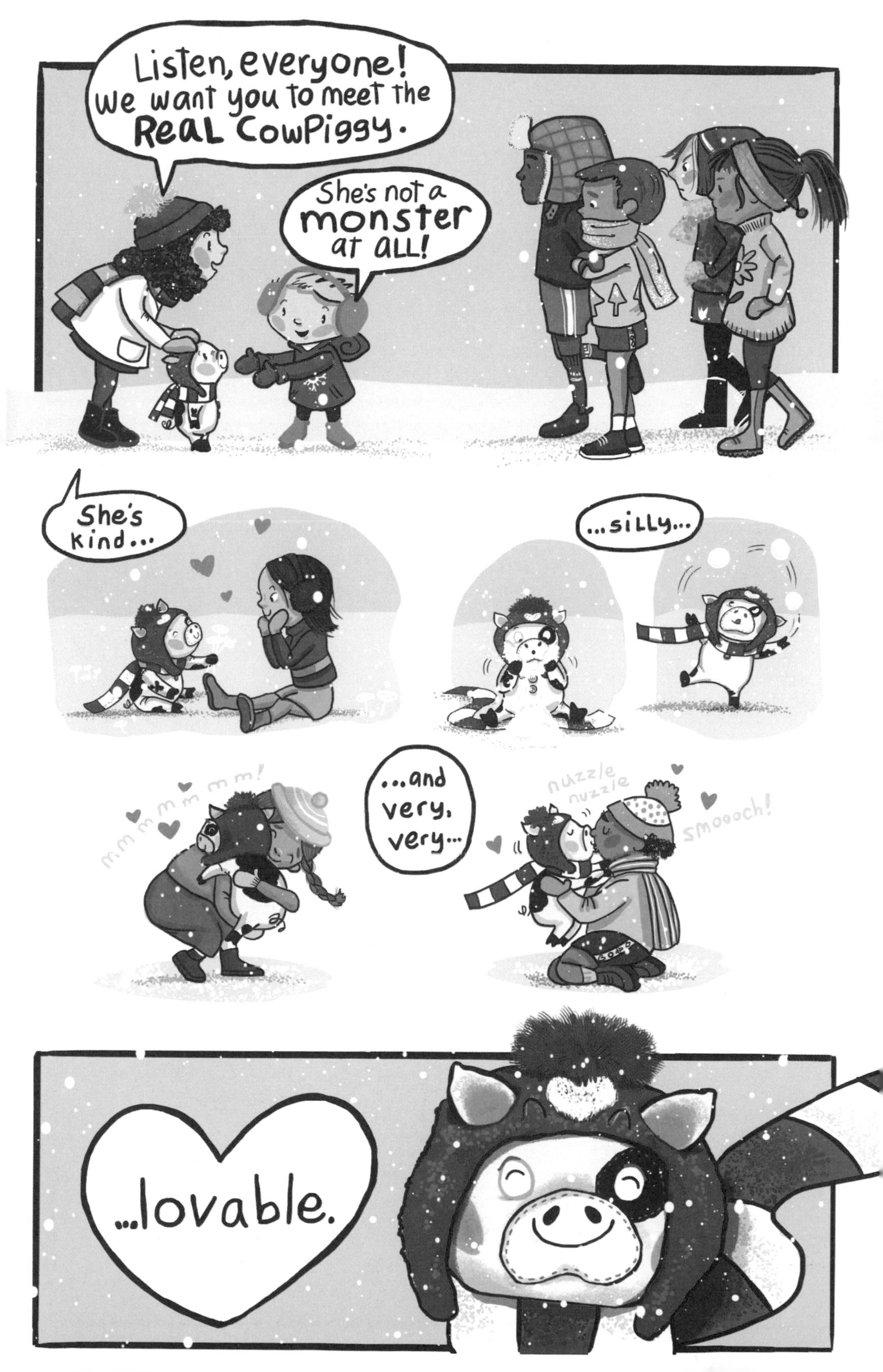

Listen, everyone! We want you to meet the REAL CowPiggy.
She's not a monster at ALL!
She's kind...
...silly...
mmmmmmm!
...and very, very...
nuzzle nuzzle
smoooch!
...lovable.

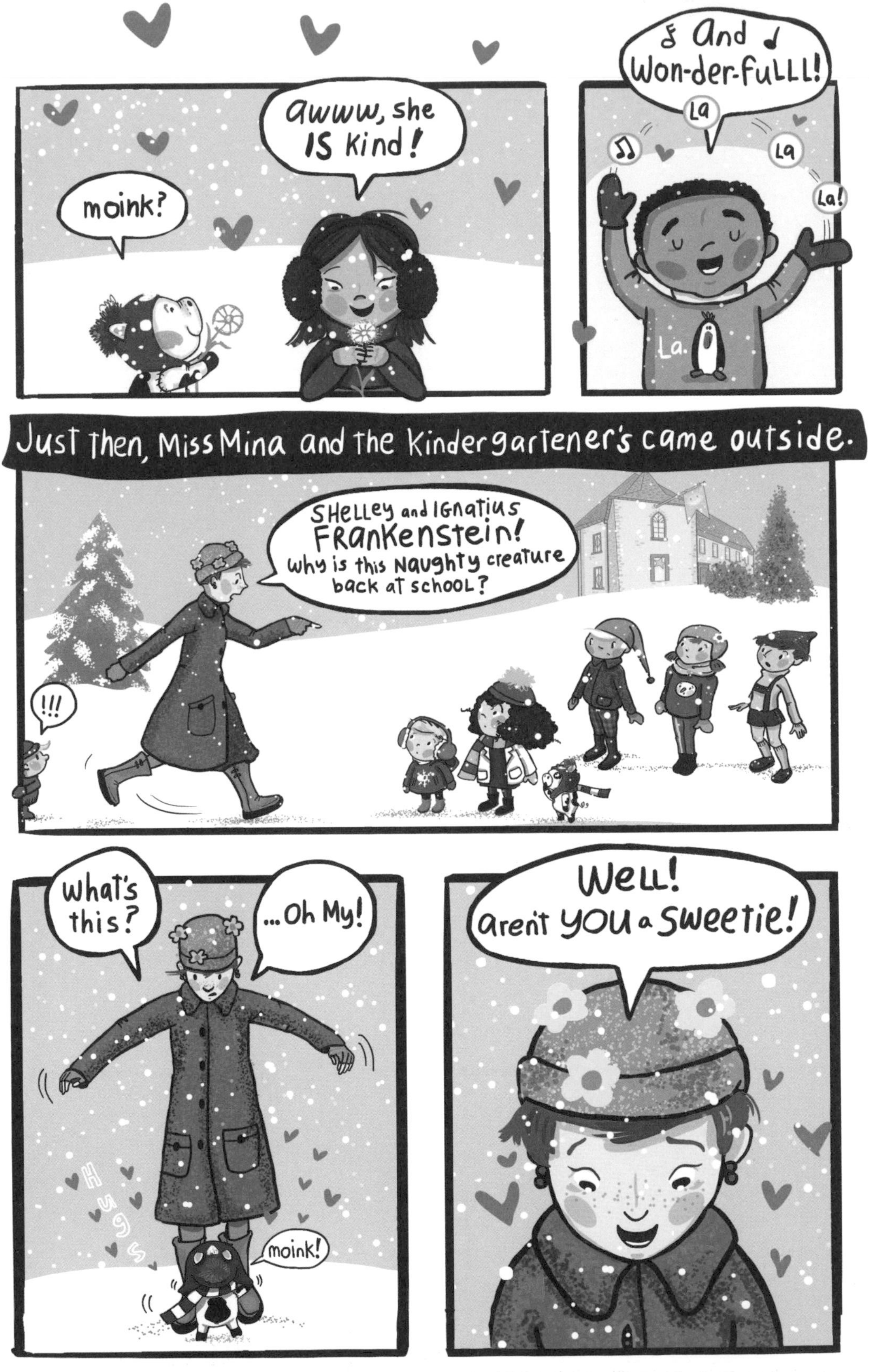
moink?
awww, she IS kind!
And Won-der-fuLLL!
La
La
La!
La.
Just then, Miss Mina and the Kindergartener's came outside.
SHELLEY and IGNATIUS FRANKENSTEIN! Why is this Naughty creature back at school?
!!!
What's this?
...Oh My!
Hugs
moink!
WELL! aren't YOU a Sweetie!

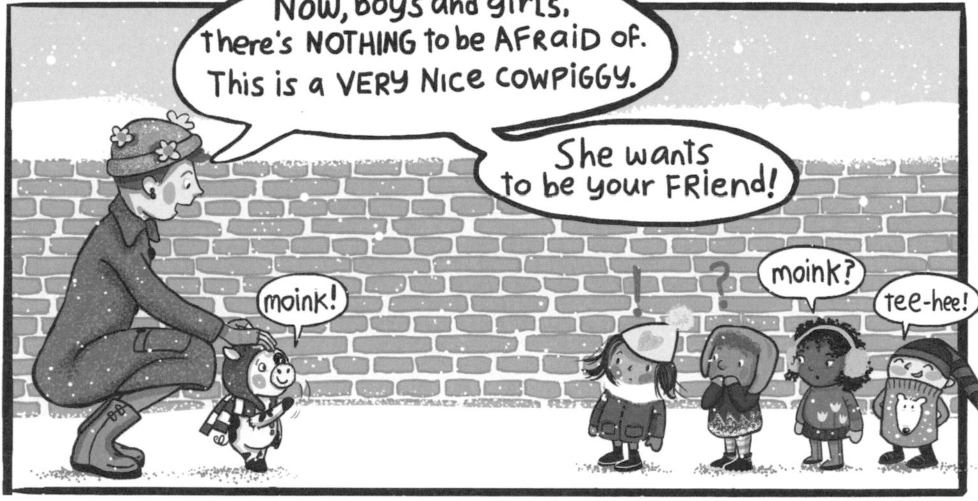
Now, boys and girls, There's NOTHING to be AFRAID OF. This is a VERY NICE COWPIGGY.
She wants to be your FRIEND!
moink!
!
?
moink?
tee-hee!

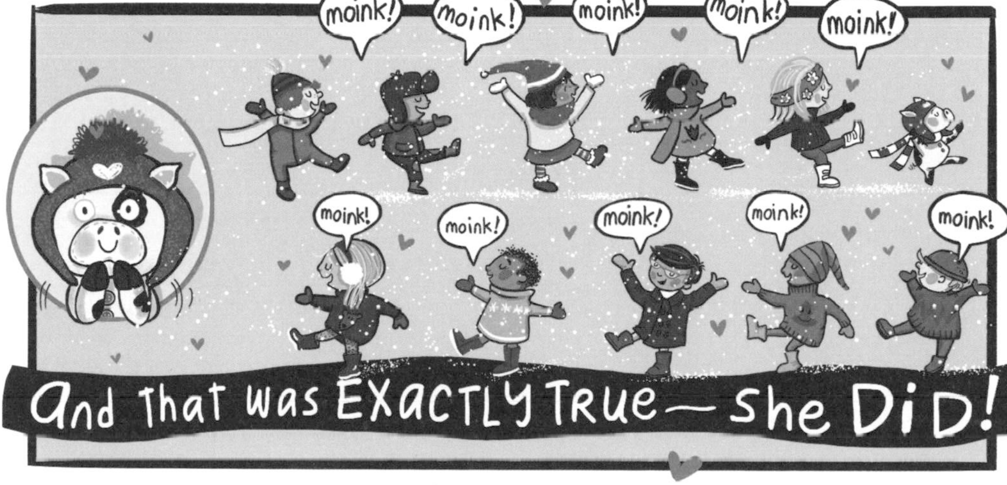
moink!
moink!
moink!
moink!
moink!
moink!
moink!
moink!
moink!
moink!
And That was EXACTLY TRUE— she DID!

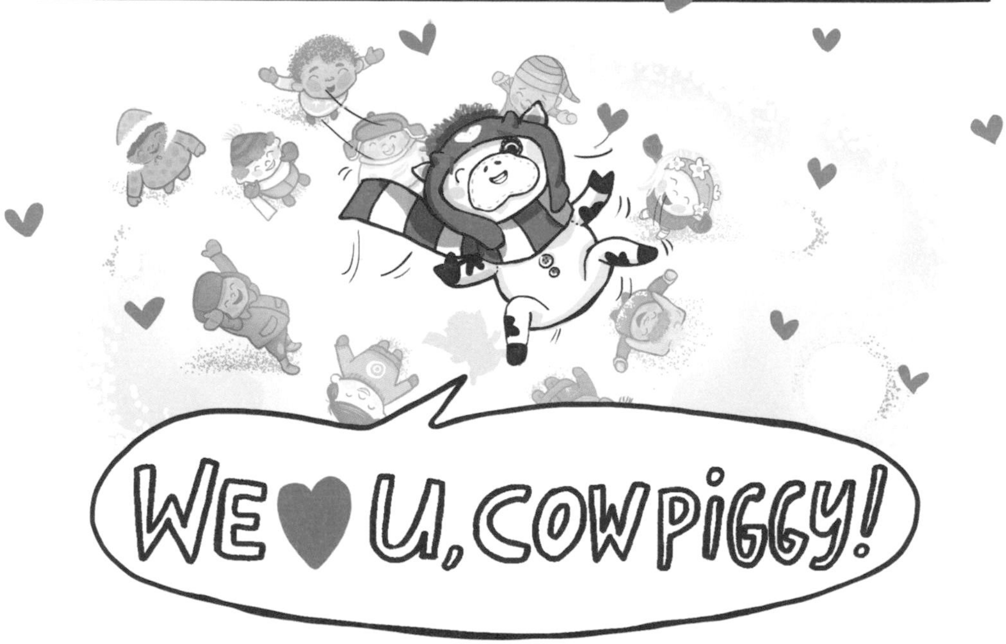
WE ♥ U, COWPIGGY!

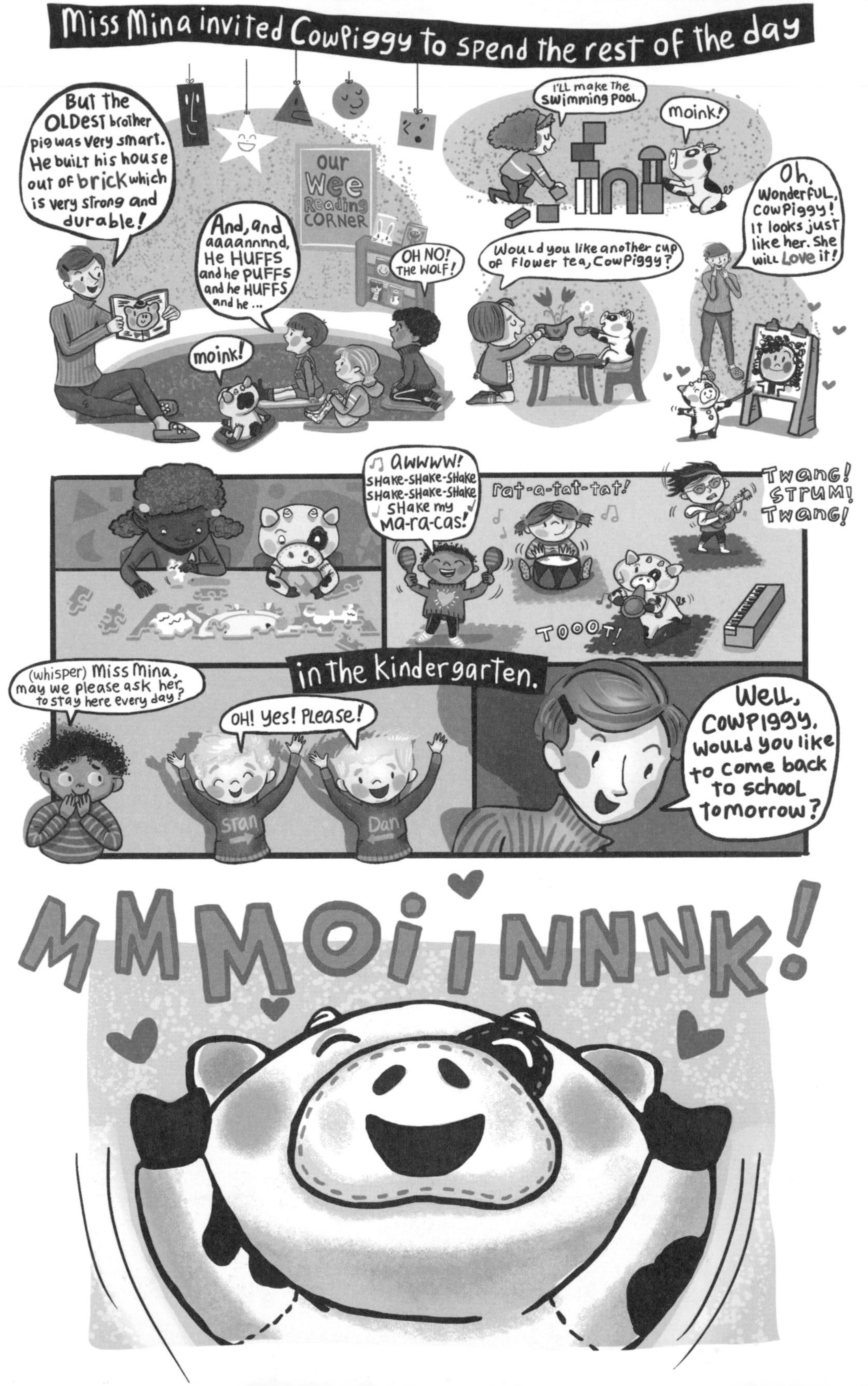
Miss Mina invited CowPiggy to spend the rest of the day
But the OLDEST brother pig was very smart. He built his house out of brick which is very strong and durable!
Our Wee Reading Corner
And, and aaaannnnd, He HUFFS and he PUFFS and he HUFFS and he ...
OH NO! THE WOLF!
moink!
I'LL make the swimming pool.
moink!
Would you like another cup of flower tea, CowPiggy?
Oh, Wonderful, CowPiggy! It looks just like her. She will Love it!
awwww! SHake-SHake-SHake SHake-SHake-SHake SHake my Ma-ra-cas!
rat-a-tat-tat!
TWANG! STRUM! TWANG!
TOOOT!
in the kindergarten.
(whisper) Miss Mina, may we please ask her to stay here every day?
OH! Yes! Please!
Stan
Dan
Well, CowPiggy, would you like to come back to school tomorrow?
MMMOIINNNK!

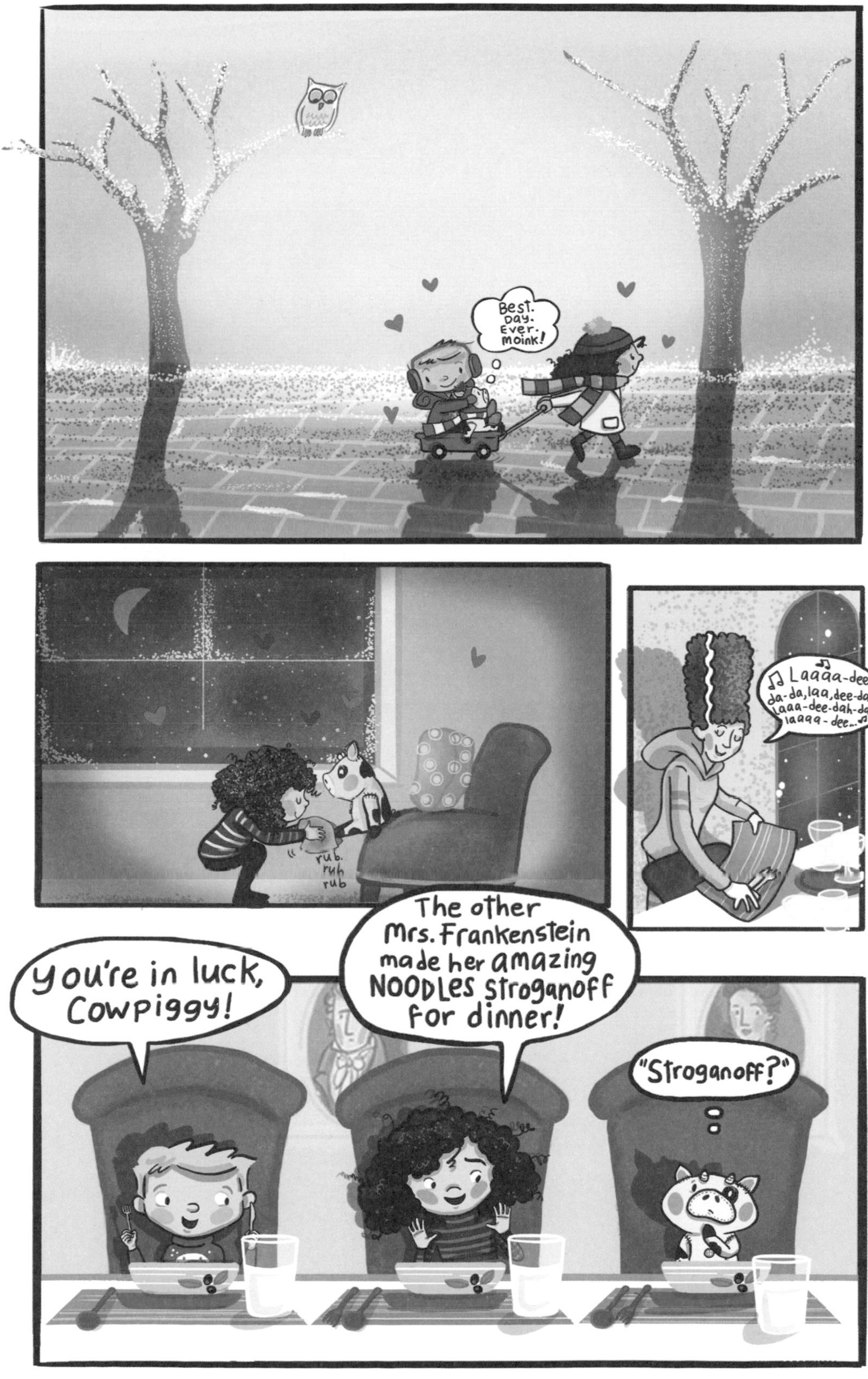

Best. Day. Ever. moink!
rub. rub rub
♫ Laaaa-dee da-da, laa, dee-da-da laaa-dee-dah-dahh laaaa-dee...♫
You're in luck, Cowpiggy!
The other Mrs. Frankenstein made her amazing NOODLES stroganoff for dinner!
"Stroganoff?"

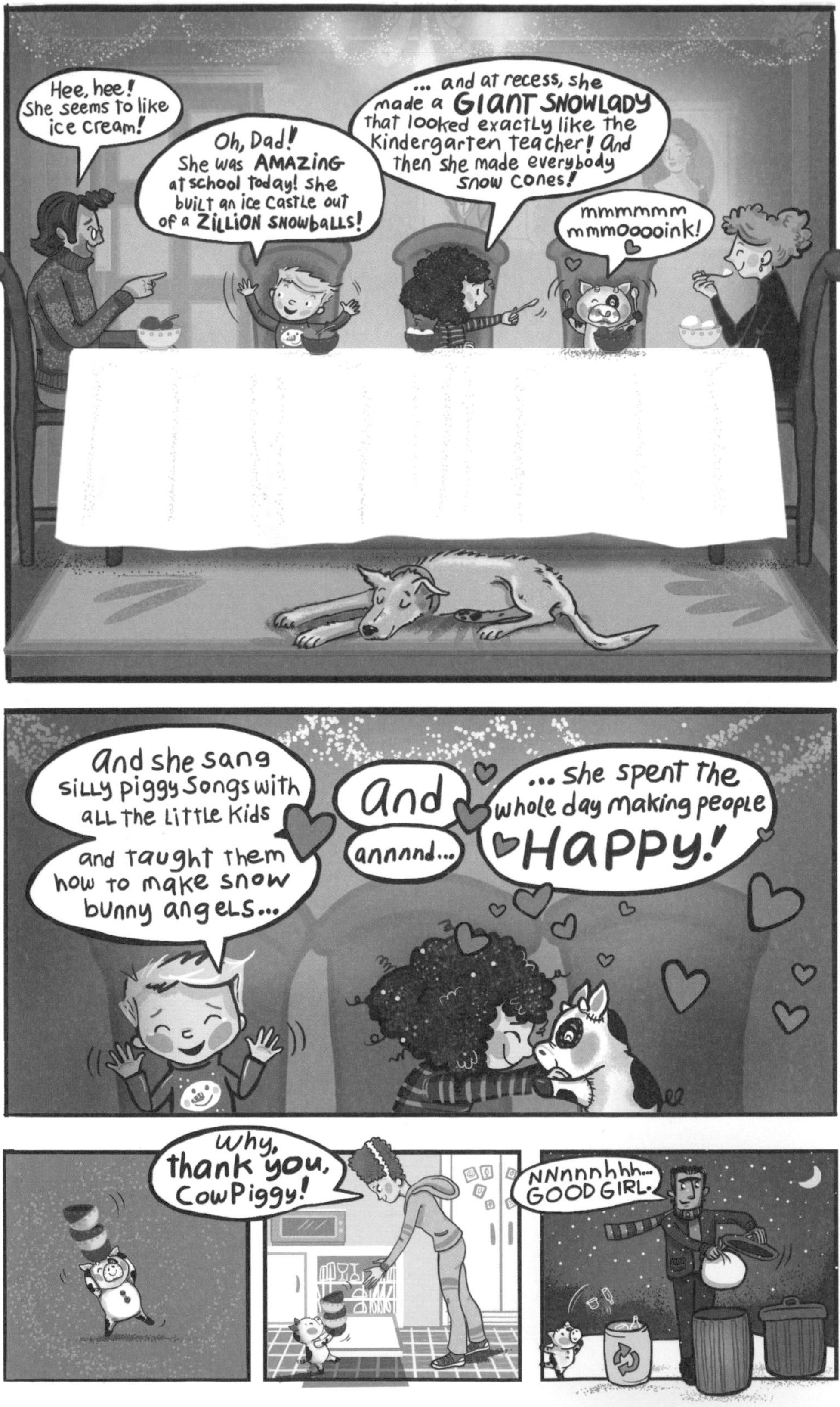
Hee, hee! She seems to like ice cream!
Oh, Dad! She was AMAZING at school today! She built an ice castle out of a ZILLION SNOWBALLS!
... and at recess, she made a GIANT SNOWLADY that looked exactly like the Kindergarten teacher! And then she made everybody snow cones!
mmmmmm mmmoooooink!
And she sang silly piggy songs with all the little kids
and taught them how to make snow bunny angels...
and
annnnd...
... she spent the whole day making people HAPPY!
Why, thank you, CowPiggy!
NNnnnhhh... GOOD GIRL.

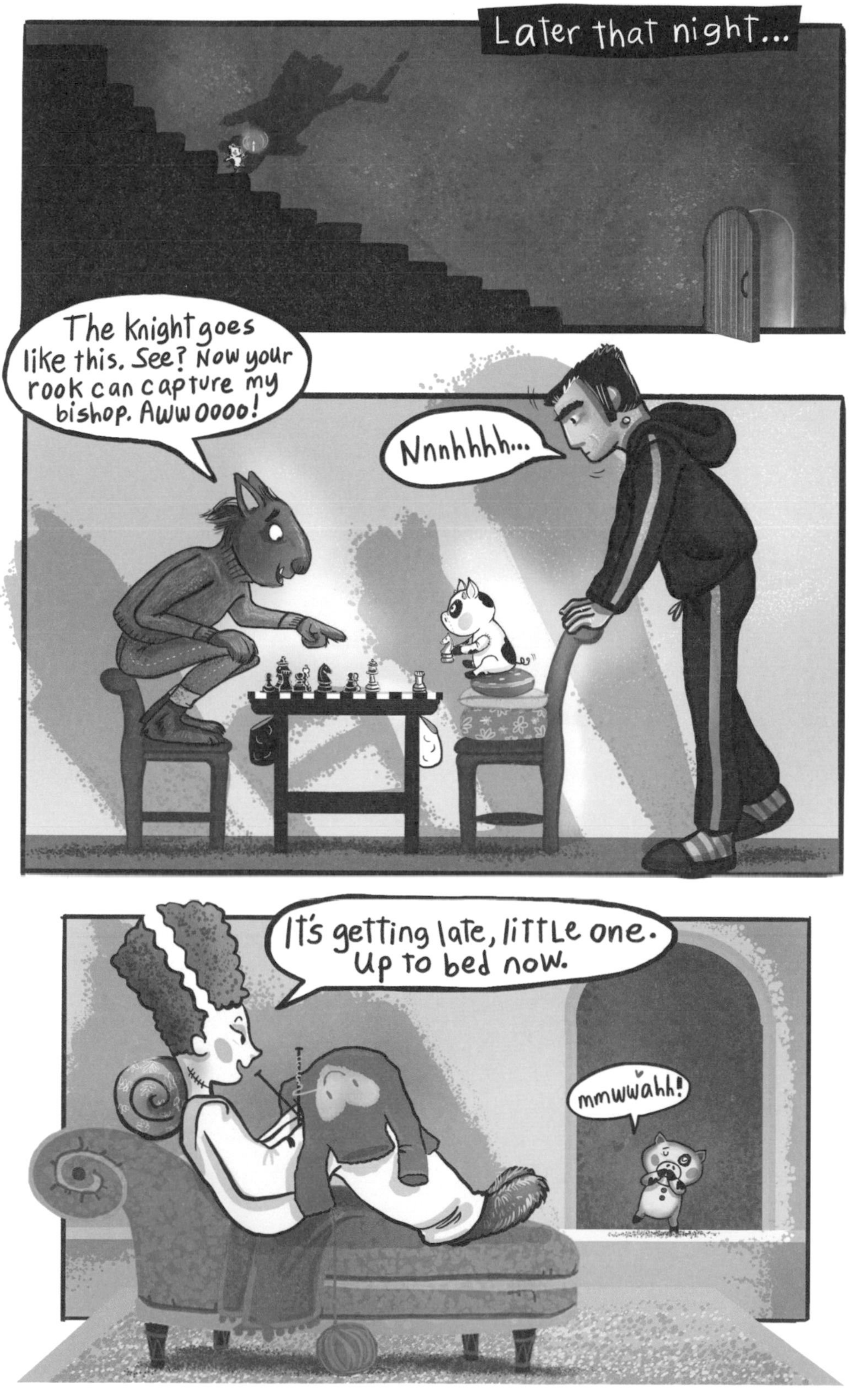
Later that night...
The knight goes like this. See? Now your rook can capture my bishop. AWWOOOO!
Nnnhhhh...
It's getting late, little one. Up to bed now.
mmwwahh!

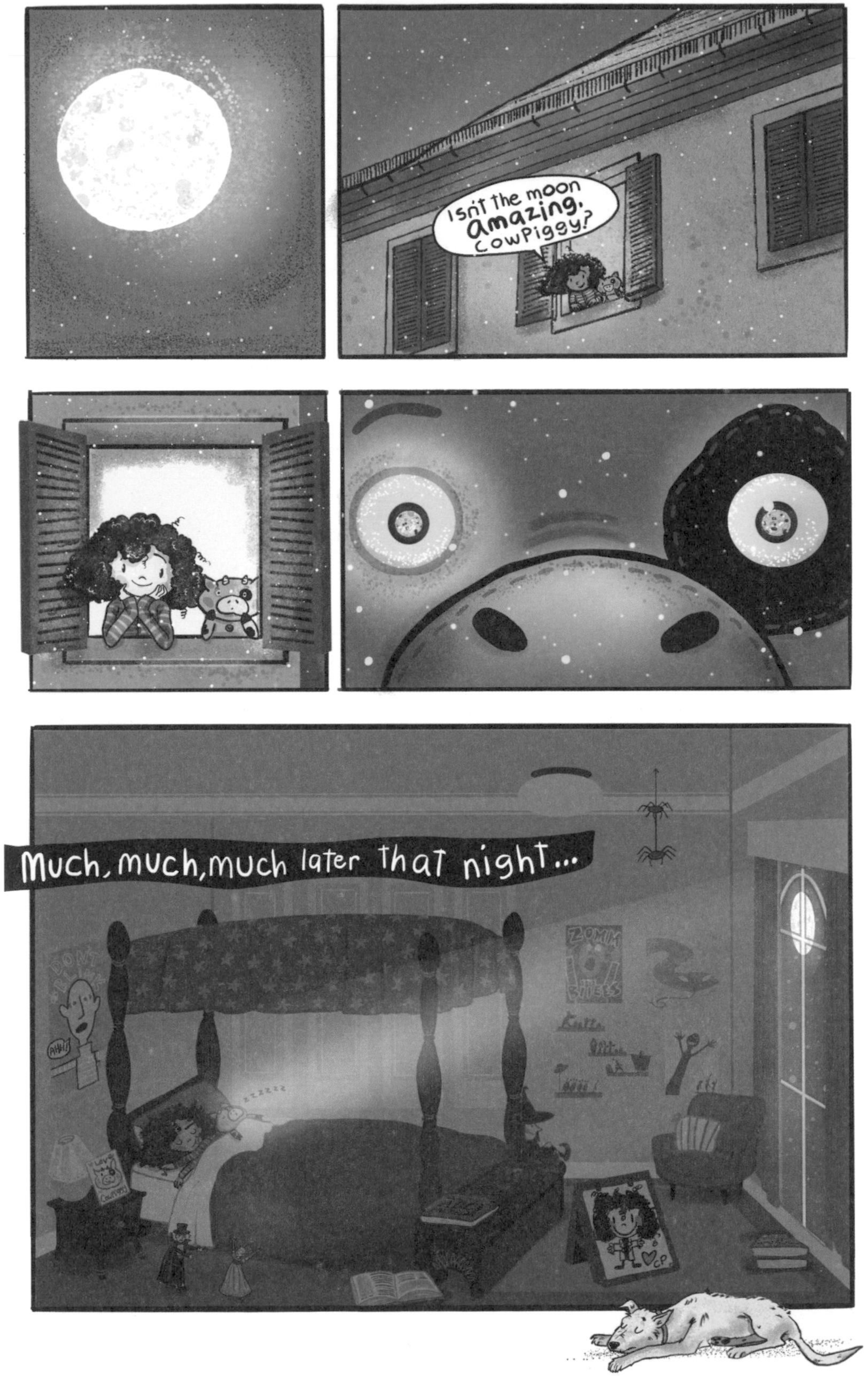
Isn't the moon amazing, CowPiggy?
Much, much, much later that night...

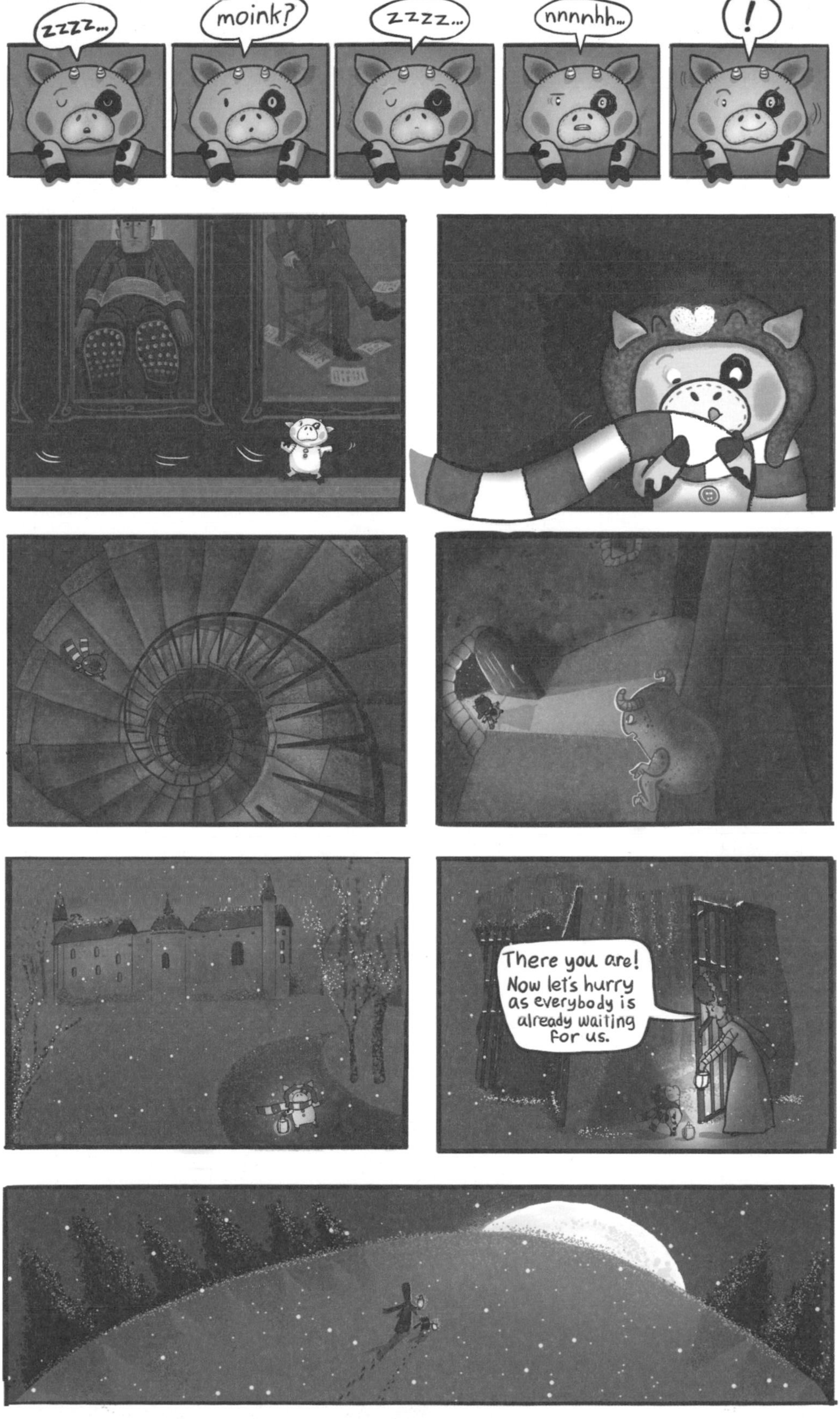
zzzz...
moink?
zzzz...
nnnnhh...
!
There you are! Now let's hurry as everybody is already waiting for us.

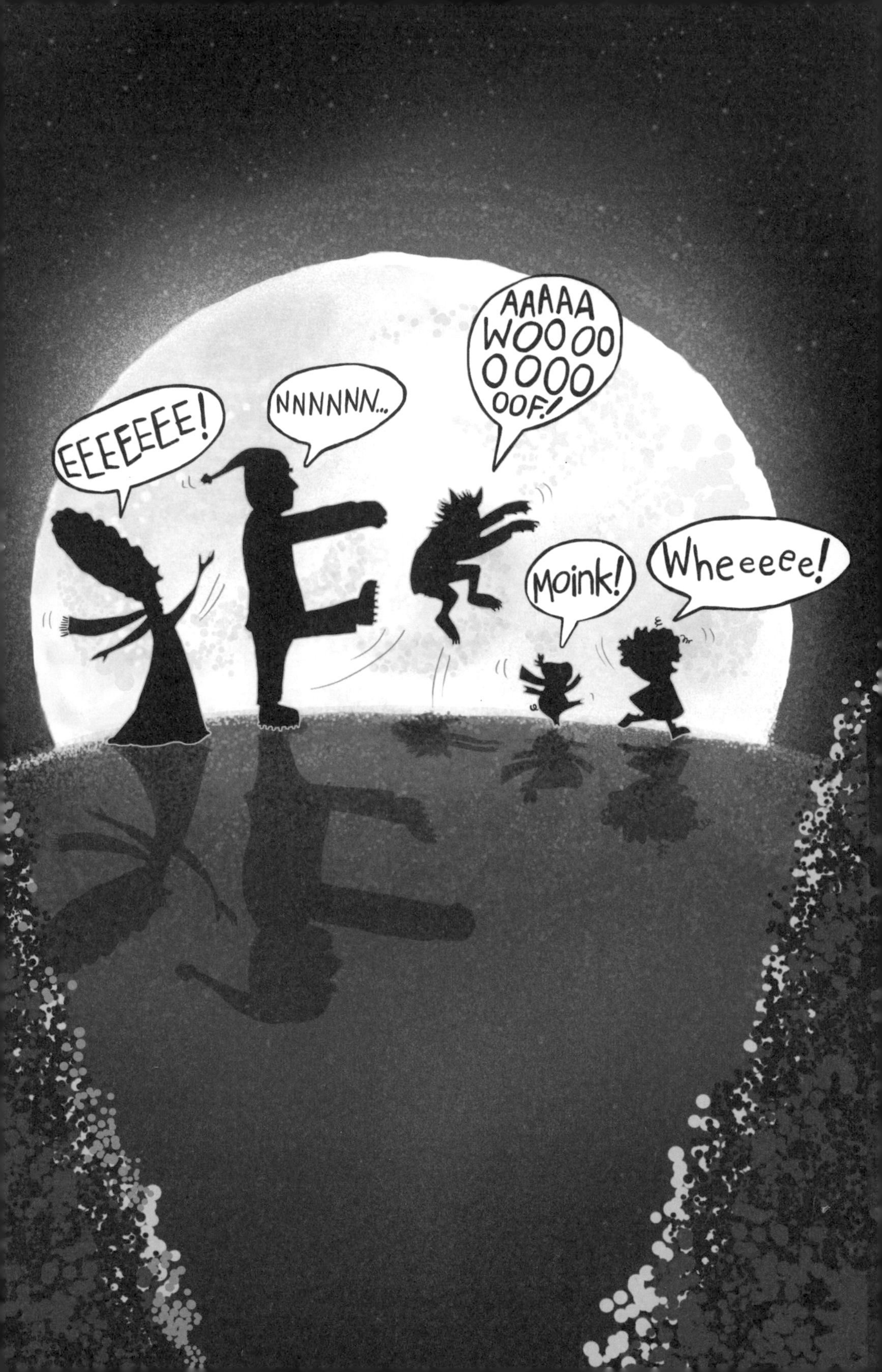
EEEEEEE!
NNNNNN...
AAAAA WOOOO OOOO OOF!
Moink!
Wheeeee!